MW01178566

OCEAN TIDINGS

BY

J.R. TEASDALE

PIEEYE Publishing Inc.
www.pieeyepublishing.com
Tel: 1-888-4pieeye (474-3393)
Fax: 1-888-421-9450

Here's pie in your eye!
Grab a piece while it's hot.

Published by PIEEYE PUBLISHING INC. with offices in Montreal, PQ and in Plattsburgh NY.

Book cover design by: Maxime Masse
Editing by: Laura Duke
Typesetting by: Pieeye Publishing Inc.

ISBN: 09759435-2-9
Printed in Canada

Gilles,

My love stands by the ocean shore,
wistfully watching the ebbed tide.
Soon the ocean will swell,
roar and roll joyous tidings to my love.

J.R. Teasdale

Look for us online at:
www.pieeyepublishing.com

Reach us on line at:
1-888-4pieeye (474-3393)

Inquire about us:

Canada
43 Samson Blvd.
Suite 333
Laval, PQ H7X 3R8

USA
116 Consumer Square
Suite 333
Plattsburgh, NY 12901

Other books by J.R. Teasdale:

IMMEDIACY, suspense visionary with a metaphysical twist.
The first in an upcoming trilogy.

MELODY INTERRUPTED, first in the pink series of hot romances.

CHAPTER ONE

Baltimore, 2000

Augustino Milan had met his match. He sat in the boardroom of his law office at the head of a gleaming cherrywood table—its polish obscured by the clutter of pocket PCs, pens, paper and twelve latest copies of the *Baltimore Sun*. He had just flown in from Miami to chair the emergency Monday morning meeting.

One of his young protégées, Brad Swell, was expressing with flourish why he thought the firm should tackle the strangest case of sneak and deceit ever to find its way into a lawyers' boardroom. "Once this information goes public," Brad argued, "we will be council for defense in one of the largest instances of fraud to hit the city core in ten years." It was their duty, he stated in lawyerly fashion, to represent Quartain Tech. "They are a high profile, government subsidized, state of the art engineering firm whose contribution to the community and the country at large more than warrants our legal help."

Augustino, his back to the other lawyers, elbows burrowed deep in the padded armrests of his high-backed lounger, reflected on an unrelated topic. A more formidable adversary sprang to mind. And it had nothing to do with Brad, Quartain Tech's high-handed rollers or his law practice. The morning's dark thoughts churned knots in his stomach, producing the same discomfort that had held him hostage most of the weekend.

Steepled fingers gently rubbing together, he exhaled deeply, continuing to ignore the pregnant pause his silence splayed around him. His only escape—to stare out the floor-to-ceiling windows with a mind's eye still fixated on palm trees, clear blue skies and miles and miles of sunlit shoreline. And nestled at the forefront of this landscape postcard peered the dark soulful eyes of a temptress—a striking one.

Even now, as sophisticated and blasé as people deemed he was, the mere recall cranked his pulse up a notch. That's how he had felt the night they met when he had lugged around his barefaced wish to dance with her—like some pathetic teenager paralyzed with the numb of a crush.

Tall, willowy and athletic, with a smile that could have launched those thousand ships, she had not appeared to notice him. Yet even though his heart had trounced what little cohesion his brain had summoned, he had spent the evening watching her dance with his friend Emilio Arroyo.

To Emilio, the young woman was simply subject matter

in the investigation of the death of his father. An informant's tip had dragged him, Emilio Arroyo and his sister Conchita, and Gary Flint—his longtime friend at the FBI—to to the celebration of the unveiling of the statue of Simon Bolivar—the *Libertador*—and of Alexander Petion, both men honored by the Haitian and Miami community that night.

The young woman attending the millennium party at the Miami City Club, on the previous scorcher of a Thursday evening had registered as Fiona Christian. The mole's insinuation was that influential Fiona Christian was an important link in the long-time operation of smuggling Cubans across the border; Cubans the FBI suspected mercenaries were packing off to camps to train as potential terrorists the minute they hit United States' shores.

But in the varied circles they frequented, many names had surfaced as early candidates for frontrunner renegades. They had never found any conclusive proof against any of them; and too often in this elusive game of tag, innocent people were routinely rounded up and blamed—framed—whenever it suited the tormentor's purpose.

So even when the young naiad had registered at the heavily secured guest quarters as Fiona Christian, had handed over the ticket with her name on it when asked by the guard, Augustino had weighed the information cautiously, especially against the circumstantial evidence of a paid informant. "No way can this young thing be your mysterious white tiger," Augustino had said. Dressed in a pale yellow sheath, her dark hair clipping a soft curve about her delicately sculptured face, she had emerged youthful and fresh. "She has stars in her eyes. Just out of college at best. And I can tell you," he had added stormily, a stubborn glint in his eyes, "she does not fit the bill—you're making a terrible mistake."

That's when Gary Flint had stepped in to ease him out of the way—peg him down a notch or two. "Better stay out of this one, Augie. I think you've met your match with this looker," he had laughed—the laugh more meant to mask his surprise at his friend's unusual reaction.

Augustino supposed the strange mellow weakness that had invaded his limbs as he had watched the beauty glide over the dance floor had been flagrant enough to flag Gary's attention early in the game. Gary who knew him since university. Gary who was used to his legendary nonchalance when it came to gorgeous women staking his hide as a trophy.

It was a known fact. Augustino could run circles around most women—the reason he had never been caught in a matrimonial headlock. A succession of beautiful sophisticated women had tried, brandishing the gilded noose at one time or another. All had failed, sparking nothing more in him than a vapid interest to play.

Gary had added, "Emilio'll handle her, Augie. If there's any information to worm out of her, he'll get it done."

"I'll get her liquid and fluid—get her to talk, or submit to any other cooperation I can *squeeeeze* out of her." Emilio had agreed eagerly, grinning like the Cheshire cat of the famous fable. He too was rattled by Augustino's odd behavior.

With Emilio and Conchita's father recently killed in that war against terrorism, and because of the tacit approval of his FBI friend, against his better judgment, Augustino had agreed to go along with the charade, supporting instead the heavy weight of Conchita's infatuation for him dangling on his arm the whole of that evening.

"It's your turn to vote, Mr. Milan..." His young legal secretary Lisa Harrison prompted in a tentative voice.

Slowly Augustino twisted his chair to face the assembly and veered his blue-grey eyes on Lisa.

She blushed from the piercing gaze and the fixed half-smile. Augustino Milan resembled one of those sexy European models women drooled over, attractively pictured between the folds of Cosmo Magazine, Lisa Harrison thought. More than he did a high-profile corporate lawyer, she rued, with his long tanned face and the sensuous clef in his chin; or with those broad shoulders and long arms leading to well tapered hands—the sight of them more than once lending her the shivers. The thought had first struck her when she had met him during her job interview—and then every day since. She swallowed hard when she lowered her eyes and took in the long slender fingers, wishing he would find interest elsewhere.

Augustino was barely aware he was staring, and only distantly conscious he was making Lisa uncomfortable. The party in Miami had fazed him, jolted his universe. A banal affair like so many others, but the mere thought of it endured. Or...the mere thought of her...

He covered his eyes with a hand that rubbed the dreams out of them. He disagreed with Brad Swell and with a laboured shrug, anchored his jaw to face the music.

He took a deep breath and faced Brad with enough

energy to make any man shrink. "When Vincent Morello approached Frank with this," he nodded toward Frank Just, one of the lawyers he had agreed to hire seven months earlier, "we both thought it might be a great idea. I've consulted with a couple of people since then...." He paused and took a deep breath, addressing the twelve associates seated at his table. "It's not a known fact yet...but their company logo was recently found on auxiliary power units, amidst the exhaust ports in the rear fuselage of aircraft confiscated in northern Iraq and Samangan—a province of east Afghanistan." His tone was measured and deathly quiet.

"That's not much to go on," from Ron Cheney, one of Augustino's oldest partners. "Logos are easy to come by."

"This one has a unique format—the letter Q crossed with a T—very subtly embedded into the APUs' envelope used to mount the units. Probably overlooked by whoever built them."

"Or kept there on purpose...for a frame perhaps?" Frank supplied shyly.

"My knowledge of avionics is limited," Ron added. "But I'm guessing they didn't follow the criteria for the 'integrity of the APU's critical parts' guide...for optimal security." He sneered at his own joke. "Still, very little to indict here. What does Vince say about all this?"

"Vince Morello appears to be one clueless CEO. Apparently they found this same logo on ammunitions carriers. Still, Vince maintains he has no idea of what's going on." Augustino hesitated. "He might be telling the truth; my man maintains there's a higher ranked puppeteer pulling the strings."

"Who's this mysterious contact?" Brad wanted to know. "Or is it political clout that's scaring you away, Augie?"

Augustino chose not to answer. Instead he gave Brad a tolerant but condescending leer.

"Come on, Augie." Brad was already losing ground under the vigilant glare. "This is a media-hungry case. We can draw a lot of publicity from it...."

"The boy's right, Augie. Let's talk publicity! You want to see publicity?" Ron flipped to the first page of the newspaper in front of him. "Quartain Tech, the newest wonder kid on the block...searching for ways to fund their most recent version of an undersea robot technology named Kevin...just accepted a two hundred million dollar grant from the US government's coffers." Ron continued to read excerpts of the article. "The robot will measure weather vagaries and map any changes to the environment of the ocean floor, helping us to predict intemperate storms and hurricanes...will even remember its own original location...blah, blah, blah. Forgive the pun; but, gentlemen, we can ride this publicity wave."

"You're right, Ron." Augustino sat up in his chair, elbows leaning on the table, his white shirt and dark tie reflected in the well-buffed veneer. "And ten years from now, this city will still be...submerged by this wave."

"Exactly my point. A blast of a party...," Brad interrupted rudely with a know-it-all smirk on his face.

Smacking his hands flat on the table, Augustino stood so abruptly the sudden motion sent his chair rolling toward the window. Brad's lingo was not lost on him, having spent months helping him kick a highly toxic, very expensive habit. "Walk out of the *Explorer Club,*" he gritted under his breath. "Long enough to realize that no one's keeping *score* here. I don't need to tell you how unproductive that would be." Augustino stared at Brad to check that the hidden analogies had reached their mark. No one else would question his words. They didn't have to. Brad sobered immediately, shifting his eyes to the files in front of him.

Augustino softened his bearing. A tentative smile hovered on his lips. "As I was saying, in very little time," he added much calmer, retrieving his chair, "the firm who defends them will have to start rowing in the opposite direction just to avoid the draw...."

Brad recognized the determination in his mentor's clenched jaw, swallowed the ready reply he had prepared and opted to sit this one out; wait for some other schmuck to say his piece.

"How do you know this?" Ron pursued, swiveling in his chair at the end of the table.

"Trust me, Ron." Augustino assured him as he sat back down. "This...little problem Vince exposed to us is like a runaway train with no means of stopping."

Ron cocked his head, waiting for more.

Augustino said. "Senator Paul Greensand was the first to launch an investigation into the matter. A quiet investigation. So quiet, that this is not known by anyone else but a handful of agents at the Bureau. The team of Jim Dunbar and Fred Lowman are investigating."

"Reliable team," added Frank, seated to the right of

Ron. "They did some investigative work for Metzger and James when I was with their firm—in one of the counter-fraud suits they headed a couple of years back. Very impressed with their work."

There was a pause around the group as Augustino allowed his team to draw their own conclusions.

"Paul Greensand was killed—in a suspicious car accident, I might add," breathed Samantha Craig, a young lawyer seated next to Augustino. The frown on her brow spoke volumes as she stared at the others.

Ron added. "How far up the ladder do you think this goes?"

Augustino shrugged. "Big government funding, planes in our enemy's hands—not to mention weapons and industrial robotic software that bore the same coat of arms..."

"You wouldn't let political muscle scare you...would you, Augustino?" Sam was thinking out loud. "I'm sure you wouldn't," she answered her own question.

"God knows I love a political snub as much as the next guy, Sam; and I've never been one to back away from a fight. But I draw the line at boarding a sinking ship—or taking the rest of you with me." He glanced at the twelve members around the table and cleverly assessed he had more than half of them convinced—enough to win the vote. But he felt he owed his team some form of explanation. After all, he was the one who had instituted this democratic fair march of choosing the bigger clients. "The young man who wrote the article you just read, Ron...Scott Tobin, he's all of twenty-seven. He's been pushing to make these inquiries public—ever since

Paul Greensand died. This is his first piece, to be followed up with nine articles due to conclude with the dirt on what he and Greensand found. Nine articles that will never be written. All of his notes have disappeared...." Augustino paused for effect. He looked around at the others one by one. "Scott Tobin was pronounced DOA this morning at Greater Baltimore Medic. He accidentally drank quinine water."

The tension around the room could not have been sliced with a knife, so thick it was.

"ID?" Ron asked, a helpless angry look in his eyes.

Augustino nodded. "Medic-alert bracelet...still had it on."

Sam drew a breath. "The killer was sloppy. Didn't even bother taking it off."

"Sloppy or...cocky?" Ron added.

Augustino continued. "Quartain's second in command, Henry Williamson, is cornered and about to confess." He paused to let his announcement sink in, repressing a long soulful sigh. The air around him taut, he toyed with the platinum-trimmed Mont Blanc on his binder, his eyes seemingly glued to the motion of twirling the pen just right. "I guess there's no need to tell you, you're all sworn to secrecy," he added, still not eyeing anyone. "Not one word of this leaves the room. One hint to anyone, an incidental leak to the press, and they'll find you—find you and have you up on charges—trumped up or otherwise...."

"Anything else?" From Ron who appreciated the full gist of it. "Why Williamson? What's in it for him?"

"Immunity is in the workings. Always a big hook...

that's all I can say for now."

"If you ask me, immunity is nowhere near his wish list," Ron added. "Although, he's too crafty to give up something for nothing...kind of makes you wonder."

Augustino stared at Ron long and hard. His eyes imparted avowal of Ron's comments. But noticing the others hanging on to their every word, he held his tongue.

"You're right about one thing, Augie," Ron admitted. "This bloody situation is a royal mess."

Augustino straightened in his chair to the full breadth of his shoulders, glancing at each one of them assembled there for the sole purpose of this decision.

The other lawyers looked at each other. They knew Augustino Milan was not one for theatrics or prone to exaggeration. He had built this firm with applied shrewdness and a reputation for fair play. If he suggested they walk away, then they would consider the path in earnest.

Samantha Craig nodded her understanding. "Can those of us who have already voted discard the result and start again?"

"If everyone else agrees that this is a valid solution... by all means." Augustino answered with a shrug. His attitude contrasted sharply with the tense calm draped over the boardroom. He knew his demeanor would dictate play. And he needed the win.

Two weeks later, Augustino was meeting with Samantha Craig. They were pouring over the staple documents in one of her new cases.

Lisa knocked, entered and apologized for interrupting them. "Emilio Arroyo is on the phone and urgently needs to talk to you, Mr. Milan."

"Thank you, Lisa. What is it, *amigo*?" he answered, motioning to Sam that she could stay.

"I have a shadow. I can't reach Gary. Can you let him know I need back up, my friend? Oh! And I have obtained nothing from the *Lolita* I dated on the night of the party."

"I'm not surprised. Gary said she is not Fiona Christian. They found the real one. She is a social director for the City of Miami shelters. The FBI paid her a visit this morning and it turns out that her purse and its contents..."

"Let me guess. A ticket to the party..."

"...was stolen over a month ago."

"So, we are right back where we started, 'cause I was unable to get any information from that girl. If she did not steal that ticket, then she is a plant for whoever did, and she is one cool avocado."

"It's cucumber—and you spent the night with her...I can't believe you didn't get any information. Where's that legendary Arroyo efficiency?" Augustino mocked, hiding his deep disappointment of the results.

"Don't get your back up—jealous? Want details?" Emilio laughed greedily as if reveling in some secret. "Relax, *gringo*! We got to the motel and she passed out—honestly. I got her undressed and watched her sleep—waited for her to wake up."

"And?" Augustino did not like the sound of that.

"She looked like an angel!" Again, Emilio laughed

sensing Augustino's frustration. "All soft and sensuous, with delicious curves..."

"Get to the point." Augustino ordered gruffly.

And Emilio was bright enough to know when to quit the game. "I think maybe she drugged me or something—at the party..."

"Drugged you! Think, *amigo*. You're talking about a girl who wasn't clever enough to turn you down—to refuse all that champagne you had her imbibe..."

"Well, how do you explain that once we got to the motel, I dropped faster than the Miami sun in the December sky? First thing I knew, it was morning and she was gone, man."

"You didn't get a name—an address—anything?"

"No*, amigo. Nada.*"

"Nothing in her purse?"

"An evening bag. *Vacía*. A lipstick, a compact, a twenty-dollar bill..."

"Unbelievable..."

"Too unbelievable. I agree. Anyway, I spent the last two weeks describing her to the taxi drivers of this city. Maybe she was picked up by someone, 'cause nobody's seen her. She is a ghost."

And Gary was worried Augustino would bungle the mission. He suddenly longed to know her name. Some little clue as to who she was, where she lived. Without this basic information, the girl was gone, out of his life for good.

"*Dios!* I think they've caught up with me." Emilio's tone was sharp and angry.

Augustino sensed fear in Emilio's bravado and

realized this call had little to do with the disappearance of one girl.

"Stand pat, *amigo*," Augustino countered. "I will get someone to cover you. Are you out in the open?"

"Visible enough. So far, I've managed to steer clear of him...or them. I don't know how many are out there. But don't worry, man. I can outrun them if I have to." Emilio was trying to make light of his situation. "People, I mean. Bullets I don't outrun—too small and too fast; but they can do damage."

"Don't do anything foolish, Emilio. Be patient. They can't get to you if you don't move. I will call the local police if I have to. Where are you?"

"Somewhere near the market. I've been walking in circles trying to lose them. I think my car is two blocks east."

"I'll find you." He hung up with Emilio and yelled out in the intercom. "Lisa! Please, I need you."

When Lisa got to his desk, a little out of breath, he was copying a number from his private agenda onto a notepad. "Please, get me Gary Flint or Bob Farrell on the phone—anyone you can find in that department actually—at this number." He handed her the yellow piece of paper.

"What's going on, Augustino?"

He raised his hand, signifying for Sam to wait—for Lisa to be out of the room. *Hold on, Emilio. Help's on the way.*

He recognized Sam's concern. She was the only one he had confided in. Actually, she had wormed the information out of him during the one night they had spent together. Working late a few weeks ago, while he was moody over the turn of events in Miami and obviously grateful for her support at their board meeting, they had shared some laughs over their paired hunger pains as they had left for the evening.

In sync, they had agreed to defy the summer downpour and run across the street to the nearest deli just to grab a bite. The cozy coyness of a safe haven against thunder and lightning, the quiet hush about the place—usually brimming with eaters—had led to sympathy…then intimacy…straight to the spread of bare confidences.

Sam was excellent at gleaning the truth out of people. That was her job and she performed it well. One thing had led to another—he wasn't exactly sure about the sequence of events—but they had ended up in bed together.

That's when the pillow-talk discussion had sprung the master-mind plan he, Gary and Emilio had been working on for almost a year now. The undercover juncture that was going nowhere and had them stumped—again. But he had not uttered word one about the mystery lady. The sin of omission was preferable to the remorse of having Sam feel bad about their encounter. Not to mention that this instant relationship with his right-hand lieutenant fanned all the colors of a one-night stand.

He could not commit—he had apologized between caresses that taunted and grunts that moaned and groaned their way inside her. What else could he do? He was holed up as a prisoner of soft sensuous arms that would not let him rest.

She had agreed, speaking the words haltingly as her tongue had hungrily snaked its way between his legs—as if her hunger pains had not been sated, he had thought while willingly giving up to the ecstasy—as if he had been the choice morsel on her menu all along.

Luckily, they had picked up their work relationship without skipping a beat. He knew she had feelings for him—superficial or otherwise, he couldn't tell and didn't care. That she was waiting with baited breath for him to take her again? Perhaps. At least she had said as much, candidly, without guile or malice, taking advantage of the privacy of their tête-à-tête in his office the next day.

That's when he had endeavoured to set her straight. He was not looking for romance or any kind of stickability. The most he could offer was a sleep-over now and then.

She had smiled and declined his blatant attempt of a save and rescue mission. They would remain friends and excellent collaborators in their field, of course. And they would never speak of their tryst again.

He had admired her brave chin-up performance. Not even a tear had glistened in those beautiful hazel eyes. Still, he had vowed never to mix his personal and business drinks quite the same way again.

"Emilio is in trouble. He needs the cavalry riding over the hill on this one."

"How serious is it?" Samantha asked haltingly. And when the reply was slow arriving, she watched Augustino wrestle with his emotions as he paced in front of his desk.

He was some prized catch; she caught her breath as she gauged the length of him from head to toe. And she was willing to reel him in ever so carefully—even if it meant tempering her intentions wisely. She had made the *faux-pas* of jumping between the sheets with him far too early. Who could resist, she had argued in her own defence. The man was wealthy, charismatic, extremely sexy and her intellectual equal. Her name was strictly branded on his forehead, she had decided. She would bide her time. She would weave some clever silent trap. He wouldn't suspect a thing. Most men, she had long ago concluded, had no armour against a woman's manipulative and sensuous wiles.

"For Emilio to call—he's very proud—he must have exhausted all other possibilities...." He clipped his sentence and stared at her instead, telltale grey eyes rapidly conveying more than words could. Deciding quickly, he grabbed his briefcase and strode to the front office abutting his own.

Samantha ran to keep up with him.

"I can't seem to reach anyone at the number you gave me, Mr. Milan." Lisa spoke gravely, a bare thread in her voice and an earnest frown on her brow. "Only an assistant who says she'll relay the message. Is there anyone else I can call?"

"Never mind, Lisa. Contact the South Miami police. Speak to Chief Alejandro. Tell him to contact AirTech. He has the number. They supply Arroyo's vehicle with a GPS antenna. Ask him to have them do an AVL sweep. He's not far from his car. You'll need to keep the lines open, Lisa." While he was speaking, Augustino had already pulled on his jacket.

Lisa was furiously taking notes. She knew this was urgent—that she would work late this evening.

"Sam, call Raoul. Tell him to have the plane fuelled and standing by. I'm going to Miami..."

“You’ll never get a cab at this hour. Let me drive you to the airport.” Samantha was eager to participate and already heading for her purse.

He shook his head. “You’ll be more help to me here, Sam. Manuel drove me to the office this morning. He’ll be downstairs with the car.”

“How do you know?” Sam asked; a little miffed at the stern brush-off.

For a couple of long seconds, Augustino stared at her while she bravely supported the steel blue gaze that imparted how much he detested having his privacy probed. Then she saw him glance at his watch.

And just as Samantha Craig thought he would not deign to answer, he grudgingly complied as he walked toward the door. “Had classes all day—just around the corner. He’ll be there.”

*****

The white of Emilio Arroyo’s eyes shone as bright as twin flares lighting up his dark accoutrement—the only tell-tale glint against the backdrop of an alley so murky, even the sliver of moon refused to acknowledge it. His curly black hair was stamped matte and damp against his forehead. It matched the color of his irises riveted to the shadowy space from where he had last detected movement. His mood was just as gloomy as he labored to heave a constricted breath and stifle the noise through parched parted lips.

Gun cocked in his right hand, the barrel rubbing

against the stubble on his cheek, he crouched behind a column and backed-up against the wall as much as he could as he waited for a sign from the enemy. A faceless foe trapped him there; a yellow coward, underhanded hypocrite—who shot first, without warning, without reason—a fact that made him white-hot mad.

If only he hadn't run himself into a corner. He should have listened to Augustino and stayed put. *Augustino*! How long had it been since he had spoken to him? One hour? Two? It had to be around 8:30...or later. The sun had gone down ages ago...or minutes ago. In his state of mind, it was impossible to tell. He had prudently tucked his watch's green dial inside his sleeve. He could not afford to let anyone see him. The only indicators of time passing were his thirst deepening with each raspy breath, and stabs of hunger threatening to echo rumbling noises through the night. *How many of them were out there?*

Slowly he redressed, biting back the pain from the influx of blood that shot pins through muscles gnarled from crouching too long. He needed them strong and ready—his knees sturdy should he have to bolt.

He was furious and the heat of helplessness churned his Latin blood to a boil; enough to flush fear to the background and have him consider bolting again, making fie of a rowdily thumping heart pumping adrenaline galore into his system. As he took a peek from behind the slab of stone, two shots buzzed passed his temple. Frightened, he drew back trying to assess if the sharp whistle resounding in his ear was from that overflowing adrenaline or from the strident resonance of the bullets that had nearly nicked him.

Impatience and fear was not a good pairing. Together, they worked as Machiavellian rivals greedily feeding on each other, souring in a man's belly—till the double dose of disparity could well cost a man his life.

Impatience was the first chump to seize him by the scruff as the lengthy waiting game jabbed at his nerves. He was an eager Spanish buck. Pinned down at the mercy of some intruder's whim was not part of his plan. He would make a run for it. He would use the starless darkness as a cloak and fake the courage he needed to spring to safety. He prayed to god to allay his fears, to bless his moves and make him silent.

As he sprang to dash the fifty yards to cover—hoping to get to the street and out of trouble—he heard a hail of pops. He felt a violent pounding in his back, so strong that it lifted him off his feet and sent him crashing to the ground. *Madre de Dios* were Emilio's last thoughts.

By the time Augustino got to the Bayside Market, the area was crawling with people and police. He and Raoul had to shove their way through layers of onlookers, dozens of police officers fiercely guarding the scene from being trampled, intent on shoving these two strangers back away from the core of the raucousness.

"Let them through!" Augustino heard the voice of Gary Flint screaming some fifty yards ahead of them. "It's okay. They're with us."

In the middle of a poorly lit alley stood a tight little

group of men composed of Chief Alejandro, Gary Flint, Bob Farrell and four medics—packing up their gear. On the dark pavement, beneath the glow of a makeshift spotlight, a lone bundle lay curled up with a cloth draped over it—the only evidence the clump was the body of a man by the sole of his shoes sticking out from underneath a gray raincoat.

An earlier sudden downpour had rendered the search of the place impossible for the time being. The men were wet, disheveled, busily giving orders and asking questions of any bystanders they suspected might be a witness to the shooting. Clues would not be easily gathered.

Augustino bent beside the body and curled back a piece of the raincoat he knew was covering his friend Emilio. Emilio would have been the first to run and cordially greet him had he been able to do so. But even as he knew what to expect, there was no preparation against the stark truth of uncovering a warm friendly face suddenly turned to stone. He bit his bottom lip, willing it not to tremble. But his mind, amok with a forceful pervasive will of its own, reeled a gamut of familiar pictures and sounds that filled and violated every ounce of space in his head. He could hear Emilio laughing and chasing him down some alley. The echo of their boisterous dreams was as clear as if they'd occurred the day before. He spotted the shadowy surroundings of his old New York neighborhood ghetto, the one he had sworn to leave a hundred times during his youth. He remembered college and their discussions of the world at large in vivid animated detail. Then there was the night at a frat party when, high on life and their youth, they had secretly brandished swords made of foil, taking a solemn oath to make the world a better place to live.

Meanwhile, Augustino had gone off to Harvard to learn how to battle evil in the courts. Emilio had enlisted with the FBI to battle evil in the streets. Now, their Don Quichotte puerile ideals had brought them to this crossroad. Except that this time, there would be no discussions on the subject. All topics were closed. No words would ever be exchanged again—corny or otherwise—no explanations. Nothing of what had occurred this evening...all that had been shared between them, Emilio took with him.

He shuddered when he saw Emilio's baby-face profiled lifeless against the rough rocky pavement. He took humble comfort in the fact that there was no pain in the young man's features. Only surprise. He labored to close the one eye that seemed to be staring into space before slowly replacing the coat over Emilio's head.

When he rose, he drew a troubled breath and vowed that he would get whoever had done this. Whatever it took, he would do it.

"I'm sorry, boss. I know he was a good friend." Raoul had seen him and Augustino hang together for the last little while. He understood what Augie was going through. He laid a comforting hand on Augustino's shoulder.

Gary walked up to them. Tall and angular, his thin blond hair appeared dark and dirty, wet as it was and plastered against his forehead. There was a haggard look on his face and his chin jutted outward defensively against tears he was desperately trying to withhold.

Augustino knew he was a kind person who detested

violence. Emilio and he had often laughed at Gary's sensitivities. How a gentle soul such as his had wound itself into one of the toughest government departments, they would never know.

"I'm sorry, Augie," he mumbled, heaving a deep sigh. "I was his back-up for the last hour. I tried to contact him but he never picked up his cell...."

"It's not your fault, Gary. I told him to stay put..."

"We found his cell four blocks west of here, in the street..."

"I guess he must have dropped it when we last spoke." Augustino explained. "He called me about three hours ago. Must have been around 6:30 or so. He was trying to get to his car...."

"That's his car over there." Gary indicated with a toss of his head the shadow of Emilio's Mustang. "About 300 feet from where he was shot." Gary stopped talking. Deeply troubled, he shook his head, deploring the sudden loss of a friend and colleague, the shameful waste of Emilio's youthful death. "Did he mention anything urgent when he called?"

"No clues. Nothing that really mattered. Just that he'd been trying to locate the girl from the party—that he wanted back-up."

Chief Alejandro, running toward them, yelled triumphantly. "We caught the guy who did this!" He stopped in front of Augustino. "So far, it looks like a lone hitter," he stammered, a little out of breath. "Unfortunately, he is not going to be able to tell us who his friends are. He ran a roadblock five miles north of here. His car took a spin.... When he got out he started spraying everything in sight." Alejandro looked at the dejected faces surrounding him. Contritely he added. "When he drew his semi-automatic on one of my officers...his partner had no choice. He had to shoot...to kill."

"Great!" Gary added sarcastically. "Emilio must have been onto...something. Why else would someone risk so much just to shut him up? The question is what?"

"Could be revenge...a vendetta of some kind? It almost looks like a mob-style hit." Bob had just returned from directing the officers from the morgue to the designated area. He had signed the papers. And now all evidence of Emilio had been wheeled away.

The four men stared at the empty space where Emilio's body had lain. For the next minute, none of them said a word.

"Or a warning," Gary added. "He'd been searching for that girl. So far, that's the best reason we have. Maybe someone thought he was getting close."

Augustino shook his head. "Impossible. He told me that she had completely disappeared. She was a ghost. No one had seen her. No one had even recognized her."

"That's just it. Maybe someone did. And whoever did, panicked, thought Emilio was getting too close. Murder never makes any sense, Augie."

"Or it could be anyone from half of a dozen cases Emilio was working on." Augustino added gravely. "He told me about one of the brothers he had jailed– about the death threats."

Gary looked at Augustino, putting a hand on his arm.

"Listen, this may not be the time or place to discuss this... but think, Augie. The girl has to be a player...to be that invisible? I'm not saying she's the puppet master, Augie. I agree with you. Too young...too...inexperienced. But she has to be a player."

Augustino just stared at him, his eyes inscrutable.

"I know it's not something you like to consider; but I think she's part of the game...a game that just got...close and very personal."

Augustino kept his feelings to himself. There was no point in adding anything that would just be more conjecture. His years in the legal arena had taught him the futility of guesswork and empty theories. And to put up a fight tonight, in this rink of twisted logic, took too much courage. The kind of courage he knew he did not possess at the moment.

The same courage that drained out of him completely during the days that followed. They were strange and eerie days, spent between the wailings of Conchita's expansive fiery grief, the poignant sobbing of Emilio's brothers and sisters, nephews and nieces, and the teary well wishes of friends and colleagues.

Sitting in the small Catholic church in South Miami where over two hundred people had gathered for the funeral ceremony, Augustino stared at Conchita's proud expression. She was leaning on her husband's shoulder this morning, her eyes finally dry. And he noticed how Juan Sanchez was making an effort to appear contrite for the occasion. He usually favored a blank, impassive expression—as if protecting what he did not wish others to read in his eyes.

Glancing at Conchita and Juan's four children sitting next to them, Augustino was reminded of how young Emilio had been. A baby, with only a baby's-teeth bite into life. Barely two years younger than he was, like himself, Emilio had not had time to jump-start love in his life, the kind of love that demanded he settle down and raise a family. Some had commented how lucky it was there was no widow—even luckier no children were orphaned. How tragic that would have been.

Following the funeral cortege, Augustino could well imagine himself in Emilio's place. It could have been him lying there had circumstances been different. And different it would be if this procession were leading to his final resting grounds. For one, there would be no family to bid him goodbye. Just colleagues and a few friends. No widow—certainly no children. Lucky for them, he supposed; perhaps not so lucky for him. And strangely, at this odd hour, the beautiful face of a young stranger came back to haunt him. As he stabbed at the jab of tears burning behind his lids, he still refused to believe she had anything to do with his best friend...now being lowered six feet into the ground.

CHAPTER TWO

Miami 2004

Amanda Cole parked her white Beetle at the edge of Bayside Market in front of the statue of Simon Bolivar, the *Libertador*. First time lucky, she cheered. She usually needed fistfuls of quarters to plug the meter and a half mile walk on better days.

She stared at dear old Simon with a smile on her face. She had attended that party in the summer of 2000 when the Haitian community and prominent Miami politicians had celebrated the unveiling of their patron Liberator. She would forever remember the ritzy do that followed. From the tallest building in Miami, looking down on the gazillion lights of the harbor below, champagne flowing by the buckets, some boy and she had danced the night away. Both bedazzled senseless, they had spread July's heat to the sheets in the early hours of the morning with steamy, sexy, impetuous lovemaking—at least, from what little she remembered.

The first time she had ever taken any form of alcohol, she recalled—the embarrassment of being drunk senseless still stinging, years later. She had awakened to find her dress neatly folded on a chair beside the bed and a tousled dark haired young man, snoring louder than a hibernating bear, next to her. Out cold to regain his strength, she had thought. What she had not been able to figure—could still not figure after all those years—was why she had still been wearing her underwear. She shrugged, giving up on the riddle while wondering for the umpteenth time whatever had happened to that boy. She couldn't even remember his name.

Twice unlucky, she had concluded at the time—well, three, if a six-month stint with a warm-blooded Spaniard who cared more about his looks than his tepid performance at lovemaking counted for anything. Johnny the-jock-behind-the-bleachers-after-the-game had been the first man in her life—the first for a full ten minutes. Then there was this nameless, faceless, what-had-they-done blank. Well, not quite faceless. Piercing blue eyes floated in and out of a memory pieced together in inebriated remnants—just not affixed to any particular face. Still, she could not give up on finding Mr. Right just yet. He had to be out there somewhere.

She clutched her large canvas purse in one hand, the other quickly stowing her miniature pinscher Dino into it. "Please be quiet, little boy, or that nice guard at the Bayside Marina will kick us out." She gave him a peck on the nose, and as if on cue, Dino scrunched down amidst her personals and remained still and silent. She grabbed her other canvas bags stuffed with canned goods and boxes of miniature goodies, piled them in the folding trolley she had hauled out, locked her car, and saluted the statue as she hurried through the market's park entrance.

She felt like Cinderella running from the ball, clutching her mendicant-belongings, especially dressed as she was in scruffy, baggy work attire. Even so, there were many offers of help from the local yokels and self-appointed Casanovas. Smiling, she plowed her way through the invitations she politely ignored and made her way east toward the gate.

Amanda paused, took a breath and gazed at the familiar crowd of habitués populating the Bayside Market's entrance. Jake and his pet snake were at their booth on the plaza, thrilling and scaring the children. Also attracting his share of onlookers was Tom, supporting on each shoulder a greenwing macaw, rivaling their brightly colored plumage with his brash neon-yellow shirt—he leasing them out to tourists for twenty dollars a picture. Carlos Hernandez and his lady were hooking passers-by with flyers for their weekend Bahamian getaway cruise. And beyond the shops and restaurants, the wide-stroll sidewalks, lay the marina with the hustle and bustle of the intercoastal canal and its four hundred boat slips.

Amanda's favorite pastime was studying people, their behaviors and their interactions. That's why when Fiona Christian, the supervisor of her work unit, had suggested she moonlight cleaning and tending a yacht, she had readily agreed. She thoroughly enjoyed the outdoorsy freedom that working at the marina two hours on Tuesdays and Thursdays afforded her, not to mention the one hundred dollars a week it paid her.

"Never go on Friday," Fiona had insisted. "If you must, make sure it's before 4:00. The owner is a stickler about privacy and doesn't want any maintenance personnel gawking at him or his party unless he has screened them personally beforehand."

That was fine with her. She didn't give two hoots about some scoptophobic geezer-owner. She was happy tending the ship. And whenever some little voice of reason reminded her that she was no more than a glorified cleaning lady, she would focus on her love of the ocean, the keen experience it offered and on the extra cash to subsidize her meager wages as a social worker with the City of Miami.

She tucked Dino's head inside her purse, shushing him as she did. It wouldn't do for Bert the patrolling guard to spot him. She had heard how adamant he was about forbidding all pet owners from strolling onto the grounds with any type of animal.

Busy studying her entourage, Amanda missed Bert the guard studying her. He smiled when he saw her settle the moving lump inside her bag. She was not the only one who enjoyed surveying people. He liked it too, especially watching her. He focused on her long brown hair with one slim mesh of gold the sun drew attention to as it swept the side of her tanned face. Every Tuesday and Thursday about this time, he looked forward to feasting his eyes on the tall shapely silhouette of the spunky young temptress. Gazing into those immense dark eyes is what he enjoyed most—like looking at the ocean on a moonless night, he would fancy—ominously dark, one could sense the sultry depth and turbulent passion that brewed there. But it was those lips, he had long since concluded, full and beautiful with their accentuated pout that had people dance to whatever tune she played, begging to do her bidding.

"Where you running to so fast, Miss Amy?" Bert asked, tipping his hat.

"Same place as always, Bert. Slip 44."

"This is not your usual day. And you seem in a big hurry. You runnin' errands or something?"

Amanda nodded hurriedly.

"Need any help with that cart?"

"Thanks, Bert." It wouldn't do for him to spot her dog. "Don't bother." She flexed her nicely toned bicep. "I'm as tough as nails," she answered before quickly pushing past him.

"Be careful not to choke your little dog," he shot to her back.

She froze, turned, and asked him breathlessly, "What did you say?"

He smiled. "You'll catch heat stroke...if you jog," he rephrased with mischief in his eyes.

She nodded, relieved yet puzzled. Frowning, she continued apace, checking back toward Bert once or twice only to find him walking in the opposite direction.

He was right, she realized when she got to the yacht with her shirt soaked with sweat. It didn't pay to hurry. Good thing she had brought a change of clothes with her. They were usually for after though, for when she left.

Amanda strapped her purse to her shoulder and backed her cart up the plank onto the boat's high-gloss wood floors. She wheeled it to the wide white double doors and unlocked them both, hauling her bags inside. Before closing the doors, Amanda glanced at her surroundings—the blue sky, the hazy heat rising off the canal and the moored neighboring crafts bobbing up and down from the ongoing traffic. She liked this particular ship, the Grand Banks Aleutian 64, and as always, wondered where it had gotten its name, *Milan Milend.*

Shrugging and taking a deep breath, she reentered the cool air-conditioned interior and shivered from the cold dampness of her shirt. She had not been there since Tuesday and she was glad when a quick survey showed nothing had been disturbed. The kitchen was spotless. She had an hour maybe 90 minutes' work at the most. But first, she was going to change her top.

Picking up Dino in her arms, she petted the little dog and told him to stay close by as she put him on the ground next to her feet. Then she rummaged inside her bag and surveyed the peach ribbed top she had brought for wearing later. She hesitated. If she put it on now, she would have nothing clean to wear in a couple of hours when she was meeting big sister Meg downtown for supper. On the other hand, if she peeled off her wet khaki shirt, she would still have her bra. It was colored, flowered, and could easily pass for the top of a bathing suit.

She removed the sweater, dumped it into her bag and realized that the bra she had donned that morning was completely see-through, except for a flimsy lace-trim up and down. She sighed, extremely annoyed. That's what came from dressing in the dark. From trying not to wake a roomie with nothing but a measly Chinese silk divider separating their one cramped bedroom—the damnedest blow to privacy, she sighed.

Well, it was not as if anyone was going to see her. And she was not about to step out anywhere. She was stocking the cupboards and the small refrigerator with goodies, cleaning the heads and tidying the master stateroom—then she was out of there.

She got to her tasks swiftly, put on the television as background noise and imagined how wonderful it might be to just sail away. She had never been to the Caribbean—or up the coast, for that matter. To get away on this boat would be heaven. Amanda smiled as her eyes took in the salon equipped with curving settee and plasma television, regular headroom and wide windows that provided light and space. The galley was fitted with a side-by-side refrigerator-freezer, dishwasher and all the amenities faced in gleaming cherrywood finish. There were even a couple of bracketed vases complete with colorful scented bouquets. She had spent many hours pretending she kept house on this ship. It was actually roomier and brighter inside than her apartment—certainly cooler.

She bent to reach for the glass cleaner in the cupboard under the sink cupboard and, as she stood, a voice made her jump out of her skin.

"Hey, Amy! What are you doing here?"

"Shit! Jeff. You scared me. Don't ever sneak up on me

again. I'm liable to knee you in the groin next time you try a stupid stunt like that." She placed her hand holding a spray bottle over her fluttering heart, glaring at him as she did.

Jeff Nicholls owned the sporty 366 moored at dock 48. He was young, wore his curly brown hair cheek length, and possessed wide faded blue eyes and a pale complexion he tried to cover up with a thin beard and goatee. He had been openly flirting with Amanda ever since they had met a few months ago, when she had borrowed some cleaning products from him. Ever since, he would lurk nearby every Tuesday and Thursday, his persistent question lingering between them.

No. She would not go out with him. It was not that he was bad looking. He was actually cute in an odd sort of way. He was of medium build, her height, and pleasant company. She just was not interested in sleeping with him. She had sworn off sleeping with any man who did not absolutely and irrevocably send her libido spinning and her mind reeling, and she had not met anyone that fit that description in a long time. Not that he wanted any sort of commitment from her—just 'a meeting of great bodies between the sheets' was what he had actually proposed.

"I'm speechless," he said. "I'm ready when you are." He smiled, staring at her bra.

She followed his eyes and just remembered she was not wearing a top. "What! You act as though you've never seen breasts before. Are you that immature?"

"I've never seen a more beautiful pair before," he smiled at her.

Hands on hips, the spray bottle ominously aimed at

him, she decided she was not going to let him embarrass or bother her. "What are you doing here, anyway?"

He smiled and pointed to her chest. "Looks like they're...up and ready for action."

She looked down and rolled her eyes, disgusted with the moment, with him, and opted to turn her back on the whole mess—face the galley's sink instead of his childish comments. Betrayed by rock-hard nipples was the last straw.

"I could ask you the same question," he said. "What are *you* doing here? I thought you weren't supposed to be here on Fridays."

Amanda ignored the question, scooped up brushes and scrub pads and dumped them in a pail with the cleaning sprays she needed. It wasn't any of his business if work had delayed her the day before. A new family at the shelter desperately needed help....Besides, it was only three o'clock. She had another hour before she needed to be out of there. Wait a minute; she had never told him she was not supposed to be there on Fridays. Or had she?

When she turned to face Jeff again and ask him that question, he had gone. She spotted the back of him as he walked down the plank.

She cocked her head to one side, surprised by his behavior, and considered that maybe she ought to prance around him half-naked more often. Whether it intimidated him or not, it certainly had gotten rid of him in a hurry, which served her purpose just fine. She had no time to play today. And although Jeff could be charming, his attitude had just reinforced her decision to have nothing to do with him.

She scrubbed the bathroom clean, dusted the dressers and the top of the berth and put some scented heart-shaped soaps in the walk-in closet. The wooden doors to the closet matched the rest of the room, a light oak, Venetian in style, so the odor would delicately waft through the room.

Quickly Amanda freshened up and flipped on her peach top, changed her grungy pants for a short white wrap-around skirt and grabbed her bags, cart and purse. She locked the doors behind her and ran along the plank and the cement alley toward the exit.

"Finished so soon, Miss Amy?"

"Going home, Bert. Have a nice weekend."

Bert looked at her strangely. He put up his hand for her to stop. "That purse looks a little flat," he said. "Forget anything?"

Amanda stared, nonplussed.

"Your dog. Where is it?"

She put a hand to her mouth, her eyes widening. "You know...!"

"My reputation as a bad ass is on the line. I won't say anything if you don't." He smiled at her surprise.

"Here I thought I was so clever....How many other people are you doing this for?" She tilted her head, giving him a slanted grin.

"Counting you? One," he said, raising his finger to emphasize the comment.

"Thanks, Bert." She kissed him on the cheek. "You're a prince."

"Go on and get him before he thinks you've abandoned

him. I'll watch out for your things." Bert urged her on. That kiss made it all worthwhile.

Amanda got to the boat and unlocked the door. She called out for Dino but could not find him in the salon or in the kitchen. He had not climbed upstairs to the pilot station. She retraced her steps to the last place she had been. And there he was, behind the stateroom doors she had closed to allow the floral scent in the closet to permeate the room.

"Oh! My poor baby," she picked up his trembling little body and lodged him in her neck, against her cheek, kissing his little nose while cooing him to calmness. She trembled herself, thinking about what had almost happened. She would have remembered in the car. By then, it might have been too late. The boat might have sailed with her little precious on board.

She looked at her watch and knew she had to scoot. As she closed the bedroom door, she heard people boarding, the distinct plunk of footsteps stomping on the bridge, the ladder clanking with the sound of heels. She heard voices, a feminine one thrown in, muffled and alien—although she thought she recognized Jeff's nasal nag.

Now what? They were early, was all her mind froze on. She panicked. She could not just leave without someone noticing. And she didn't want to lose this job. She could not afford it. She was already in hawk with several projects she had vowed to make good.

She held Dino closer to prevent any whimpers. Suddenly, the leisure to decide vanished. Voices were approaching quickly. She re-entered the master bedroom and scoured the area for a place to hide. She opted to duck for cover in the stateroom's walk-in closet and hoped that although she could see through the louvered slats, they could not see her. And more importantly, would not need the closet anytime soon.

As Amanda held her breath, she wondered about the thump of her heart so loud in her ears. Then, curiosity taking over, she opened her eyes to catch a glimpse of the two people who had just entered the room.

A tall man stood his back to her. His hair was short, black, sleeked-back while curling-length tendrils ran down the nape of his neck. He was wide across the back, his shoulder breadth impressive. He was wearing a beige short-sleeved shirt and a loose-fitting pair of dress pants.

The woman had her arms wrapped around his neck and wormed her ruby red fingertips down the back of his head.

"You're already drunk, *cara*, and it's still two hours to dinner."

"I'm not drunk." The woman slurred her words. "I just needed a little pick-me-up to be better prepared for you. I know you like it when I'm ready and warm inside, easy to pry." Her tone was sultry, her accent Spanish and there was no mistaking her intentions.

She's Spanish, but he has to be Italian. Cara means sweetheart in Italian, Amanda pondered. But she could not decide if the woman's behavior was a deliberate, sensuous weapon to gouge the man's passion, or if alcohol was really to blame for her wanton posture. In any case, she wished she would move so she could get a better look at her face.

No sooner formulated than she got her wish. Much more than she had bargained for. She not only gazed upon a beautiful face, hot, sultry eyes and parted red lips, but a voluptuous body that was slinking, contorting and writhing in ways Amanda had never dreamed existed–to get this man's attention, obviously.

"I'm going to be as soft and willing as a kitten," she purred, "with the bite of a tigress," she added, picking up his right hand and sticking his third finger in her mouth, doing a complete number on it. "Now, you know where this finger goes, don't you," she breathed, removing her sheath of a dress over her head, baring all except for a jewel-studded thong.

Femme fatale extraordinaire then turned her back to him, gracefully bent from the waist as she told him. "Remove the thong, *querido.* I am waiting; and I cannot wait any longer." She pretended to pout, presenting him with a smooth, well-rounded tush.

Oh my god! Amanda could not believe her eyes. The man grasped the woman's arm and yanked her to face him. He clutched her against him, strapping an arm around her waist. "I need you to be sober this weekend," he muttered between clenched teeth. Then he showed her the finger she had sucked on and jabbed it where she had asked him to put it.

Amanda closed her eyes. This was much more than side-glancing at those porn flicks Meg and Jerry loved to watch. This was real, going on not two feet in front of her. She suddenly wished she was miles away from there. Because as tightly shut as her eyes were, she could not help hearing naked lady's squeals of pleasure; her moans and groans and pleas for him to remove his clothes and take her completely. So convincing were this woman's pleas, that she caught herself peeping through her eyelashes. Then she opened her eyes wider when finally seeing the man's face. He turned to face her as he held the woman up—barely supporting herself on what Amanda imagined would be weak legs by now.

She stared at his face, not believing how handsome he was. Not pretty handsome. Ruggedly so. Dark lashes, what looked like steel grey-blue eyes, a long Mediterranean face with a dark tanned complexion. A smile hovered over his playful mouth traced with tempting, sensuous lips. She could not believe how familiar he looked—as though she had seen him before. Maybe he was an actor she couldn't quite place. She also couldn't believe how cold and detached he was. Even she, recoiled and remote, willing to be elsewhere, stood there with her legs crossed, unconsciously flexing her thigh muscles, utterly aroused by the sight of his hand deftly driving this woman senseless and closer to orgasm with each passing second. Did he have ice water running in his veins or what?

She had always thought a woman was irresistible to a man—any woman, whether he liked her or not—especially one looking like that. That was what the whole James Bond persona exemplified. The hero for good going down in the trenches with the arch enemy beauty. And even before James Bond, as far back as biblical times, there was Adam and Eve, Anthony and Cleopatra, Samson and Delilah—and all those other love-hate couples in between.

Worse, as Amanda was certain the wanton partner was about to come, the man withdrew, picking her up and laying her down on the bed. Even she knew how painful that had to be.

"When you sober up, I will finish this. Until then, dress for dinner. We have guests."

The woman began shouting profanities at him. They were serious threats. "And behave yourself," he admonished, only slightly winded, "or you will get nothing later." His threat seemed to work. She quieted down almost instantly.

As for him, he wiped his hand on his handkerchief, straightened his tie and just as Amanda was set to believe he was a total monster, she saw the bulge in the front of his pants. Well, perhaps just a monster of self-control. He had to be severely aroused or dangerously well equipped or both, because that was some bulge and those were loose pants.

Just then she heard a noise in the engine room. Another bout of panic seized her. What if they left while she was on board? Where could she hide? The engine room! She remembered. An emergency door in the head behind the shower led to the engine room. Once there, she could easily take the stairs to the side deck, then sneak out by climbing the emergency ladder at the front of the ship.

She simply had to wait for this man to leave the room. Then she would try to sneak into the bathroom before the woman recovered. She had lunged across the bed, face down and softly moaning.

Gently, Amanda opened the door to the closet, and keeping a hand securely wrapped around Dino's muzzle, she inched out of her hiding place. Delicately, she tiptoed to the head and turned the gold handle, praying that clicking sound would not be too loud.

Once inside, she had a little more flexibility to maneuver. She opened the hatch to the engine room and started running between the giant Caterpillar motors revving in preparation for departure.

The noise was deafening as she surreptitiously ran along the narrow white corridor leading to freedom, hoping and praying no one else was there.

She dove for the door, climbed the stairs two by two and checked the coast headlong before emerging from her hiding well. She waited and listened for a sound, any sound other than her fibrillating heart and rakish breathing. Damn it, why did she need so much air? Where the hell was it all going?

The coast seemed clear. She unlatched the door leading to the lower deck and stepped out along the narrow, gleaming white passage. She walked toward the front, toward the side ladder to the deck. She was ill equipped for the hustle of the vertical climb with Dino in her hands. She tucked him in securely against her chest and delicately, silently took the metal rungs one by one, slowly. Finally she could see the deck. It looked abandoned. She flipped her leg over the ledge, being careful not to smother Dino too tightly against her, and eyed the outside plank to freedom....

"What are you doing here?"

She screamed, turned and encountered the tall man from the cabin. Facing her, towering over her, he looked so much more potent than he had in the room not five minutes earlier. The full force of his eyes delved into hers and she glimpsed recognition in them. As if he knew her. She noticed his bottom lip tuck in and thought she caught his chin trembling. Amanda shivered under this sustained gaze, and she was not easily intimidated. But all she could visualize was his impish hand lavishly foraging between that other woman's legs. She swallowed a nervous twitch in her throat and noticed he did not inquire as to who she was.

She turned, hearing Jeff walk out to meet them. He clucked at her teasingly. "I thought you were long gone. It would have been better if you'd left."

All of a sudden she noticed how precarious her situation was. These guys might be drug dealers or smugglers or... white slave traders for all she knew. Who would come to her rescue? Who even knew she was here? This was more than about keeping her job. This was about leaving. Now!

"If you'll excuse me," she smiled. "I have a dinner engagement, gentlemen." She made to leave, walking toward Jeff; but extending a hand the stranger grabbed her from behind and pulled her toward him with his arm wound tightly around her waist. She could feel how rock-hard it was as he yanked her back flat up against him. Annoyed more than mesmerized, she felt his breath brush pass her ear.

"You're going to have dinner with us," he said, barely audible as he caressed the lobe of her ear with his lips.

Jeff laughed, nervously backing away from them as if sensing that his partner was now putting dibs on this fine glass of wine. "Can I have the other one, then," Jeff asked with a wry look in his eyes.

There was no answer.

"Augie! You can't have 'em both. You choose, man. But you leave me one."

So, his name was Augie. What kind of name was that, she wondered. "I can't stay, gentlemen," she gasped bravely, her back still tucked in tightly against Augustino's rock-hard torso. "Not that your invitation doesn't flatter me; on the contrary. If you wish, I can come back...next week—if you like..."

"Inside!" Augie told her, bodily backing her through the open door.

As she struggled with him to head in the opposite direction, Amanda saw that the woman from the stateroom had come up the indoor stairs. They could see her through the galley windows, heading to the salon where Amanda spotted three more men sitting on the settee.

"Jeff, tend to Connie. I don't want her saying the wrong thing to our guests. She's drunk."

"Aye, aye, skipper." He laughed at Amanda.

No doubt he's excited by my predicament, buoyed by my helplessness, the louse. Amanda bore her eyes into Jeff's back—as if this was going to make a difference. "Why do you want to keep me here?" She asked, turning her profile toward the stranger who still had her wrapped against him, the slightest catch in her voice.

Augustino backed away from her enough that she was able to turn and face him. He looked at the dog she was holding and whispered in low tones. "You can be *my* pet for the weekend. You can play house, do my bidding. I will be your keeper. Would you like that game?"

She stared at him hard, not even realizing she was

holding her breath. There was something so familiar about him. It was the eyes, she thought. They were insistent and probing as if trying to reach deep inside her.

"Would you, *cara*? Are you a player, I wonder?"

He had spoken softly, under his breath, and Amanda could not tell if he was goading her or seriously considering this. She took a long quivering breath and shook her head for good measure. Just in case he was to get the wrong idea. She might be hypnotized by the depth of his eyes and the gentleness she thought she had glimpsed lurking there, bowled over by the way his powerful hands had caressed that woman, but that did not mean she was willing to play cat and mouse with him.

"Miss Amy?" Bert was calling to her from the edge of the dock. "Are you all right?"

Bert! She had forgotten about him. He still had her things and was probably waiting for her to show before he left his shift. Might even be worried about her.

"I'm fine, Bert," she answered, daring Augie to say otherwise. "I'm coming down promptly." She had the nerve to tilt her head at this redoubtable man before walking off without looking back. She was aware somewhere behind her of the commotion caused by an irate Jeff; but otherwise, the tall stranger did not lift a hand to stop her. Only once in Bert's presence did she risk looking at where she had stood.

The man called Augie was now sitting on the back door to the boat's ramp, his bent right leg sandwiched between his arms, avidly staring at her as if willing her or desperately waiting for her to return.

Amanda looped her arm into Bert's and thanked him profusely as they walked away, still unable to stop staring at the man. "Do you know who this owner is?" she asked him, her heart still aflutter.

"I can poke around if you like, Miss Amy. Did he scare you or something?"

Amanda shook her head. "No. He didn't scare me, Bert. Just made me curious. You know me," she smiled at him, flexing the arm with the purse and Dino's head in full view, "tough as nails."

He had not scared her. He had bewildered and excited her. From somewhere, a little voice had assured her he could never really hurt her.

Augustino returned to the coolness of the ship's salon and welcomed the air-conditioned atmosphere on his burning, hot forehead. He was wound up, agitated. After all these years of searching—hoping—opportunity had placed the lovely woman at his doorstep. Opportunity? Could the meeting have been set up to look like an accident and be none other than an elaborate plan? Staring at the little confab in his salon, he gathered all his physical strength to remain composed. He eyed the people assembled there.

Connie was sprawled on the divan like a wanton siren—her eyes scorching at will anyone who dared look her way. *Pouting—she's trying to make me jealous*, thought Augustino ruefully.

Gary Flint was relaxed and sipping a glass of gin and tonic, his eyes drawn to Conchita's every move. Mistrust or good old fashion lust? Augustino was not certain.

Bob Farrell, dark and imposing, sat hunched over the coffee table, flipping through the latest issue of a magazine on boats and trailers, relaxing and out of his usual bureau uniform.

Jose Arroyo, older brother to Emilio and Conchita, was waiting for the meeting to start with barely concealed impatience. Twice in ten minutes he had changed his seat and was now standing at the end of the settee.

Augustino imagined what the men's reaction would be when confronted with the news he had just learned. Telling them would be like lighting a torch under a volcano, threatening to reopen a wound that had not yet healed—for anyone. Relishing the peace he knew would soon be shattered, he considered remaining silent about the girl—for no other reason than to have the leisure to prove them wrong. Quickly he dismissed the thought. He desperately needed to believe there was nothing to hide, nothing to prove. Telling them about the girl would establish this and would reaffirm his loyalty to both camps. To double the strides that they had made in the past year with this case, they needed to work in unison.

Augustino sighed as he entered the salon; raw and on edge, he was in no mood for Connie's antics. By now, she was stretched like a cat, and she wore the tight skirt of her dress in a slinky ringlet at the top of smooth, silky thighs. "Jose, tell your sister to behave. We need to talk—privately."

Jose glanced at his sister then eyed the men with an angry leer. But when he faced Augustino's adamancy, he nodded nervously and rose to accompany Connie out of the room. She protested in slurred Spanish, threatening to make a scene if he forced her to leave.

But Jose could be a terrifying little man when he chose to be. In Spanish, he threatened to have her physically removed by his bodyguard Anton. A block of a man with a deadened leer in his eyes, he was Jose's shadow—always there—rarely visible, lurking in a corner somewhere.

Jeff came down from the pilothouse. "Augie, Captain Lutz never showed. And Raoul doesn't want to take her out too far—not until he's more used to her."

"Very well. Tell him to cut the motors. We'll stay docked." Augustino finished pouring himself a scotch then sat down beside Gary. "Oh, and close the double doors once you're up there. We need privacy."

"You satisfied, Milo?" Jose asked, sitting down again with the others. "I hate fighting with my sister. You had better have good reasons to exclude her from this meeting," he told him aggressively. He was never one to openly cooperate. Emilio's death had not sweetened his disposition. "It's her war too. And she has been an excellent collaborator—risking everything to help you. You people!" He complained. "You never bring family into the picture. You protect your loved ones and hide them under rocks while you leave us vulnerable and exposed. It is my family being destroyed bit by bit..."

Bob Farrell added. "We know, Jose. We understand. That's why we have allowed you to share a bigger role in what we are implementing."

"Nonsense...," Jose vociferated.

"You didn't hear me very well, Jose." *The man can be*

deaf when he chooses to be. "I meant for you to assist your sister and go with her. I need to talk to Bob and Gary—alone."

There was a stunned pause all around as Jose waged a staring match with Augustino Milan. He knew Milo's will was unbendable, and the stubborn glint he saw there made him jump up, causing him to spill part of his beer on the floor. His face had reddened a couple of shades. He was quick tempered but his demeanor was beyond anger; he was fuming with rage. The two evils he despised the most—being insulted by having to take orders, and being kept out of the loop. "You have something to say to these bozos, you say it to me!" Jose articulated at the top of his voice, his Spanish accent strong when he was irate. He stared at each man in front of him with daggers in his round dark eyes. "First my father, then my brother...."

"Relax," Augustino urged. "It's nothing that concerns you. We can have our meeting later...."

"I will say what concerns me!" He shouted, his body shaking with rage. "You will not have secrets—none." He waved a finger, not two inches from Gary's face and Augustino had to check his own growing irritability, visible in his clenched jaw and dark expression.

"Let him stay," Gary shrugged tentatively, more to diffuse a potentially explosive situation. They needed Jose's cooperation. They could not afford to thwart him—not yet. "I don't mind, Augie."

Augustino shook his head mildly, trying to convey to the two that he had confidential information to hand them. But Gary had a goofy *doesn't bother me* expression on his face while Bob was staring at his shoes inexplicably aloof all of a sudden, as if this was a domestic dispute in which he had no business taking sides.

Augustino sighed. There was another staring match between him and Jose. He knew he needed to capitulate—and capitulate he would, but on his own terms. "Very well. Let's get on with our meeting."

"Proceed with the information you wanted to hide from me," Jose taunted. "If there is going to be trust between us, Milo, you need to bare a little of yourself to me. We have laid our family's troubles at your feet, Milo, having no choice but to believe in you and your friends. You will do me the same honor."

Augustino recognized the logic behind the statement. After all, the encounter might involve details about Emilio's murder, and perhaps some clue as to who had shot him and why.

Augustino took a sip of his scotch, trying not to let the others see how shaken he was. "I have just had an encounter—aboard ship a few minutes ago."

Gary and Bob looked at each other, only now just sensing how vital this information might be.

"The last girl to dance with Emilio. The young woman at that party four years ago. She was on my ship just now, leaving as we boarded. Trying to sneak away actually—unsuccessfully." He downed the last dregs of his scotch. The event was real now. There was no escaping the storm.

"My god, man! Why didn't you stop her—arrest her or something?" Gary stood up, absolutely stunned.

"I tried. She had someone waiting for her outside. A guard—from the complex."

Bob finally found his voice. "The mysterious white tiger we've been looking for high and low these past four years was just aboard your ship? Why the hell didn't you call for back-up?"

"White tiger, white tiger!" yelled Jose. "That's all I've been hearing about these last years. I told you before and I will tell you again," he yelled, getting up to pace, hands deep in his pockets. "My brother would never have allowed some pretty *chica* to kill him. A gang of thugs did it. The Havana Club. They are our fiercest competitors; and they are picking us off one by one while you guys are letting them do it!"

Bob tried to quiet him down. "We investigated the Havana Club. They traffic in illegal products just as you do, Jose. They have nothing to gain by killing your people. Besides, they were never near either area when your father and brother were killed."

"Or close to any of the other two murders," added Gary.

"A lot you know, *gringo*. I happened to know more. And you are *loco*. We do not traffic in illegal guns and weapons. Only products that people need. Our operation provides services and jobs for many of my countrymen."

"Do you know her name?" Gary asked, only caring about the news Augustino had dropped in front of them like a hot potato. "How to reach her—where she lives?"

Augustino shook his head. "But Jeff does. Apparently she's been tending my ship these past few months."

"Unbelievable," Gary muttered.

Jose was seamless in his rantings. "Besides, the people-smugglers—whoever they are—cannot be killers. All they do is trade money for taking people out of Cuba. The worst your white tiger lady can be accused of is being an illegal travel agent, lending mercy to my people trapped in starving parts of Cuba."

"How do you know these smugglers aren't killers?" Augustino wanted to know.

"Ah! Had you allowed Conchita at this meeting, she would have told you. She knows one of these smugglers—very well, she does. She came across the information by accident... a few weeks ago," he finished lamely, as if realizing he had said too much.

"Who is it?" Bob was suddenly very interested.

"You will have to ask her yourself." Jose was smirking, content to finally have the upper hand and everyone's undivided attention. "As a *familia*, we stick together. Something you people know nothing about. You wrap your families in cotton balls to protect them. You isolate them; alienate them from your lives. I will not do this to my sister."

Augustino sat there, somberly thinking how the onus to extract the information from Conchita would rest on his shoulders. She was insatiable in her demands and her sexual appetite was like a bottomless pit; but it was her constant need for a firm commitment on his part that was troubling him—growing to alarming proportions.

"You're right, Jose. We often do jeopardize our familial relationships by keeping them at arms length of our affairs."

Augustino agreed.

"What the hell are you talking about...?" Gary found it odd that Augustino should agree with Jose Arroyo—especially on this nagging subject Jose was forever toting around, like some bad penny he was trying to pawn.

"Don't give it another thought," Augustino told the three men. "I have a plan. Meanwhile, we should explore the new information we've just uncovered and decide on a plan of action."

CHAPTER THREE

"You've barely said two sentences since we got here. What's wrong, Amy?"

Meg was the eldest. Tall, blond and blue eyed with an easy smile, her looks were striking. Theirs was a family of three girls and two boys. And while the rest of the clan lived in New Jersey, Meg had married down here and had agreed to care for baby-sister Amanda who, as a devout sun-worshiper, craved to live near the ocean.

Meg's maternal instinct was popular during Amanda's early days of college. But now that Amanda was twenty-five, had her own apartment and thrived in a budding career as a social worker, she was somewhat more reluctant to confide in older sis.

"Just thinking." Truth was she could not get that man out of her mind. "Miss, could you bring some water for my little dog? Thank you," Amanda smiled when the girl nodded.

They were sitting at an outside café in South Beach, catching up on all the news from friends and family as they always did on the second Friday of every month.

"Then why are you so fidgety? You can't seem to sit still."

That much was true. Amanda could not get that man's eyes from boring into her, still. He sure had her libido overheating. "You know that feeling you get after lying in the sun all day? Your skin gets all tight and tingly?"

"Tell me about it..."

"You get the chills from cooling down too fast. And you know that no matter how many showers you take or how much cream you rub on, by morning your burn will have gotten worse. It's like the sun got under your skin somehow and is cooking you from the inside—and there's nothing you can do about it," Amanda sighed.

"Last week, Jerry Junior..."

And while Meg went on about her son's beach burn, Amanda could not help wondering if Augie had been serious about her playing house on his boat. What did that mean exactly? Something deliciously sexual, no doubt. Did he want her to cook for him and his guests? Help with the dishes? He mentioned being her keeper. For her to do his bidding. A roll and a toss in the sack were probably on the menu. He wanted to sleep with her, she was certain—but then what about that beautiful woman she had seen? He had promised her some relief later that evening—assuming she sobered up, Amanda remembered.

He struck her as the type of man who could easily

take them both on, one after the other—hopefully not together—that would be strange. Maybe he just needed new fare. If Bert had not shown up, would she be in his arms this very minute? She sighed, imagining the brutal force of his overpowering kiss. Nope, she was not scared. She would have given in to him and not because of fear. Being frightened was not part of her make-up. She had fought her share of bullies growing up; not to mention that for a long time, she had held the reputation of being the neighborhood's toughest tomboy.

When turning thirteen she remembered that her mother had cautioned her with mysterious words of wisdom. Her beauty was beginning to show, she had told her. And beauty, she had added, coupled with audacity and buoyancy, was a man-magnet. And in becoming a woman, these qualities, unchecked and unleashed, might get her into trouble some day. Amanda sighed. Pray that the day had arrived, she smiled. And that trouble resembled the man she had just encountered.

No, she decided. She could not tell sis about the man. She would wag her finger and tell her that this is what came from being the baby of the family—with everyone spoiling her rotten. In fact, for better or for worse, she enjoyed having more nerve than was potentially safe. Especially that it meant she was free to tackle any kind of problem head on. That's why she had become a social worker—to make a difference. Nope. Augie did not scare her, not one bit.

"...They think they're invincible to everything and anything. Sunscreen's not cool! Kids today...Amanda, wait a while before considering a family." Meg had talked herself into a frenzy—or into a corner. She, the mother incarnate, trying to get pregnant again for the past two years, was warning her against having children.

"I lost my yacht job today," Amanda sighed as if she had just lost her best friend.

"How come? You said the owner never goes there."

"He showed up, unexpectedly."

"What does that have to do with too much sun? Did you get caught tanning on his boat?"

Amanda shook her head, her eyes in the distance. She was caught all right—burning under his gaze.

"Then what does one have to do with the other?"

"Nothing. It's a sad song—Unchained Melody," Amanda sighed. "Except that it's all tied together and...mixed up."

"Well, I say good riddance. I didn't like you hanging around those docks anyway."

"Meg, you say that like it's these downtown loading docks where commercial ships peddle anything from coffee grounds to hot cars. It's the Marina. It's filled with million-dollar pleasure crafts. People are friendly, cooperative." *Most friendly and cooperative.* "It's a literal, littoral playground." Amanda smiled at the play on words then wrinkled her nose in lieu of an apology. "Besides, I was counting on that money. There's this little boy in one of the families I'm taking care of...well, it's his birthday next month. I was saving up to get him a bike."

Meg shook her head, giving her the eye. "How are you ever going to make a nest-egg, sweetie, if you keep giving your money away. Your job is to find new money trails, not to try to feed everyone from your meager wages."

Meg was right, she knew. Still, there would be hell to pay on Monday. Fiona would be furious. She wasn't likely going to let her live it down. She hoped it would not jeopardize their working relationship too much. She would hate to lose her trust.

* * * * *

In a high-rise on Williams Island, a gathering of another sort was taking place the following day. Saturday afternoon and four people sat on the terrace of a 24th floor balcony, overlooking the south-west view of the island all the way to the ocean.

Neil Sinclair was complaining that they were playing with fire. Tall, thin and gangly with a pale complexion, the hands in his pockets accentuated the fact that his hips were wider than his shoulders. Standing dangerously close to the edge of the railing, he was looking down at the bobbing ships and the white trails they left behind when sailing out of port.

"You thinkin' of jumping, Neil? Looking to drown your troubles?"

Neil didn't have to look back. He knew Fiona was enjoying a good laugh at his expense. She was not weak like he was—at least, not like he felt. With her short frilly skirts and see-through blouses, she wore the balls he lacked. She pulled the strings and manipulated people and events to suit her wishes. She was fearless. Neil walked back to where the other three were sipping their drinks. He was nervous and dejected about the latest turn of events.

"Don't worry, Sinclair." Henry Williamson smiled from his chair. He sat comfortably in a garden rocker, his long legs sprawled across the deck. "Haven't we sent them scurrying in every direction for the last four years?"

"Still," Neil Sinclair added. "I liked it better when Milan wasn't in the picture. Those Bureau guys are easy to fool. Him...now it's almost as if he's running the show."

"Don't worry." Williamson turned to face the other man that was sitting on his right. "Brad here keeps us abreast of what goes on with Milan." He laughed loudly. "I can't believe the klutz still hasn't figured it out..."

"Hey." Brad told him with a childish frown on his very round baby-face. "Good for me that he hasn't. Good for you too. You'd be wise not to get so cocky. The man's no fool."

"I won't be cocky if you quit admiring him as much as you do." Williamson shot at him, pretending to be angry. "I'm the one you love, remember?" He smiled and mussed up Brad's fine brown hair. "As soft as a baby's bum, this cute mug of yours," he added to soothe his number one ally. "You're lucky I have to go back to my wife tonight," he winked at Brad, "or I'd give you something to kick about."

Brad looked down at his shoes. He hated when the man was this explicit in front of others.

"What about Bob Farrell?" Fiona put in her oar. "He might have put two and two together a few months ago—when he spotted me leaving Quartain's headquarters. If he sits and thinks about this or if something triggers his memory, he's liable to hit us hard. Do we have anyone covering his comings and goings?"

Henry Williamson twirled the pale liquid of his yellow parakeet cocktail. "I've got Bob Farrell in my pocket. He was at our house for dinner two weeks ago. Played tag with Ritchie and Martha, even included our dog Fairway in the lot. Secretly pines for the wife, Marsha—or her cooking. Difficult to tell with these Bureau men. Not the most romantic chaps in the world."

"What was he doing at your house?" Fiona wanted to know.

"On an errand for pal Jim Dunbar—or as we like to call him, Jim *Dumbo*."

Brad laughed at the moniker, always playing the pleaser.

"Don't you think the line between Farrell and Dunbar is too thin for comfort?" Fiona gave him a weary look.

"Without the close and dangerous, where would be the sport?" Hank replied.

"So what's the plan—you know, now that there's been visual contact between the girl and Milan?" Sinclair asked as he sat down at the table across from Fiona. He considered the event a blowout error and could not shake the unease it stirred in him.

"More to the point," Fiona added, "come Monday morning, I'll be expected to get into role."

Neil Sinclair, unable to sit still, shot up like a wound-up coil and began pacing the small patio. "I don't know what you were thinking sending that child to Milan's ship. They were bound to meet. It was bound to happen."

"Wait a minute." Brad stirred from a delayed thought. "How did you people find out about the two of them...bumping into each other—so fast? Is there another informant working for Augie that's also working for you, Hank?"

"Aha!" Williamson exclaimed. "There it is. That all-consuming jealousy that feeds my ego." Williamson stroked Brad's arm. "Don't worry, no one else can fill your shoes, dear boy."

"What do you think modern technology is for?" Fiona laughed.

"Or a little piece of apparatus tagged onto a phone line?" Continued Henry Williamson.

Brad nodded. "Okay. I get it. So who put it there?"

Williamson looked at Brad with a satisfied grin on his freckled face. "A most important ally, dear boy—Miss Amanda Cole herself." Reverting his glance to Neil, he continued to smooth his attack of nerves. "An important audio aid, wouldn't you say? And more incriminating evidence. By now, we've planted enough circumstantial evidence in this girl's life to have her put away for a long time—should they try to fry us."

"Well done." Fiona raised her glass.

"That doesn't mean they'll believe any of it. When push comes to shove, she's just a kid..." Sinclair whined.

"A kid that's just as easily framed as the rest of them." Fiona added. "Sending her to the ship was twofold. Having her fingerprints all over the yacht will establish that she's been there—snooping..."

Hank said. "Or for whatever dreamy set-up we decide

to concoct."

"...And now, she's in a tenuous position with the Bureau guys who already suspect her of murder—the girl who waltzed off with Emilio Arroyo. It's perfect." Fiona turned to Hank. "So, what do I do come Monday morning?" She repeated.

"Stall." Williamson answered. "A few days at the most. I'm securing a deal as we speak. Plus...a few more witnesses to help the cause." Williamson smiled. "Nice feeling when you know you can't lose—when you can see the stacked deck."

From Fiona who preferred her men strong and silent. "Don't be so sure. You're still asked to testify against Quartain Tech committee members from time to time. One wrong move, one misplaced word and all of us would be compromised."

Hank Williamson laughed heartily. "Most of Quartain Tech's undesirables have been tried and convicted. And now I have a free hand with many of their ex-contacts. Great times await us, lady and gents." He held up his glass to refill it from the pitcher and toasted them with it. "Monday will be business as usual, Fi. You take your cue from Milan. You can bet your round, sexy little bottom he'll be calling you."

* * * * *

On Monday morning, Amanda sat in her office with an inordinate amount of trepidation. Unable to get rid of that man occupying her inner most thoughts all weekend, she figured it was probably for the best if she never set foot there again. The only hurdle left was facing the recriminations Fiona was sure to hand her—freely.

She settled some visa problems two of her families were having with the immigration services, answered her e-mails and prepared her brief for the MADD—Mothers Against Drunk Driving—chapter she was addressing that afternoon. And later when she returned to the office, there was still no sign of Fiona. She spoke to Maria in personnel who confirmed that Fiona was off sick.

Tuesday morning, still no sign of Fiona. Amanda began to worry. Did she or did she not still have a job? She didn't feel like heading out there if there was trouble, or if she had been fired.

She called Fiona at home, figuring that she would test the waters. "How are you feeling, Fi? Is there anything I can do for you?"

"No. Thanks. I'm just very stuffed up. The doctor says a few more days should do the trick. Can you take over my group tomorrow? You're the only one I trust, Amy."

"It's an AA group. I don't have a lot of experience with that yet."

"You'll be fine. Oh! By the way, that nice man Augustino Milan called me yesterday."

Amanda was happy not to be facing Fiona; she felt the telltale sign of nerves tighten her face. *Milan, the name of the ship. Augustino, the long form for Augie.* So, at last they met. She nodded, taking a deep breath—quietly. "Who?" She hated having to pretend.

"The man who owns that yacht you're tending."

"Interesting. I had no idea you two knew each other. I thought you'd told me he was a friend of a friend."

"That is how we met, four years ago. But we've since become good friends. He's a very exciting man, Amanda. And he tells me that he appreciates you—well, not you per se, but the person I chose to take care of the light work around his yacht. He raved about your attention to details—those little snacks you leave behind. He mentioned little soaps in the closet..."

Amanda closed her eyes, remembering her last episode as a guest of that particular closet. The all too familiar feeling of arousal was back—proof it had never totally dissipated. "Did he mention anything else...?" Amanda wanted to know if Augustino Milan had mentioned running into her.

"No. Just that his work is more and more demanding. He's looking for additional help, someone he can trust...anyway, one thing led to another..."

"I hope you didn't dig up more work for me, Fiona. I have more than I can handle as it is. I have two new cases... difficult ones and..."

"Don't be silly, Amy. Augie just thought it might be nice if you could assist with the menu preparation, act as a hostess one of these weekends—you know, for his on-board guests. It's quite an honor, you know."

"I don't think that's a good idea, Fi. Not at all. You should have discussed it with me first."

"I didn't say you'd do it. That's up to you. I just told him I'd mention it to you."

"Good." Amanda was breathing again. "I can't find

time to do one more thing. Even going to his yacht four hours a week is already a bit much..."

"Do me a favor? Wait until he asks before you refuse. I don't want to have to be the one to disappoint him. It'll be better coming from you. He may not even bring it up—ever. You'll most likely never encounter him. He is very elusive, travels a lot."

Obviously Augustino had kept her secret and said nothing about their meeting. Well, thought Amanda, at least this cleared up the question of whether she needed to go there that afternoon. She hadn't planned to head out there today, so the conversation with Fiona brought nothing but mixed feelings. She hadn't brought Dino with her because of a morning presentation. Ginette had the double shift at the hospital. The poor little creature would be alone until six. She would make some calls. If need be, she would put off going until Thursday.

"Ginette, sweetie, it's me. Did you have time to put Dino out before you left?"

"I did. But I left so early, I don't know what good it did. But hey! Don't worry. Your friend came by to pick him up."

Amanda's legs went weak. "What friend?" she slowly articulated.

"A tall hunk of man, a looker. He came to the door and said he wanted to see you. I said you'd gone to work. He saw Dino and told me he'd bring him to you."

"You gave my dog to a total stranger?" Amanda's tone had risen by several decibels. She suddenly felt faint and dizzy.

"Amanda! He gave me his card, his phone number, told me he'd last seen you on Friday. That's not the MO of a dognapper."

"Think, Ginette. Did he say where he was taking him?"

"Amy, what's going on? I know you and I have some catching up to do...I'm supposed to be your friend and roomie and I don't know a thing about what's going on in your life. I just thought he was your beau or something."

"It's okay, Ginette. Just try to remember what he said."

"He said he was meeting you at the yacht today, like every Tuesday."

Amanda was able to breathe again. "Did he say his name was Augustino Milan?"

"Yes. That's exactly who he said he was. I thought it'd be better than leaving little Dino alone on his own—for so long..."

"It's okay, Ginette. Don't worry. Let's have dinner on Friday. We'll catch up then."

Amanda hung up and began pacing her office. She was furious. How dare this man go to her apartment—take her dog—insinuate himself into her life—take her dog! She couldn't believe her little Dino was in the hands of that maniac.

She sat down and fought to regroup. She needed to focus on why he was doing this. Obviously, he wanted to make sure she would go back there today. And she had worried about being fired!

First she would get her dog back; then she would get an injunction against him, if need be. He had gone too far. Never mind that he had disrupted her entire weekend...boy, did she feel stupid for having thought of him all weekend. In a twisted way, he had just done her a big favor.

Amanda had a 1:00 she could not reschedule. She would have to remain calm, get through it, change and head for the yacht first chance she got.

"Miss Cole," the receptionist buzzed her on the intercom, "Mr. Sanchez is here to see you. And he brought Mrs. Sanchez with him."

Juan Sanchez was an old case Fiona Christian had handed down to her. As per Fiona, the Sanchez family was a large one that needed help finding sponsors. They had money, wielded power and owned status in their country. Unfortunately, these elusive items were not easily stacked in the bottom of a suitcase. Most of their fortune would have to be left behind or whittled in at a snail's pace. And they needed help squaring the matter of their immigration against the stricter laws meted out these days.

Fiona had admonished that she take good care of them. The family, she had told her, was comprised of many brothers, nephews and nieces and that, in time, she would need to place them in the working community. Some of the younger members were already attending Miami Dade high schools. So far, Amanda had only met Juan on a few occasions. He was polite, well educated and willing to work hard; he was just persona non grata in his own country. Amanda sighed. Where did Fiona expect to find jobs for all these people?

Amanda rose and welcomed the pair into her office.

"*Señorita* Amanda, this is my eldest daughter, Maria."

"But they told me at the reception that she was your wife, *Señor* Sanchez. You never mentioned an older daughter." Amanda surveyed the meager file that Fiona had handed to her—to sift through very carefully, she had stipulated. For a case that she had been toting for years, there sure wasn't much to go on in the grand total of ten pages.

She looked at the young woman scantily dressed in a clingy, short summer outfit and thought her too old to be his daughter. A mistress perhaps...by the way she was greedily clawing long red nails into Sanchez's arm, but not a family member.

"She needs help also, *Señorita*. That is all. Her papers are in order, I can assure you."

Amanda silently called on a dose of patience. Status and power often meant nothing other than a short fuse for applicants faced with rules and regulations. "I will be the judge of that, *Señor* Sanchez. Meanwhile, we still need to meet with your wife and son before we can proceed with any potential sponsorship—with helping you find a job. This...daughter will have to register with our office in a separate file. I am certain she is over twenty-one."

"I don't need a sponsor. Just a visa. I can pay—over time. Besides, I was promised legal entry for all of my family, including my twelve brothers and fifteen nephews and ten nieces."

"*Señor* Sanchez, Rome was not built in a day. We will

have to proceed with all of their papers individually…"

"Mrs. Christian has promised that they would be filed as a group. Seems to me, she is much more resourceful than you are. You obviously do not know what you are doing. Please check with her."

"Uh-huh. First, we will start with your immediate family." *Nice attitude, pal.* Amanda filled out the forms for Maria—whose last name was also Sanchez—*probably as popular as Smith is in America.* But as Sanchez had mentioned, her papers were in order, properly stamped and duly processed by INS; though her birth certificate indicated she was twenty-eight—much too old to be Sanchez' daughter.

It was not always an easy job dealing with people's feelings and requests. Her task was to assure their entry into the city was as smooth as possible, and their integration into Miami society trouble-free. The applicants themselves often made her job harder than it actually was. They did not understand the need to comply with policies and sets of laws and were definitely out to get the most that they could—any way they could.

Ignoring Sanchez' little tantrum, she took her time explaining to the couple the next steps to broach and the time-frame to respect. She read the manual of compliance to them, underlining the particulars unique to their case—which by then had Juan Sanchez wearing a hole in her carpet, trotting in front of the desk.

"You do not have to lecture to me as if I were a child, Miss Cole. I already know all of this. It has been read to me many times." He had begun this process previously with Fiona Christian some years back. Why it had been interrupted or was not yet processed, Amanda could only imagine it was so that he could bring with him as much of his Cuban possessions as possible. She couldn't be sure—not from the little amount of information Fiona had handed her.

"Relax, *Señor* Sanchez," Amanda soothed, deploying all her people skills to get his face to revert to a paler shade of red. "I know very little about what was done previously. I have no other information to go on but this thin folder..."

"That is a lie!" he barked. "I was there when Mrs. Christian handed over two boxes full of my files."

What the hell is he talking about? "Let's not waste precious time arguing, *Señor* Sanchez. Mrs. Christian is not here today. I will clear this matter with her as soon as she returns."

"Mr. Sinclair is a good friend," he continued. "He will hear of your incompetence. You have obviously lost my papers and do not wish to admit this."

"*Señor* Sanchez, I can assure you I have lost nothing. At the most, I am repeating instructions you have already heard." *Big deal. I have a day too, you know.* "This will all be ironed out for our next meeting," she smiled.

He tugged on his friend's arm, signifying for her to rise and that they were leaving; and proudly he straightened to his full 5'2" height, his chin jutting an extra inch. "Good day, Miss Cole. Next time," he added as he turned from the doorway, "please make sure you are properly briefed on my case."

For the first time in her young career Amanda was

glad a session was ended. She was unhappy with Juan Sanchez for trying to pull a fast one by bringing this new relative Maria into the picture. But commingling with her anger was an odd sensation of confusion. She was not inept by nature. She was efficient and good at her job.

Mechanically, she looked around for any boxes that might have been lugged there without her knowledge. Her office was a narrow little cubbyhole with barely enough room for a desk and three chairs. There was a filing cabinet in the corner, a coat hanger beside it; and by the tall, drapeless window a small fern battled the heat as it bathed in the torrid midday light. But no boxes.

She walked over to the window and fingered the fern as she looked out at the traffic humming in the market area. True, she had not been quite herself these last few days, with all this business about being caught red-handed on that yacht. There was something disconcerting about the whole affair..., which brought her mind back to an even more disturbing present. She remembered poor little Dino; and she worried about one tall stranger and his wide possessive hands on her helpless little dog. He was her next port of call.

Quickly she collected her thoughts and shed her funky mood. She was going to show him, she thundered, storming out of the office.

She didn't even bother to change into her dingy cleaning fatigues. Let him think what he wanted. So she would show up with a pleasing appearance. Didn't mean it was for his benefit. He had kidnapped her dog, for shit's sake. He knew she was not going there to satisfy any need of his and doubted he expected she clean there ever again. *Little soaps in the closet...*she was going to show him little soaps...

She parked a few blocks down. Tuesdays were usually busy. She walked fast, plucking away at the rhetoric she planned to hurl at him, promising it would be spicy.

When she entered the grounds, she scoured the place for Bert. She had already decided she would use him as an ally. Accompanied by a witness, Augustino Milan could not detain her any longer than it took to give him a piece of her mind, snatch her dog and leave in a huff—for lack of any door to slam.

She hated putting Bert in that kind of situation and certainly did not intend making him a part of her demise. She would only ask him to come along as a friend and impartial observer, mentioning that with his cooperation this man would not be able to detain her any longer than he had to—with idle chatter. Well, even if Bert suspected there was more to it than that, at least it was a plausible excuse. One he could use sincerely in case anyone ever inquired about his presence there.

But as her eyes swept past Jake and his snake, Tom and his parrots and the mishmash of booths in spherical rows, there was no Bert. That was odd—you could usually set your time by his schedule. Amanda checked her watch. It was earlier than usual for her. She had run there disregarding her normal routine. And while the part of her that felt like running headlong to dock 44 was being forcefully held back, perhaps by some clever magnet of reason, she nevertheless started in that direction.

As soon as she spotted the bow of the *Milan Milend*, she picked up the pace. She was so relieved. She had worried he might have left or sailed somewhere. Now all she hoped was that this alpha-dominant male was aboard.

She climbed the plank, already expecting to see him there on deck; but there was no one. She turned the door's handle. It was unlocked. She entered the salon, looked toward the kitchen and stretched up the flight of stairs to catch a glimpse of the pilothouse on top. There was no one there either.

"I'm down in the office," Augustino called out to her.

He must have heard her board, she thought. She walked down the stairs, but before she could reach the bottom, a smooth, sleek little bundle jumped right into her arms.

"Oh, Dino! My sweet little pet...my cute little precious...!" Amanda was laughing and cooing at him as though he was a long lost pal, cuddling and kissing his trembling little body.

"Where do I stand in line to get that sort of treatment?" she heard Augustino say. He was sitting at his desk, smiling and looking up at her with amusement in sharp, steely blue eyes.

Amanda looked at him properly. He was wearing a low-cut tank top, copper colored—almost the same color as his bronzed skin—and tight cream colored jeans. She had forgotten how damned handsome he was. She had not been stupid at all, yearning for him all weekend. Nothing but natural is what it had been, she consoled herself, now that gazing at him brought on the familiar stirrings in the pit of her stomach.

"I have a bone to pick with you," she muttered at him, unafraid and itching to fight.

He rose to his full height slowly, giving her the full span of broad shoulders.

"There's no bone there. Just muscle." He looked down at the bulge in his jeans, then smiled wickedly when he noticed her jaw drop and her dark eyes widen with anger. "I apologize about your dog. I needed to make sure you came today. Don't worry," he continued, as Amanda was speechless with rage. "He was very good company."

Amanda put the dog on the floor.

"You are to stay away from me and my dog. My friends, my co-workers and everyone I know will be warned about you. And if you ever come near me again, it's the police I'm going to alert."

He grabbed the wrist she was waving at him menacingly, which only served to enrage her more. So he grabbed her other wrist to stop her from slugging him.

"Let go of me! You're hurting me," she spat at him.

"Not until you calm down."

"You don't tell me what to do. And if you don't let go of me this minute, I will scream bloody murder. Someone will hear me."

He smiled, his eyes locked on hers. "No one will hear you," he spoke softly. "Because you are not going to scream and you know it." He waited, giving her the chance to disprove him. When she did not and as she still stared into his eyes, he added. "This is exactly where you've wanted to be ever since you laid eyes on me. And if you deny it, I'll know you're a liar." He pulled her flat up against him, letting her wrists go to encircle her waist so that her arms fell limp by her side. He bent his head, rubbing his cheek against her forehead, gently kissing the side of her temple. "And the reason I know this," he added as a soft whisper, "is because I feel the same way."

The next thing Amanda felt was his hand on her hip—his bare hand against her bare hip. He must have slid it up her skirt, she thought in a soft and hazy torpor. Because he was caressing its curve, applying the span of his palm against her panties, gently rubbing and mashing her into him so she could feel his arousal. Oh! She breathed—and so very aroused he was. Where was her will power? All that angst, that healthy rage she had stomped there with, just minutes ago? Instead he had her squirming in his arms, completely at his mercy.

His lips brushed her cheek as softly and lightly as a warm waft of wind. Then he let go of her, stepping back enough to look into her eyes. He cupped her face with his hands and smiled when he witnessed the wonderment in her eyes. "Thank you," he said. "Thank you for being honest. I couldn't have endured lies or pretense—or any sort of wide-eyed coyness." His hands on her shoulders, he plopped her away from him. "That's what I admired most about you the other day—your pluck, your sincerity; your absolute lack of airs or pretension." He smiled at the curiosity in her eyes. "No questions?" he added, a finger brushing across her lips.

Amanda's eyes were nothing other than puzzled. And many questions popped up readily. Who was this man? Mr.

Rev 'em and Leave 'em Milan. Was that how he got his kicks, she wondered. Seduce a woman, abscond and leave her high and dry?—well, down and wet was a better description. She was not about to beg him to continue like that other woman had. Okay, maybe that's what she had originally wanted to do. But sincerity and integrity did not mean lack of decorum or absence of dignity.

"Why are you doing this?" She was finally able to mouth.

"I have a business proposition for you," he told her, fidgeting with a book on his desk. "I want to hire you. Not to clean my boat or any such nonsense. I think your time is too valuable to be polishing heads and staterooms or shopping for tidbits. No. I intend paying you directly for your services. I will need you most weekends, some evenings...and I am prepared to pay you $100 an hour."

"You must be crazy," she whispered.

"Okay. You're right. I realize that a weekend job is a huge dent on your social life and...I can be a nuisance at times," he smiled. "Episodes like the one you've just encountered are likely to resurge—each time they do, it means I'll be unable to keep my hands off of you—which, let's face it, may turn out to be often." This time his smile was a wide grin. "So I'm prepared to up the ante to $200 an hour."

How dare he smirk at me with that proposition? She was incensed. "I am not some floozy you can just pay to ease your conscience," she breathed. "Nor am I some high-priced call-girl you can order around. I cannot and will not be bought." She raised her chin and the stubborn gleam in her eye defied him to argue.

He laughed at her. "Relax! I'm not looking for a sex kitten. Although if I was, you'd do," he added, brushing his eyes up and down her slim silhouette—those eyes he seemed to be able to turn on and off at will. "On the contrary. I'm looking for someone who will provide me with a certain amount of...legitimacy. A hostess for my guests and a female presence—beautiful and young enough to discourage...talk, rumors and amorous advances from other female contenders. I am securing sensitive business dealings for the next couple of months. The last thing I need in my life right now is for the wife or...the mistress of one of my business dealers to..."

"Undress in front of you and demand you make love to her?" She could not resist adding.

He cocked his head and *his* eyes reflected interesting questions for a change. Whether he chose to ignore the jibe or did not understand the allusion, he brushed his hand against her cheek and continued as if uninterrupted. "One look at you and all other females will know that there's no contest."

Amanda was amazed how incredibly charming and persuasive this man could be. Of course, she had to remember that his compliments were nothing more than that—compliments angled perfectly at hooking him whatever he wanted.

"You seem to forget, Mr. Milan. I have a full time career. To accept your proposition would mean that I'd be *working* sixty hours a week."

"I'd rather hoped that a big part of your *work* would be enjoyable." His eyes dared her to speak the truth.

"You're right. A big part of your proposition would be

very pleasant." She spoke in alluring tones, her eyes caressing his face. "I've always wanted to sail to different ports and I love the ocean. The only difficulty I foresee is the probable recurrence you spoke of earlier." She raised her eyebrows. "You know, the episode you said might *resurge...*"

His eyes darkened and he lost his smile. "Don't lie. Don't disappoint me, Amanda."

It was her turn to smile smugly. "I didn't say it would be unpleasant—just very difficult...to withstand...—as I said, a lot of work."

He bowed his head slightly. "Touché, Amanda, touché. Now do we have a deal?"

Amanda looked at him squarely. She was fairly surprised. He seemed to be more than anxious for an answer.

"Think of all the people you'll be able to help with all this crisp new money."

She shrugged. "I don't know. I'll have to think about it," was the safest answer she knew to hand him. He couldn't just blink and expect her to jump and do his bidding. Who did he think he was, anyway? And how did he presume to know what she intended doing with that money? It was none of his business.

CHAPTER FOUR

Friday night Ginette and Amanda were having supper together as planned. With their respective work schedules they had not conferred in weeks.

Ginette was serving and decided she would cut to the chase. “So, what are you going to tell him?”

Amanda shrugged. She cuddled little Dino on her lap and tried to side step the famous question, hacking at her for the last four days.

“Two hundred dollars an hour! Do you realize how much money that is?”

“I can count, Gin; thank you.”

“Of course you can, love. But how many hours does he deem a weekend to be? If you’re at sea, you can’t just go home after supper. You’d have to sleep there. We’re talking 48 hours.”

Suddenly, the reality of this predicament dawned on

Amanda. Where would she sleep? If all the staterooms were occupied—and if she was going to be known as his girlfriend—did this mean they would have to share sleeping quarters? "I don't see how I can accept his offer. I don't care about the money," she stated categorically. Then as an afterthought, "Ginette? This guy never said, but...do you think we might have to pretend all the way to the bedroom?"

Ginette dished out pasta and bread and her wry face spoke volumes. "I can't help you there. I have no idea." She sat down in front of Amanda, tucking a napkin on her lap. "Guys can be such phonies. When Jill and I were growing up, my no-show father was always chasing some girl back to her crib..."

Amanda gave her skeptical raised eyebrows.

Ginette crossed herself. "I swear. I kid you not. Some girl always young enough to be his daughter. And in the small town where we were raised, that was like bait to those old cronies who never had anything better to do than gossip their life away." She took a sip of her wine.

"Sorry, Ginette. That couldn't have been comfortable for you."

Ginette tossed her head. "My sister and I didn't care. In a sense, we were lucky. He never came after Jill and me; know what I mean? Tore my mother's heart to shreds though..."

"Is he still around?" Amanda poured dressing on her salad.

Ginette shook her head. "He taught at the local college. One day, he left with one of his students. Didn't even pack a bag. We found out from Priscilla Lodge. She called to deliver the news to my mother. I remember how brave my mom was. She never cried, just handed us extra portions of pie that night."

"I'll admit that was pretty bad. But not all men are the same, sweetie," Amanda told her between two mouthfuls of spaghetti.

"I beg to differ," Ginette said sarcastically. "I remember my sister and I used to go to the park near our house. We didn't have a television and my mother didn't have the patience to entertain us....Anyway, we used to stare at the couples on the benches. We got real good at knowing which ones were going to make it and which ones were doomed at the gate."

Amanda smiled. "Where was this?"

"Madawaska, Maine."

Amanda laughed. "That sounds like the small New Jersey town where I'm from."

"One day, Jill and I—we're sitting there 'cause we just got kicked out of the house by my fractious mother—we hear this guy on the bench next to ours, chatting up Mrs. Blanchard."

"Who was Mrs. Blanchard?" Amanda asked after a particular long pause.

"Our music teacher. She was in her late thirties. Her husband was coach of the women's basketball team. Anyway, this man was doing a number on her..."

"What do you mean?"

"You know, rattling on about chapter and verse. Jill and I could tell the guy had been rehearsing. He was a lonely, phony-baloney, story-telling leech. And the more he fabricated, the more Mrs. Blanchard's face lit up. I mean, she was soaking it up like she was dry biscuit and this guy was gravy."

"So what happened?"

"They ended up having an affair. Two months later, the guy's gone and it's all over school. Her husband eventually divorced her—a very sad story—all 'cause she wanted to do some guy some favor."

"This a true story? Really?"

"Swear to god! That's the summer I decided to become a nurse. I wanted to cure all those sick bastards and send them packing before they dogged down all the other Mrs. Blanchards of the world."

Amanda's eyes looked at her warmly. "Is that when you decided you preferred women over men?"

"Ouch! You could out me with a little more sensitivity," Ginette mildly protested, a willing smirk on her face.

"It's okay. I've known for a while," Amanda reassured her.

"Yeah! Well, keep it to yourself. I'm not ready to go public yet. And when I do, just for the record, you are so not my type!"

"Gee, thanks—I think," Amanda laughed. "So what you're telling me is that lonely men will gab about anything to get a woman's attention? That is what you're saying."

"Something like that." Ginette gave her a half-smile

"Only one problem. I can't see Augustino as being the lonely type." Amanda's dark eyes silently queried Ginette's expression for support.

"Don't look at me. I can't tell. I just saw him when he picked up your dog; and hell, I totally believed the crap he told me. Is he a fast talker?"

Amanda laughed. "Let's just say he's a man of few words. His attributes are more the physical kind when he demonstrates what he wants."

"Ooh! Talked with his hands!"

Amanda nodded, rolling her eyes to indicate the mass of that understatement.

"Where exactly?"

"I'm not going to discuss that with you—or anyone else." Amanda was smiling but adamant.

"Fine. But just to be on the safe side, we're going to run a little test—anonymously—you don't have to say anything." Ginette withheld a telltale smile. "I'm going to describe a few erogenous places a man usually likes to clutch and tell *you* what each particular gesture implies..."

"You're crazy," Amanda snorted.

"No, no. This is good, you'll see. This'll give you some inkling into what kind of guy he is. For instance, if he grabbed your breasts it means he's insecure, looking for a mother and the easy take—you know, grabs the first thing that sticks out."

Amanda laughed, shaking her head.

"Next is the thigh man. He slowly slithers up a woman's thighs, all the while seeking that treasure we women defend beyond our lives. He is usually Mr. Lusty—not in love, uncaring and quickly disinterested. Avoid at all costs. Then there's the alpha-dominant male who swoops in from behind—get it? Behind?"

"I get it, I get it." Amanda rolled her eyes but could not prevent laughing.

"He's usually dominant, very possessive and often falls for one woman and one woman only. Very bad news for whoever is NOT that woman." Ginette downed her wine, trying not to laugh. "Is this helping any?"

Amanda was laughing but still refused to let a hint drop as to what type of man Augustino was. "Where did you get all this mumbo-jumbo? Sounds right out of Hustler."

"Sweetie, the things you hear in the wards....Hustler would do well with our material."

"What about the man who kisses?"

Ginette's eyes widened with shock. "Is that what he did!"

"No. Don't be silly. Why? What does it mean?"

"Men rarely kiss a woman they hardly know, especially an open-mouth kiss. It's...too personal; too transparent; and much too indicative of a guy in love."

Amanda ate her food without savoring it as she usually did. She was tired of having the onus of this answer hanging over her head.

"Just remember, Amy that this guy will be in the perfect position to take advantage of you anytime he likes. You won't be able to protest since, in a way, it'll be part of your job description. However," she added when she saw the grimace on Amanda's face, "let me remind you why you still want to do this so much." Ginette nodded, twirling pasta onto her fork. "First, it's money for your causes—God save your causes; you've got tons of them. Then, you need to show this guy who's the boss. I mean, where's the spunky, in your face, cool Amy I know and respect?"

Amanda gave her a shoulder nod.

"What's the worse that can happen? You guys do it. You get to have this raunchy sex—repeatedly—any time you snap your fingers he's on you like syrup on a pancake. So you live a little—sail around in a million-dollar yacht and meet interesting people..."

"You make a good case, Gin. Oh! But that's not the worse that can happen," Amanda sighed. "The worse I foresee happening is that I accept his proposition. I do what he asks while he remains all stiff and nothing but business." Amanda flashed Ginette her dark brown eyes. "And I become as pathetic as that woman I saw on the bed, having to beg him to pay attention to me because I can't stand to have his body next to mine not caressing me every minute of every hour. I swear, Ginette. This scenario would be equivalent to a fate worse than death. Unrequited lust. Don't know it; don't want to."

"You have a point. The guy does seem to have monumental self-control. But hey! So do you! You have just as much self-control as he does. You're as tough as nails, remember?" Ginette flexed her arm the way Amanda always did.

Amanda laughed and let out a noisy gut-wrenching sigh. "Okay. I'm open to suggestions. What do you propose I do?"

"Hey! He's the one who raves about honesty. Have it

out with him. Tell him what you've told me—not everything you've told me." She forestalled Amanda when she saw her about to interrupt. "But *not* on his boat. Somewhere neutral. Somewhere you can leave in a hurry without him being able to stop you."

"Of course! That's a great idea." It was normal, she thought, to ask Augie for specifics. His proposition didn't draw the typical yes or no response. There were too many blanks. Amanda got up all excited, reached for the business card he had handed Ginette and dialed him at the table. Besides, this was one great excuse to see him again—without any strings tugged in either direction.

"I didn't mean this exact minute." Ginette shook her head at Amanda's impetus. She was a one-track-minded dark beauty.

Amanda waited as the phone rang, holding her breath and praying for him to answer. Then she remembered it was Friday night and most people had a life—some place to go to, someone to go with.

"Milo."

The voice was gruff and sounded sleepy. That name was not familiar. For an instant, she was tempted to hang up. What if he was lying in bed entangled with some *señorita*? "Is this Augustino?" She asked in her most pleasant voice.

There was silence at the other end.

"Hello?" she repeated, thinking that since it was a cell, he might have bad reception.

"What is it that you want?"

There was barely a question in that tone. Amanda

couldn't believe how short he sounded. Then she remembered she had not introduced herself. There was no rule that said he had to recognize her voice. She had never spoken to him on the phone before.

"It's Amanda," she answered. "Amanda Cole."

"I know who it is. Why are you calling, Amanda?"

There *was* a rule that said he had to be pleasant—at least if he wanted to entertain a conversation with her. "I'm sorry. Obviously I've called at a bad time." That was the only plausible excuse to explain his rudeness. "Call me when you feel the time is more appropriate," she added primly. She was about to hang up when she heard the same forceful question.

"No games. Just say what you want."

Spoken so low, this succinctly, she came close to answering *you*. Luckily she stopped herself just in time. "*You*... handed me a proposition the other day. I thought we should get together and discuss the pros and cons. There are too many variables to allow me to make an educated decision."

"If you must. I'm on the yacht for the night. You may come and join me at any time."

"No. I thought we could meet in town, have a cup of coffee..."

"I don't eat little girls, Amanda. It's safe to come on board."

Amanda pulled the phone away from her ear and cursed it silently with her closed fist. Rolling her eyes, she shook her head at Ginette, indicating this man was impossible. Then she remembered her training in working with people—difficult cases. It was easier to calm a bear spooning him honey than throwing him rocks.

"I thought it might be nice to meet elsewhere—get to know each other. You know, a different perspective," she added in her most conciliatory tone.

"So, you're asking me out on a date?" he queried with derogatory undertones.

Sure, why not? She sighed, "I guess I am. Where would you like to go?"

He laughed. "By letting me decide, aren't we right back where we started?" By now he was openly jeering. There was no mistaking that fleck in his voice.

"Listen," she answered, barely disguising her mounting temper. "It's 6:30. Can you pick me up in an hour?"

"The reason I asked you to come to me, Amanda, is that I can't leave here this evening. If you're that frightened of me, then I propose we meet tomorrow night. I will pick you up around 8:00 and we'll go somewhere downtown where there are tons of people and lots of noise. Does that suit you?"

"That suits me fine. Oh, and I'm not at all frightened of you. I just think neutral grounds will be a more convenient place to...talk."

He laughed silently and hung up without saying goodbye.

"Would you believe that man!" Amanda hung up the receiver and turned toward Ginette who had listened-in on the portable.

"He seems pissed. I don't know. His attitude doesn't wash—not your typical behavior. Certainly not the *thank-*

god you called or *I'm so glad to hear from you* euphemisms."

"That's it. I'm calling him back and canceling the whole bit." Amanda was fuming. "Better yet, when he comes tomorrow night, I won't be here."

"I don't know," Ginette answered, contorting her face. "I wouldn't get this guy angrier than he already is. If you really don't want to see him again, I'd tell him—before tomorrow night."

"You're right." Amanda dialed his number again. Tapping her foot on the ground, she waited for the phone to ring four more times before a feminine voice answered. This floored her. She never dreamed there would be another woman there—not after his invitation. She took a deep breath. "May I speak with Mr. Milan?" she asked politely.

"*Un momento, por favor.*"

Amanda waited with renewed rage, ready to rap him with the brunt of it when the woman came back to the phone and robbed her of the pleasure. "If this is *Señorita* Amy, he cannot come to the phone. He says you come here now or he sees you tomorrow." Promptly, the woman hung up.

Amanda stared wide-eyed at Ginette. She stared at the phone in her hands as if her angry eyes could filter through the handset, reach in and squeeze his neck. *Ooh! The gall of that man.*

She sat back down to cold noodles and a warm soda and wondered why she had spent the week haranguing over this stupid man. "He must think I'm a complete idiot. It's Friday night. I practically order him to pick me up in an hour—

as if he doesn't already have something better to do. I call him back—after he agrees to see me tomorrow night, to play along, to humor me—only to be told by some female that he can't talk to me right now; that if I'm in such a hurry to see him, I should go there." She raised her hands in desperation and shook her head vigorously. "I blew it. I totally blew it. If he was laughing before—and he was, believe me," Amanda stuck her finger out for emphasis, "by now, he must be holding his sides to stop them from splitting."

It was Ginette's turn to burst out laughing. "Good point." She continued laughing. "What? You made a joke and it was funny..." Ginette pinched her lips to repress the laughter, an apologetic glint in her eyes faced with the thunderous omen in Amanda's dark ones.

"I have a good mind to go over there and tell him off in front of his...his Lolita whoever she is."

Ginette shook her head with a wry look on her face. "Personally, I think that all your bright ideas concerning Augustino should be shelved for the next twenty-four hours. Right now, you are anything but the keen-eyed intuitive I know and love. You need a breather. What do you say we go to a movie? My treat, your choice."

It was certainly better than moping around the house until 8:00 tomorrow night. "Okay. I want to go and see that gig about all the ways to dump a guy," smiled Amanda. "It's so very appropriate. I may even learn how to get rid of mine."

Ginette cheered Amanda's return to a sassier mood. The two dressed casually, Amanda in low-rise jeans with a small sleeveless top, her hair braided at the back. Ginette wore flared pants with a knitted top and brushed her blond hair to one side, tying it in a thin ponytail. The two of them resembled precocious teenagers rather than young professional women. And as they walked hand in hand to the nearby Lincoln theatres, they got wolf whistles and ready invitations to party that they nonchalantly ignored.

The evening was as warm as the day had begun; and no promise of relenting heat blinked down from the millions of stars and orange moon streaking the Miami sky. Not tonight, not for many nights to come. July was finally here, Amanda's favorite time of year. And while tourists left the area in droves—some for cooler climates—she relished this blissful peaceful sense of summer. Summer meant longer days, sunnier days and holidays. Walks on the beach at all hours, the warm spray of the ocean on her feet in the early morning and the low *gaws* of the Mangrove Cuckoo's call—a wooden sound indicative of sterling peace. And fervent for it all, the always-popular Floridian native ambling down the pedestrian streets half-naked and shopping for bargains.

Stuffed with popcorn and sour candies, Amanda and Ginette laughed out loud remembering some of the vivid movie scenes. The dialogue had been witty and unexpected, funny enough to relieve some of Amanda's week-long tension.

"I wish I was more like you, Ginette," Amanda said as she hooked her arm into her friend's. "I would give up men in a heart beat and never look back. They are a bother and a holy nuisance."

"Oh, right! Like you've had so many men in your life.

What's the count today...let's see...one?"

"There's been more than one," Amanda answered hesitantly, not wanting to bring up the fiascos in her life.

"Holding their hands to help them cross the street doesn't count," Ginette laughed at her. "Anyway, forget about it," she said, squeezing her by the waist. "It would never work."

"And why not?"

"I don't mean you giving up men. I mean you and me. You're much too bossy for me and way too horny." Ginette threw her a sidelong glance and laughed at the comical face of denial Amanda put on. At least she was back in full form. "So who's this man you're thinking of dumping?"

"What are you talking about?"

"When we left. You said that the movie might give you suggestions on how to leave yours..."

"I did, didn't I?" Amanda knew she had meant Augustino. He was the only man in her universe right now—and for a long time to come, she suspected dejectedly. How had she become enamored of a stranger—a rude overbearing one at that? Perhaps, as Ginette had so cleverly pointed out, because of the missing count of more than one, which added up to zero experience. And since practice made perfect in all fields, even in matters of the heart and areas of sexual attraction, she was an ingénue of colossal proportions. "Someone at work I don't want to talk about."

"Yeah, right." Ginette was not going to argue the point. Amanda would come around when she felt the time was right. Meanwhile she had her cheered up. That was what mattered.

"Notice how many hot glances we're getting from passers-by?" Amanda retorted in a jovial mood. "People think we're lovers."

"Two girls holding each other by the waist means nothing. Now if it was two guys...that would be different."

"I don't know about that...this *is* South Beach." Amanda laughed as they crossed the side street in front of their courtyard apartment. But a loud honk made her trip on the edge of the sidewalk and nearly had her fall flat on her face, dragging Ginette down with her. She slapped the hood of the car, angry with the rude driver's manner. "Honking at two defenseless girls at 11:00 at night is tantamount to war—or getting arrested." She scanned the area for a police cruiser. They always lurked around the place, especially on Friday nights.

"Leave it," urged Ginette. "It's too late to start a fight. Besides, you won't win. Not with the driver of an XJ Jaguar." There was admiration in Ginette's tone.

"I don't care if he's driving a lunar module. We all deserve a basic amount of respect."

But then the car's door opened and slowly there emerged the tall, well-built, charismatic figure Amanda recognized immediately as Augustino Milan. She was breathless, and though she tried to cough up enough venom to cut him to size, the words jammed somewhere between heart and throat. She was not about to ask him to volunteer the Heimlich maneuver.

"Mr. Milan!" Ginette was quick to intervene. "We

meet again. Only now, let me warn you. I'm on to your...prevarications."

He cracked a half smile, his steel blue eyes hitting their mark. "I did exactly as I told you I would."

Ginette backed down from the chill of his demeanor.

"I would like to talk to you, Amanda. May we have some privacy?"

Her gut reaction was to turn her heels and head in the opposite direction without uttering a single word. Her instinct warned her, however, that it was best to confront him now and get the whole matter settled quickly. She would get less friction from him and be done with the man that much faster.

"Very well," she answered, very much on her guard. She turned toward Ginette and showed her the span of one hand. "Give me five, hon."

Ginette nodded and left.

Augustino indicated the car with a tilt of his head. Amanda cringed at the thought of the two of them in such close quarters. Nevertheless, she agreed. When she reached for the front door he indicated the back seat. Only then did she remember that he had gotten out of the back himself. This could only mean that another was driving, which alleviated some of her trepidation. With a chauffeur looking on he would likely be more of a gentleman.

Once in the car, no sooner had she admired the oatmeal colored leather and posh interior than the engine roared to life and the doors automatically locked.

"Where are we going?"

"You wanted to go somewhere to talk."

"Earlier, yes. Do you realize how late it is?"

"Are we going to talk or argue?" He stared at her; and even in the shadows she reveled in his handsome looks, the soft piercing eyes stubbornly staring at her, the mobile mouth with the sensuous lips, soft and pliant.

She wished he would stop staring at her. As she tried to ignore his eyes, she peered out the window to better gauge in which direction the car was heading.

The driver seemed oblivious to them while Augustino, bent on bestowing on her his undivided attention, was beginning to make her feel uncomfortable. She shifted under his gaze and heard his long rakish sigh revealing he was just as uncomfortable as she was. He remained mute. Probably waiting until they reached their destination, she thought. She fleetingly wondered where he was taking her, not daring to ask. Asking meant speaking and she didn't trust any words coming out of her throat to be louder than a whisper. She noticed the car sped southwest toward Coral Gables. Itching to say something, she opted for silence. She would know soon enough, she figured, trying to think of a restaurant still open at this late hour.

But after fifteen more grueling minutes, the car turned down a narrow lane. From the little she could see there were perhaps four or five properties lining the edge of a private road, each one more elaborate than the next. The car pulled up a well-lit circular drive, displaying a large courtyard and a huge house of Italian design spread on each side of the drive. Three garages on one side and two on the other were surrounded by tall bougainvilleas and flanked by an ornate shrubbery fountain in the center.

He got out of the car and waited for her to do the same. He did not offer his hand or help of any kind and Amanda wondered if this was a new resolution of his—physically backing off to make her feel more secure.

"Where are we?" she now had to know.

"My villa," he answered curtly.

He had a villa? In the middle of the city? And all the time she had wondered where he went while not on his boat. Of course, he had to own a place in town. To call it a place was understating it. This house had to be over seven thousand square feet in size; shaped in the form of a half-moon, each wing displaying its own private entrance.

"May I borrow your cell phone? I left mine. I need to call Ginette before she sends the police looking for us."

He smiled and handed her his phone. "I see you're not too worried?"

"Not one bit," she answered, her chin inching up slightly.

She explained to Ginette where she was and asked her not to worry. She was detained, not against her will, and she would keep her posted. She added the last part of her sentence in a louder voice so that he would know someone was standing by, waiting to hear from her.

He led her to the entrance on their right. It was a double oak door fronted with a large bolt. He unlocked it, after which he handed her the key.

Once inside, he flicked on the hall lights and she

stared in awe at marble floors, inlaid millwork and a circular marble staircase with wrought iron railings. Huge tapestry paintings that looked strangely like the works of great masters hung in the immediate vicinity of the foyer, and small camera eyes hiding in the foyer's corners moved as they did.

She stared at the key he had placed in the palm of her hand and palmed it tightly, the warmth of his hand still imprinted on the metal. Did he intend for this key to be hers? She wondered. It was far too personal if he did. She would slip it onto some smooth surface first chance she got before she left. She was too rattled and it was too late for her to argue about it.

There was a small parlor on their left and he suggested she have a seat. He pressed an intercom button and a man answered at the other end.

"Can you bring us some tea, coffee...?" He glanced toward Amanda. "What would you like?"

She shrugged, still overawed.

"Are you hungry?" He suddenly appeared kind and solicitous.

"I'll have whatever you're having," she answered demurely.

"Use your imagination, Albert." He smiled. He sat on the chair facing the sofa where she had perched herself on the edge, attempting not to show she needed to collapse from nervous exhaustion.

"I'm angry with you," he told her simply, removing his jacket.

"Is this why you were unfriendly on the telephone?

Not a very nice attitude for a mature adult. Nor is it very smart for someone seeking a favor from an intended party to risk turning that party against him." This felt good to heave off her chest. She instinctively relaxed and sat back into the sofa cushions.

"I, not mature–not nice!" He undid his cuffs' buttons and rolled up his sleeves. "I ask you one simple question, offer you a king's ransom–not to mention my trust," he added in soft caressing tones, "and you ignore me for a week, letting me stew in my own juices, making me worry like an idiot school boy. I was terrified that you would refuse me." He looked at her intently. "Still am."

There was that feeling again, lodged in the pit of her stomach. "Is that why you wouldn't take the phone when I called you a second time?"

He laughed. "I knew you were angry–fuming probably. I wouldn't have it. And I was dying to see you. I was hurrying with my visitors so that I could meet with you tonight. I waited for an hour outside your door."

Albert entered, wheeling trays of refreshments. There was a kettle, a porcelain ewer filled with water and a tea decanter. There were biscuits, slices of fruit and cheese and a plate full of cold vegetables. There were even a couple of bottles of red and white wine with the appropriate stemware in readiness on a separate tray.

Amanda swallowed the funny lump in her throat. This is not what she had imagined he would say. She had prepared a speech and was on the verge of hurling it at him. Now, this humility, this candor...it disarmed her and left her vulnerable. She was grateful he was sitting in his corner and wondered if he felt the same way, if this was why he had made certain to keep his distance.

She looked at him frankly. "I didn't know you were expecting an immediate answer. I...I've never...no one has ever asked me to be their...hostess or pretend...girlfriend before. That's all I was able to think about all week. Your offer overwhelmed me..."

He smiled his eyes kinder than she had seen them, ever. "You thought about me all week?"

She nodded, raising her eyebrows to emphasize.

"I guess I should be flattered. I thought you had forgotten about me and my crazy plan, or you'd tossed it, putting off deciding until later." He smiled, stretching to pick up one of her hands in his. He looked at her fingers, weighed them carefully, caressed them lightly before letting her hand go. "Thank you," he mouthed softly.

Those lips! She could understand that woman wanting him as much as she had. A fate worse than death; it was clouding up to look like that more and more. She smiled, accepting the cup of lemon tea he handed her, willing the saucer not to shake, and wondered how she was ever going to walk away unscathed and unharmed.

CHAPTER FIVE

Amanda opened her eyes, smiled and stretched lavishly, tossing the blanket with one foot. Another hot day on the horizon. Even their AC was lazy. But she didn't mind. It was Saturday, a little leisure time in store for her and she had had the yummiest meeting with Augustino last night—or rather until the early hours of the morning when he had driven her home.

Poor Ginette; she had had to answer three of her reconnaissance calls, until sleepy, grumpy, she had told Amanda to stop calling her and to do it already. But Augustino had behaved like the perfect gentleman, she recalled, also remembering her disappointment at the time. He had talked about his early days in Brooklyn, growing up with a single mother. His mother, Adele Cromwell, had married Valentino Milan, an Italian salesman from Sicily. When Adele's father, the British tycoon Alistair Cromwell had found out about their elopement, he had disinherited her. It was only after Valentino's sudden death that he and his mother had come to America—Augustino was five. He had told her about doing time at NYU—as he put it—and completing his law degree at Harvard. When Amanda had inquired about his mother he had simply stated that she had died during his last year at NYU. The only good derived from his mother's untimely death, Augustino contended, was that the shock had brought on the death of his grandfather. "The old bastard deserved it—for the way he had treated her."

Amanda had not asked but wondered if the money he apparently owned in such abundance came from the Cromwell estate. It would make more sense than fees received from a lucrative law practice—especially since he did not seem to work or have any use for a precise schedule. A world-class philanderer with a law degree might be a little more tenable, she conceded, although she had noticed he was not too forthcoming with other details.

He had reiterated how he appreciated her qualities, her honesty, for instance, and how he needed someone with her spunk and élan on his team. They had discussed money; and when he had mentioned two thousand dollars per weekend she had cringed, absolutely refusing that much money. So he had included a couple of nights work a week when she was free, and when it didn't impede with the work she did at the center.

The only physical contact there had been between them was when he had stepped out of the car to open her door—below her apartment window at 4:00 in the morning.

He had lightly bent forward to brush her temple with a kiss. She had closed her eyes, hovering, hoping. But he had smiled and sent her on her way.

Amanda sighed as she got up to brush her teeth. The memory of that tender moment would have to do, at least for now. Looking in the mirror at the glow on her face, she smiled thinking that her first assignment with Augustino was tomorrow afternoon. She had the whole day to prepare and look her best. For the first time in a while, she found herself singing in the shower the only *Moon Over Miami* verse she knew, thinking that maybe, like the song, she would be lucky enough to get a little love and not so little a kiss on the shores of Miami, in the arms of Augustino Milan.

When she padded into the kitchen in robe and slippers, Ginette was already sitting at the table in front of the Saturday paper, drinking black coffee and cursing at the world affairs section.

"You should read the comics," Amanda told her. "They're much more entertaining."

"Your sister called. At 11:15 precisely."

"Last night?"

"Uh-huh."

"What did she want at that hour?"

"Oh! Come on, Amy. You know that every Friday night you guys aren't together, she checks up on you. She's pathological."

"Don't be silly. She's not that bad."

"What are you talking about? She detests me. The woman hates my guts. I never did anything to her."

Amanda noticed how grumpy Ginette was. This was no time to argue with her. Especially that she felt partly to blame for having wakened her more than once the night before.

"She probably concluded the same thing you did about me and worries that I'm going to corrupt you or something." Ginette added.

"I'm sorry I woke you last night. I was afraid you might be up, worrying."

"The first time, I can believe. The second time, we can chalk up to simple mistake—I won't even guess why you needed to call me a third time."

"It just dawned on me that you might not have his number. I had his card with me and...why are you such a grouch anyway?"

Ginette shrugged, noisily flipping the paper's page and refusing to look at her. "I don't know. I just saw the way this guy looked at you...." Glancing up at Amanda, she ventured. "Do you think I'll ever have that with anybody?"

"Sweetie," Amanda sat down beside her, rubbing her back. "Of course you're going to find someone. You're a beautiful, smart, funny person. You'll find someone who will love you forever. Besides, I don't *have* this guy. Had you found a way to be there last night, you would have been, without a doubt, the most bored fly on the wall. He was all business—just as I'd suspected..."

"So, are we saluting the fate-worse-than-death flag?"

Amanda nodded, a pout on her lovely face. "Yep. And it's flying high, billowing in the wind." Amanda threw Ginette a side-glance and noticed that she had at least gotten a smirk out of her.

"I'm sorry to rain on your parade, sweetie." Ginette added. "I'm not usually this bitchy. Put it down to PMS rearing its ugly head."

"Hey, don't worry about it. I'll soon have more funnies to cheer you up. I'm actually going through with this charade. My first assignment starts tomorrow." Amanda rose to her feet quickly and raised her right hand to her forehead in guise of a salute. "I'm joining the Augustino Milan infantry division of LL WAACs."

"You're crazy," laughed Ginette. "I shouldn't ask, but what the hell does LL stand for?"

"Lusty Losers—women's auxiliary army corps—get it?"

"I get it. You're nuts," Ginette laughed. She really was nuts if she couldn't figure how much this guy had the *hots* for her. She would find out soon enough, she figured. It was all part of that sweet process of discovery, Ginette thought, which sometimes was the best part of a relationship.

Amanda shuffled her popped toasts from hand to plate and sat down at the table to spread strawberry jam on them.

"So, did you get to see the whole mansion?"

"Nah. He gave me the dime tour. But hey!" Amanda continued excitedly. "He has a dock at the back. And it's not a yard, it's more like...grounds. He has a helipad, two tennis courts and a huge saltwater pool...at least as he described it."

"Why does he moor his boat at the marina? He could just anchor it to his own dock. Take the popular long walk a short pier every morning; that would be perfect."

"Don't know." Amanda ignored Ginette's sarcasm. "It was dark, I couldn't really see. He may have another boat docked there. But judging by the little that I know of him, I would think he's a stickler for privacy. Since he uses his yacht for business, I'm guessing some of the sponges he hangs with wouldn't be welcome at his home."

"Well, there you go. That's the first place he took you. I'm telling you, Gidget; this guy burns for you."

"Nonsense. The man trusts me to say nothing about his home, is all. He actually swore me to secrecy on any matter that concerns him and that he confides in me. So," Amanda zipped her lip and twisted it, "mum's the word, Ginette."

"Hum!" Ginette made an exaggerated loyal face, rolling her eyes. "Wild mermaids couldn't drag it out of me." Then she shook her head at Amanda's enthusiasm. "I swear if you weren't such a cutie, you wouldn't be getting your way with this guy."

"If I was getting my way with this guy—as you say—I wouldn't be here this morning having breakfast with you." That ought to clamp any further discussion, Amanda thought.

And it did. Ginette snorted a little of her ill mood but stuck her head back into the morning paper, leaving Amanda the leisure of drawing a mental list of all the errands she had to run.

She had not mentioned it to Ginette, but Augustino had insisted she take at least half of her first weekend's pay. He wanted her to go shopping for clothes. Of course she had not taken a dime from him. She was more than capable of buying herself the few items she needed. Besides, shopping was not exactly her forte. She would enlist her sister's help as a second opinion. She needed a bathing suit—maybe a couple of them. And she couldn't think of another single item of clothing she needed. She shrugged, sticking her nose in her coffee cup, attracting Ginette's attention.

"What are you so quiet about," Ginette asked her.

"Just thinking of the gazillion things I have to do today."

"Shopping for that WAACs wardrobe, no doubt?"

Amanda nodded. "I'm going to ask Meg to help me. I don't know the first thing about shopping for fancy clothes. As far as I'm concerned, I've got all I need."

"Tell that guy of yours, if he wants to parade you around as his own personal Barbie doll, he should at least provide the fashion consultant."

Amanda drew a breath. "How did you know...?"

"I wasn't born yesterday, Amy. Obviously he took one look at your Sears...department store wardrobe and thought, quick, let's get this girl dressed. So much more fun to undress...,"she added between clenched teeth.

"Well, he's going to have to take me as I am. I'm going to buy a bathing suit and maybe a new wrap. If he doesn't like it...then...he'll just have to show me what he wants."

"That's quite a threat," Ginette smiled.

At least she was smiling, Amanda thought. "Hey, come with us. It'll be fun."

"With your sister there? No way."

"It's the perfect opportunity for you two to get to know

each other. She won't dare be rude to you in front of me, Gin. She'll have to be nice; and she'll grow to love you just as I do."

"Sweetie, I have other goals in life than getting your sister to like me. Besides, I have a day too. You go and enjoy."

It was just as well Ginette didn't accompany them. Meg was cranky, complaining most of the afternoon about Jerry Junior's latest capers, Jerry's indifference, and the litany wore on from Burdines to Bloomingdales non stop. She even recriminated about not finding her home when she had called the night before. But Amanda did not *set her straight* as Ginette always insisted she do. She was used to lending an ear to other people's problems. She had made a career of it. Her sister was certainly no different, and a priority in her life. She didn't mind paying attention while she steamed out part of her wrinkled, dirty laundry.

The shopping trip was a bust anyway. Amanda couldn't find anything she liked; or rather, she couldn't find anything she thought Augustino might like. Dressing to please someone else was different, she found, and extremely difficult. He would just have to accept the package as it was—without the frills. She certainly did not intend redoing this little exercise on a daily basis—which is the frequency she would need to apply over time if she was to stock up with any kind of a decent wardrobe.

"I'm heading home," Amanda told Meg.

"I'll give you a ride. Are you sure you don't want to look in on that little guru shop down Ocean Drive?"

"Whatever for, Meg? I told you. I'm looking for designer wear. Something flashy."

"What's gotten into you? Is there a new beau in you life?"

Why did everyone think they had her number? Probably because they did, she sighed with frustration, hating that she was this transparent.

Meg did not press the subject. She knew Amanda's generous nature could stand just so much shoving and prying.

She drove her home and when Amanda offered her a cup of coffee, Meg looked up at the apartment—as if to gauge if someone was present—then politely declined.

"Gin doesn't bite, you know," Amanda smiled. "I don't understand what you find so threatening about her."

"She doesn't bother me, Amy. I just thought you'd want your privacy and all—unless you're ready to introduce me to that tall, manly outline I just glimpsed in your living room window." Meg smiled. "From down here, he looks yummy."

Amanda quickly peered through Meg's window—Meg barely had time to move her head out of the way—but she saw no one in her window. "I don't see anyone. It's probably a friend of Ginette's." She pecked her sister's cheek and leaned back, collecting her one bag and purse. "Call you later," she added as she stepped out of the car.

Amanda waited for Meg's car to speed away before crossing the street. As she did, she spotted the familiar Jaguar parked in front of her bug. Her heart instantly fibrillated its own raunchy little tune. Augustino was here—in her apartment. What could he possibly be doing there? This meant Ginette had let him in.

She ran the rest of the way, took the stairs two by two to the second floor, then paused in front of her door. She wasn't going in there out of breath with her heart beating hip-hop. She closed her eyes, visualized a smooth lake and counted to ten. As she meditated ebullience to a calmer tempo, the door opened—quietly. Opening her eyes and reaching for the handle she came face to face with Augustino, standing in the doorway with a telltale smile on his handsome face. Why did she know she was going to cringe when remembering this moment later? Why did he have to be so damned handsome?

He wore nothing out of the ordinary, a casual pair of khaki knee-length shorts and a sporty beige shirt. "I heard you climb the stairs," he told her with a glint in his eyes. "I was wondering what was keeping you." *I couldn't wait one more second before feasting my eyes on you.*

"Just rummaging...trying to think if I'd forgotten anything..." That was so pathetically lame it was more embarrassing than being caught in the throes of a very personal Hatha Yoga purging stance. "What are you doing here?"

"Won't you come in, please?" He was laughing at her as he moved aside, tilting his head as she entered.

Ginette was in the background making pitiable, diffident faces at her. Of course, this did not augur well and did nothing to calm her nerves.

"Is this the result of your frantic shopping spree?" he asked her, staring with raised eyebrows at the one little bag she had just dumped on a chair.

She threw him a knowing glance while directing her tirade at Ginette. "What makes you think I went on a *frantic* shopping spree?"

"He wormed it out of me. I swear." Ginette raised her hand.

"Well, for your information," she returned her eyes to the man in front of her. "It was anything but frantic and I bought strictly what I needed, nothing more." She raised her chin, trying to look down at him which was difficult to do from her five foot ten to his six foot three height. As she walked past them to stroll calmly to the refrigerator, she felt the stamp of two pairs of eyes branding their hot mark on her back. Silently she poured cold water from the pitcher and drank slowly, her back to him and her eyes riveted on the window over the sink, supremely happy she had decided to purchase as little as she had. She would have been mortified if he had seen her come home with loads of bags.

"I think we can do better than this," he told her, lifting from the bag on the chair the one-piece bathing suit she had bought. Obviously, this was not the proper way to grab her attention. The instant he saw the hard glint of disappointment in her eyes, he knew he had committed a major blunder.

Amanda stomped toward him with shock on her face. She could not believe he had gone through her bag. "Is this what you mean by respecting a person's privacy?" She eyed him, hands on hips, trying to display the right amount of temper. He had handed her that big speech the day before on how important privacy was to him.

Augustino met the fiery brown eyes that could not

manage anything other than sensuous warmth, the full-pursed lips and the stubborn upward slant to her chin, and relented, cursing his urgent need to know everything about her. "You are right," she heard him say, incredulously. "I apologize. I shouldn't have looked through your bag without permission," he added softly, his eyes speaking a language of their own.

"You're forgiven," she answered, wishing she was tougher and meaner. "Why *did* you come here?"

He smiled a bright wide grin. "I came to tell you not to fuss or bother with new clothes." He closed the few feet that separated them, and tilted her face up to meet his with a caressing hand under her chin. "You are perfect just as you are," he whispered. Then he turned and walked toward the door. "Oh! Also, Manuel will pick you up a little after one." He nodded toward Ginette and was gone, just like that.

By the time she regained enough of her senses to ask him what she should wear or bring, he was in his car driving away.

She collapsed in the nearest chair, unhappy with the way she had handled the situation and wondering if she would be able to pull off this sophisticated woman-of-the-world role he so wanted her to play. "How long was he here?" She asked Ginette.

"He just got here, maybe ten minutes before you arrived. I was glad you got here when you did. This man has a way of weaseling out the most intimate secrets from a person..."

"Why?" Amanda asked, suddenly worried. "What else did you tell him?"

"Nothing else." She put up her hand. "But he got me on the shopping bit; he tried to trap me on a few more of your sentiments, not to mention my own—didn't succeed," Ginette added quickly. "Still, Amy, the man is like the devil incarnate. I'm telling you. You'd better watch your step with this one."

"Kind of gets to you, doesn't he?"

"Girl, I'll never undermine your predicament again!" Ginette shook her head. "Just don't leave me alone at home with him ever," she countered. "Personally, I don't think any amount of money you guys agreed on is enough—whatever it is."

"You think he's too much man for me to handle?"

Ginette looked at her long and hard. "I don't think his type could ever be handled—by anyone, Amanda. I also think there's more to him than meets the eye—much more. Details, in fact, you might not want to know about him..."

"A dangerous side," Amanda answered pensively. "I already sensed that; the first time I met him and...last night—when he spoke of privacy. There was an edge to his voice. Gave me the shivers."

"Are you still going through with this, Amy?" Ginette sounded concerned.

Amanda sighed, shrugging and at her wits end for some form of easy solution. "Whatever happened to all your good advice about the worse case scenario not being so bad?"

"I hadn't met Mr. Tall, Dark and Dangerous. Scratch that." Ginette added. "It was pretentious and stupid of me. I gave you frickin', flippant advice. I wasn't being the best of friends, I guess. I'm sorry, Amanda." Ginette's wide blue eyes stared at her, ill at ease and contrite. "Will you at least attempt to reconsider?"

Amanda toyed with the graduation ring on her right hand finger, the only jewelry she ever wore aside from her watch. "I'm still going through with it, Ginette. I gave the man my word. He's counting on me. You should have seen how angry he was when he thought I'd given him the brush-off."

"If you're doing this because you're afraid of what he might do if you don't..."

Amanda shook her head vigorously. "It'll be okay, Ginette. I'll keep my eyes and ears open tomorrow. If I feel the least little twitch out of place, I'll call it quits. Okay?"

Ginette did not answer but looked at her sternly. "At least now I know why you called that third time last night. You were trying to show him that I was there, counting the minutes and standing by for you—in case he stepped out of line. You were scared of him." And when Amanda tried to protest. "You were—are—scared of him," she emphasized. "And me, like the idiot fool that I was..."

Amanda stood and wrapped her arms around her. "Hey! You shush. You worry too much. I was fine last night, wasn't I? It means I'll be fine tomorrow. You'll see." Amanda gave Ginette a little squeeze. "Thanks for caring."

CHAPTER SIX

The temperature was sweltering. Even at this early hour of dawn the deck was the least comfortable place to be. The night's humid heat had not relented and, with the Aleutian docked between two large ships, the air space was tight and thick.

"Have you heard about our boys-in-Washington's calamitous proposal to limit the tourist visa to 30 days? Combine this bright idea with their new power of shipping people back to wherever they came from—without so much as a warning..."

Augustino put up his hand to elicit Bob's silence; Bob Farrell had just come on board and was not aware of the latest drastic turn of events. To emphasize the request, noticing the puzzled look on Bob's face, Augustino placed his index finger across his lips.

A hefty man in a blue uniform appeared from around

a corner, sweeping the deck. He was carrying a rectangular box equipped with a long black hose and a metal nozzle, allowing the tune of a homing sound to lead him by the nose.

Bob approached Augustino and whispered. "What's big Clarence doing here? You got fleas?"

Augustino nodded. "Gary suggested he visit us when I complained of finding a small tick late last night," he mumbled just as quietly. "A small tick that can carry scraps of details a distance of 35 miles."

"You're lucky there's not much traffic at this hour. Our Clarence is conspicuous. Doesn't look like your typical maintenance man."

Clarence turned off his counter surveillance unit and placed the black container down near the flight of stairs leading to the lower deck. He took off his blue fatigues, draping them over the unit, and climbed to meet with Augustino on the upper deck. "That's the lot of it. Now all you need to do is check your cell phones—make sure they haven't been tampered with."

"Are you sure there was nothing else—anywhere?"

"Positive. This baby," he indicated his trusted equipment with a proud gesture "is the utmost in detecting devices."

"What's the bit about cell phones?" Bob was curious.

Clarence shrugged. "There's no need to worry if your cell phones have never been out of your sight. But these days, there are chips they can add to a phone—in a matter of instants. They work with any SIM card."

Bob and Augustino looked at each other. "Don't look

at me," Bob retorted. "I've been extra careful—with the company I'm keeping these days."

"What are we looking at?" Augustino asked thinking prevention was worth more than the traditional pound of cure at this point.

Clarence shrugged. "Takes less than a minute to program. They key in their contact number, push a few buttons and sesame! Allows them to hear any sound in the vicinity of the phone...and both parties' conversations. *You* assess the damage."

"Distance?" Augustino demanded, intrigued.

"Clear across the country." Clarence nodded at both men's surprised expression. "Follows you anytime, anywhere; home, office, bedroom..." He grinned as he left the phrase unfinished.

"I would call that a *nice to know,*" Gary added, startling Bob and Augustino who, deep in thought, had not heard him arrive. He had been on deck long enough to hear the warning. "Any other tidbit of information we should be made aware of?"

That was a lot of sarcasm for Gary this early in the morning, thought Augustino. Perhaps due to the fatigue he glimpsed in the thin man's eyes.

"Hey, we only come up with 'em when we find 'em. It's blind pursuit at that. Picking up the crumbs the bad guys leave behind—when they're stupid enough not to cover their tracks. Hell, that's nothing new. I reckon you guys know about that." He threw them each a jeering glance as he prepared to leave.

Of course they knew. They were also conscious that

the whole department was aware of the ham-fisted length of their operation.

"Any way to tell how long that bug's been here?" Augustino questioned when he saw Clarence bag the device he had retrieved and drop it in his suitcase. When he got no immediate answer, and the tension grew tighter than a drum between the four of them, he persisted. "Are you going to lift prints?"

This time there was a shrug from Clarence on his way down the ladder. He turned to address them. "A dual prong telephone connector...could've been there forever if you hadn't noticed the malfunction of your phone line, Mr. Milan. As for prints...like I said. If they were stupid enough not to cover their tracks....My gut tells me they wore gloves; but you can never tell."

The three men watched in silence as Clarence resumed his downward climb, packed his gear in its case–his blue overall neatly rolled-up beside it–and donned sandals to stride across the plank, turning once to signal a polite wave as he disembarked. Walking toward the entrance in colorful garb, his stout frame would soon be lost amid the early morning traffic.

"And the frickin' fog thickens." Gary threw both men a disgusted leer.

"What's eating your craw?" Augustino smiled at the usually affable character that was his friend.

"That asshole's attitude is what's gnawing at my stomach lining. Him and the whole damned department; they're laughing behind our backs. Come to think of it, they're doing it pretty close to our faces these days, like the jerk just did."

"Hey, don't let them get to you, Mother T. We'll show them." Augustino slapped an arm across his back. "Haven't we made giant strides these past seven months?"

"That's right," Bob chimed in. "We've got the dope on Senator Rolland and Sam Biggelow. They're cooking together and involved up to their eyeballs."

"You're forgetting one vital piece of the puzzle, people." Gary replied. "Proof. We have no proof—a lot of loose ends, but no conclusive proof."

"Sure we have. Thanks to Sheila, we know Attorney General Biggelow owns that subsidiary company that acts as a training camp for our friends, the illegal Cubans....Soon, we'll have enough to indict..." Augustino continued pensively. "The hard part is letting innocent people go to jail so as not to blow our cover." He eyed Gary, wondering what might be the real cause of this bout of temper. Even in their darkest hour Gary was usually laid back.

"Hey, don't worry about it, Milo. They'll all be reassessed once this is over." Bob assured him. "But you're right. The hard part's having to wait. Besides, fine people are going out of their way to help. Our friend Sylvia, Rolland's girlfriend for instance. She is taking enormous risks...those Rolland letters she copied." Bob had detected that his partner needed cheering up.

"And we've planted bugs of our own." Augustino reminded him. "Sam Biggelow is tapped to the hilt. And we've secured his aide's help—enter Sheila Purdue. Want me to tell you every scrap of juicy detail I performed to ensure her cooperation?" Augustino smiled, trying to coax Gary into a better mood.

"Like it was some terrible form of punishment," Gary scoffed, shaking his head. "The woman puts Jessica Rabbit to shame."

"That she does." Augustino breathed. "Still, we've made progress. We know the range of territory they cover, some of the companies they infiltrate. We have a pretty good idea how they do it." Augustino urged the two men to follow him down to his office on the lower deck, to a more temperate climate and away from the growing traffic around the marina.

"Yeah, you're right," Gary conceded, going downstairs behind Augustino. "It's just that sometimes I wonder if these bums won't always be one step ahead of us, and I'm thinking maybe all this evidence we're suddenly finding—stumbling onto left and right—is just another plant. God knows we've been down that road more than once," he sighed dejectedly.

Augustino poured them each a cup of coffee. "I don't think so. It's different this time. I can actually see the dots connecting. And Jose is not that dumb when he rants about the Havana Club."

"What do you hear?" queried Bob, who had not been briefed in a few days.

"Turns out that Tony De Marco..."

"Big Havana boss himself?" Bob asked.

Augustino nodded. "Turns out he had several luncheon dates with Lowman and Dunbar's whistle-blower friend, the trusted Hank Williamson—after the first series of trials began." He sat down on a bar stool across from the two men.

Bob was counting on his hands. "Hell, Milo. That's over a year ago. We're just learning about this now? What the hell do Hank Williamson and De Marco have in common?"

"A very good question," Augustino answered.

"And why didn't Jose tell us this last week when we met on your deck—instead of all that rehashed garbage about the Club?"

"He did," Augustino nodded, his eyes solemn. "He coughed it up; you had just left."

"Nice!" Bob shook his head.

"According to Jose, they met several times in out-of-the-way places, flanked by body guards, while a gang of thugs from both sides hovered nearby."

"Sounds like an unholy double-dealing piece o' peace." Bob answered. "Except, it's a piece of what? How do these two connect?"

"All trash hangs together," Gary added. "I've been trying to construct this puzzle ever since I heard about it the other night. Nothing fits. One is an international mess; a heavily funded scientific corporation accused of espionage, intrigue and supplying equipment found in terrorist terrain. The other, *our* bloody mess, is smugglers and people shipped off to...terrorist camps..." Gary's eyes opened wide as his expression showed the dawning of an idea.

Augustino smiled and nodded. "My thoughts exactly when I heard. Here we are rounding up suspects in one corral and...wouldn't it be strange if both corrals were trampled by the same people?" Augustino's smile broadened as he raised his coffee mug. Still not convinced Gary was over his hump, he added as a way of encouragement, “Jim Dunbar and Fred Lowman have been investigating Quartain Tech a long time—just as long as we have been looking for the *white tiger* and her bunch of traffickers...”

“Yeah. Except that they’ve been tying nooses for a while. We’re still scratching our heads,” Gary added.

“Who cares?” Augustino told him sternly. “If there is a hell-pact between their case and ours, let’s find it. Once we do, not only will you two get the kudos, but we can maneuver it if we play our cards right.”

“I’ll get on it, Augie. We’re going to start comparing notes, dates and places,” Bob supplied.

When no response came from Gary, whose eyes were downcast and moody, Augustino had to know. “What’s really troubling you, my friend?”

Gary took a sip of his coffee. He looked at Augustino with eyes that spoke volumes. Instead, he simply shrugged. “Nothing special, Augie. It’s just that I’m wondering; why did Jose wait so long before coming clean with this information? Had we known this months ago...”

“Just be glad he did.” Augustino told him, his eyes brooding. “Jose has had a lot of setbacks these last few years. We’ve come to an impasse once too often. His father, his brother....As a result, there is a measurable lack of trust in the air he trails. Right now, my vote is he’s attempting to gauge which side is the strongest.”

“He wouldn’t consider taking on the Havana Club on his own, would he?” Bob was suddenly concerned. “That could jeopardize the safety of a lot of good people.” He was thinking about all the extras that were quietly going about their lives collecting information for them.

Augustino added. "One reason he was late coming with the intel was he knew we'd be livid. Having the informant in an FBI investigation followed without anyone's knowledge... that was enough to get himself clobbered—not to mention putting our credibility at risk..."

"I came within two hairs—two of the thin hairs on my head—of having him soused and tied to a pyre." Gary spat, his eyes reflecting the close call with his angry side. "If it hadn't been for Augie, the guy would be knee deep in shit right now."

"Hey, Mother T, we're too close to the finish line to start fighting amongst ourselves." Augustino added. "Still," he shook his head, giving Gary and Bob a stern look, "he believes De Marco had his father killed, eliminated Emilio and is slowly plotting to do away with the rest of his lieutenants."

"Aye, mates; competition is fierce in Cuban waters," Bob snorted.

"Jose doesn't care one iota about the illegal entry of his compatriots into our country—hell, it suits him perfectly," Augustino admitted.

"Well, he should care, the idiot. There's the little fact about them being smuggled here to be trained as mercenaries," Gary retorted, lending an imaginary Jose his most disgusted look.

Augustino gave the men refills. Then he called Albert on the intercom. "How much longer to breakfast, Albert?—Thank you. We'll be up in five." He downed the rest of his mug. “Worse, if Jose gets the least bit close to proving his theory, there will be no stopping him.”

“Hey.” Gary asked. “Do you suppose the Williamson and De Marco meetings might have been pay-offs?”

The three stared at each other while Gary’s comment became a whole other person between them.

“Holy shit!” Big Bob Farrell snapped, banging his fist down on the bar’s countertop. “That makes sense. A pay-off for...? How many times did you say they met?”

Augustino shrugged, deep in thought. “I just assumed they might be plotting together on some side deal—exchanging favors...goes with the territory. That’d be considered some kind of compensation—an exchange of some sort...but what if...” Augustino rubbed his face with his hands. He had not had the leisure of much sleep these last few days. Eighteen hour shifts were beginning to creep up on him.

“Are you going to share that with us, Augie?” Gary asked impatiently.

“Well, I’ll have to corroborate with Jose. But what if these meetings were just good old fashion payola? After the trial...for the trial....this could mean that...”

Bob nodded. “Yes. I hear you. We could run a trace between jury members and De Marco. See who matches.”

“Which would mean Sheila Purdue lied to me?” Augustino eyed the other two with a sheepish glint in his cool blue eyes.

“Which wouldn’t be the first time a gorgeous woman lies to a man—to get ahead?” Bob countered.

“Or to get head.” Gary added more to himself. “What?”

He asked when seeing the other two give him the eye. "You're right. Won't be the last time some female lies to get...her way," Gary edged in with loads of undertones, staring Augustino in the eye—undertones that Augustino quickly seized.

Bob intervened. "How do you know she lied?" He asked to distract Augustino.

Augustino tore his glance away from Gary's stubborn glare. "She specifically told me that Biggelow was the only one behind the scenes—the mastermind in charge of those companies fronting the employment racket. She specifically said that he had no back-up plan. That not even Digby had known about it..."

"Who the hell is Digby?" Bob wanted to know.

"Digby used to be Biggelow's associate a little over two years ago—his right-hand man. They worked together for almost ten years."

"Heard about them splitting up. A sudden parting of the ways...a change of heart?" Gary asked.

Augustino shrugged. "You might say that—although no one really knows what happened between them." Augustino stared at both men. "He was also a jury member at the Quartain trials."

"Whoa!" Gary exclaimed. "Way too coincidental."

"Maybe Sheila was just shooting from the hip—trying to impress you," Bob supplied.

Augustino shook his head. "The first rule of planting a lie. Make sure the question is asked before the answer is given. I never asked her if there'd been help from anyone else. We didn't even know these two events might be connected before Jose brought it up." He raised his head and eyed the other two. "She volunteered—and convinced me that no one else was involved."

"Sloppy. I can't believe she actually mentioned the name," Gary mumbled to himself.

Augustino nodded. Then he shook his head, amazed this hadn't dawned on him before.

"There you go. Now we know." Bob reinforced. "I'll call in and get some man power on this right away."

Gary was the first to rise and shuffle his feet up the stairs to the dining quarters. The delicious smell brought the other two up the rear.

Augustino elbowed Bob, throwing him a headlong nod in Gary's direction, wondering what was ailing him.

Bob raised his eyes and pinched his lips, shrugging as he did. The comical expression on his face asserted he knew, but wasn't talking.

The table was simply set. On an off-white percale tablecloth rested orange juice, eggs, ham slices, pineapple and more coffee. As the men seated themselves, Albert entered with a tray, deploying stacks of pancakes and two full decanters of maple syrup.

Augustino passed the ham plate to Gary, who forked a small slice in silence. Without further ado, as if the information he was concealing was a fever he needed to purge, he blurted out. "Bob told me about your plan." He refused to look at Augustino, either to sum up courage or diffuse potential resentment. Instead, he became preoccupied with serving himself while staring at the food on his plate.

Augustino, waiting for Albert to leave the area, shook his head, ruefully snorting his amusement at the same time. "I see." He gauged Bob's lift of one shoulder to mean that he had been forced to tell him, and turned his attention to Gary Flint.

"You see! That's all you have to say?" Gary was stunned. "Don't you think that by flirting with Amanda Cole you'd be repeating the mistake you made with that Sheila? According to the documents we found, Cole is at least knee deep in this quagmire, if not more..."

"This from the guy who complains about forever stumbling onto *planted evidence*! Yammering about people who are always one step ahead of us."

"It's not the same thing..."

"Isn't it? Don't you think the documents we found in Rolland's file—by sheer coincidence this past week—are a little too pat?"

"Hey, wait a minute." Bob almost swallowed a big piece of ham whole. "That would mean that he is onto us. That he knew we'd be looking at his files?" Bob shrugged, not knowing what Augustino meant.

"I doubt it. It means he's being set up—by someone trying to stick him as a patsy," Augustino answered.

"Can't be." Bob was adamant. "The one who brought us the file was Brad Swell, your altar boy; and it matches the letters we got from Sylvia Preston, Rolland's girlfriend."

Augustino did not immediately answer. He had begun noticing stranger and stranger behavior from Brad. He had simply put it down to his resurging need for weed rearing its head. One thing he was ready to stake his life on. Swell was no innocent. A few minutes hung in the air between them before he admitted. “That’s right, Bob. I’d forgotten about the source of that file information. It was Brad that clued us on to it.”

“What are you saying now? That Brad can’t be trusted?” Mild-mannered Gary was fuming. “That Sylvia is a double agent?”

“I can’t speak for Sylvia. I don’t know her—although a girlfriend’s testimony might not be the safest bet.” He glanced at Bob, who lowered his head and raised powerless shoulders. It was clear he didn’t know either. “As for our little group, we’ve always known there was an inside leak. We just never knew from where....” Augustino trailed.

Deep in thought, he foraged in his brain to remember Brad’s attitude over the last few weeks—months—years. Taken in this particular context, there were many unexplained circumstances. Brad’s solicitous demeanor whenever he was caught eavesdropping on him and Gary’s discussions. His strange habit of knowing his location when Sam swore she had not divulged it. His need for information about cases he maintained could not be handled by other firm partners—just to get close to Augustino, get a fix on his bearings—like the time he had shown up at the yacht....He would need to go back and rethink this carefully.

“Leaks! They’re everywhere,” Bob mumbled, his mouth full of pancakes. “We’ve had one in our own department ever since we started this bloody war...”

Gary threw him a sobering glance.

“It’s okay. Milo knows.” Bob answered with a shrug.

Gary shook his head. "Augie, don't try to think out of the box here. That's how they get to us every time. I'm sorry. I just don't trust the girl. Just something about the way Emilio died. And now she resurfaces four years later—on your yacht!"

"Tell you what," Augustino added, deciding that the path of least resistance would be the better bridge to span. "Let's say you're right, Gary. Amanda Cole is part of the junta we're fighting. Wouldn't it make sense to keep her as close to us as we can—isn't that the first rule of observing the enemy?"

Gary and Bob looked at each other, at a loss for words.

Gary was the first to recover. "This is either an extremely horny and desperate attempt to screw the girl, or..."

"I'm right, aren't I?" Augustino held their eyes, defying an argument. When none was forthcoming, he continued. "My plan is twofold. Fraternize with Amanda using tactics that will elicit her total trust—getting to the truth that much faster. Second, allay Jose's fears by showing him that not only do we not suspect the girl anymore—meaning we're lending credence to his story about the Havana Club—we consider her part of our circle of friends; plus, as you know, I intend to raise the commitment bar on that friendship. This will also show him how strong we are, how utterly secure we feel and that we too are brave enough to recruit family within our midst."

Bob nodded. "He did think we were bedwetting wimps for blaming her. Still, Milo, your plan's farfetched. You've to get the girl to agree to this without seeming suspicious, and technically, the two of you have just met."

Augustino smiled. "Leave that little detail to me. All I ask is that you two play along."

Bob shrugged. "Do you suppose the juggling act might make him reconsider going after the Havanans on his own?"

"It's a possibility. If nothing else, he'll be as pleased as a peacock that we're lining up behind him." Augustino smiled ruefully.

Bob agreed. "He'll be more apt to stay out of our way, I'm in. What about you, Gary?"

A long drawn-out sigh was Gary's reply. "Do I have a choice?" He looked at the other two. "Looks like I'm outvoted." He shook his head, staring at Augustino. "All I'm going to say is, this had better not be your dick talking, my friend. I don't want to lose you, Augie. I swore Emilio was the last friend I was going to bury for a while."

Augustino smiled. "Don't worry about me, Mother T. I intend to live long and prosper..." He put up his hand to stall Gary's next retort. "Not another word, please. Anyway, we've got bigger problems lurking on the horizon." He continued eating his eggs without looking at Bob and Gary, waiting for their curiosity to peak.

"Out with it, and spare us the drama," Gary snorted, thinking Augustino simply wanted to redirect their attention elsewhere.

Augustino acknowledged with a dour expression. "Drama?—you be the judge." Once he knew they were both riveted to his words, he added. "Have you considered that since Sheila lied, letting it slip about Digby—about no one else being involved, perhaps..."

"Holy shit!" Bob was floored. "That means she lied about Biggelow's implication. Think about it. Why would she point the finger at him if she was lying about Digby?"

"Because someone else is pulling the strings at a whole other level." Gary answered, breathless. "Goddam it! If Sam B. is innocent....Who has more power than Attorney General Biggelow?"

The three men looked at each other.

Augustino nodded, a knowing grin dawning on his face. "Don't look for someone with more power; look for someone in the shadows dreaming of more power."

"Huh?" Bob made a face at him.

"Since we're considering Jim and Fred's case being tied to ours, remember the Morello trial? Every day sitting at the back of the room, diligently taking notes?"

"That idiot clerk from Jenkins' office? Pete Schneider is a weasel, a first class ignoramus." Gary supplied.

"Ah! But who does he represent?"

Bob shook his head. "Augie, Judd Garrison doesn't have the money to employ all these bozos. He'd need big time bucks to pull this off—commandeer an army of loyalists this size?—big time bucks."

Augustino nodded. "He has the clout and the influence. Plus, he is an avowed political enemy of Sam Biggelow. All he'd need to carry this off would be money makers, investment bankers hungry for power and set on keeping their little terrorist wars erupting all over the place..."

"For bankers to create more money, they need to spend the money they create...makes sense." Bob finished.

"Might even be the link that ties our friend Hank to the traffickers..." Gary mentioned.

Augustino added. "Our greedy boys want more political clout—to influence the military budget—I am certain of it. Think of it. It's been going on a little over four years. Ever since a Republican party came to power..." Augustino was thinking out loud.

Bob added as an afterthought. "Isn't Judd Garrison a Republican?"

"Exactly. And if he's undetected, who's going to know? Blame it on the opposition. Or on an extroverted leftwing liberal. Plant enough evidence..."

"Sam Biggelow. Yeah, I get it." Gary nodded. "By the way, great going, Augie." Gary slapped Augustino on the back. "But this in no way clears the Cole girl, I hope you realize this."

Augustino gave Gary a stern glance. "I'm in charge of the girl. Leave the matter to me. Have you thought about the fact that...?" Augustino paused for a few moments, reluctant to open a new can of worms.

Bob nodded as he told them both. "I'm way ahead of you, Milo. I took the initiative of having Fiona followed—ever since your little announcement of the girl leaving your boat. When Jeff told us where she worked. I figured that being in Fiona's employ was just too large a coincidence."

"And when were you going to share this with me?" Gary asked him, fatigue paling the outraged look on his face.

"We have two sets of people following Fiona Christian." Augustino smiled in Bob's direction. "Raoul's brother has been following her ever since that night—in part to protect Amanda."

Bob nodded with admiration in his eyes as he met Augustino's glance. "I don't imagine asking her how she got the ticket to that party is part of your plan?"

Augustino shook his head. "I worry about starting her thinking process about that night. I doubt she would remember...just don't want to chance it. For now, the less she knows the better."

Bob agreed. "We'll have to compare notes."

"What am I in all of this?" Gary shook his head from one to the other.

"Frankly," Augustino told him pointedly, "I didn't know that I could trust you with this idea." He put up his hand to forestall Gary from posting a defense, "—and I don't want this information rehashed past this timeline. One misplaced word or crooked look in front of the wrong person..." Augustino was thinking of Connie always lurking around him. "We've all agreed to go ahead with the plan; we've also agreed that the question of her guilt or innocence is a moot point—for now."

Gary nodded, rolling his eyes. "Of course, now this means we'll be examining a whole new set of assholes. Not to mention that this sends the message to our Bureau friends that we've been idiots all these years," Gary said dejectedly.

"Not necessarily," Augustino answered. "Jim and Fred didn't find the connection, we did. Think how grateful they'll be that we're helping them with their investigation."

Augustino saw Gary's face light up with the thought. "And don't forget that we had already investigated Fiona Christian at length and found nothing. These people aren't stupid. They are bright, resourceful and thoroughly without scruples. They've taken pains over the years to stack an awful lot of mirrors in front of us—just to avoid detection. Why? Because the solution's an easy one. Now that we know who the key players are, the rest won't be hard to unravel."

"Guess who's going to need to get back on top of Sheila—or is she the one who likes it on top?" Gary was grinning from ear to ear. The situation was clearing up and he felt better now that their operation was headed in the right direction.

Augustino smiled at Gary. "I guess you'll know soon enough, Casanova. I'm out of commission for a while, remember?"

CHAPTER SEVEN

Later that morning, Augustino's visitors were boarding ship.

"Hey Milo, what do you hear from your contact in Alice Town?"

Augustino shook the stout man's hand as he boarded the *Milan Milend*. He motioned him to speak quietly, as people were milling about the quay. The dark-haired Cuban had just docked five slips down and was coming aboard accompanied by an entourage of three—a petite woman in her late forties, round and brunette, and a younger man who looked related, owning the same eagle-dark eyes and red complexion as Jose. Anton, the impassive sculptured block of a bodyguard, closed the procession.

"This is my girlfriend Maya, and my boy Lupe. I am training him to take over my operations some day." He laughed, slapping the back of the adolescent's neck with the palm of his hand. "He's a quick study."

Augustino prompted Maya and Lupe to join the other two men in the salon. He showed Maya where the drinks were and told her they should help themselves to any snacks they wanted. Then he followed Jose and his bodyguard down to his office below deck and closed the door.

"You need a bigger boat, Milo; especially if you're going to conduct all this business here," Jose snickered unattractively.

"Conducting business on my boat is my last priority—as you already know. I'll be glad when we come to the end of this bloody situation." He sidestepped the small liquor cabinet he kept well stocked, took two tumblers from the cupboard, checked them for cleanliness and poured two fingers of scotch in each of them. He knew Jose's bodyguard would refuse the drink. He sat in a corner sipping on a tall glass of iced tea he had just poured himself from the pitcher on the desk. "It's coming up to four years that we've been running this operation. We're just now able to see the light at the end of the tunnel."

"Meanwhile, good men have perished. It's taken too long, *amigo,* much too long." Jose dropped two ice cubes in his drink, straddling one of the low bar stools.

"*Because* good men have died," answered Augustino. "Each time, the operation had to be recalibrated and recoded on the wires. Four contacts have died in the same number of years, each time forcing us to change our course of action."

"Did the fink in Alice Town ever surface?"

Augustino smiled contentedly. "Let's just say we found

him. One of the captains-for-hire pointed him out to us."

"Is he singing?"

"Somewhat. We've arranged a meeting with him in the Bahamas next week. It's confidential, Jose; so keep it to yourself."

Jose tossed his right shoulder. "Who am I going to tell? I'm not some punk you have to tell what to do, Milo."

"We've taken extreme precautions for this trip, Jose," Augustino told him, taking a seat himself. "We're not even flying there. No outstanding log to worry about..."

Jose laughed. "What are you going to do? Swim across, Milo?"

"Never mind how we're getting there. What's important is that the fink has vital information to give us and won't do it any other way. He's scared."

"I bet he is. *Madre de Dios*, they kill finks—and their entire families."

Augustino searched Jose's face. "Who are *they*?"

Another shoulder shrug. "The Havana Club. Who else? Do I always have to repeat it? Who else is running the show?"

Augustino ignored the tetchy remark but vowed to keep an eye on Jose. "Anyway, we did manage to extricate from him the name of one of the portals they are using."

"And?" Jose had waited a long time to disband the organization he deemed responsible for killing his father and brother. Never mind that the financial gain outweighed his revenge. That his band of hoodlum-traffickers would shout for glee at the decimation of their biggest rival's leaders.

Nevertheless, he understood that to pull the strings too soon would mean retrieving only minor players in this drug cartel war. Especially that the drugs were a front for illegal arms and dreadful terrorism—the deadly duo that stemmed from his country to travel all over the world. He no longer wanted the shame and stigma of harboring these people on his island, he had stated. When reminded of his own contribution to smuggling, he had raised an outcry. He was trafficking in goods and produce—to help his people and supply jobs.

"Too soon to tell." Augustino forestalled his impatience with a raised hand, eying him forcefully. "Trust me, Jose. You will have the burden of knowing soon enough."

"Very well. I trust you, Milo. I know you will find who did this—bring them to justice. If you don't, I will find them and subject them to my own brand of *venganza*."

Augustino knew the threat was an empty one. Although Jose and his band of merry men had hindered their discovery operation on more than one occasion, he also knew that none of them possessed the information necessary to bring down the cartel or block their forays from widening their illicit ventures—not by themselves, without their help. It would have to be a team effort. "At the meeting today, Jose, you may ask a few questions. But be prepared to receive even fewer answers than usual. Gary and Bob aren't too pleased with the fact that you withheld vital information for so long—you know the one I mean. And be forewarned; they will strongly solicit your full cooperation and added contribution where your people are concerned."

"Haven't I always complied with what your leaders

wanted?"

Augustino noticed how Jose deliberately ignored the reproach he had just handed him. He nevertheless opted to keep his mouth shut. Jose's comment was a keg of powder; one he could've easily ignited into flames. To boot, any argument would make Jose look like an idiot. Diplomacy had Augustino smile instead. "Let's just say, most times you have."

"When are we going to meet this girl of yours?" Jose laughed forcibly, his attention span short and rudimentary. "When you told me about her on the phone, I laughed so loud—ask Anton." He pointed toward his bodyguard who nodded imperceptibly.

Augustino realized that Jose's jocularity rose from having his wishes finally exulted. He simply nodded—gave the Cuban the chance to rub it in a little more.

"Put your family on the line for once. *¿Si*? You Americans are too chicken. You keep your loved ones protected under lock and key." He laughed, humorless noise meant more to jeer and insult—"take Lupe and my Maya, they are so brave"—added friction in an atmosphere Augustino was determined to ease.

Better now with him, he conceded, than later in front of Bob and Garry. He found himself wishing Amanda was already there, sitting beside him.

He had considered his motives carefully and from every angle before he had asked for her help. That weekend he had spent on the boat after she had run from him under Bert's protection had been a difficult one. For too many years he had worked up a sweat at the thought of never seeing her again. Now he could hardly believe she had found him. He had been shocked to discover her there, on his boat. Of all the people Fiona could have hired for him...

As he listened to Jose's ramblings about the new lady in his life, he wondered how high Fiona's assignment of Amanda to his ship scored on the coincidental scale. Of course it had been deliberate—part of that elaborate plan the enemy had been weaving these past four years. The one stranger he had fallen in love with one hazy, torrid July evening suddenly appearing on his ship. The one stranger he was NOT supposed to love. He didn't think Amanda was aware of the effect she had on him. He doubted she would even remember who he was, even with a little prodding. Hot sustained glances across a crowded room was all there had been between them. Strange, he pondered, how fast he had fallen. What was that saying about the bigger they were the harder they fell...? He was big at avoiding commitment, and aloofness stretched across him like a second skin.

Now that he was weaving and plotting to never let her out of his sight, his biggest moral dilemma was his conscience accusing him of being selfish, of so desperately needing to be with her he had not stopped to consider her safety. Then again, she was closely working with the enemy. The closer he kept her, the better he could keep an eye out for her. Plus he knew Amanda had backbone and courage to spare. She had the experience and knowledge to deal with anyone and any situation circumstances threw her way. She had proven that by working at the shelter. She was not only beautiful, she owned a great deal of personal charm. He was right about her. She would not disappoint him. She might hate his guts for the rest of her life when he finally told her the truth—by far the biggest risk he had of losing her—but this also he had to chance.

"So now you know all about my Maya. Tell me about your girl, this...fiancée!" Jose laughed and downed his scotch. He tried to bring Anton into the game—to jeer at Augustino's choice of words.

"My fiancée is on her way here as we speak," Augustino told Jose. "And you already know her. She's the last girl Emilio took home four years ago..."

Jose's smile vanished. Suddenly he frowned, his dark eyes suspicious slits. "You serious about this girl? Or you putting her through the wringer?"

"I agree with you, Jose. I knew Emilio. This girl had nothing to do with his death. Had she wished to kill him, she would have had many opportunities to do so that evening—especially while alone with him in a motel room."

"Ha!" Jose exclaimed triumphantly. "Finally, we are making progress. *¡Finalmente!* Did you hear that, Anton? Someone believes me." He nodded his head, gazing at Augustino with an approving grin. "Give me a refill, *amigo*." He handed his empty glass to Augustino who promptly filled it. "But still...this girl...your fiancée! Ha! That is a trick difficult even for you, *amigo*. Women wish to be courted, *Señor* Milo, before they will consider our advances."

"True, Jose. Quite true. Still, there's a special connection between her and me." Augustino chugged the last gulp of his drink. "She is quite a catch. A veritable charmer who has swept me off my feet. And I don't have to tell you, Jose, how much women love commitment... "

Jose nodded for emphasis. "*Si*, Milo. No need to tell me this. Maya is proof enough. Still," Jose chuckled, "when I meet her, I will beg for your forgiveness." Jose stood and took a deep bow, clearly still doubting Augustino. "Milo, if this is true, then you will have my undivided loyalty. Those men in there are idiots—assholes. We are just waiting for them to take a wrong turn..." He laughed, once more bringing his bodyguard into the game. "I don't care what those men do in there. You show me family and we will support you," he crossed himself, "you have the word of Jose Arroyo."

Augustino tilted his head and raised his glass. He knew family would bring these people around. And god knew they needed them and their contacts playing on the same field. Now all he needed to do was to hand the news to Amanda and hope she didn't choke on the bauble. "Come on, we've kept them waiting long enough." Augustino stood and led the way upstairs.

When the three men reached the salon, they noticed Lupe and Maya seated by themselves, communicating with each other in quiet Spanish, avoiding the two suits sitting in the opposite corner. Augustino knew fences needed mending.

"Gentlemen, we all know each other. Just so that everyone is clear on whom everybody is," stated Augustino, "this lovely lady is Maya, *Señor* Arroyo's good friend, and this young man is his son, Lupe."

The two men rose and shook Maya and Lupe's hand.

"*Señora*, Lupe," added Augustino, "Agent Bob Farrell and Agent Gary Flint, both with the FBI. If you will start the meeting, Gary," Augustino prompted.

"Thank you, Augie." Flint cleared his throat and broke into what was obviously a rehearsed speech. He didn't stand. He sat on the edge of his seat with his hands sandwiched together as if in prayer, striving to swallow what he considered was Arroyo's treason and Augustino's loss of reason. "First I would like to thank Augie here—we are good friends. That is why he allows me to call him Augie." He smiled, trying to ease the tension. "We want to thank you for the use of your boat. It is risk free to be meeting here and we appreciate the hospitality."

Jose raised his glass to the host.

Augustino appreciated the polite manner Gary was fronting to better induct Lupe and Maya into the group.

"Also, we wish to thank you, Jose, for all the efforts you and your family have made in working with us to solve this problem. The reason we are here today is to ask for your continued support." He paused, taking a sip of his water. He glanced toward Augustino who gave him a small comfort nod. "We have recently found a key area where the dissidents are being processed before they are able to integrate our system."

"From the fink in Alice Town ?" Jose interrupted.

"Unfortunately, we can't reveal the source of our information at this time. But we need your cooperation, Jose, for your men to continue sending us any piece of reconnaissance they come across."

“Why so formal? I’ve been doing this all along. You of all people should know.”

Gary bit his tongue, and when he stared at Bob and Augustino, they both gave him an unctuous smile. He sighed and nodded. “Of course you have, Jose. Meanwhile, we always suspected the trail left from somewhere inside Cuba—thanks to some of your contacts. We now know that their point of departure is deep within the province of Camaguey. They launch from Punta Cruz and instead of heading toward Andros Island as we’d originally thought they did, they traipse through the Bahamian archipelago and head for the shores of Eleuthera—north Eleuthera to be more precise.”

“That’s suicide. Why go all the way there?” Jose wanted to know.

“Probably to avoid detection. We know they’ve boated out there on a couple of occasions, most likely when an inexperienced sailor was at the helm. They called in a captain-for-hire to help them cross the shark infested waters of the Devils Backbone, at the northern tip of the island. We located that captain…”

“How did you know about the captain?” Jose asked.

“Well, when your informants told us they were seen headed away from Andros, we thought of Nassau, but the port authorities are as fierce in New-Providence as they are in Freeport. They’ve assured us that they maintain a tight net on anyone coming in and leaving their islands. The process was one of elimination—took us months to conclude. Then when we finally narrowed it down to Eleuthera or Exuma, we knew that in the case of Eleuthera, they might’ve needed help at some point or other to sail to the tip. So we began scouring for captains-for-hire. We got lucky. Anyway, he's given us a name and a description. That's how we were able to trace a new informant and...one other name..." he paused, not knowing if he should have mentioned this last part of his sentence.

"If you're trying to spare my feelings with regards to Conchita's husband, don't bother, *amigo*. I know that she told Milo what she had heard." Jose eyed them all, one by one. "Each morning I wake up with the wish to kill him—slowly—with my bare hands. It takes me the rest of the day to fight this urge."

Gary nodded, looking contrite, but said nothing. Silently, he was asking for their cooperation, and not simply because Jose's posse had eyes and ears everywhere. Mostly, he wanted their cooperation and promise that they would not interfere with their investigation.

Augustino got up—a sign to Gary and Bob that they should take a breather; a sign that they'd said enough. More was not necessarily better.

"So what do you need from us?" asked Jose, his interest to probe and discover.

"That you continue collaborating with Milo," answered Bob, "and keep the channels open between your key people and the three of us here."

Jose weighed this for a few minutes. Then, relishing everyone's attention, he stood and walked over to where Augustino was standing. "Milo here has promised to introduce us to his fiancée," Jose derided, drawing the others into his game. "When he does—or, pardon me—" he laughed loudly accompanied by Maya and Lupe, "IF he does, he will have my undying devotion. I have already given my word. Jose Arroyo has only one word." He smiled a white toothy grin while two gold crowns caught the glare of the sun. Then he chugged the rest of his scotch, wiped his mouth with the back of his hand, smiled and handed his glass for a refill.

* * * * *

Amanda was hurrying to get ready. She had packed a small bag with a towel, a bathing suit and a change of clothes. She had tried to call Augustino repeatedly all morning. He was conveniently unavailable. Meanwhile, Manuel was waiting downstairs and she was rounding up the last of her personal items.

She kissed Ginette on both cheeks and told her for the umpteenth time not to worry. She would call her as soon as she got there and give her a number where she could be reached—should her cell be out of range. Then she bent to let Dino lick her face. He was wagging his little body, expecting to go with her. She explained to him that she would be back soon. And Ginette promised she would take good care of him.

When she got downstairs, Manuel stepped out and ran to open the rear passenger door. He greeted her warmly, stating that he had just received a call from Mr. Milan who had asked her to stay in the car once they arrived at the marina. He wished to come and greet her himself, to walk her to the yacht.

Finally, Amanda thought. Perhaps now she could get a word in edgewise with him before they boarded. She didn't know if the summer dress she was wearing was appropriate, nor if any other accessory in her accoutrement bag was to his liking. She knew he expected her to follow some natural etiquette—a uniform of sorts—as required by the job. And she did not mind him telling her what to wear. She did mind him leaving her in the dark, at a complete loss and guessing, sorely sensing her inadequacy at the task.

"Thank you, Manuel."

He smiled at her in the rearview mirror as he maneuvered out of the small space he had almost boxed himself in while waiting for her.

When they got to the marina, Manuel punched the coded number on the car's mobile and asked her to wait. That Mr. Milan would be there shortly.

She peered out of the window, mentally counting slowly to a hundred to calm her nerves. He sure knew how to make an entrance. She forever seemed to be waiting for him somehow.

When she first spotted him, the weak legs, the palpitations and all the other painfully familiar sensations of an overworked heart trounced back. And she was not the only one ogling him; he was attracting a good number of onlooker's stares as he walked to the car. She noticed he appeared to span wider shoulders than she remembered in a creamy-white polo shirt. She was also happy to glimpse blue Bermuda shorts. Thank god! He was dressed casually.

He opened the door and she took a deep breath before stepping out of the car. At once he surveyed her, his smile waning as he took in her appearance. Her heart sank. What did he not like about her dress?

But Augustino was overwhelmed by her youth, her beauty and by the blatant trust he read in her eyes. He wondered again if he was taking the right tack with her. Her dress' bodice was tight fitting and low cut, with only a very thin strap caressing her tanned, sculptured shoulders. The curve of round breasts was appealing, and as he held her hand to twirl her around, he glanced at her bare back and shuddered. Delicately, he sidled up to her and planted a kiss in the back of her hair. The silky scent of her dark mane compelled him to wrap his hands around her small waist.

But she writhed and twisted to face him, still apprehensive about the dress she had chosen. "Is this okay, Augustino? You never gave me any specifics of what I should wear today."

"You look...peachy, *cara*." He smiled, referring to the white dress' peach flower pattern. "I especially like the way the skirt falls. It's light and airy; the pleats hug your beautiful body." He looked down. "It's transparent slightly."

"I know. But this is the nicest dress I own...well...the only nice dress I own. I thought it would be okay."

"It's perfect," he uttered, looking into her eyes. "I have something for you," he told her, reaching into his pocket "something that will complete your outfit. You see, while you were out of the room this morning, you were sort of...promoted."

He smiled, reaching for her left hand. He kissed it gently, sensuously nibbling at her fingers and she allowed it. She would have to accept many of his caresses and kisses if they were going to carry successfully the pretense of being lovers. She glanced toward Manuel who was smiling at them, viewing them as the perfect couple. She guessed the task would not be too difficult to swallow. She would just have to be careful not to bury herself in the part. But when he slipped a diamond ring on the fourth finger of her left hand, she not only protested, she stepped back, yanked it off her finger and stamped it back into his hand as quickly as if she had been burned.

"What are you doing?" She was shocked. Glancing toward the car, she tried not to let her face register too much astonishment.

Augustino flinched at her reaction. He turned toward Manuel and thanked him for his kindness, dismissing him until later. Then with his face an inscrutable mask, he took her by the hand—the diamond ring lodged in his left fist—and walked with her toward the entrance gates. With a nod of his head he directed her toward one of the benches that overlooked the canal.

"Sit," he told her peremptorily. "Please," he added when he noticed the mutinous glint in her eyes.

Amanda agreed to listen, massaging the wrist he had almost crushed as she sat diffidently on the edge of the bench.

"I didn't mean to hurt you," he muttered apologetically. "Please forgive me. Your reaction surprised me—caught me off guard. I didn't mean to startle you with this mock proposal–it's merely part of the charade. I had no idea you would take it to heart..."

"I didn't...I'm not. I know it's not personal," she said haughtily. "But Augustino..."

"You may call me Augie if you wish," he told her gently. "My close friends all do."

"I'm glad they don't call you Gus. Personally, I like the sound of your full name..." She smiled ruefully when detecting urgency in his features. "You have to understand; this is an expensive ring–or is it glass?" she asked, suddenly comforted by the thought that perhaps it was. Since this whole engagement was nothing but a hoax he had surely opted to have the ring mounted with a glass bauble.

"It's a four carat princess-cut flawless diamond, Amanda." He smiled, noticing her panic-stricken wide eyes. "If you don't like it, I can take it back to Tiffany's and have it reshaped, or perhaps have a few emeralds added to the mounting..."

"Are you crazy?" she breathed. He had to be out of his mind to trust her with a ring like that. He knew so little about her.

He sat down beside her, tentatively slipped the ring back on her finger, a pleading request lurking in the depth of his eyes. She couldn't decide which had more blue brilliance and multi-faceted lights, his eyes or the gigantic stone. "I mean, Augustino–I mean, Augie..."

"It's okay to use my name," he whispered, his lips on her temple. "My mother was the only one who ever called me by my full name," he added, softly rubbing his face against the veil of her dark hair. His hand slipped underneath her hair and toyed with the soft flesh at the back of her neck.

She closed her eyes, just for a moment, trying to remember what objection she had had when he first slipped this ring on her finger. But his touch was so gentle, so sensuous that she wondered if this wasn't his method of having her accept this situation without further protest. She opened her eyes to see his Adam's apple constrict as he swallowed and knew she had to shake herself out of her stupor.

"Augustino, I can't wear this—not that I don't appreciate it—even though I know it's just pretence. What if I lose it...? This must be worth..."

He sat back to better look at her. "It's insured. You have nothing to worry about."

"But I can't wear this all the time. Certainly not when I'm with my sister—or at work, for that matter. There would be too much explaining to do—trust me."

"You have to wear it all the time. You never know who you're going to meet. The only place you need to be inconspicuous is at work. No one at work has to know *who* your fiancé is."

"No, they don't. But my sister Meg....You don't understand; I'm the youngest of five children. They'll all want to know who the fellow is...my mom, my dad..."

"Just ask your sister to be discreet for a little while. Tell her you would like to keep it concealed for a couple of weeks. Then when it's all over, she won't have to know why. You can simply tell her it didn't work out."

Strangely, Amanda could almost sense how telling Meg about her broken engagement with Augustino might taste—a nervous, bilious mouthful worsened by the bloody flavor of a broken heart.

"I guess I can think of something," she added sadly, toying with the ring on her finger. She sure had not envisioned that her first marriage proposal would be a bogus one. But then again, she had never hoped for someone as terrific and incredibly charming as Augustino Milan to want to marry her. He was the man who came once every several lifetimes—a man women secretly wished was theirs.

"Good girl," he smiled, pecking her on the forehead.

Surely this giant effort deserved some form of better reward than a brotherly kiss on the forehead, she thought. "Aren't you taking awful chances?" she suddenly rallied a gleam in her dark eyes. "I could decide never to return this ring—never to break our engagement." She stared at him, unflinching.

He gave her a crooked smile and bent his head close to her cheek. "Don't tease, Amanda," he whispered next to her ear, his tongue barely caressing the soft part behind her lobe. Instinct had her stretch her neck to help him continue unhindered. "There is a thin line between illusion and reality that is too easily crossed..." His fingers radiated a trail of fire from the base of her neck all the way down her shoulder blades. Sliding his hand downward, he applied pressure to the small of her back for her to rise with him. "Come, Amanda; there are some people I would like you to meet."

She stood, unsteady but determined not to let it show. Her pretext as she fell against him when her legs gave out was to curse her new sandals. "I'm so not used to these thin heels. I haven't worn them in over a year."

"You'll be fine," he answered, buoyed by her willingness to please. "Just hold onto me whenever you feel you are losing your footing." Saying this, he slipped an arm around her waist and led her toward the boat. "I won't let you fall, *cara mía*. I promise."

She knew how to walk on those heels just fine. It's tiptoeing around him that found her tipsy and holding on to him liable to make her lose her footing. Steadying her step to his, Amanda glanced at the ring on her hand and mentally juggled with what she was going to tell her friends and her sister. Its size, its beauty and its brilliance had her hypnotized. She direly needed to remember that this was merely a role, a juicy one at that, but still just the lead in a play. She wasn't really engaged, she sighed. They stopped in front of the *Milan Milend*. "How did you know my size?" she asked him, suddenly realizing the nice fit on her finger.

"At my house the other night—when I picked up your hand. I looked at your fingers."

"Wow. You're very good at this. You must've been practicing."

He shook his head. "First time," he glanced at her tenderly.

"Oh! I'm sorry then," she whispered, absented-mindedly staring at the ring.

"Why? Because you've had more practice?"

"No. I'm just sad that your first time isn't more...real."

He turned her to face him. "Is that how you feel?" he asked with a frown on his brow.

Amanda saw he was concerned, astounded even. He had not considered the aspect of sentimentality. He was a guy, as Ginette would say. Men didn't attach any importance to such trivialities and often did not fully understand the women who did. She certainly did not want him to think her maudlin.

"It's fine," she told him, "—really," she added, seeing he was not convinced. "I suppose it's rather like the first time an actress wears a wedding gown on the set. She can't help but wonder...you know? I mean, being a bride is a notion drummed into us from birth, probably encoded in our DNA," she laughed. "Honestly, Augustino; once I step into character all my root teachings, my preconceived ideas just...swish," she gestured an easy-glide motion, "all slotted into proper little tumblers—all my priorities in order—really, just perfect." She smiled, her eyes upholding his inquisitive stare.

Augustino was not convinced. For a moment he thought he had spotted some strange gleam in the back of her eyes—a tear...he could not be sure. Of one thing he was sure; he could not bear it if his insensitivity was responsible for her tears. He deeply regretted having sprung this on her as suddenly as he had. It was no wonder she was upset. "I'm sorry, Amanda, for blurting this out to you without any warning. It was stupid and inconsiderate of me. But I promise, by the time your assignment is over I will have made it up to you tenfold," he smiled.

"Gees! You're paying me enough money. Who's complaining?" she told him, trying to restore some distance between them. The only way to prevent her heart from being trampled and beaten was to protect it with a veneer of indifference. For weeks to come this would be her focus, pretend to pretend.

CHAPTER EIGHT

"*Encantado, Señorita.*" Jose kissed her hand, his button black eyes quickly surveying Amanda's slender round curves, her smooth complexion and immense dark eyes dipped in a delicately sculptured face. "You are most beautiful, Miss Amanda," he ventured. Glancing tentatively at Augustino, he added. "Charming, most charming, I agree."

"Thank you, *Señor* Arroyo," she smiled while he stepped back dramatically as if wounded.

"You must call me Jose, please. Such a beautiful smile," he enounced, visibly impressed.

Augustino introduced her to Lupe. He too was taken with Amanda's beauty. His smile was bold, bordering on boorish, and Augustino slipped a hand around Amanda's waist, staring at the young man squarely—tightening the grip on his claim. Amanda sensed the tenseness drawn thick in the small group, especially in Maya's eyes that were dark belligerent slits. She sighed, deeply content to have the perfect excuse to lean into Augustino's hard body. When he felt her nestle, he gave her a possessive little hug and kissed the top of her head, all the while his eyes never leaving Lupe's avid glance.

It was Gary Flint who finally broke the stalemate. He approached with a polite smile and extended a hand. "I'm a friend of Augie's. We go way back." He nodded as Augustino released her just enough so that she could shake his hand. "It's nice to finally meet you," he added with loads of undertone only Bob and Augustino could detect. He shook the hand she tendered vigorously. "Augie was right about you." He raised his eyebrows, feigning surprise. "I should have known it's not like him to exaggerate."

Amanda smiled and wondered just what Augustino had been saying about her. Obviously he had planned this for some time. Unless, she thought, his friends were aware of their little dramatization. The only problem she foresaw was that Augustino had not told her about them. She didn't dare say a word.

Augustino planted a sensuous kiss on her temple and she could not help thinking how she loved him constantly caressing her—enjoying his nurturing and loving attention—even if it was for the gallery. "These are the two FBI agents—and friends I told you about, *cara*." He spoke in silk tones and as she lifted her head toward him in surprise, his lips brushed her cheek close to her mouth; she found herself shivering from the slight pressure of an almost kiss.

Augustino felt her tremor and worried that the fact Flint and Farrell were agents had scared her. He suddenly realized how quickly and inadvertently he had dragged her into this caper. He had been wallowing in the mess for months—years even. She had just been introduced to it a couple of days ago and had no facts. His remorse had him tighten his grip on her as he walked with her to the sofa. He would need to initiate her to the bigger picture as soon as possible. This was his most dreaded project. She would have tons of questions and he would have but a few answers. On a need-to-know basis, she would have to trust him implicitly. Would she be strong enough to continue supporting him while fearing the worse? People always feared the worse when knowing very little. Ignorance bred fear—this he knew. He had agonized over it often enough.

Left on her own as Augustino prepared refreshments, Amanda felt cold as the stark reality of her precarious situation slowly penetrated her pores, like the night dampness after a hot day lying on the sand. FBI agents, she wondered. At least they were friends of Augustino's, which meant that he was on the good side of the fence.

She had begun worrying about illicit activities, worrying that his actions deploying the need for subterfuge—like a false fiancée on his arm—bordered on the verge of illegal. She was relieved to find his loyalties in the right arena. She did experience a jab of betrayal, however; he should have trusted her enough to volunteer a modicum of information. She had been more than accommodating, darn right patriotic as it turned out, and there was no fit reason for him to leave her completely in the dark.

She promised herself she would attack the subject as

soon as they were alone together. Her eyes darted toward him and caught his gaze. She saw that he knew her silent request as he nodded surreptitiously.

As it turned out Amanda did not have to wait long. An hour later, Farrell, Flint and the Arroyos left the boat. Bob and Gary went under pretext of friends to attend. The Arroyos debarked simply because Augustino ousted them politely yet firmly off his boat, somehow managing to send them packing. Now he stood on the plank watching them leave, his back to her, hands in his pockets and toying with the means to broach a conversation with the beauty in his salon.

Amanda watched him shuffle back with a frown knitted on his brow. She knew he was searching for words.

She patted the seat beside her as soon as he reared his head inside the cabin. "Don't make talking to me seem like such a bad case of stage fright," she half smiled. "Fiancées have no secrets; or has no one ever told you that?"

He winced at the designation she used for them and stared at her ominously. "You would do well to help me remember our pact is just a game, *cara*," he said mutinously. "You be saccharine sweet to me when no one is around, I'm liable to forget you're acting and consummate this union."

He stood directly in front of her, his knees touching her own as he towered over her, his eyes as dark as a night sky.

She had a mind to tell him that it took two to consummate an engagement such as theirs, but remembered the power he had unleashed the first day she had met him, in his stateroom, and decided some truths were better left unsaid—especially the tentative ones.

"All I'm asking for is an explanation. You surely can't begrudge me that," she emphasized. "I've been nothing but cooperative with you since the minute I met you—well, at least not long after I met you," she thought it best to clarify. "You, on the other hand, have been secretive and extremely non-committal; almost as though I'm the last person in the world you could ever trust." She had gone from pleasant and alluring to perching on the defensive. She didn't quite know the best tack to take with him. As a result, she sat there looking up at him with wide eyes, unwittingly pleading and unavoidably charming, her full mouth slightly parted.

Augustino looked away, his mood not improving. He sat on the edge of the sofa at the complete other end, elbows on thighs as he steepled his hands to support his face. All he felt like doing was kissing the hell out of her, crushing her against him and covering her sensuous mouth with his. He took a deep breath and let it out in a tired, bedraggled sigh.

She slinked over to him and gently placed a hand on his arm. "Is it that difficult to explain?" She asked in a small voice.

"You can't be this clueless, Amanda," he pronounced in a low, barely audible tone. Summing up courage, he turned to face her. "There's a reason I'm sitting at the far end of the sofa. Would you like me to demonstrate what that is?"

Amanda stared at him innocently enough, then, as the gist of his words slowly dawned on her, she lowered her eyes and meekly retreated to where she had been sitting at the other end of the couch. Why did he have to possess so much self-control? She berated his damned aloofness and wondered sadly if his type took lessons on how to avoid a girl's charms? Instead of stirring in his arms, which is all she yearned to do, she would have to veil her desire carefully to avoid flagrant humiliation.

"I apologize," he said immediately. "I don't mean to wipe my foul mood on your gracious, precious help. I'm just at a loss for words."

He turned to face her and she glimpsed such soulful pain in his eyes, she barely held back from lunging at him and kissing the hurt all better.

"I know I'm overdue with some kind of explanation. It's just that most of the material we are working with is still classified; and I am on a very tight leash...as to what I can and cannot say."

"I already know that the FBI is involved. That in itself, I don't mind saying, is a big comfort. I was beginning to worry about the nature of your set-up."

He registered surprise. It never had dawned on him that she might have a problem with the secrecy or clandestine reason for playing the part of his girlfriend. He might not have to give her much information after all; he felt relief—at least, not today. "Of course, I guess the fact that the government is involved legitimizes the situation....We've been working on this project for four years, almost to the day. Four wonderful people have died on our way to discovering the truth; and we still don't have all the facts."

"Murdered?" She whispered.

He nodded. "I'll understand if you want out, Amanda.

But just for the record, I would die before I allowed anything to happen to you."

"Four years! What's taken so long?" She asked tremulously, more absorbed with holding her hand back from stroking his face than any concern for her life.

"People are coming into the country unseen, unheard... like ghosts in our system." His eyes stared into hers. "They infiltrate the fabric of our society through various methods, different routes—all of them leading to terrorism. Then..." he shrugged, "we lose them. They become proverbial needles in the haystack. We're close though. We're closer than we've ever been."

"I guess that's good..." she answered, deep in thought. "So where do I fit into all of this? Why recruit me—what can I bring to your organization?—and don't tell me that I am some kind of female buffer..."

"You are. That man today, Arroyo, has promised to give us his undivided cooperation because you exist—because I dared bring a loved one into this mess."

"So that's why!" She bit back her bottom lip, willing it not to quiver. "That's why you couldn't afford to bring in someone you truly love—not to risk their life. You needed a stranger to do your bidding."

His eyes bored into hers and for an instant, he was tempted to kiss those parted trembling lips, just to show her how wrong she was. He hung there so long, staring at her mouth, that Amanda felt he had mentally kissed her.

Instead, he rose and began pacing. Turning his back to her, leaning against the bar's counter, he declared in a gruff voice. "There is no other love in my life, Amy."

He had just called her Amy, she thought, as a tremor ran through her limbs. And what did that mean, other? Was one of the past four years' casualties his wife, his girlfriend? Was that why he had so adamantly proffered he would die before he allowed anything to happen to her?

"I want to help," she reiterated, her basic generosity once more at the helm. "I just don't want to be taken for granted or...misled; can I at least have that?" It was a true question and she waited for his answer.

He nodded from where he stood, without looking at her. When he did turn to face her, he avoided staring directly at her. "I have one more request of you," he stated in a formal tone, clearly stepping away from raw emotions. "I would like you to stay the night."

She smiled. "I can't. I...tomorrow is a work day," she said.

"I realize tomorrow is Monday, Amanda. Are you saying you can't stay because you have to work?"

She stared at him in silence for a couple of seconds. "No, I am saying that I can't because we have an arrangement. An arrangement that states weekends and some prespecified evenings."

He smiled. "Are you scared of being alone with me on this boat?"

It was her turn to smile, thinking if he only knew how easy it would be to seduce her. How she would even be glad to help if he only let her. "Not at all. I just didn't come prepared. I have nothing to wear—things to do—a life..."

"You have three weeks holiday starting tomorrow. Enjoy!"

"It's two weeks. I'm taking one week in...so your question about me working tomorrow *was* a trick question." She figured Fiona must have told him.

He nodded.

"I knew it was," she added. "I almost told you that I was—working—just to see your reaction. I still can't stay."

He walked over to her slowly and took her hands in his, hoisting her up to meet him. "Please," he asked, arching her arms behind her back and laying her flat up against him.

She gazed up at him, not two inches from his face, compliantly allowing him to mold her even closer to him by tugging her in at the waist. She heard his low groan and noticed his eyes become cloudy. Frankly, it amazed her how this charming man, as aroused as he obviously was, as so used to getting his own way as he had proven he was, so failed to recognize how ready and willing she was to be totally and completely his. She certainly was not about to fall into the trap of initiating any next move—not so he could discard her in total humiliation as she had seen him do before. The most she could muster was a half-hearted protest. "Is this how you're going to solve all our arguments?"

She felt him exhale a soft, hungry laugh at the base of her neck. "You just give the word and I will step away faster than lightening."

She nodded. "Okay. The *word*," she whispered. She looked up and he had stopped smiling. This was the only way she knew to keep her heart intact. If he continued turning her legs to putty and her loins to liquid fire, she would end up begging him to make love to her just as that woman had. And she knew where that led. "You were the one who asked me to help you remember that this is all a game. That I not be...I think the word you used was, saccharine sweet, when no one was around."

He released her, a wicked smile back on his lips. He tilted his head. "Nice to know you are in complete control." He let go of her wrists, backed away a few inches and glanced down at her hands as she steadied herself with both palms against his chest.

She could feel his heart thumping loudly through his shirt. She pressed her right hand against it to feel the rapid beat a little better, looking up at him as she did. She noticed the nervous twitch in his left cheek and unable to support his gaze, looked downward as she extricated herself from his hold. It was then that she noticed, staring at the floor, that he had not yet regained one ounce of his control—his muscle still taut and hard. Turning her back to him and hugging her arms to ward off the sudden chill, Amanda repeated gently, "I told you, Augustino. I have nothing to wear." She waited, not knowing what to expect of him. She knew that in the process of protecting herself she had wounded him—or at least his damned ego.

"Come," he said softly, clearing his throat. He left toward the stairwell and looked back to make sure she was following. "I just want to show you something," he confirmed with a pale smile. "I promise to behave. I'll be the perfect gentleman, Amanda."

She sighed; just the threat she did not want to hear. She followed him to the master stateroom and hesitated before entering it behind him.

"I promise not to bite, Amanda," he smiled. "Allow me to ease your fashion fears," he added, signaling she should come closer.

Amanda followed him to the closet and took a sharp breath when she saw the amount of clothes hanging there. She distinctly remembered her famous hiding place as being bare. She quickly foraged through the expensive summer dresses, the stretch pants and the blouses and tops—all of them with price tags still affixed—and whistled appreciatively. "Your girlfriend has exquisite taste, Augustino. Or maybe she's a fashion expert. These outfits are classy."

"Good! I'm glad you like them. They're yours—all of them." He laughed softly at the shock on her face.

"Why would these be mine?"

"Easy. First, I don't have a girlfriend." His eyes bored into hers. "Then, I thought it would be easier if I supplied the props. Why should you go to all the trouble of shopping incessantly? After all, it's my game, my invitation. It's the least I can do."

"I'll let you in on a little secret," she breathed erratically. "We women love shopping incessantly—believe me, it's no trouble. However, never in my life would I have purchased such expensive clothing. I mean, how much is all this worth?" she asked, noticing the accessories and fine lingerie as she continued scouting through the cedar closet's drawers.

"Money is no object—and stop bringing it up please."

He picked up a dress and placed it against her, trying to match the peach color to her golden skin. “Louise, an artist friend of mine and a fashion student is coming aboard in an hour. She will go through all the items with you, help you decide which colors you want to keep, which look best on you and she’ll make a list of any item you want changed or added.”

“This is too much, Augustino. I mean, I know you say that money is no object, but I can’t ignore the consequences, not on my rudimentary salary. There’s no way I could ever repay you for this.”

“You are not meant to. They’re yours, Amanda. Are you so proud that you don’t know how to say thank you?”

“Of course I can say thank you.” She lifted her head with a hint of bravado. “It’s nice to see that some men take pleasure in dressing up their...intended, rather than constantly thinking up ways of undressing her.”

He laughed boisterously. He enjoyed her quick wit and blunt comebacks. Her spitfire personality sprinkled spice in his life and helped to arouse him almost as much as her slender sexy figure did. “Is this your way of accepting to stay the night?”

“It all depends. Where will you be sleeping?” He had roped her into staying. She could not very well say no to his pressing invitation after he had spent a fortune and a half on a wardrobe for her. But his lavish display of generosity simply reinforced the fact she needed to keep her guard up. She was not for sale.

He eyed her up and down, glanced toward the king-sized berth and gave her a wicked smile. “I don’t suppose you would want to share your sleeping quarters with me?" he asked softly.

It was her turn to smile coyly and with a slight hint of mischief, she relished adding, "That also depends—on whether you can sleep beside me without stirring. I'm a light sleeper. Any tossing or turning or...heavy breathing...would likely wake me." There, she had practically accepted him wholeheartedly. How deaf could the man be?

But again he laughed, flicking the tip of her nose. "You needn't worry. I don't intend disturbing your beauty sleep. I'll bed in one of the upper bunks in the crew quarters. It's accessible from the engine room. I can get there by the door behind the shower of the master head. I can come and go without being seen."

Of course, she thought. Once more he had teased her into thinking that he demanded more of her than sensuous smiles and sexy innuendos—to no avail. And Amanda wondered if this handsome dashing man even liked women. Maybe he was more of a man's man. Without noticing, she sighed, a little frustrated, and he called her on it.

"You don't like the arrangement?"

She thought she read expectation in his eyes, but she was not going to chance looking like a fool with an answer that would only make him laugh again. "The arrangement is fine. As always, you have thought of everything."

He nodded, searching her eyes; then turned to walk away, leaving her to her own devices. Before crossing the threshold he turned to remind her, "Louise will be here shortly. I'll let you inventory what's here. You'll be caught up that much faster." He smiled. "Don't stay away too long."

Shortly after leaving Amanda, Augustino and his mate, Raoul, welcomed Captain Charles on board. He was there to assist them with plotting charts and courses for their upcoming Bahamian trip.

Augustino said. "I appreciate you doing this, Captain Charles. I am still a novice with the instrumentation. I don't want to get us stranded on the reefs."

"I told you. I'd be pleased to go along with you to lend a hand."

"Well, if I need you I'll call you. As Gary told you, we're heading a delicate operation. The least amount of people involved the better." He'd gotten too much precious information on the enemy from another captain-for-hire. This also meant the reverse was possible.

The trio strode up to the upper deck gleaming bright white in the mid-day sun. They entered the pilothouse and Captain Charles surveyed the instrumentation panel.

"The boat possesses a high class chart-plotter system," Charles noticed. "I guess you know the functions of these digital knobs?" As he described the panel, Augustino pointed out that he was familiar with most of them. "On this board here, you have your speed, your depth gauge, your wind direction and wind speed, two freshwater monitors, gray and black water monitors, and your fuel gauge. Down here, the all important latitude and longitude meters."

"I've operated a boat previously, Captain Charles. I've just never used this one over such a long distance."

"They're all the same, really. Except that this system

will allow more tricks. You can set up alarms to ring along certain parameters—even tag them on to your cell phone or landline. You can download the software to follow you on your computer and attach as many as...I think eight camcorders on your system—to record...you know, whatever you feel least comfortable with."

"I guess the best way would be to take her out for a spin with you on board," Augustino added.

"That, or use another less sophisticated craft," Charles replied.

"The other boat I have moored at my dock is simpler to sail, but smaller. It won't do for what we want to accomplish."

"Very well. I can be here on Tuesday morning. We'll take her out to sea for a couple of hours—for the day if you judge necessary. Can you manage that?"

"Sure. I've taken her out before. I've gone to Palm Beach and back, and down to the Keys—but that was during the calm season, last October; and a friend was the main pilot." Augustino pointed to Raoul. "Meanwhile, you can show Raoul how to load and operate part of the Vision software. Give him some pointers on the system as well. Raoul is well acquainted with ships." Augustino patted the stout Raoul on the back. He was as smart as he was strong, and Augustino relied on him as a bodyguard and as a proper tactician.

While Raoul and Captain Charles went down the stairwell to the office below Augustino stayed on the upper deck, poured himself a drink and soaked up some of that bright sun while he made a few important phone calls. He needed to test some of his theories with regards to Brad Swell and make more demands of one Sheila Purdue. While it was agreed that Bob would discreetly attempt to confer with Sam Biggelow to gauge his cooperation, Gary would run a trace on jury members and perform a thorough search of Sylvia Preston's activities as well as coordinate with Fiona's tailgaters.

Just as he had hung up with Gary Flint, Augustino spotted Connie rounding the top of the pilothouse stairwell, clad in nothing but a tiny bikini, a huge hat and spiked high heels. Her smile brightened with undisguised pleasure when she encountered Augustino and immediately she removed the top of her bikini when she noticed he was there alone.

He smiled. "Connie, you're incorrigible. Put your top back on. We have guests."

"I know. Louise and I came together. She's downstairs in your stateroom with something she deems a secret project she said you gave her..."

"No. Raoul is here..."

"He's seen me many times. I like Raoul."

"...and Captain Charles." He picked up the top she had discarded on the ground, threw it at her and told her to get dressed. "Plus I have a special guest today." He looked at her as she slipped her top back on, glancing at the thong she wore as a bottom. "You'll have to be on your best behavior, Connie. This guest is my new fiancée."

Connie opened her dark eyes wide with anger and outrage—a mixture that spread quickly to her face as she ran to where he sat and made a motion to strike him with a vicious right hook. "You bastard! How dare you! I'm going to kill you!" she yelled.

He stood and wrestled her to calmness, twisting her wrists behind her back. He had tried to map out umpteen scenarios of the many ways to tell her. He had finally opted for the direct route—the traditional ripping-off-of-the-bandage pull. Yes, she would flare up. She was like a wild filly that would never be tamed. And yanking her out of his life would be vicious, for both of them. But doing it quickly would sooner have it over. "Aren't you the one who said you would do anything to help me get to the truth? The one who has been indispensable with the information you've already given me?" He yanked her against him and spoke inches away from her mouth.

She eyed his lips and his eyes and seemed calmer. "You know I will do anything you ask, *querido*. But I will not be a party to you loving another woman—much less marrying one." She turned her head to the side and spat on the floor defiantly. "Next time, I spit on you," she warned.

"You will trust me, Connie. I am simply pursuing my investigation."

"Who is she?" Connie asked, her chest heaving fast.

Augustino remained silent. "You've already met her, Conchita. She was Emilio's dance partner four years ago."

"How can you bring her here?" She demanded, her dark eyes on fire.

He cautiously added. "This is just the next step in the ladder. You'll have to trust me. You have been a major ally in our foray so far, *cara*. It would be a shame to have to part ways this late in the game." He knew that Connie needed him as much as he needed her. He knew she would take a back seat if it meant pleasing him.

"What you're saying is that you still need me—even though you have this...fiancée?"

"That's exactly what I'm saying." He smiled, bent and kissed the top of her head.

"What is this girl to you, *querido*?"

The question surprised him. He could only stare at her with no ready response, his arms falling by his side, suddenly limp.

"Do you love her?"

And when still he did not answer, she propped her freed hands against his chest and pushed him as hard as she could. "You *loco* bastard! You can't even pretend that you don't. I will kill you before I see you love another woman." She uttered her threat quietly and, casting him a murderous set of black eyes, she tottered to the ship's railing, grasping it firmly, leaning over the edge. Connie needed the saltwater breeze to cool her head. She felt used and punished.

Augustino walked up behind her. "I never meant to hurt you, Conchita." His hands on her shoulders, he drew her back against him. "You are married. You have a family. You and I were never supposed to be...a couple." He spoke softly in her ear. "You insisted I make love to you, if you remember well. Please, I don't wish to fight with you. You are too valuable to me." He felt her collapse against him, her stance yielding and soft.

"Are you telling me that this fiancée doesn't satisfy you the way I do?" She sniffed.

"Don't put words in my mouth. You're too smart for that. But I will admit that you have undeniable charms that are vital to this investigation."

She remained silent, staring out at the canal for a long minute. "You will prove this by coming to visit me this evening?" She breathed.

He spun her around. "I have nothing to prove to you, Connie." He stepped back to better rally her attention, holding on to her hands. "I have enjoyed our time together, Conchita. But here is where it must end." His voice was persuasive and gentle and he knew her anger was subsiding. "If you're a good girl about this, I will make it up to you."

"Tomorrow night then." Her breathing was shallow and rapid. "And not just for a couple of hours; the whole night—until dawn." She gave him her best soulful eyes. "As a farewell performance."

The prospect of making love to Connie was an easy and mechanical form of pleasure. But he was not about to jeopardize what he had worked on for so long. "You have chosen not to hear a word I said." He shook his head, gazing into her eyes. "I've just finished saying that you and I are in the past. I can no longer make love to you. I am engaged, Conchita. And," he added, putting more distance between them, "you will be friendly to her. For me?"

Her eyes darkened once again. She was on the verge of another fit. But staring into his eyes, she mellowed. "I will do as you ask—because that is how much I care about you, Milo." She nodded reluctantly, looking even more rebellious. "I promise," she added when she saw him cock his head, desperate to remain on his good side. She knew how painfully aloof Augustino could be when he did not get his own way. At least now, she could step in the minute he was finished with this lukewarm girl and take her rightful place beside him.

She scooted past him, grabbed the first towel on the stack by the small sink and draped it over a lounge chair. She would soak up some sun, aft, by the side of the dingy. She gave him one last look before sitting down, facing him on the lounger. Adroitly she flipped up the top to her bathing suit, carefully dabbed lotion on her limbs and paid particular attention to her breasts. She repeated the motion on the rest of her body, deliciously aware that he was staring at her. Contentedly she decided that lazing naked under the sun's warm rays would ward off the chill he had just instilled. The fact that she was basking under his glance, whenever he looked up from his charts, was a double sensuous pleasure.

She was forever digging up new ways to please this man. There was no better lover in all the men she had bedded. And the count, she realized with an unctuous smile of satisfaction, was an exorbitant one. Yes, this strategy satisfied her. This battle might be lost, but the war was far from over.

When thirty minutes had passed, she rose from her lethargic position and asked him to apply lotion to her back.

She was a devil, this one, he thought. He shook his head and smiled at her transparent guile. Of course he would have to oblige. There was no other way to keep her happy. He rose from his seat in the shade and walked over to where she was waiting, already lying on her stomach. He applied lotion to his hands and began rubbing it on her back and shoulders.

"Do my lower back, ah! Yes...lower still," she cooed, "...and my thighs while you're at it." She smiled, making contented little sounds as he deftly massaged the lotion into her skin. His hands were strong yet gentle. She loved his silky sensuous touch.

"You could've done most of this yourself, Connie. I don't know why you insist on being so demanding. Most women wait until they are asked."

"Most women do not know what they want, Milo," she told him. "I do."

He was still rubbing down her thighs when he heard a feminine voice clearing her throat. Augustino startled, turned abruptly, barely managing not to look like the child whose hand is caught in the cookie jar. There stood Louise who had drawn their attention, with Amanda who had walked up to the deck beside her.

Amanda frowned, briefly disoriented. She stared at Augustino—could not define the look in his eyes because of the glare of the sun—but recognized the lady on the lounger, the one whose eyes were staring at her wide with curiosity. She was the rejected naked lady she had felt sorry for that first night she had encountered Augustino Milan. No longer rejected, she was veritably pampered, Amanda realized. She also remembered that she was not a real fiancée. She was playing a role, she schooled herself, and Augustino owed her nothing—no loyalty, no love, no explanation. She smiled at him and his lady friend. "Hello, I just came up to tell you that Louise and I are all squared away. She's a real find, Augustino. Thank you."

"Thank *you*," Louise added. "You're the one with the fabulous taste, Amy."

Augustino wiped his hands on Connie's towel and got up slowly. "Have you seen Amanda's ring, Louise?"

"I'm sorry. I forgot to mention it," Amanda said, flashing her fourth finger toward Louise's excited expression. The omission coursed a little jolt of consolation through her veins. It was face-saving comfort to let him know that this engagement did not occupy a larger place in her life.

He moved toward her out of the sun and under the tarp, and cornered her with intent blue eyes. He did not even have the pleasure to see her squirm. She was strong, he thought. "You've met Louise, *cara*. This is Connie, a good friend and an important collaborator," he told her, his raised eyebrow urging Connie to be on her best behavior.

"*Hola*," the other girl said indifferently. "Any friend of Milo's..." She lay back down on the lounger, not bothering to continue the sentence—or the conversation for that matter. Amanda smiled to herself. This girl thought of her as competition. To Amanda's people-trained eye, Connie's retreat simply meant that she was writhing with jealousy and striving hard not to show it.

Amanda picked up Augustino's hand and squeezed it gently. "How about taking me home?" She ventured in front of the others. She could not see the reason for him to keep her here—now that her identity was firmly established.

"How about you show me the result of your wardrobe

choices," he replied, giving her the benefit of a silky smooth smile. He was not going to let her deter him from his previous demand. He led her downstairs to the stateroom in complete silence and said nothing before he closed the door behind them.

A cloud ran across his eyes. He was angry, this she saw. Why?—she had no idea, except that perhaps he was miffed for the way she had forgotten to tell Louise that they were engaged and had smugly confessed to the deed in front of Connie.

"You and I are engaged to be married. That is a $35,000 ring on your finger. The idea is for you to let people know about this little detail."

"The marriage or the price of the ring?" She was being facetious and deliberately obtuse—probably courting danger. But she needed answers. And if the only way to obtain them was to goad them out of him, then this is what she intended to do.

"You are playing a dangerous game, *cara*." His voice was low and very deliberate.

"Not any more dangerous than the one you're playing, *caro*. You who asked me to become your pretend fiancée to keep unwanted female attentions at bay, and to persuade your scoundrel buddies that you are a good, dutiful family man. Then the first instant my back is turned, you are rubbing suntan oil on a gorgeous, extremely horny female—who I am sure fits the profile of the sort you said you most wanted to avoid."

She flashed him warm brown eyes and all he could do

was gaze at the full lips of her pursed mouth. And while massaging Connie's anger had been mechanical and had left him indifferent, he suddenly craved to melt Amanda's anger away by delving deep into the sweetness of her opened mouth. Without even realizing it as he advanced toward her, she had backed up and was standing against the wall, wide-eyed with shallow breath. She found his eyes disturbed her to the point of having to toil to haul air into her lungs, of being dizzy...

He leaned his body into hers, supporting himself with his hands flat against the wall. She had a fleeting moment to wonder if he was always as hard and ready for other women, when the room went dark as he covered her face with his in a soft deliberate kiss.

At first, it was a bare touch as he gently slid his lips over hers, forcing her to clutch his open shirt for balance. Her grabbing fistfuls of his chest hair made him shudder and he managed to groan. "Please..." against her lips for her to open wider and allow him inside. He was too weak to fight the urge to taste her mouth but still too reverent to subdue her.

She moaned as she parted her lips and allowed his tongue to take over her senses. As the kiss deepened, wave upon wave of feverish tension seized her, compelling her to arch her body and hungrily press it against his—her will that of a cotton doll's.

She didn't know how long the kiss lasted or when exactly he scooped her up into his arms. Perhaps it was when his tongue wrapped itself around hers, stroking her palate and prickling the back of her throat. The back and forth hunger of his mouth drew her immediate response and she began exploring his own mouth, needing to give him the same sensuous pleasure. She wondered how long she could withstand this delight without collapsing. And where was this monumental self-control of his?

Augustino was out of control. The sweet juices of her mouth drove him mad. And as he squeezed her against him, his hands hungrily stroking her bare back, all he could think of was feeling her soft skin against his and wedging himself inside her for as long as he could.

There was a repeated loud wrapping against his cabin door. "Augustino, are you in there?"

Slowly he extracted his tongue from her mouth, swallowing hard. He stared at her with haggard eyes and heard her complain as he withdrew his lips and found his breath.

Amanda noticed his mouth was dripping wet. He did nothing to wipe his lips. Instead, he ran his tongue over them, pressing them together as if to savor the sweet lingering taste of her mouth. With eyes closed, he answered in a rough, broken voice. "I'm here. What do you want?"

"Captain Charles is leaving..." There was hesitation in Raoul's query as he spoke through the door. "Do you need to talk to him?"

"No. I'll see him Tuesday morning." He stared at Amanda's expectant face, heard her short gasps for breath and knew he had gone too far. He placed his hands firmly on her hips and pushed her away from him. "I'm sorry," he whispered. "Please forgive me. It wasn't my intention to seduce you, Amanda."

"I sort of hope I participated a little..." she didn't

recognize her voice. It was soft and childlike.

Her tone only served to make him swear and clench his fists. Unable to support her eyes, he turned from her altogether. He walked toward the door. "Please stay the night. You have my word I will not step out of line again." He stayed poised on the threshold with his back to her, waiting for an answer.

"I will stay, Augie, if it means that much to you."

He nodded. Then, as if he needed to look at her almost as much as he needed to breathe, he turned and said. "Can you forgive me?"

She shook her head. "There's nothing to forgive, Augustino. It was just as much me. I don't think I can easily forget though. Can you...?" She needed to know.

"I have to; if I want to stay sane."

With those few words he was out the door, affording her the freedom to flop on the bed, dizzy, confused but elated. Doubly elated when she remembered Gin's comment about the kind of man who kisses a woman and how the reason behind the kiss exposes him to be vulnerable with a transparent kind of love. Being a pragmatist and an honest one, however, she stared down the barrel of a more sober realization. Augustino was certainly *not* in love with her. He hardly knew her. He was a man faced with perilous odds and surrounded by a bevy of beautiful women. Hormones had taken over. She had just been the nearest candidate when they had. Reality finally gripping her hard, she wondered dejectedly how many other women he had kissed like that in the past few weeks.

There was a knock at her door. She jumped, heart

thumping and head buzzing. He was back. "Come in," she answered, hurrying to the door.

But it was Louise with a bright smile on her face. "Raoul and Augie are taking the boat out—not far, just a couple of miles to the ocean and back. Raoul wants to show Augie something he's learned...I'm not sure what. Put your bathing suit on. Connie and I are tanning on the upper deck. It'll be fun."

Louise had rattled on in a single breath. She seemed to think Amanda needed coaxing; probably because Amanda was still getting over the disappointment of Louise standing there instead of Augustino. Not to mention that the prospect of lying beside the likes of Connie did not impress her one bit.

"Sounds like a plan," Amanda smiled. "I'm going to change and meet you up there."

Alone, her legs gave away to the sensation still hovering in the pit of her stomach. She marveled that he could just pick up his affairs where he had left them and recover as quickly as he had. She supposed he had more practice than she did with these types of situations. Still, she had to make an appearance up there or he would wonder about her. She had to show him she was just as quick at moving on as he apparently was. She ferreted through the clothing she and Louise had opted to keep. There were a couple of nice bathing suits, one mini-bikini—she automatically discarded—and the one-piece suit she had purchased on Saturday. She chose a banana-yellow two-piece flatterer that Louise had earmarked as the best of the bunch. The color complimented her tan and the gold mesh in her hair. She completed the outfit with a long wrap skirt and flat heels, grabbed her sunglasses and lotion and headed up the stairs to the upper deck.

The afternoon sun was tipping but still ruled strong. She put on her sunglasses and noticed Louise waving to her. She waved back, grabbed a towel from the rack and looked toward the pilothouse where Raoul and Augustino were checking the instruments as they backed the boat out of its slip. She ignored them and walked towards the girls.

Connie was sitting in the shade. She had had enough sun, and when she noticed Amanda she picked up a magazine and parked her face behind it mutinously.

Louise knew how Connie felt. She tossed her shoulder at the other girl to indicate that Amanda should ignore her and to come and sit beside her. “Isn't it brave of Augie and Raoul to take the *Milan* out?”

“It is,” Amanda agreed, dabbing lotion on her long limbs and silk-smooth body. “Kind of wish they'd put it to a vote, though. Luckily, I'm a good swimmer.”

Louise laughed at Amanda's wry humor. She loved this girl's punch.

“Well, Augie is a good sailor,” Connie snapped. “He doesn't need our approval. He knows best.”

The dark woman gave her a murderous leer and Amanda now knew to keep conversation to a minimum around her. She was in no mood to start a catfight over Augustino. And somehow she had the feeling Connie was aching for one. Was this why he had wanted her to stay—so she could set this girl straight as to who was the new queen of the hill—to fight his battle? Her apathy would be a shocking surprise to him, she thought. She did not intend wrestling Connie or anyone else for his affections. That was not in her job description. She rolled eyes at Louise, her telltale expression self-explanatory, and another bout of laughter from Louise confirmed she at least had an ally. She lay face down on the chair, glad for the rest after the day's commotion. At least this way she could kill two birds with one stone—exert a presence, making Augustino happy, and sleep—all in the same neat little package.

"Do you want me to rub lotion on your back?" Louise asked her. "The sun's rays have unusual stamina for amplification on this deck."

"Thanks, Louise. That would be nice."

"With or without a tan line?" Louise asked, flexing the strap on her back.

"Without would be nice."

There was the lapse of a minute or so before she felt strong hands deftly undo the clasp of her bathing suit. Cream was squirted directly onto her back.

"Ooh! It's cold, Louise. But it feels so good." Amanda sighed as the sweet girl went out of her way to properly massage all of her back. She was surprised to feel how big and firm the girl's hands felt, still smooth though—even sensuous. They gently rubbed the back of her neck, thumbs scooping the knots between her shoulder blades. "That is fantastic," she moaned. "Ooh! It's soo good! Where did you learn to do this?"

Louise giggled and Amanda opened an eye to see her stretched out beside her. Quickly she turned in her chair, holding her top in place, and caught the intent gaze of Augustino, his unsmiling face cautioning her to temper her startled expression. His hands were full of lotion and he'd clearly been the one dutifully massaging her from the beginning.

"Don't look so surprised," he warned her gently. "I saw you stretch out on your stomach and worried about your back frying to a crisp."

"I'm not surprised," she lied. "But I can't help thinking who's manning the boat?"

He smiled. "Raoul and I have taken her out. The rest is easy. Anyway, I'm just here for a couple of minutes—to make sure you're all right." He gazed at her through eyes she knew remembered intently what had just happened between them. She realized this was his way of checking up on her.

"Don't let me interrupt your maneuvers, Augustino. I happen to know first hand that interruptions can be heart-wrenching." She paused, letting her words hit their mark.

He gave her a half-smile and nodded. He understood.

"But aside from that, Augie, I'm fine. You needn't worry."

"I guess these lovely ladies are treating you right?" He glanced toward Connie who stubbornly hid behind her magazine.

"We're all getting along splendidly," she answered, overly cheerful.

He understood the gist of that also. He heaved a sigh and told them he would see them at dinner. He bent and kissed Amanda's warm shoulder and left to rejoin Raoul.

Dinner was lovely. Augustino and Raoul had managed

to take the *Milan Milend* out to deep waters, past Government Cut, and the boat was hardly moving—practically stopped—while the lapping of the ocean's waves crashed softly against the hull. The sun bled its fiery red onto a sky turned pink, its shape seemingly melting as it tucked into the deep purple ocean. Far and wide, the streak of rose spread in the western distance, deferentially unfurling for them the day's end.

Augustino had ordered victuals from the marina's concierge the day before. They had a full stock in the galley.

Amanda sat beside Augustino—his presence quiet and overwhelming. She enjoyed her portion of red snapper and a tossed green salad. "Who's the cook?" She asked, pleasantly surprised by the gourmet quality of the meal.

"Tonight it is Augustino who prepared the meal," Connie answered. "He is my favorite chef—he knows how to... cook, very well," she added with loads of interesting undertones.

Augustino's eyes were loaded weapons as he stared down Connie, and Amanda thought herself lucky not to be on the other end of that barrel. But Connie seemed to revel in it. She was obviously very adept at bending his will to her needs. And again, Amanda perceived that instead of a buffer to the many female advances a man like Augustino Milan might attract, she was there more to defuse the raging desire of one particular person—Connie...she realized she did not even know her last name. Already he was vacillating in his resolve to be strict with her as Connie stared right back at him, her eyes just as defiant.

Dinner a pleasant memory, Amanda stood by the ship's

aft deck leaning against the balustrade; and her dark strands of hair toyed with the wind while she listened to the soft drone of the motor as they traveled through choppy waters. Mesmerized, she stared at the clouds of sea foam trailing behind the ship's powerful draw.

They were headed back to shore. There was no sign of Louise or Connie. They were somewhere below, sharing the guest stateroom. They had used the pretext of the evening being chilly.

She drew her shawl around her bare shoulders. The new blue sheath she wore clung to her perfectly and had fetched her many compliments during dinner. But it was ineffective at keeping her warm in the cool sea air. She should have retired, she thought. She just did not know what was expected of her exactly. She had not seen Augustino since the after-dinner brandy and figured he was piloting to get in before total darkness. Still, should she simply retire? Wait for him...she thought. Would he even join her? Had he not promised to use the crew quarters?

She considered joining him in the pilothouse, but there would be no privacy. Raoul was there. She finally opted for going down to the room. She would change and read or watch television. He would turn up eventually. He needed to explain the next day's agenda.

But as the hours wore on, Amanda's initial disappointment turned to dejection. A long cream-colored satin negligee accomplished nothing if she was the only one to admire it. He had found a way to retire without being seen, she concluded, absent-mindedly twirling in front of the dresser's mirror.

The satin frock hugged her every curve, accentuating her figure, just transparent enough to leave the rest to be imagined.

"It's lovely, but you're a thousand times lovelier." She heard a voice speak behind her and she jumped, jolted more than frightened.

"Augie." She could not repress a smile even though she was angry with him for having startled her—for having kept her waiting. "Whatever happened to knocking?"

He stayed where he was, fear of coming closer etched in his poise to leave. "I thought you might be sleeping...I didn't want to wake you. I came through the head. I just needed to pick up a few of my personal effects." He showed her the small bag he was carrying. "Are you all right?"

"I'm fine. I came down here not knowing...I hope it was okay?"

He nodded. "You've been a real trooper, Amanda. Thank you. I'll take you home tomorrow morning after breakfast."

She felt dismissed, unwanted. She should have been happy, but the sudden strange feeling of loneliness had budded. "You mean Connie is leaving and you no longer need me to keep her at bay?" She could hardly believe she had said it, but there it was. And she couldn't take it back. Not even when she noticed his face tighten and his eyes become hard and dark.

But after what seemed like interminable seconds he took in and let out a long breath, and his features softened. His eyes became a gentle and mesmerizing blue. He smiled.

"Good night, sweet Amy." He turned and left the way he had come, leaving her with such a sense of loss, she had to hug herself not to tremble.

It was not a good night. She tossed and turned for most of it. Sleep came fitfully, interrupted by the heave of the ship, the whistling of the wind, the strangeness of new surroundings and the king-sized berth—empty on one side.

CHAPTER NINE

Aboard Jose's 80' Hatteras yacht, docked at the other end of the marina, Conchita was entertaining Augustino Milan, having invited him to dinner.

Augustino knew he was on the dessert menu. But he attended the late evening engagement to tactfully retrieve new information Conchita had unearthed about the traffickers.

Tonight the dining room was quiet and subdued. The server was discreetly standing by—in a whole other area of the ship—and Connie was wearing a slinky dress that left very little to the imagination. The table's African mahogany gleamed with the flicker of candlelight, centerpiece to an array of dishes and cutlery set for two.

Augustino wore a suit and tie for the occasion—like a hangman's noose, he ruefully fancied as he slipped two fingers between his Adam's apple and the tie's knot to loosen it a little. While eating his cucumber bisque, he mentally prepared the platter he would serve Conchita to stuff her enough, just enough, that she might consider not ordering dessert.

"You are extremely quiet tonight, *querido*. You are playing with your soup, teasing it." Conchita bent toward him and whispered, "I enjoy it more when you devour what you eat."

There was no mistaking her meaning. Augustino smiled at her wickedly. "Just make sure we're still discussing the meal..."

She moaned hungrily, running her bare foot up his pant leg. "You can leave the soup if you don't like it," she crooned. "That's not what I want you to ravage...in that greedy way you do—so deliberately...so completely..." She twisted in her seat, fanning her legs underneath the table. "I am *open* to all your suggestions, *querido*," she laughed softly. "I will do anything you wish—give up anything you want..."

Augustino lifted her hand from the table and brought it to his mouth. "How about giving up the information I asked for, several days ago." He kissed each one of her fingers, looking into her eyes as he did.

She nodded. "I will. Then, will you...gorge yourself on everything that...comes...your way?" She smiled as he tilted his head, his piercing eyes making liquid fire of her loins. He was an unbelievable lover and she would do anything to belong to him—even if it was a last performance.

"I told you, Conchita. I'm engaged...you and I...making love...it's out of the question..."

"She need never know. And it's not making love. It's... exchanging services. I serve you with the information I have and you...serve...me," she laughed teasingly. "In your language it is called *tit for tat.*"

Augustino sat back in his chair. To say that he was immune to Conchita's charms would be lying. There was a sensuous allure about her tonight that was extremely heady, especially since her offer was so willingly bestowed. Shaking the funk that was slowly making mud of his good intentions, he sprang from his chair and turned his back to her. He walked the few steps toward the curved window and stared at the midnight ocean. A pair of dark eyes suddenly emerged from its sultry depths to taunt him, floating on top of a beautiful smile; and beyond the waves, in the distance, Amanda's sensuous silhouette danced on the ocean's crest.

"So, I will tell you what I know, *sí*?"

He heard her rise from the table. He knew she was desperately trying to seal their deal. Except that there would be no deal. They had snatched their last moment together. That day Amanda had run from his ship, he had selfishly spent the night tearing through Conchita, fiercely hungering for Amanda. Somewhere in the haze of their moans and groans that evening, he had promised himself never to compromise again—each time he came, in fact. To cheat on one promise was bad, but to cheat on several...

Tightened fists by his side, he turned to face Conchita.

A brief survey of his face and Conchita raised her chin, abandoning her seductive pose. The determination in his clenched jaw, the coolness of his eyes—too easily recognized. She crossed her arms about herself, shivering from his sudden remoteness. He would not be hers—not tonight. She had the upper hand, though. She could avoid telling him all she knew—keep him dangling.

"For your own sake, *cara*, I think you should share what you know," he told her simply. He also knew her well enough to detect the mutinous façade signaling capitulation. Tonight she was sober, and much too proud to plead with a man she knew wanted nothing to do with her.

"I am not afraid, Milo. Should anything happen to me," her chin trembled and her voice quivered, "my brother knows what to do."

He nodded, resigned to not knowing. He walked toward her with deliberate steps, circling the table slowly. As he came closer, he saw she was holding her breath. "I never meant to hurt you, Conchita." He smoothed the few rebellious strands of hair combing her forehead. "You and I should never have slept together. We were friends once—good friends." He thought of Emilio and the happy times the three of them had shared. "Remember? We met when you first came to enroll Emilio at college."

She nodded, biting down hard on her bottom lip. Augustino was difficult to resist when this gentle and relaxed. Or perhaps it was the memory of Emilio that softened her stance. She also thought of the favorite brother taken from her too soon. She knew it was Emilio's death that had served as the catalyst to their affair. "Emilio would wish us to continue to be friends," she told him softly. "I do also."

Augustino smiled and held his breath. Could there be peace between them?

"Come," she took him by the hand. "Let's finish our

meal. I will tell you what I've learned during dinner." Her smile was genuine with only a hint of sensuality. "You will be shocked by my news."

Augustino agreed, remaining silent. Then his cell phone rang. "Milo."

"It's Bob. I just thought you'd like to know. The results came back from the lab on that little tick Clarence picked up last week. Only one set of prints other than yours. Amanda Cole's—social worker for the city of Miami."

Augustino fought to keep the concern from invading his expression. Connie was friendly and cooperative. He needed her to remain so. "Thank you," he said simply before putting his cell away, cutting off any other information Bob might have to tell him.

But her mood had not swayed. A quick survey of her face showed him she was still at peace with their arrangement. In fact, seated back at his place, he kept his eyes on the next course that was being served. This was the Connie he had first made love to, the rapt and sensuous woman who had created havoc in his life for a time. Better she not read in his eyes how more attractive was this version of herself.

* * * * *

Same time across Miami, in a two-room apartment off Kendall Drive, Gary Flint was tying the holster of his gun just below his chest. He was haggard and tired. Purple blotches traced half-moon circles beneath his eyes—the only color to his blond complexion—that and the red on the bridge of his nose from yesterday's surveillance done from his car in punishing heat.

He was meeting with Bob by the sand dunes at the height of 17th Street, on Ocean Drive. At 1:00 in the morning they would be undisturbed. Anyone coming or going, they would spot immediately.

He was amazed at how fast events were lining up before them. This time, they were solving the riddle. They actually had a list of suspects as long as his arm and all of them fit the mold to a tee.

He sped across the deserted streets until he reached the popular South Beach drag. Miami nightlife was humming like a hive even for a Tuesday night. Parking on the strip was a challenge.

He left his car with one of the valets at a restaurant lining the beach and checked his back before running for the shadows of the moonlit sand, past the fountain and under the wooden boardwalk.

Bob was already there, dressed in black and comfortably seated on a little mound of sand, having an animated discussion with his cell phone.

"What's up, big guy?"

Bob shushed him with the wave of his hand. "Are you sure?" After a few more silent minutes, Bob closed his cell and stared at the lapping of the ocean's waves in the distance.

"Please don't say anything is wrong..."

"No, no. Nothing like that..."

"And why are we meeting out here? This better be good. I'm dead tired," Gary complained.

Bob nodded. “We’re here because I ended up on the beach when I finally shook my shadow. Don’t want to move in case he catches up with me again.” He took a long breath. “That was Jim Dunbar on the phone. We spent the last couple of days together pouring over files and documents.” Bob turned to look at Gary’s worried, tired face as he scrunched down in the sand beside him. “Remember how we always thought that we were hunting down a bunch of traffickers?”

Gary nodded. “Traffickers...murderers...and the infamous white tiger and her killer cubs...we’re about to land the bastards, flush them out. Why?”

Bob watched Gary squeeze his sandaled feet into the sand. “What if I told you that the traffickers and the Quartain Tech arm dealers and smugglers are the same people...?”

“So—it’s official. The two camps are linked on this.”

Bob shook his head. “Yes. But more than that. They apparently do everything together, like one big happy family.”

“Impossible. We’ve been after these traffickers for years. We would have known...a trail between the two is plausible, sure...” Gary stopped talking. There was foregone conclusion in Bob’s eyes.

“Fred and Jim on the phone...” Bob waved his cell phone to drive the point home.

“You said that already. What else?” Gary noticed Bob was having a hard time wording what he’d just discovered.

Bob nodded. “It’s official,” he added in a haze. A few minutes passed before he was able to stare at Gary. “Hank Williamson had meetings with Judd Garrison.”

"Geez! No! That's gotta be bull. All this goddamn time when they've been investigating Quartain and those allegations into foreign contraband? Those murders...? We've compared our shit before. Hell, we're the ones who supported their theory about Vince Morello, the clueless princess."

Bob shrugged, at a loss for words. "It seems we weren't thorough enough. Jim just phoned. They worked under that assumption today. Got hold of a patsy Hank ran over last year during one of the trials. He swears Garrison and Hank are bosom buddies." Bob eyed Gary with a hound dog look on his face. "*Mea* fuckin' *culpa.*" He jabbed at his torso with his fist.

Gary knew that for Bob to air out his anger, he had to be incredibly upset. "I guess this means that the lead between the jury and Hank panned out..."

"You think? What if I told you that the payola was lives—taking lives!"

Gary's shoulders slumped and his face dropped. "Not..."

"They needed Greensand out of the way. So the Havana Club did the deed. Guess who really runs the Havana Club?"

"De Marco...everyone knows...that..."

Bob shook his head.

"...Judd Garrison?"

Bob nodded, although he knew Gary had already scored the right conclusion.

"The payola to the Havana Club for having killed Greensand was for Hank's men to...off someone on the

Club's side—like Armando. They killed Emilio as a debt to Havana for Tobin's murder. Emilio's life was owed. Each time one member had to die on one side, the other would have to even up with a likely candidate from the opposite side."

"Goddamn it! Now you're pissing me off. Are you saying that Judd heads two groups?"

"No. Jim and Fred's stoolie friend Hank Williamson heads the other one. He had Emilio killed."

"Geezus marcus! I'm going to kill the son of a bitch." Gary got up and began pacing.

"Sit down. Are you trying to get us killed? They're out there, combing the city trying to find us. Talk about your devil genius," Bob added. "That's why we could never match the killer with the murder."

"I can't sit still, Bob. I feel like I'm going to hurl. I've never been this angry." Gary stooped and bent in two, his hands groping his knees. "I swear, if the son of a bitch Hank was standing in front of me, I'd kill him, so help me God. I'd strangle him with my bare hands. Why in hell's name are we just finding out now about that schmuck that Hank screwed? Why didn't he spill earlier?"

"Hank was forever promising this guy he'd vouch for him—get him off." Bob shrugged. "I guess it took him a year in the dark—behind bars—to see the light." Bob stared at Gary. He was in shock, his mind spinning and weaving with the morbid ridicule of their situation.

"Forgive me if I don't laugh," Gary added, just as shocked. "Do you realize how much shit we're in?"

Bob nodded. "We've got to lie low. That means saving

our strength and not wasting one single brain cell. At least, until we talk to Milo. That also means not doing anything stupid." He eyed Gary, silently exhorting him to sit down. "What about Fiona?" he asked.

"Fiona is..." It was Gary's turn to feel stupid. "She's Sinclair's number one girl. And we know Sinclair's been cavorting with fuckin' Hank—FUCKIN', FUCKIN' Hank!" Gary yelled out into the night.

Bob just stared at him, feeling his pain. "That would also mean that Jose was right about the Havana Club. They didn't murder his family, but their debt did."

"—wait till Milo hears." Gary couldn't come to terms with the huge nightmare they had just uncovered.

"And Brad?"

"Still waiting to hear," Gary added absent-mindedly. "I don't think we should go back to our places. We've got to start out-thinking these bastards. We can't afford to make one wrong move."

"That's why I called you out here in the middle of the night. I have a friend nearby. He's not tied to any of this and he's agreed to put us up until we leave."

"What are we waiting for? Let's get some of these guys indicted." Gary's voice was tinged with desperation.

"Too soon. Augustino still has to worm information out of Conchita..." He checked his watch. "Just about now—hopefully. Anyway, all that matters is getting to the fink in the Bahamas. He's been promoted to *muy importante*. He has proof that supposedly ties all these A-holes together."

CHAPTER TEN

"Will you stop moping around?" Ginette was fed up having to watch Amanda loafing around the apartment in slippers and a bathrobe. "He's going to call you. We're only Wednesday and you saw him Monday morning, damn it."

But she wasn't getting any response from Amanda who was standing at the front window, looking outside through a crack in the curtains.

"Open the drapes will you? Please? And get some sun. You're on holidays. Go rollerblading down Lincoln—you love that. Or...or go to the gym. You haven't been in a week... Amanda? Am I getting through to you?"

"Yes, I hear you—loud and clear. Stop nagging already. It's *my* vacation. I can do what I want."

"You're right. It's your life," Ginette added with sing-song caution. "But if you get flabby and fat, you'll be giving him an excellent reason not to call."

"How can I get fat or flabby? I haven't eaten in two days."

That was true. Ginette had been pushing food down her throat whenever Amanda complained it all tasted the same. "Kiddo, I'd kill to get your tight ass and sculptured thighs. But you don't get those by sitting around depressed and pining for the invisible man—no matter how little you eat."

Amanda stared at the ring on her finger. "Do you suppose it's that last sentence I said to him that made him angry?"

"Sweetie, we've been through it all with a microscopic sieve. Forget about it and live your life already. Besides, you're walking around waving thirty-five grand of his money. Odds are he doesn't forget about that little detail."

Amanda sighed. "Might just send someone to retrieve it." She came to sit at the breakfast table where Ginette was finishing reading e-mails on her laptop. "Aren't you late for work?" she asked, tired of having her discomfort so damned transparent. If she wanted to have a good cry or walk around depressed and do absolutely nothing, it was her prerogative. "You'd be more of a friend if you left me alone to do what I want," she snapped at the shock registering on Ginette's face.

"Yes, I am late for work. The *reason* I am late for work, is that I dread leaving you here to your own devices, not knowing what the hell you're likely to do. Excuse me for caring."

"Well, care in a helping way—not...not by trying to reason with my brain about what's right...what I should do...or... or how much of an idiot I am. It's my heart that needs fixing.

I already know what I'm doing is stupid. Surprisingly enough, knowing doesn't seem to do a thing for me. Imagine that," she added, a mocking smirk on her pretty face.

"Okay." Ginette rounded up her computer, her bag and her purse. "I'm out of here. You're on your own, kiddo. Just make sure if you use the razor it's to shave those gorgeous legs of yours, and don't use the gas burners other than for cooking." She ducked as Amanda threw a muffin at her head. "One more thing for you to do around here," she smiled mischievously, "clean."

Amanda couldn't help smiling. Ginette was right. The kitchen was a mess. Pots and pans were piled up on the counter and sticky gooey tomato sauce had splattered and dried on the top of the range. The floor needed mopping and the whole apartment, though small, needed freshening up. Because of Ginette's every other week double shift schedule, it was her turn to clean—had been for the last three days.

The phone rang and startled her out of her introspection. She closed her eyes and took a deep breath—what if it was him...?

She ran to pick up, stubbing her foot against the desk as she did. "Hello?" She grimaced in pain, jumping up and down and rubbing her aching toe.

"Miss Cole, this is Mr. Sanchez. I need to tell you that I have three other nephews that have been approved to the program and we need to have them processed as soon as possible."

"Mr. Sanchez! How...I mean, I'm on holiday. This is my home number. Maria is taking over the paperwork on your case for the next two weeks...how did you get my personal number?"

"I've always had it—as an evening number. You are the one who gave it to me."

"I certainly did not, Mr. Sanchez. And I can't help you right now. I'm going to have Mrs. Christian call you and coordinate with you."

Amanda was forceful, concise, but it still took her twenty minutes to get Sanchez to stop arguing and hang up the phone. By the time he did, there was another phone call from another one of her clients. She would have loved to know just what was going on and where these people were getting her private information. Ginette was going to kill her. Now their number would have to be changed.

"Fiona, I'm telling you. These people have my home number. And no, I did not give it to them. I'm not crazy. There has to be a leak in the system somewhere."

"Come on, Amanda. I've been here ten years. No one's ever gotten my private home number. I'll have to ask Mr. Sinclair to investigate. If they have your number, it means they might also know where you live."

Amanda was startled. She hadn't thought of that. "While you're at it, ask Mr. Sinclair about Sanchez. He kept referring to him as a reference. Even had the name of our agent, the contact that is arranging the interviews with the different firms. I don't think that's normal. All this information is catalogued as confidential in my manual."

"Of course it is. All this is extremely strange, Amanda. We will definitely look into it. Just take your phone off the hook for now and enjoy your vacation. If any other calls come in, just tell them they have the wrong number."

Taking her phone off the hook meant perhaps not getting the call she most expected to receive. She hesitated as she surveyed her tired slippers, worn dingy bathrobe and the mess around her apartment—all contrasting the sunny gorgeous day outside—and snapped. She was on holidays; it was a beautiful day and she was through feeling sorry for herself. If Augustino could not reach her, then it was his bad luck.

She laid the receiver to one side. Here was where she turned a new leaf. No more longing for a man who did not deserve her. She picked up Dino and marched to the bathroom, where she drew herself a bubble bath. First order was to restore some neatness to her frumpy, wrinkled appearance. She would worry about the kitchen later.

But as she lay relaxing amidst the frothy mousse, her right arm draped over the tub as she petted little Dino, she worried about what was happening at work. She had been there four and a half years, ever since graduation in fact, and she had never come across any leak of information—especially one of this magnitude. She would make sure to check with Fiona later. The whole business about people maybe discovering where she lived was extremely unsettling, and the only positive note about it was that it trounced all thoughts of Augustino to the background. He was no longer a cherished priority.

She did not know how long she had lain there in the hot scented foamy water, but Dino's incessant barking finally drew her from her torpor—or had she been sleeping?

When she glanced in the direction he was growling at, she screamed, sitting up in the bath. "Augustino! What are you doing here?" He was standing in her bathroom, staring at her with a smile and a strange look on his face. Quickly she plunged back into the tub—a lot of good that did her, as by now most of the foam had cleared and she was an easy target through the milky water's transparency. She made a vain attempt at covering herself with her hands.

"I'm sorry," he gently laughed at her predicament. "I've been trying to call you all morning. Your line was busy and now," he pointed to the receiver beside the phone, "I know why. Plus your bathroom door was open. I didn't expect to find you sleeping in the tub," he mocked.

"Well, get out," she admonished. "You're still standing there in my doorway when you should've already excused yourself and left," she told him angrily. "And please close the door on your way out," she added, the initial shock of finding him there not yet evaporated.

He gave her a little hand-salute as he left and closed the door. "By the way," he added, his voice muffled by the door, "I hope you haven't made any prior engagements. I meant to call you yesterday but I got tied up."

"I'm sorry. I can't hear you," she told him, running the warm water. "Can it wait?"

He opened the door slightly. "Take your time, relax. I'm in no hurry."

"I'm sure you're not," she answered teasingly, throwing a brush at the door.

He laughed as he closed it tight, the brush crashing

against it.

By the time Amanda emerged from the bathroom, she came into the kitchen to see Augustino with her flowered apron tied around the waist of his Hugo Boss pants, bent over their sink filled with suds and doing the dishes. He had piled up the clean ones in the second sink and had rounded up all the soiled ones from the table and the adjoining counter. She noticed he had also cleaned the stove and the top of the table.

He turned to look at her, continuing to scrub a stubborn stain in one of the pans. "Don't we look domesticated," he told her, eyeing her bathrobe.

She shrugged by way of an apology as she looked down at the dingy chenille robe that had seen better days. At least she was squeaky clean and smelling sweetly of raspberry lotion.

"It's okay," he told her. "I've just seen how beautiful the girl is underneath the bathrobe." He smiled from ear to ear.

She gave him a defiant glare betrayed by a little half-smile, unable to resist completely his sensuous charm. "Turns out you're pretty domesticated yourself. Who would have thought? I imagine you usually have people do this sort of thing for you—I was even one of them."

He laughed good-humouredly. "The proverbial only son of a widowed mother, that's me. I've done more than my share of chores around the house, including dishes, ironing too, and even some sewing on occasion." He looked at her raised eyebrows and knew she was still in a teasing mood.

"What do you say you come and give me a hand here?" He picked up a dry cloth and threw it at her. "Hard to believe there are only two of you living here. Is it a house rule to do the dishes only once a week?"

She gave in and laughed. She had tried not to but could not resist it any longer.

He stopped and stared at her. It was the first time he had heard her laugh. It was pearly and pretty and it caused him to focus on her mouth. Remembering their last encounter together, he turned quickly, wiped his hands on the hand towel and let the water out of the sink. "I'd better help you dry or we'll be here all day. Better yet, what do you say you go get dressed while I finish this?" He stared at her with kind eyes, waiting for her reaction.

Amanda weighed the cloth she had in her hands and nodded. She would go get dressed. "Casual?" She asked.

"Casual is good," he answered. "Not anything as casual as that bathrobe," he added teasingly.

She turned and draped the damp cloth over his head before hurrying out of sight, laughing.

"Miss Cole, you're asking for it!" She heard him yell. When she got to her room, just for safety measures, she locked the door behind her, out of breath and stricken with a bad case of giggles.

By the time she got dressed, hair brushed, light make-up dabbed on and was standing in the hall ready to go, Augustino had put away the dishes, mopped the floor and cleaned the counters. He was sitting in the kitchen waiting for her, Dino comfortably nestled in his lap. Amanda took in the picture the two of them painted, and her heart tugged at the soft way his strong hands were petting Dino—who surprisingly enough had readily accepted him. He usually ran and hid from strangers—especially men.

"What have you done with my dog?" she asked him, trying not to laugh. "He doesn't like...men."

He smiled. "I thought you'd be more concerned with what I did with your dishes." He extended his hand to show the tidy kitchen. "You may never find them again. I put them where I guessed they should go."

Amanda bit down on a bout of laughter when she imagined Ginette cursing while searching for the pots and pans. She opened a cupboard and saw that even the glasses were on the wrong shelf.

"You can't really blame me," Augustino said. "Your armoires were empty, virtually. I had no clues to go on."

Amanda choked on another little laugh. "We best leave. I wouldn't want to be here when Ginette discovers she has to rearrange the whole kitchen cupboards. Where are we going anyway?"

"Bahamas. We'll be gone for the rest of the week." It was his turn to have a laugh at the comical look of surprise on her face.

"I'll have to bring Dino." Amanda looked at him, her wide eyes beseeching.

"Is he potty trained?"

She eyed him with mock contempt, thinking he was lucky to be so handsome. "Since when are dogs ever potty trained? I trained him to go in a litter from time to time."

She waited, but he still had a dubious look on his face. "I can't leave him, Augustino. Ginette has a double shift this week. He'll be alone too long."

He stared at her warm sensuous eyes and the lovely full mouth and gave in, as he knew he would. "Bring anything he needs. I'll help you." And as she walked away he held her back, grabbing her arm. "Nothing's too good for my fiancée."

Amanda noticed he was not smiling or jesting, and as she stared into his eyes she grew disturbed by their message. She felt much safer surrounded by the banter they had just exchanged, by his quick wit and wry humor. That she knew how to handle, how to dole back. Joking with him felt friendly, familiar and much less likely to kindle arousal in her. If she was going to spend a week with him, she wanted it to be as friends. He was not a lover, not a real one. He obviously did not want to be, despite all his innuendos to the contrary, and frankly, she was not sure she would ever survive a casual fling with Augustino Milan. She had painfully learned this during the past few days. "Let me know who that is when you find her," she answered, smiling to alleviate the mounting tension between them.

"I will, *cara mia*. I promise."

His blue eyes lit up with meaning, she noticed. What that meaning was, she could not—would not—guess. This man was a master at creating illusions. Gin was right. She would have to tread lightly around him if she did not wish to lose her heart completely.

Nestled in the bucket seat of his Jag, she focused her attention on Dino. He was on her lap, wiggling his little body, excited by everything he saw out the window. It was safer than glancing Augustino's way. She had so many questions she did not dare ask. Where was Conchita? Who was she and why did he think it important to humor her as much as he did? Why travel to the Bahamas? And why, more importantly, did she need to go with him? Questions that would remain unanswered for now as she silently, stubbornly, continued to stare out her window. It had felt so natural to have him doing the dishes in her little kitchen and she had felt calm in his proximity. Now, seated beside him in the car's tight quarters, she felt once more overwhelmed by his magnetic presence. She suffered little tingling sensations each time she glanced at him handling the stick shift.

"You're awfully quiet," he attempted, glancing her way.

"It's not from lack of questions. They're all fighting to be posed first."

"Shoot," he smiled good-humouredly, petting little Dino as he stopped at a light.

"Who is Conchita? I mean, who is she to you?" She looked at him, the red traffic light allowing her to capture his full attention. She butted against a teasing glint in his eyes.

Both hands on the wheel as he faced the road once again, a knowing smile hovered on his lips. His answer was long in coming. "She is the wife of a prominent suspect in our investigation," he finally said, negotiating traffic. "She is also the sister of one of the men who died."

"That would make for warring families, would it not?" Amanda was curious. "Sort of a Spanish West Side Story?"

"Not exactly. The husband was bought and paid for long after they were married. She only found out about it recently—a few weeks ago, actually."

"And the other question?" Amanda smiled hesitantly. She feared sounding too personal.

But he did not seem offended. He smiled as well. "She's nothing to me other than a friend. She has four children. Her eldest is fifteen years old. With the death of her brother, it was easy for me to convince her to help us. I guess that's when she and I overstepped the line one night. At the time she told me that our love-making gave her the courage to go through with it—the spying, the relaying of information." He shrugged at the inevitable. "She was scared—mostly for her children. She's a good mother. Now...I guess you might say our affair has run its course."

"In other words, you made love to her to convince her to rat on people...on her friends?"

His face grew somber. Gone was the pleasant smile. "It served a dual purpose. She craved the attention; I got the information I needed."

At least he was honest, she thought. "Did you ever consider that she might be in love with you?"

He glanced at her quickly, surprised by her question.

"And you know what they say, Augustino. Hell hath no fury....How quickly can an informant become a liability? Even from my limited experience with that sort of thing, to hazard a guess I'd say...in a heartbeat?"

"I'd say...you're probably right. Although sometimes, my lovely, reversing a process creates just the momentum needed to propel that process forward."

"So if she warns her husband—out of spite...or belated loyalty..."

"She risks two things. He banishes her and she never sees her children again, or has her killed and she never sees anyone again. No. She wouldn't sound the alarm. But she may try to play both sides against each other, in which case, she would unwittingly alert us to who this other side is."

"And them to you..."

"Any way is fine. They already know who *we* are. That's been our disadvantage from the outset."

"What do you mean?"

He sighed, sounding tired all at once. "There's a mole inside our organization—several of them, we just found out—which would explain why they've been one step ahead of us for the last four years. Only recently did we begin to make inroads into their schemes. Information is leaving our camp directly to that of the enemy's. We're just beginning to suspect who these informants are."

"It took you four years to find that out?"

"In our defense, the investigation did take twists and turns. We only discovered this once we got the names of a few key individuals."

They had arrived at the marina and Augustino drove to the guest quarters at the back to have the valet park his car. As they got out of the car, Augustino gave the young man a twenty-dollar bill for him to bring the bags in the trunk to slip number 44.

Amanda tucked little Dino away in her large bag and

walked beside Augustino. He did nothing to show her the least bit of physical attention.

"So where do I fit in this brilliant plan of yours? I mean, for someone as cunning as you are about the situation, surely you've mapped out a juicier role for me than that of posing as your fiancée. And why me?"

"We've already gone through that." He answered curtly, his drawn face proof he would not address the subject again.

Well, she thought, none too proud. He had just summarily dismissed her. A loud curt order to shut up would not have been ruder. Each time she let her guard down and allowed herself to inch closer to him, he would slap her back to reality. She supposed she ought to thank him. This was the surest way of remaining whole with her heart intact. Still, she had been on roller coaster rides that felt safer—and tamer. She grabbed his arm, intent on having him slow down. Even for her, he was walking fast. "Why you? You told me you were a lawyer. Are you officially with the Bureau?"

They had arrived at the boat. He paused before taking her hand to climb the steps to the plank and eyed her up and down distractedly as if deep in thought. "My best friend was killed in the line of this investigation. I decided to take his place," was all he said. He preceded her onto the ship and opened the door to the deck for her.

So much for the loads of questions he'd told her she could ask. Meanwhile, Amanda was surprised to find Albert the butler and Manuel the chauffeur on board. Raoul was there as always. She extended a polite hand to each of them and Augustino told her he would meet her downstairs in their room.

This was a quick way of sending her off. He obviously needed privacy with these people. But as she was about to turn and head to the master stateroom, he caught up to her, strapped an arm around her waist and kissed her on the mouth. "Wait for me before you come up, *cara*."

She nodded as her heart and mind raced—in opposite directions—her heart loving the salty pliancy of his lips, her head warning he could turn the charm off and on at will. *Be sensible, girl,* she cautioned her better judgment, *he's hamming it up for the audience.*

In the stateroom she found the clothes she had left behind. She had told Augustino that it was easier hanging them there, handy when she needed them, than lugging them to her apartment each time she left. This way, she had consoled herself, the clothes weren't really a gift. Once this...assignment ended she could leave them. Something told her that once Augustino was out of her life she would rapidly need to scuttle any reminder of him.

She unpacked Dino's toys and food, changed into a bathing suit and topped it with a short red blouse gathered at the waist and a long flowered sarong, slit in the front. She dabbed her face and neck with lotion. She piled her hair on top of her head, pinning it with a big white comb, and sat on the edge of a chair, wondering how long she'd have to wait before Augustino came to get her. It was already 1:00 and she could hear the motors rumbling in readiness. She decided to call Ginette at the hospital to let her know she was going to be away. She picked up the phone on the small dresser, and pondered that Ginette could reach her at this number she had given her previously or at least call her cell phone. Christine, the head nurse, took the message. Ginette was out doing her rounds. She would be pleasantly surprised, thought Amanda. She hung up the phone and a couple of minutes later thought she would try Fiona Christian's private line, but when she lifted the receiver, she noticed someone was already on the phone.

"I told you, Conchita. You cannot come with me this time."

Amanda noticed it was Augustino talking to Connie. She should have replaced the receiver. She would...eventually. For now it was just too tempting.

"I hate that bitch. Does she know you are on to her?"

Who was Conchita talking about, she wondered. Clearly not a fan.

"Watch your language, Conchita. We are all part of the same team. Just last night we had an understanding, *cara*, remember? I hope we can remain friends."

"I am your friend. This is why I will be there in Harbour Island. You cannot stop me from going, Milo."

Amanda delicately—very delicately—replaced the receiver. So, he was still communicating with Connie. Just last night, he had mentioned. Still placating her and seemingly doing it in secret. She wondered if this was the reason he had sought privacy.

She was about to despair not being on deck to watch the boat pull out of the dock when she heard a knock on her door. She sprang to open it, Dino in her arms.

"Ready?" He asked her with the usual Cheshire smile on his face.

"Ready?" She answered with raised eyebrows. "I've been waiting for the past twenty minutes. Why is it necessary for me to wait in my cabin? Why do I apparently have to be escorted?"

"Albert has prepared a surprise for you. He wanted to add the final touches to it. I hope you don't mind. All I ask is that you act...surprised—and grateful, of course." He smiled, offering to help her with Dino's things.

"I thought we could put his litter box up on deck," Amanda said. "This way, since he's used to asking for the door, it'll be easier for him to get accustomed. At home I keep it on the terrace."

"I'll bring it," he told her. "By the way, you look sensational in that outfit."

"Thank you," she answered simply, remembering the dark mood that had invaded him in the car. He truly was a master of illusion. He'd missed his calling. He could've been an actor—an Oscar-winning one.

Upstairs, Albert had laid out quite a spread on the galley's counters and the dining room table. She spotted lobster tails, crab legs, copper marmites brimming with fresh mussels, plates of crudities—some of which looked like smoked eel—crusty baguettes and several platefuls of green salads. There were even a couple of bottles of white wine from the refrigerator. She certainly needn't *act* surprised. She *was* surprised. "I thought we were pulling out?" She asked

Augustino, a bemused look still on her face.

"We are. Raoul and Manuel are quite adept at operating the ship. We went out yesterday with an experienced captain. You met him the other day. Captain Charles?"

She nodded, also remembering the incident that took place in his cabin—the mighty kiss that had kept her awake and dejected for the past few days.

"Raoul and I piloted the *Milan* out to sea and back without any problems."

That was reassuring, she guessed, knowing nothing about sailing and wondering more about the story behind the ship's name than how it fared at sea.

"She'll do quite well, even while we eat. She's extremely steady—you'd never know she's equipped with a fiberglass hull. Even in the choppy weather we're liable to confront at this time of year..."

"Why this time of year? It's summer. Shouldn't it be calmer—the ocean, I mean?"

"Quite the opposite." He paused for a minute as if searching for an easy way to explain the combination of the sweep of trade winds mixed with direct solar exposure. "The ocean in summer is a little like the slowly simmering salted water in a giant soup kettle. It gets hotter and tends to...bubble over. This brings on winds to varying degrees and with them, inevitable high tides. That's why the best time to cruise is between October and May." He smiled at the look of concern on her brow. "But don't worry. *Milan* will do just fine. She is straight yet nimble and can maintain 22 knots on a light load of fuel. Although, I doubt Raoul will bring her up to speed until we've crossed Government Cut and left the Florida Straights. Here, have a seat." He pulled out a chair for her and sat down beside her.

It was clear to Amanda that he was proud of his boat. "I noticed you refer to your ship in the feminine tense," she smiled, staring into his eyes. "What's the reason for her name?"

He picked up a plate, handed it to Albert who consulted with her on what she wanted and then did the same for Augustino. Albert poured the wine and then quietly left for the crew's quarters below.

"I named the boat after my father. It was his dream to sail one day...and...for the place I was born, Mile End—a district of London. That's where we were happy once, as a family..." He trailed off, scooping a mussel from its shell.

Amanda swallowed the lump in her throat, practically wishing she hadn't asked. It was clear he'd come a long way from the little urchin mopping the streets of London with the seat of his pants. But it was also clear that the memory of those days was still as deep and saucy as the ocean at high tide. And she saw by the hardening of his jaw that he was sandbagging the flood gate she had innocently pried open.

"What about you?" he asked, his immediate concern obviously to change the subject. "What is the beautiful Amanda Cole all about?"

She finished a mouthful of shrimp salad, washed it down with a gulp of white wine—for courage—mentally exhorting herself to be brief. "I'm the youngest of five—the baby as my sister Meg calls me. I come from a little town called

Pleasantville in New Jersey, about five miles from downtown Atlantic City. So in a way, I grew up enjoying a part time ocean..."

"Part time?" He paused, interested by the analogy.

"You know—two months, three tops. Then the cold season starts."

He nodded. "You come from a large family—all girls?"

"No. Meg is the eldest, then my sister Susan, my two brothers Michael and Shawn and then me. Being the baby, everyone assures me that I was spoiled rotten. I don't know that that's true exactly." She shrugged. "Anyway, when Meg married Jerry Springer—a native Floridian who wouldn't leave if you paid him a million dollars, I begged her to take me with them..."

"To finally meet up with that full time ocean."

She laughed. "Meg is very sweet—mothered me to death when I was growing up. So, here I am."

He wiped his hands on a wet towel. "I also agree that you were probably spoiled rotten, growing up."

"Watch it!" She scrunched her face at him. "Them's fighting words, Mr. Milan," she smiled.

"You must've been loved to death. That's how you can give so much of it back—to people at the center, to others in your life. You've made a career of dispensing goodness and kindness to everyone around you."

She frowned at him with a dubious expression.

"No false modesty. It's true. I've watched you, Amanda Cole. You have a good heart. You're always finding ways to please people—anyone—often in spite of your needs. You roll with the punches, are an extremely good sport and can't stay mad for more than...half a second?" He smiled, his eyes gently stroking the stunned expression on her face. "You were even pleasant and accommodating to me, a perfect stranger with outrageous demands...even a few minutes ago," his voice softened, "when those big brown eyes empathized with my difficult childhood." He stroked her face with the back of his hand. She appeared transfixed to the spot with no words, shocked by his profound insight into her heart. "When you were sorry you'd even brought it up..."

"Well!" She shook herself from her stupor, embarrassed eyes no longer able to support his gaze. "I can see I'm going to have to chalk in my outline a little. I seem to be transparent where you're concerned."

He took a sip of wine and wiped the corners of his mouth with his napkin. "May I kiss you, Amanda?"

And while she stared at him with wide eyes while wondering what to answer to that loaded question, he laughed softly at her bemused expression and pressed his lips against hers in a light and reverent kiss. "My point exactly," he murmured against her mouth.

CHAPTER ELEVEN

The weather cooperated as they sailed across the Gulf Stream toward the south side of Bimini Islands. For the remainder of their trip, Amanda intended sitting on deck watching the white froth of waves jauntily trailing the ship's wake. She loved the low drone of the engines, taking charge of the hull they propelled forward while splashy echoes of the ocean lapped the sides of the ship as they berthed a path for them.

She wasn't sure how fast they were going, but they'd passed several smaller crafts along the way. Augustino would know. But he was upstairs in the pilothouse, relieving Raoul who was eating in the dining room with Manuel. And staring at the water kept her mind occupied and Augustino-free—not that she didn't enjoy it—on the contrary, it was the biggest adventure of her young life.

She thought of heading upstairs to keep him company. It was the proper thing to do. She'd even have a better view, although she wouldn't have the benefit of the ocean spray from time to time, cool and refreshing.

The men in the dining room had peered her way a few times with curiosity on their faces, a sign she should be up there with her intended, she supposed. But as he had earlier revealed how transparent she was, how well he could read her, she worried he would sense how attracted she was to him. Still, a nagging interesting little voice told her he was apt to read more into prolonged self-exile and likely to pose more embarrassing questions than if she was to follow normal protocol. He was too clever not to.

She sighed and got up from the chair, slipped into her wrap skirt and short blousy top she had discarded to tan, and proceeded to climb the outside steps to the upper deck—barefoot and loving the feel of the warm wood against her feet.

She reached the upper deck from the aft section, and stared at his back for several minutes. She took in his wide shoulders, his strong broad back—more imposing with the billowing of his open shirt—and she shivered in the hot sun from the tender chord his lonely image struck in her. He was standing erect, facing miles of ocean, deftly directing the wheel and checking the instrument panel; and he suddenly seemed so alone that she felt guilty for having left him up here without any company for so long. All she wanted to do was trail a hand down his back and plant a kiss on his rugged, salty cheek.

"Hey, a penny for your thoughts, Miss Cole," he startled her. "Actually, I'd give a king's ransom to hear your mind ticking away at this exact minute. I won't even begin to tell you what I saw in those beautiful brown eyes when you first showed."

She smiled brightly to dispel any ill ease she felt for any smug interpretation he might be harboring, although there wasn't much point to that and the thought relaxed her. He still had his back to her. "There's not much to see," she quipped. "Not unless you have eyes behind your head."

She approached him, determined not to let his charisma intimidate her. He turned to look at her and she briefly wondered how she could have mistaken his stance for a lonely one—even for a second.

"I have this mirror on the right side of the panel—see?" He pointed to the damning evidence. "It allows me to spot anyone coming up those stairs at the back. It's good too when you want to converse with guests seated at the back table. So how about you sharing those thoughts," he urged her with a tantalizing smile, grabbing her right arm with his free hand to hug her closer to him. "There, now you're my prisoner." He spoke urgently, his lips against her cheek. "You'll have to confess," he teased, unknowingly creating more havoc inside her than would twenty-foot waves to the *Milan Milend.*

"If you must know, I was thinking that you shouldn't be alone on such a glorious sunny day." She trailed off, staring at the view below. "It's breathtaking from up here," she whispered.

"I'm glad you share my love of the ocean, *cara.*" He strapped an arm around her waist and nuzzled her hair. "Hum! You smell of those tall sweet reeds that grow at the sea's rocky edges."

She briefly thought he was getting into the habit of demonstrating affection to her, even when no one was around, and she found herself questioning the good sense of such comportment. It would make for heavy losses later, when the charade was finally over. Nevertheless, she spontaneously kissed him back—a peck on the cheek. She was through behaving like a schoolgirl around him and any contribution she brought to the role she was playing established her as a player—not a wounded party. And she just couldn't resist the tremor of pleasure that coursed through him whenever she touched him.

"In honor of you and I both enjoying the ocean, I have planned a surprise for you tomorrow."

"Where are we headed, anyway? I've been meaning to ask you since I got here. I'm always interrupted for some reason."

"As I started explaining to you at dinner, we're headed for the southern tip of the island of Bimini. There is an airport there. We're picking up Gary Flint."

She was dying to ask why, but didn't dare. "Then where are we headed?"

"Well, we're going to circle south of Cat Kay and head for Berry Islands via the Bahamas Banks. We're going to make a small stop there. Gary is picking up papers. Then, we go on to Nassau's Paradise Island."

"Sounds lovely. How long will all this take?"

He shrugged. "We've picked up speed. We're traveling at eighteen knots. If you calculate that one knot is equal to one mile per hour, and that we have another hour to Bimini, we should be able to make our dinner reservations at the Atlantis on Paradise Island for eight this evening, including stops."

"Is that the surprise?" She had edged away from him, as he needed both hands to steer at one point, and was sitting on the tall stool beside the panel, dangling and swinging her feet.

He glanced at her through his mirror and smiled. "You are very beautiful, Amy."

She was taken aback when in a heartbeat she caught a glimpse of his eyes staring at her in the mirror. She had forgotten about that telltale mirror. She scolded herself to be more vigilant. "It's the sea air," she smiled back at him. "It's very flattering..."

He laughed at her outright, shaking his head at her innocence and lack of pretension.

"You never answered my question," she replied, a little short, feeling much too vulnerable under his glaring scrutiny.

"Have you ever scuba dived?"

Her eyes rounded with surprise. She shook her head. "I've never even considered it. I hear there's lots to learn, and...don't you have to be certified...?"

"Would you like me to teach you?"

"Yes," she stammered. "I would love to learn. Do we have time?" She jumped off the stool and unconsciously moved toward him, delicately placing a hand on his arm. "That is a surprise. That's the surprise of a lifetime. I'm telling you...Augustino...scuba is something I always thought was out of my reach, you know, for other people."

He smiled and nodded. She was so damned adorable. He didn't trust himself to speak. All he wanted was to scoop her up in his arms and drink in her excitement, feel her heart pounding against his chest. He noticed Raoul coming up the back stairs. "Come to relieve me already, pal?" he asked.

"Yeah, sure. I love to drive. Go and take in the sights with your girl," he admonished gently. "I'll let you know when we're getting close."

"Thanks, Raoul." Augustino relinquished the helm.

Taking Raoul's advice to heart, he pulled Amanda into his arms. He held her tightly, content simply to feel her presence against him.

When he released her, his eyes held a mocking, teasing glint Amanda didn't know how to interpret. What had her hugging him revealed? No doubt she had shown him another glimpse of her heart.

"Come," he told her softly, leading the way to his office. "I'll show you some of the equipment we use for scuba. I even have a few books on the subject you might want to browse through."

Amanda excitedly picked up two picture books on diving and followed him to the mid-deck. She listened intently as Augustino explained the basic patterns of weather and the ocean's reaction to them. He explained about the best formula to swim parallel to any rip current. He used their surroundings to show her how to check for current. He briefed her on evaluating optimal weather conditions for a dive and how best to watch for varied wave patterns. "Take a look portside," he told her, hanging over the rail. "Here, use these binoculars. Now, can you see way down that there's a wave crashing, seemingly in the middle of nowhere?"

"Yes. I see that. There are several waves. A big one, then closer there are smaller ones breaking down in front of it. How strange!" Amanda continued timing them through her binoculars.

"Not strange. Very easily explained. You see, waves break in water only slightly deeper than their height..."

"I get it. This means that the ocean's bottom is higher there. The water is shallow."

"That's right. Sometimes it's due to an offshore reef or a sand bar—could be several reasons. And after the wave breaks, it flows back into the ocean under oncoming waves. This is what causes undertow, or what many people call back-rush. In itself, it's not too dangerous. Most undertows dissipate in three feet of water. But if the beach or the incline is steep, as in the side of an underwater crag, the undertow would be stronger and seemingly bottomless. Plus, the deep crashing motion of the waves would tug you in different directions, making it difficult for you to maintain your balance."

"You mean, the waves would push me toward the shore...or the reef, and the undertow would tug my legs in the opposite direction?"

"Very good!" He was impressed with how quickly she was seizing the gist of her first lesson. "You'll do well," he told her. "There's a lot more to becoming familiar with the sea, of course. Even for a dive master like me, the thrill of discovery on a dive is always changing, forever different. Each time I head out I learn something new."

"There's a phone call for you, sir." Albert was handing Augustino the headset and phone.

"Thank you, Albert....Milo—Jeff! Where are you?"

Amanda watched him as he listened intently to the caller and wondered if Jeff was the one from the marina.

"No. We're not going to need his help after all. —I don't care. Just tell him there is no deal. —I'll see you when I get back." Augustino hung up the phone promptly.

"Is that Jeff Nichols—from the marina?"

He nodded curtly. It was obvious to Amanda that he didn't want to discuss it. "So, why do you call yourself Milo?"

He smiled. "When I was a boy people referred to my father as Tino—he being Valentino. They couldn't very well shorten my name to Tino. So, they called me Milo—not to confuse us." He shrugged. "I began using it a few years ago as a means to anonymity. I guess I still use the moniker with guests and business partners. Most of my friends call me Augie."

"Augie," Raoul called out to him, "I can see the islands."

Augustino looked around him and noticed the traffic had increased tenfold. There were a lot of fishing boats and tall ships headed to the islands. "I'm going up there to lend a hand. Want to come?"

Upstairs Raoul was radioing his position to the coast guard. "I told them we weren't docking. They told us to circle around the channel to the southern island. I spoke to Flint.

He's already there."

"Good man. You've taken care of everything."

"I thought Bimini was one large island," Amanda mentioned, surprised to hear Raoul's expression.

"Sure, it is. But there's a very shallow channel that separates north from south." Raoul added. "There he is, Augie." He pointed to a motor boat that was fast coming toward them. "Manuel's at the back gate. He'll help him on board."

Augustino was checking the boat with binoculars. "He has an overnight case. I hope he has the parcel."

"I just hope he has our papers, Augie. We won't make it into Providence if he doesn't."

Ten minutes later, Gary was greeting them on the bridge; sandals wet, cotton pants rolled up, but elated to be aboard. "Am I glad to be here." He gave Augustino a bear hug. "For a while, I didn't think I was going to make it." He gave both Manuel and Augustino a strange look.

"Run into trouble?" Augustino seemed concerned.

"You could say that. We got the info though, turns out it's a small film-sized container," he shot triumphantly with a huge smile on his face.

"Did you have time to verify it, authenticate it?"

Gary shook his head. "Conchita and I ran in and out of the bank. I dropped her off at her car and on the way back to mine I nearly got my head shot off."

"Where is it?"

"Hey, this is Conchita. She insisted on keeping it. I'll debrief you later. There's a lot to talk about. Bob said you didn't let him slap two words together on the phone with you last night."

"He called me at the worst possible time, trust me." Augustino's tone of voice drew an end to that conversation. Instead he turned toward Amanda. "You remember Amanda?"

"Remember! Hell, I can't stop thinking about her," Gary smiled—a hint of mischief in his eyes as he kissed Amanda's hand.

Amanda responded graciously, trying to forget that she was the only one they seemed to want to exclude from their little secrets. Something told her that on this next leg of their journey, she'd have lots of time to study her new pastime.

"Tell Raoul not to worry. I got the *Milan* clearance all the way to Providence Harbour. I've got permits and stamped customs forms."

"So we don't have to stop at Berry Islands. That's wonderful. I guess it pays to have clout with the Feds," Augustino smiled.

"Hell, Augie. I *am* the Feds—at least I'm part of their department."

While Gary, Raoul, Manuel and Augustino powwowed on the upper deck in the pilothouse, Amanda spent her time between watching the shimmering turquoise ocean striated in varying shades of blue—as the depth of the water varied along the breadth of the Grand Bahamas Bank—and peacefully studying the vagaries of scuba. Oh! And wondering what these men could be discussing for so long, with such intensity.

Every now and then she'd hear laughter trickle down

to where she sat on the settee in the living room. Then there would be the occasional loud rants and deep voices, when she felt eight years old again and shut out from her brother Michael's clubhouse, trying to listen in with her ear propped against the branches. Something told her, though, that their little confab became silent when brewed the true ominous portent of their discussion. For instance, she would've loved to hear about Gary's brush with death.

But the tail side of the coin that really flipped her was realizing she hated not being the mirror of Augustino's entire devotion. She wondered if he was the type of man to relegate the women in his life to the balcony seats when he had important matters to settle behind the scene. Was he that much of a chauvinist?

This thought bothered her as much as the seething humiliation of what she considered extreme rudeness—of being the only person excluded from their meeting. Well, except for Albert. Was it a woman thing—or worse, a trust issue? She hoped it was neither and that he could plead his case with the defense that he was simply a man being as considerate as a teenage boy was sentimental.

At 4:30 Albert came up from below and offered her something to eat.

"That's very nice of you, Albert. But I can grab something from the refrigerator up here if I'm hungry or thirsty. Thanks anyway."

"Are you certain? I can whip you up fresh scones and croissants in minutes...to go with a nice pot of tea..."

"How do you do it? How do you manage to cook all

these fancy goodies on board?" She smiled up at him.

"May I?" he asked, indicating the free chair beside her.

"Please do. I could use company about now," she said quietly. "But then again you knew that—right?" She raised her head, looking straight at him.

He nodded. "To answer your first question," he tilted his head in old style reverence, "I freeze the dough and sometimes the partially cooked recipes. Then, I simply pop them in the oven downstairs for a few minutes and, voilà."

She smiled at his charming demeanor. He was the perfect majordomo, salt and pepper hair, pleasant face and extremely punctilious manners. "But the lobster and all the other victuals..."

"Fresh from the market this morning. Some from the day before. Mr. Milan allows me a very generous budget—open, as a matter of fact."

And there they were, talking about Augustino again. She sighed unknowingly, visibly annoyed.

"And if I may be permitted to answer your other question..." he waited for her curiosity to peak; and only when the question in her eyes became impatient did he continue. "In my humble opinion, Master Augustino believes he is protecting you by not inviting you to attend their little meeting. He is one of the most considerate persons I know. He would not intentionally hurt anyone, especially not...you." He smiled cryptically.

Amanda was pleasantly surprised. Albert was not only kind and thoughtful, but extremely insightful—or was he simply so devoted to Augustino he didn't want her or anyone else brewing bad thoughts about him?

"And you would know this...how, exactly?"

"I've been with the family since the year prior to his mother's death. I can tell you that even though he idolized her, he thought of her as an equal. Treated her with utmost respect." He nodded to reinforce his words.

Amanda was excited. Little electric shivers brushed up and down her arms. Here was someone who could dispel the mystery behind the man. He had known him since his teen-age years. She was suddenly tempted to ask him all kinds of personal questions regarding Augustino. Had he ever been engaged? Did he once have a significant other in his life? "Why did you say...especially not you?" she breathed, the only opening Albert had conveniently left her.

He raised his chin slightly, straightened his back, obviously attempting to distance his emotional views from rational thoughts to draw her as clear a picture as he could. "In all the years I've known him, I've never seen Master Augustino more head-over-heels...interested in anyone as much as he is in you. He is a changed man. And it warms my heart to see that you...feel the same way about him?"

He was insightful. "Augie head-over-heels ...!"—whatever that meant—*interested or lusting?* Whatever it was, he had not addressed any of her questions; merely spiked her interest. Did it matter how many women the man had kissed or loved? According to Albert, Augustino was...head-over-heels...interested? Albert had not used the word *love,* which was usually what followed that well-known adage. "How can you be sure, Albert? I mean, did he tell you anything? He just met me. It's too soon."

He smiled politely. "I beg you pardon, Miss Amanda. But you have also just made his acquaintance. It is early for you as well. Still, I see it plainly in your eyes."

Amanda's heart sank. If Albert could see it...

"He doesn't know. He's too preoccupied..."

"Please don't...say anything to him, Albert. I would rather he confirm his feelings first. I guess I'm just terrified of getting my heart trampled. And I'm not easily frightened. That's my one scare," she raised her index finger to emphasize.

"I understand," he stated simply as he rose to leave.

"Interested in me, you say?" She bit down on a thoughtful smile. She wondered if Albert wasn't mistaking Augustino's pretence for the real thing.

He nodded reassuringly. "Who can presume to measure the depth of the human heart?" He smiled and executed a little bow before leaving. He turned at the edge of the stairwell. "I'm glad it is you, Miss Amanda. His mother would be proud."

Amanda collapsed in her chair. Her legs felt like silly putty. Little excited shivers suddenly ran ice cold up and down her spine in the hot afternoon sun. She closed her eyes and took a deep breath. How easily she could conjure him up with just the mere flicker of a thought—his piercing blue eyes in the sculptured face, the clef in his chin and those sensuous lips. So, this was what he was doing. Protecting her. Taking care of her the best way he knew how.

She heard the commotion of the little group breaking up and the first one down the stairs was Augustino.

He looked for her in the dining area and smiled the instant he noticed her, sitting alone. "I apologize, *cara*. I did not think our meeting would last as long as it did. I am truly sorry. Were you able to get through the books I handed you?"

He smiled as he looked at her, innocently enough, she thought; but had Albert and she not had the talk, she would've been furious with him.

"I did *some* reading." She looked up at him smiling, noticing his head cocked with curiosity at the strange tone in her voice. "And truthfully, I was beginning to wonder why I had been so rudely, shamefully tossed aside—uninvited to a meeting attended by everyone else. Luckily, I had a nice chat with Albert." At this point she was the one searching his expression. He had suddenly lost his smile. There was a telltale little muscle flexing in his left jaw and he stared at her intently, trying to gauge the message behind the words. "He's quite devoted to you, Augie," she said softly. "You should be grateful to him. Thanks to Albert, I'm no longer angry with you...," she trailed her eyes back on the book.

He moved her chair away from the table—the scraping resonating loudly on the wood floor. He grabbed her shoulders, lifting her bodily to her feet to face him.

"You're holding me too tight," she breathed.

He released her, still searching her eyes. With barely audible words, he demanded. "What exactly did he tell you... to better your disposition toward me?"

Amanda looked at him and couldn't help smiling when she saw half a smile curling up the corner of his mouth.

"As if you could ever be angry with anyone...much less with me...," he whispered.

"Don't be fooled. I do get angry when I've had enough," she cooed. "I'll admit I do have a longer fuse than most people, but once it's lit there's no turning back. I can turn off...for good."

His smile stretched from ear to ear and he appeared to relax, concluding she had heard nothing out of the ordinary.

And while Amanda wasn't about to betray Albert's trust, she needed to wipe that smug look off his face, to somehow let him know she knew about his feelings, if only to help him better express them—the sooner the better, she decided, smiling up at him. "I hadn't realized he'd been with you all those years. Since you were eighteen—how many years would that be?"

His bright smile waned somewhat as his brow furrowed. "I'm ten years older than you are, Amanda. You know that."

"Actually, I wasn't sure until now. So, Albert has witnessed seventeen years of water under your bridge," she smiled. "It gives him a good sense of...knowing what and... who you like....He knows the people you like." She uttered the last sentence barely louder than a whisper.

He raised his head, took in a deep breath and stared at her through eyes that were probing slits—like a poker player assessing a worthy adversary across the table. His wavering certainty more than satisfied her and, skirting effrontery, she tiptoed closer and planted a kiss on the lobe of his ear. "Thank you, Augustino," she added, "you know—for taking care of me."

He nodded, not at all convinced she had confided the whole of it. "You're more than welcome," he answered politely, an odd look in his eyes.

CHAPTER TWELVE

Amanda applied a last coat of peach lip-gloss, gave the mirror a look-see, grabbed her evening bag and closed the stateroom door behind her. Carefully in her low-heeled sandals, she climbed to the mid-deck where Augustino was already waiting for her. He was handsome, she thought, her heart beating faster as she stared at his back. A cream-colored jacket was stretched over those wide shoulders and falling attractively over dark brown trousers. And the snug fit of his collar, a beige tone that enhanced his hair and tanned complexion, told her a tie completed the outfit. He was playing with Dino, throwing a soft toy to the other end of the deck, waiting for him to bring it back.

She waited patiently for him to turn and see her. She hoped with trepidation that she had picked the right outfit. Dinner and dancing, he had told her—and her legs were already wobbly. It was hard to believe that only this morning she had been in her apartment moping at the idea of never seeing him again. It had certainly been a long day, and now she found herself hoping—praying—that the evening would endure, trickle by slowly because the night was theirs and theirs alone to share, to treasure, to love...

Augustino turned to follow Dino's trajectory. That's when he saw her, standing with the setting sun at her back, looking like an apparition. He gazed at her speechless, awe-struck by her beauty. He advanced toward her, taking in her silky hair—she had left loose to please him—and an ecru chiffon number he found so sexy, his eyes had to sweep her up and down several times to be certain he wasn't hallucinating.

Silently he took her by the hand and twirled her to see the full effect of the dress. The chiffon gathered at the back of her neck came down the front as two separate lapels delicately pleated over her breasts. They joined collected at the waist, which left her back and sides completely bare. The material was light and pale and though gathered, Amanda's tanned round breasts were slightly visible through the chiffon. The skirt, garnered at the waist with thin piping, was bouncy and pert, falling in bell-shaped fashion two inches above her knees.

"That's quite a dress," he murmured, at a loss for words. "Or...not," he smiled as he traced a finger down the open slit at the front of the dress, fingering the contour of perky round breasts on his way down. "At least what little there is of it. You look...edible."

"Behave," she told him easily while allowing him to

continue—her rock-hard nipples proof that she enjoyed his caress. "I just hope it's not too revealing..."

"It's perfect, Amanda. You must remind me to thank Louise for her choice of wardrobe," he said.

"This one was my choice," she added proudly.

He helped her put on a rose-beige embroidered satin wrap and led her off the quay to the promenade in front of the Atlantis—one of the most posh hotels in the world.

She had heard about it, seen pictures in magazines, in advertisements. It was so much more spectacular to gaze at in person.

Augustino took her by the hand as they walked along the pier. She got a full view of all the fabulous yachts moored there, some as big as two hundred feet long—bobbing, shining and spiffed-up to look their best.

Walking toward the steps to the front entrance to the Atlantis, she was surprised to notice the volume of quaint traffic. Tourists with children ambled along with dreams in their eyes. Formally attired dinner guests such as themselves headed toward reserved seating. And all types of seafaring enthusiasts fawned and caressed their ships, happy to be ashore yet unable to abandon outright their mode of transportation. Then there was the high number of locals, tanned and smiling, many of them wearing uniforms and offering their help with a barrage of services. And though the sun was quickly setting, the bustle seemed a vigorous one as if just born for their benefit—new and vibrant like a morning *ménage*.

As Augustino led Amanda through the portals of the hotel, one by one the lights blinked on and, though she tried not to resemble too much the typical tourist, she held her breath as she gasped at the magnificence of the grand Royal Tower lobby. The foyer was a marble extravaganza with ornate ceilings and gigantic, larger-than-life chandeliers—all of them evoking a naval theme. Augustino brought her to the balustrade. Below she glimpsed the Great Hall of Waters lobby. Gently he flicked her chin upward and she saw its ceiling, a dome of golden shells soaring 70 feet high in the air.

"Augustino, this is beautiful." There was just so much to take in. The ten feet circular columns supporting the dome, the many murals painted on the walls and the Mayan life-size artifacts and figures displayed in every corner. The whole of Atlantis appeared built by the gods. In fact, so impressive was the grandeur that oozed from every facet of its walls that people circulating below resembled fast crawling ants scurrying about, unaware of life's grander mystery.

"The restaurant below is aptly named Great Hall of Waters and opens on the other side to underwater streets teeming with fish and Atlantean artifacts." He smiled. He loved the wide-eyed innocence of her childlike sweetness. "Come on, we have dinner reservations at the Bahamian Club. It's a ten minute walk down the west wing." He grabbed her hand and they descended the central staircase from the mezzanine to the marble wide corridor below, the one that connected to the various hotel entrances, to the shops and boutiques and to the many five-star restaurants.

"How long are we here for?" she asked him, gazing quickly left and right, practically running to keep up with him.

"Not long enough for you to see it all, my sweet. Tonight and tomorrow. Actually, we were due to be on our way tomorrow. I extended our trip so that you could experience your first scuba lesson here. It's easier at the beginner's basin they sponsor out back by the beach front."

They arrived at the restaurant and inside the atmosphere changed drastically. It was like stepping through the archway into another era. The headwaiter came to greet them with the usual Bahamian flourish, in bow tie and tuxedo, bowing from the waist and extending his hand for them to follow. The place was quiet, country club in essence, decorated with wooden tables and high back thickly upholstered loungers. Each table was secluded enough to form its own little island.

Augustino thanked him generously and waited for Amanda to remove her wrap, standing behind her chair in readiness.

"Should I?" She asked hesitantly. Aside from being air-cooled, the ambiance was formal and very much grand boudoir.

He tilted his head and smiled, patiently waiting for her to remove it.

"I might be cold," she told him, refusing to have him check it, draping it on the back of her chair instead. "These seats are so comfortable."

"A small show of Bahamian hospitality. Contrary to most places in America, here they want you to loll around—figure that by staying longer they can get you to eat more."

He couldn't stop admiring her. And somewhere in the back of his mind lurked the pathetic question parked there for the last few days. Where was he ever going to find the courage to resist her charms? He was barely thinking straight as it was, staring at the décolleté of that dress, at her hair, at the pure joy in her eyes. All he had to do was extend an arm, reach out and gently slide his fingers under the loose material of her dress to stroke her breasts. It would be so natural he didn't think anyone would even notice. He physically shook his head to tip those thoughts back in the box. It was early in the evening and he needed to stay focused on being pleasant and keeping his distance.

"Is anything wrong?" she asked, seeing him roll his eyes and vigorously shake his head.

"No. I think I have a little water in my ear." What a jerk he was. To think that this still-wet-behind-the-ears little girl held such power over him. It was humbling, he thought wryly, and more than disconcerting. All the mysterious and glamorous women that had literally thrown themselves at him over the years—years, he nodded emphatically. He was ten years her senior. She should be kowtowing to him.

"What's wrong, Augie? You seem to be having this whole...conversation with yourself...I wish you'd come back to the table." She smiled at him, unwittingly enhancing his plight. "I enjoy your company, you know. Besides, it's embarrassing talking to you and not having any response. People think I'm talking to myself."

"I'm sorry, *cara*. What were you saying?" he smiled.

"I asked you about the fish here, about what you're going to order?"

The waiter had dropped menus and he hadn't even

noticed. “The last time I came here I had the grouper.” He rallied quickly, picking up his menu. “It’s very good. They prepare it with a special spicy sauce and accompany it with rice and vegetables.”

“Then I’ll have the same,” she smiled agreeably.

Augustino was quiet for most of the meal. He had wished to discuss many things with her prior to arriving at the restaurant. But now he needed all his strength to keep his id in check and his libido curtailed.

Amanda didn’t seem to notice. She talked about growing up in Pleasantville, about her dog Dino, and trounced the grueling years spent getting her degree. Sharing an apartment with Ginette came on the topic, and how living alone was definitely on her agenda for the next coming years.

“Why? Don’t you like sharing an apartment?”

“Of course I do. Gin is very nice and it makes for enjoyable company. But having been the baby of a large family, I just crave going it alone for a few years. You know, decorating to my heart’s content and getting up any time I please without having to tiptoe around in the dark.” She shrugged. “That’s just the tip of the iceberg.”

“What you’re saying is you’re coveting the road to spinsterhood.” He chuckled under his breath.

“Don’t be silly. I intend to meet the right guy...one day...” she looked at him, strangely shy to continue—those damned piercing blue eyes.

“But you’ll have to tiptoe around him—in the dark. You’ll have to decorate while making concessions for his particular taste. Worse, you’ll have to cater to his...needs before going to sleep every night..." He gave her a wicked smile. "That's a lot more demanding."

She traded her prettiest, dubious smirk. "Well, I'm sure it wouldn't be...*every* night." She looked away to ignore his raised eyebrows. "Besides, when you're in love those little things don't matter as much."

He chuckled softly. "Little...things—no. They don't matter at all."

She shook her head, unable to hide how amused she was. "I have a feeling your mind is in the gutter this evening, Mr. Milan."

"I beg to differ. Not in the gutter from the angle I'm looking at," he teased, his eyes caressing her. "I'm staring at lovely warm eyes overflowing with kindness." He picked up her right hand and rubbed the back of it against his cheek, kissing each individual finger before toying with the ring he had placed there. "Kindness I know you have in your heart for a poor soul like mine. After all, you've already said yes..."

She cleared her throat, not wanting him to notice how touched and frazzled she was, gracefully retrieved her hand and thanked God she didn't have to stand on those limp, useless legs underneath the table. "Thank you, Augie. That's a very nice compliment." She perused the dessert menu and tried to ignore his ear-splitting smile she spotted between her lashes.

Dessert was a more subdued affair, especially for Amanda. Augustino simply had coffee. When he signaled for the check she hazarded to stare at him, needing to pinch herself to make sure she was truly there, out on a date on

Paradise Island with a man freshly sprung from the wishing-well of her most secret desires. All she had to do was hold it together for a little while longer. So far, she had passed her rigorous test with excellence. No begging, no fate worse than death to attest to, no white flag of her longings on the horizon. Smooth, straight sailing, she thought; enjoying the pun with a smile.

"Happy?" he asked, noticing her smile as he rose from his chair.

"Extremely," she echoed back, draping her wrap on her arm.

"Not too tired for a little dancing, I hope?" He asked her with mischief in his eyes.

Some little voice nagged that she should opt out. After the day she had had, being tired would be admissible—she wouldn't even have to feign it. But dancing with Augustino was a longer thirst-quenching sip from that deep, dark wishing well. And she intended taking all it would dole, slowly, to the very last drop. "Not at all. Where to?"

"A little down to the right, to the Dragon Club. It's lively and very entertaining. Think you can keep up?"

He was such a tease. It's a wonder he didn't have a fat cheek from getting his face slapped. "I am willing if you are..." she teased right back.

This time he was the one who backed down, darkened eyes reflecting the hit.

She was on a roll and finding more confidence with every passing minute. This was the proper setting, the one surrounding where she could shine—tons of people and noise all around. She would worry about being alone with him later. For now she could dangle the leash and spread the bait all she wanted. He would have to behave in front of all these patrons.

The Dragon nightclub was dark, lit with glimpses of flashing lasers and beams of decorative circles of light that did little to brighten the night. The white smile of the gentleman behind the bar was the brightest spot in the joint. As she smiled back at that friendly bartender, Amanda felt the pressure of Augustino's warm, gentle hand on her bare back, directing her toward him. How easily her edge could slip away.

"What will you have to drink, Amy?"

It amazed her that he assumed she would want anything to drink, so inebriated was she already—with the power of her feminine sensuality. Besides, she had gotten drunk once in her life, some gazillion years ago when she had left the Liberator Party with a total stranger. Following a phenomenal hangover and an even worse case of amnesia, she had vowed never to do *that* again.

One glass of wine with dinner was more than enough. "I'll have tonic water with a twist of lemon please."

He looked at her with raised eyebrows. "Not very sporting of you," he smiled, obviously continuing their previous topic with renewed gusto.

"Since when is it necessary to drink anything fermented to have a good time? In my book, alert and keen beats loose and sloppy anytime." This was fun. She was ahead in the score; of this she was certain.

"Allow me to hold you to that," he added, perplexing

her a little.

"What do you mean?" She accepted the drink and followed him to a table second from the back and near the DJ's booth. The tiled dance area was well lit but empty. Most couples sat by and looked on. "Why isn't anyone dancing?"

"It's too early. Unlike you, people sometimes need the accumulation of alcohol to free their inhibitions."

"Speaking of which, what did you mean earlier when you said you would hold me to it...?"

"Proving your theory—that keen and alert is better than loose and sloppy..."

Ooh! That was a *check* move. She would have to tone it down. Later loomed ominously close all of a sudden. "Needs no proof. It's a well known fact," she said a little louder, the music resuming.

"Come, let's dance this one."

"But there's no one else...and I'm not sure I remember—this is a mambo."

"Just follow my lead. If you like, you can place your feet on mine to learn the steps."

She burst out laughing. He laughed also, yanking her to the dance floor.

"The mambo is a simple two step. Whenever I spin you or toss you, at the count of two you're always back facing me." He clasped her hand and strapped an arm around her waist. Sliding his left hand down her lower back, he tucked her pelvis into his, the dance's sensuous friction letting her know with certainty he had hard inches to spare—while a dark gleaming pair of blue eyes seemed to announce he was more than willing to share it with her.

She held his gaze unafraid—loving the warm liquid it spread to her limbs. Deftly she measured her step to his as the beat enveloped them both. His leg was partially between hers, the up-and-down roughness of his knee against her thigh directing their next move, each one more daring, more surprising than the previous. All she could see were his eyes, hot and trickling lava inside her, melting her resolve by the second not to beg for his kisses. She didn't even care that the other couples were smiling as they watched them enthralled in a world of their own. The DJ spotted them with the aura of a white light and Amanda lost track of the throng of people surrounding them, cheering their every move.

"You've done this before, *cara*," he rasped, fighting to keep his smile.

"I was my sister Susan's fill-in...you know...when her boyfriend stood up their...dance lessons," she added dizzily, unable to get the words out of her constricted throat. But this was not a Lila's Little Feet mambo session. This was hot and exotic. Augustino used his body as a metronome and stuck her to it—to keep time of his sensuous pulse. She labored to breathe because her arched chest was more preoccupied with the thrill of rubbing against his than supplying her with air.

During the music's crescendo, he tipped her then yanked her back on her feet, strapping both his hands against her bare sides just underneath her arms. There was the sound of thunderous applause and, as if to appease the audience, holding her a few inches away from him, he bent and kissed her with a hungry mouth. At first, she refused to part her lips and tried to push him away, conscious of all the eyes staring at them. But he slid his thumbs under the chiffon of her dress and caressed the soft underbelly of her breasts in an upward motion until they reached the tender flesh around her nipples. He toyed with them gently, using the tips of his thumbs in a rhythmic circular motion until they pointed outward like brave little soldiers. That's when she opened her mouth wide, answering his kiss with as much compliance as she could muster.

Then as suddenly as he had greedily subdued her, he released her, his hands sliding down her bare sides to rest on her waist, leaving her to quickly close her mouth and wipe it with the back of her hand. He had just established who was boss in this relationship and the crowd loved it as they applauded again, the celebration sprayed with catcalls from some of the men, complimenting Augustino.

As reason found its way to her numbed crazed brain, Amanda choked on the realization that he had not cared one iota about the crowd. He had felt like kissing her, caressing her and touching her and he had gone ahead and done it. He was shameful.

Staring at him with angry eyes, she came close to slapping the sex-craved, wanton expression off his mug. She didn't. Ham that he was he would have loved it too much, she concluded. Instead, she smiled politely and walked away, leaving him standing there alone.

When he caught up to her at the table she was grabbing her shawl and getting ready to leave.

"Where are you going? The evening is just getting

started."

"Is it? And what are you going to do for an encore? Slip the dress off my shoulders?"

He had never seen her angry before. "They saw us kiss. That was all. You'll discover that many couples end their dance this way. No one noticed me slipping my thumbs inside your dress, Amanda—no one but you, that is. Be honest," he urged her, "you loved it."

Of course she had loved it. Had he made love to her on that floor she would not have objected. How could she? She had wanted him inside her the very first day she had met him. But she wasn't some prize he had earned. Or some bimbo he had bought and paid for. The ring on her finger did not give him the right to overstep his boundary—not unless it was of a common accord. But she *had* agreed, a small voice insider her nudged. She had opened her mouth and kissed him back. "It was wonderful," she admitted with sincerity. She looked around and rather than cause a scene, she sat back down to sip the rest of her tonic water. "I don't have your suave experience, Augustino. I've been kissed twice maybe four times in my life if you count the other day in your room...you've kissed hundreds of women..."

"I haven't kissed anyone in fifteen years, Amanda..."

"And you expect me to believe that!" She held her tongue, just. She was about to rattle on about seeing him with Connie, on the first night they met, when she remembered that he hadn't kissed her.

"I've made love to...well, I've lost count. It doesn't matter. I never kissed any of them, ever." He smiled to alleviate the tension between them. "I've had week-long relationships, *cara* that ended because of the intimacy I refused these ladies. The last woman I kissed I lived with a whole three months before we did it proper. We broke up a year later. She wasn't the first, but she was the last. And that was fifteen years ago, Amanda."

"Then why did you kiss me...? It doesn't make sense." She was still vaguely mutinous.

"Doesn't it? Is that the honest truth?" He smiled ruefully. "I think you know why I did." He stared at her with a frown on his brow, needing for her to read his heart and desperate to restore respect and camaraderie between them.

"That's just it. Kiss or no kiss, you have more experience than I do—more expertise. You were able to stop just now...whereas I..."

"Is that why you're angry?" He nodded slowly, realizing her demise. "You're angry with your loss of control? Maybe because you weren't calling the shots anymore—like you've been doing all evening?" He smiled at her.

"No." She was angry because she had promised herself she would not jeopardize her heart by accepting a situation where he could exercise *his* control—a monumental one.

"Can we go now?" she asked him, feeling the day's emotions take their toll.

"Only if you tell me that there are no hard feelings between us, *cara*."

She stared at him, deep in thought. Seeking a little victory of her own, she smiled and nodded. "I'll do better than that," she answered. "I'll show you," she whispered as she leaned into him, placed her lips on his and parted them softly to drive her tongue deep inside his mouth.

She heard his loud groan as the gesture took him by surprise and deeply contented, a few seconds later, she ended the kiss and chalked it up as victorious proof of her own self-control. "I have no hard feelings." She smiled at his perplexed expression. "Can you say the same? About no hard...feelings?" she asked, uncaring she was courting danger.

But he threw back his head and laughed dryly. "Very good, Amanda." He rose, exhorting her to do the same. "Now we are...well, not quite even as your feelings have mellowed... mine...*has* not." He stared at her, his plight humbly in his eyes and on his trembling lips.

She looked away. She would have done anything to take back her last remark. It wasn't like her to be hurtful. So he had more self-control than she did. It was normal. He was more experienced and he had been around longer than she had. "I'm sorry for that last remark, Augustino. It was selfish," she told him apologetically as she followed him out of the bar.

He kissed her temple. "It was true, and I deserved it." He took in the startled look on her face. "Don't be so surprised. You're not the only one who can be magnanimous," he chuckled, draping his arm around her shoulders.

But as warm and amenable as the evening had been, they walked back from the Atlantis in silence, holding hands under a glorious moon. On the bridge of the ship they exchanged nothing other than polite goodnights—Amanda because she was shy, Augustino because he was wounded and could not have resisted another assault. He pecked her on the cheek for form.

She asked him where he was sleeping exactly. He smiled, told her not to worry. It was all arranged, he said, before taking his leave and heading for the sanctuary of his office.

Why was he so detached, Amanda pondered as she soaked in a luxurious roman bathtub loaded with suds with the jet sprays humming full blast. She desperately needed to relax. But the evening's conversation kept emerging from the hot fragrant vapors, as did her disappointment in Augustino's coolness. Dino sat on the bath corner, wagging his tail and trying to snap at the floating bubbles. "There is no point in the contemplation of this mysterious man," she told Dino, petting his little head when she finally stepped out of the bath. "Unlike you, my four-legged sweetie, he is a veritable enigma."

She put on a short satin nightgown and padded to bed. She fluffed up the other pillow—for Dino—and smiled, ironically glad she wasn't alone on such a romantic evening. Instead, she tossed and turned to get comfortable and noticed on the sideboard clock that it was 12:00. Staring up at the porthole on the ceiling, she gazed in wonder at the gazillion stars out that evening. She remembered the moon on the walk back from the Atlantis and imagined what it might be like to stroll on deck when everyone was sleeping—to gaze at the endless stretch of sky over the marina. The Atlantis would look like a pink jewel—a vivid fairy tale memory for her to bring back.

Quietly she explained to Dino that he had to stay. Then after slipping on the matching robe to her pink satin nightgown, she climbed up to the deck. It was sparsely lit and abandoned. But she had been right; the view of the Atlantis was spectacular.

She looked up at the stars and tried to spot the constellations familiar to her. She was usually good at this but for some reason she couldn't quite find her bearings. Head veered upward, continuing to walk down the length of the deck, she bumped her leg against a metal object. She looked down to rub the wounded area and spotted a lounge chair with a lump sprawled on it in what looked to be a sleeping bag. Coming closer she spotted Augustino's tousled black hair sticking out of a comforter. He was sound asleep.

She sat on the edge of the chair, carefully, and gazed at the frown on his face even as he slept. Her heart ripped open as she glanced at his makeshift sleeping quarters, the sad look on his brow and wondered why he had not admitted to the shortage of bunks.

That was easy to surmise. He had opted not to make her feel bad. He knew she would offer to change places with him; or he knew she wouldn't sleep knowing he was out here. Whatever the reason, she sighed; he was the odd man out on his own boat. And that wasn't right.

She took a deep breath and gently nudged his shoulder. "Augustino," she whispered. "Augie." She shook him slightly.

"Hum," he mumbled gruffly.

"Wake up," she urged him. "It's me, Amanda."

He exhaled deeply, kicked the comforter off his body and turned on his back with his eyes still closed. He seemed dazed, she noticed, tired and gone. He wore a tight crewneck t-shirt and loose cotton pants. "Amanda? What are you doing here?" he uttered in a sleepy voice. "Is anything wrong?"

"I was just out taking a breath of night air when I bumped into your chair. Augie, why didn't you tell me this is where you were sleeping?"

He shrugged, finally opening his eyes to look at her, frowning from the ship's night light. "This is where I'm sleeping. Does it matter?"

"You know it does. Why aren't you in one of the other staterooms?"

"Albert and Manuel are in the crew quarters downstairs." He stretched his legs. "Raoul has the smaller room and Gary has the guest stateroom. I couldn't well take the other bunk in Raoul's quarters, or make up the queen size bed in the living room. We're supposed to be sleeping together, remember?" He stretched and yawned, recovering enough of his spirits to stare at her.

Amanda couldn't resist fingering his ruffled hair while he continued staring at her with a tensed jaw, quietly waiting for her next move. "It's not any better if someone comes out on deck and sees you sleeping here—like I did."

"It's easier to make something up..."

"We can share the room," she said quickly before she lost her nerve. "We're two mature adults so there's no reason we can't fix this. I'm smaller; I can use the chair in the corner."

He looked at her without adding anything, just shaking his head from side to side.

"Come on, Augie. Okay, so we can share the bed. It's big. It's a king size bed. You'll have your side and I'll have mine..."

He smiled, rolling his eyes. "You're precious, Amanda—you know that? If I come within one width of you while we're in bed together, I guarantee you'll be losing a lot more than your damned self-control. Go back to sleep, Amy." He turned his head the other way, closed his eyes and considered the matter closed.

Ooh! He was stubborn and smug. "And what would I be losing anyway. My virtue? My virginity? Don't bother. I'm not a virgin; and even if I were, why is it that you men always assume that we women *lose* something in the process of having sex. I mean, who made you judge and jury of what's good for me and what's not? That is so pretentious."

He drew an enormous breath to let it out in one drawn-out sigh and sat up on the cot, his arms resting on bent knees. He eyed her intently. "Is this your...round about way of inviting me to share your bed, *cara*? *Truly share?*" he emphasized, a blatant question in his eyes.

Never mind the emphasis; she knew what he meant. Only now, she heard this drum-roll in her head. She was about to officially invite him to spend the night with her. What if he said no—her dreaded fear, the fate worse than death she had promised to avoid at all cost?

"You know me," she told him nervously. "I'm all for sharing..." For a moment his eyes lit up in a peculiar way—

with a kindly light. "...if it'll get you off this chair." She regretted having added this even before she had said it. Her stupid pride shoved in her mouth again.

He nodded ruefully and laid back down, covering his eyes with his arm. "There are worse things than lying on this chair, Amanda. Useless pity is one of them."

"Fine; have it your way." She rose, tugging the belt to her robe. "At least I made the effort. I am going to sleep the sleep of the innocent tonight, Augustino. Goodnight."

She stomped off as loud as bare feet on a wooden deck would allow and hurried for the refuge of her room. Once there, she closed the door and leaned against it, her heart beating all the way up to her throat. Dino was excited to see her, jumping up and down to be picked up, and she did so, feeling the sting of Augustino's rejection like a red welt stamped across her flushed face.

He hadn't really rejected her; she tried to console herself as she got back into bed. He had just reacted to her poor choice of words. Still, she couldn't stop thinking about him, about what might have been.

She must have dozed off because Dino's barking sounded as if it came from far away. Then she felt him jumping up and down on her chest, his painful little dance rapidly alerting her to someone's presence. She appeased him with a gentle sweep of her hand, looked up and noticed the door to her room was open. Against the ship's dim corridor light she saw the trace of a man's silhouette in the doorway, staring at her. "Augie, is that you?" she asked, slightly concerned.

"Is the invitation to get me off that bunker still on?"

he asked humbly.

She nodded. Realizing he couldn't see her in the dark, she reached and turned on the small reading lamp on top of the berth. "You know it is." She smiled tremulously. "You wouldn't be here if you thought it wasn't."

He coined her half a smile and entered, closing the door behind him. He walked halfway to the bed before yanking his t-shirt over his head. He smiled when he saw her eyes widen with apprehensive curiosity. He untied the cord to his cotton pants and slipped out of them, kicking them to the side.

She held her breath as her eyes swept over the tight muscles of his clenched jaw, the broad shoulders, the lean chest, the svelte waistline and hard stomach. But she couldn't help gasping when she noticed how well endowed he was. There was no question he was ready for her. He made Johnny the jock's brave ronyon look like an overcooked string bean. She had once heard girly gossip about plus sizes—never believed it—until now.

He continued advancing toward her, his eyes dark blue and luscious. He picked up Dino and deposited him on the chair. "You don't mind if I take his place, do you?"

She smiled and shook her head. She gathered her satin nightgown and tossed it over her head. It felt good finally baring her body to him. She had wanted to for so long.

He smiled as his eyes traveled over her. He gazed at the well-toned body, the satiny golden skin and the round luscious breasts. "You're so much more beautiful without clothes," he told her roughly. Quickly he slid in alongside her, scooping her up in his arms, shuddering and groaning with deep satisfaction when he felt her soft nude body slithering against his. "I'm so sorry I misread your signs, Amanda. I'm an idiot." He ran the tips of his fingers gently down her back, her thighs, and she squealed with pleasure, rubbing up against him, unable to stay put. She had dreamed of this moment for so long—all her life it seemed— and the tall thirst-quenching glass was overflowing. She couldn't take it in all at once. She wanted to, but could not, no matter how dry and parched her love life had been till now.

He cupped her face with his hands. "You're going to have to be patient a little while longer, *cara*." He spoke with short spurts of breath, curtailing with difficulty his own impatience, feeling as though he was going to implode.

"Why?" she breathed, suddenly worried he had changed his mind again.

Her concern touched him. For an instant he closed his eyes to regroup. "I want you to lie still and allow me to discover you, slowly and completely. You see..." He interrupted to kiss her mouth, first sliding his lips over hers and jabbing his tongue through her parted lips, sliding it greedily over pearly white teeth, wrapping it tightly around her tongue—the deep throbbing motion putting an end to her question and arresting all will in her. "...I want our first time to be perfect," he mouthed on her lips, their breath fusing, clinging and refusing to part. "Can you give me that, Amanda? Will you allow me to love you and thrill you as no one has? I want you to be absolutely and utterly mine," he whispered hoarsely, his fiery fingers spreading the scorching heat below her belly.

Her mind strained to construct cohesive words—two

in a row—*yes, please*, she moaned. But words were distant effigies. She could not even formulate a mere one.

She opened her eyes and gratefully knew by the tenderness in his that he could read their jumbled language. She would afford him anything he wanted. Of course she was his for the taking. Why the question? Didn't he know?

He nodded and groaned at the smile of capitulation of her face. "Good girl," he whispered, shoving his tongue in her ear as deep inside as he could, feeling the sweet tremors of her pliant body stirring underneath him. "I promise. Be patient a little while longer and I'll show you how to drive me absolutely mad—so you can lead me around by the tip of my nose anytime you want. Make me do anything you like. Deal?" He breathed hotly against her lips, waiting for her response.

She nodded, her huge brown eyes wild and damp, thinking how sweet the breath of him was. And by *patient* she knew he meant he was about to subjugate her to such a rough rash of pleasures she would wallow in their sensations for days to come. She felt like the biblical burning bush—on fire, in ecstasy, greedily consumed yet not singed or destroyed or darkened. Love was such a miracle—although she sensed destruction may lie in wait when the doused flame would leave her cold and sadly without light. Piper would be settled then. She wanted nothing to do with him now.

Not while the man of her dreams was foraging through her with the intensity of a raging fire. Propped up beside her, he trailed his lips down her neck, twisted his tongue around the soft vulnerable part of her nipples and sucked each breast until her nipples were wet, hard and red. His free hand created havoc with soft caresses on her abdomen. He focused on discovering her erogenous zones and preyed on them mercilessly each time he heard her squeals and yelps accentuate—his cue he had found a pleasure spot.

He remained oblivious to her pleas for relief as she twisted and arched her back in an attempt to get some. "Please," she was finally able to utter. "Place your hand between my legs," she asked shyly—softly whispered against his ear. "I've been patient enough."

Her plea drove him to the edge. The best way to stop her words from triggering the explosion he was barely capping was to clamp his mouth on hers. Gently supporting his weight so as not to crush her, his tongue deep down her throat, he covered her body and rocked up and down on her sensuously, affording her some relief but deepening her hunger.

Her kiss became greedier than his did. And as he continued the delectable dance, adding his fingers to the mix, had he not had her mouth sealed to his, they would have heard her hungry cries all the way to the Atlantis. Didn't he know she was on fire and needed him inside her? She was way past craving his fullness, his aching possession and the souse of his juice to put out the fire.

He sensed she was getting angry. That he would lose her if he persisted. So tilting aside, he soloed with his long tapered fingers, exploring the soft glazed pleats of delicate skin he'd just sensuously mashed. The motion drew an enormous sigh of relief from her and she spread her legs for him, enthralled and deeply aroused as his fingers pinched and pronged their way deeper inside her.

He marveled and worried about how tight she was, even as the in and out motion finally afforded her some release.

Carefully, he added a finger and another to stretch her properly and give his dive more depth. That's when he knew she climaxed, when he heard her let out a strong, soft moan of satisfaction. Her deeply contented sighs attested to how good it felt and this moved him deeply.

But now she wanted him inside her. The burning purpose loomed stronger than ever, especially when she saw him rise and stretch for the cabinet beside the bed. She saw him open a drawer and heard him open a package. "What are you doing?" she whispered. Then she saw him dress up. "It would be okay if you didn't, Augustino," she asked more than she suggested.

"No. It wouldn't," he clipped. He was adamant, his eyes mutinous. And as she continued to beg him to hurry, he trembled, the effort of putting on the condom superhuman. He bent to her ear, licking it first with a hungry tongue. "Shh, Amy. Don't rush me. I want this to last."

That damned self-control of his. He was right. But who cared about right at a time like this. He lay on top of her and supporting his weight, he penetrated her slowly, inching in very carefully—so as not to hurt her. "You're so tight, Amanda. It feels as if you've never done this before."

He was right and wrong. She had done this before, but she had never done *this* before. *Finally*—she thought she had cried that out—but didn't—couldn't. Having completed his invasion, his fullness stretched her beyond coherence and she felt as though his throbbing would never let her breathe again.

Searching her face and her eyes for clues, he began his forward movement. The gentle friction drew rhythmic gasps from her as she instinctively moved against him to amplify the motion. At one point her motion was quicker than his. She was pointedly urging him to move faster. “Am I hurting you?” he mumbled gruffly. He worried about being too big, about splitting her.

But she shook her head impatiently, caressing and kneading his buttocks to drive him and will him to pick up the pace. That’s when he unleashed—at last. She knew he must have, because she lost all sense of balance, all sense of time as the swell of passion buzzed through her ears. Ravished with pleasure, seconds became minutes as his ardor never ceased to keep mounting. When finally he came, worn and beaten she collapsed from the tension, unconsciously still teasingly twitching against him.

Dazed, she sensed him gently get up and go to the washroom. He came back, carrying some towelettes he deposited in a bowl by the bed. He sat on the edge beside her, stroked her forehead and brushed damp meshes of hair out of her face.

He smiled at her, his eyes still darkly sensuous. She smiled back at him, her eyes drawn to the fact that he had removed his condom and washed. What she couldn’t understand was why he was still hard and prepped to go.

“Tired?” he asked her.

She shook her head, smiling back at him and content

to bask in the glow of his undivided attention.

"Did I hurt you?" he demanded to know.

Again, she shook her head, no sound coming out of her throat—except for a soft yelp when she felt him dab one of the cold wet towels between her legs, wiping her thighs, her stomach...."Lift up?" he asked her as he rubbed the soft cloth against the back of her thighs. "I thought you'd be more comfortable," he whispered, staring into her eyes.

And the next hour was a gift of sweet vindication as he taught her how to tug and pull and caress him. She was not only a quick study, she initiated moves of her own, using all fingers of both hands, using her mouth.

Yes, she had him cornered. He was helpless in her arms, she thought gleefully. She mounted him and as soon as she stabbed at him, adjusting herself carefully and halfway to succeeding, he sprang up quickly, flipped her over and removed himself. He stared at her, eyes dangerously brooding. He grabbed protection, ignoring her bitter protests before filling her to the brim once more.

Had minutes gone by—hours? All she knew was that she was exhausted. She began shivering with the cold from nerves. Carefully he held her tightly against him, providing soothing, stabilizing warmth.

She must have passed out, because when she next opened her eyes, Augustino was ferreting in the soft folds between her legs with a passionate, ravenous tongue.

No, she thought, her mind like mush, she had never done this before either. And as he deepened his foray with chin and mouth, she wondered why he had kept the sweetest, most paralyzing sensation for last. As he dispensed pleasures on her she never imagined existed, not even in her wildest fantasies, she decided she was entirely his—belonged to him from now on. She would never feel for anyone like this again.

What woke Amanda next were not Augustino's caresses. He was stretched out on his stomach, asleep. His arm was draped over her midriff. She took comfort in the fact that he wasn't snoring. He looked just as passed out as she had been, lucky to be sleeping soundly.

She noticed that Dino was sleeping at the foot of the bed. She tried to remove Augustino's arm so she could turn around, but he grunted and drew her closer. That's when she knew what had wakened her from a sound sleep. Pain. The persistent kind. A stubborn, throbbing soreness racked her lower limbs. Even her breasts were tender. She doubted she could get up to walk without feeling discomfort. Besides, she didn't want to alarm Augustino to her predicament.

She tried to inch away from him, hoping that curling her legs and lying on her side would relieve some of the pressure. She jumped when she heard his voice.

"What's wrong, Amy?" he asked, groggy; and she wondered how he even knew she had stirred.

"Nothing's wrong, Augie. Go back to sleep."

She heard him exhale a long, ragged breath. She saw him run his fingers through his hair, then push himself up to sit on the side of the bed. He remained prostrated there for a few minutes, then took a few haggard steps to the head. When he came back, he was carrying a glass of water and something else tucked away in his left fist.

"Here, Amy," he told her softly. "Two ibuprofen tablets. To relieve the pain. They'll help you sleep. You'll feel better in the morning." He looked at the clock and noticed it was almost morning. "Well, give or take a few hours."

She took them from him, surprised and grateful. "How did you know?"

"I should've realized it before—when I saw how tight you are. I'm sorry I was so greedy," he told her, lying back down and falling asleep almost immediately.

"Thank you," she whispered. With a little grimace, she propped herself precariously against the pillows and popped the tablets, downing her glass of water. He was the gentlest, least greedy person she had encountered. In fact, she was just as much to blame as he was, she considered as she lay back down on her back. As soon as she was horizontal, he turned to face her and drew her close, cuddling her against his chest with a sigh of satisfaction. "You're mine now," he mumbled, his words slurred. "You can't ever escape." He planted a noisy kiss on her temple. "I love you, Jersey girl."

Amanda wondered if he even knew what he was saying—or doing. The man had been tired and sleeping when she first encountered him up on deck. It's no wonder he was rattling on in a weird way. She hoped he would remember these last words in the morning but somehow thought they'd be gone, whimsically filtered and quickly evaporated as the sweet machinations of a dreamer often are.

Still, as tired as she was she lay awake for awhile, her heart aflutter as she stared at the disappearing stars one by one in the night's ebb, through the porthole in the ceiling. Smiling, she nestled closely to Augustino. Strange, she thought, how she now found peace and blessed sleep in the arms of the man responsible for creating such glowing turmoil inside her just a few hours ago. In the arms of the man she loved.

CHAPTER THIRTEEN

Scuba never happened. Amanda understood why they were not able to go so late in the day. Augustino and she had gotten up early afternoon, rested, happy just to lie on the beach and stare into each other's eyes. He had not repeated any sublime declaration to her, the memory of the previous early-morning confession long gone, just as she had suspected. But he was attentive, kind and veritably willing to fulfill all her little wishes.

"Let's get back to the ship. Darkness comes quickly, even in July." He held her arm for support as she slipped on her sandals. He led the way, holding her hand. "I promise we'll have time to dive in Harbour Island. There are beautiful reefs there, you'll love it."

Amanda agreed with a smile. It had been a wonderful day. Breakfast—or rather late lunch—in bed, Augustino's arm around her at every opportunity and the nice male smell of him never further than a couple of feet away, lolling on the sand and lunging in the surf together. “I’ve had a glorious time, Augie. You couldn’t plan a day like this.” She looked up at him. “Thank you.”

“I’m the one who is grateful, Amy.” He stopped and gathered her in his arms. “For the first time in...well, your... kindness, your generosity helped me forget the nightmare I’ve been living.”

He kissed her temple and her cheek while she closed her eyes, treasuring his breezy touch with the serrated breath. There were definitely deeper feelings emanating from his actions than his words. Amanda had the distinct feeling Augustino was holding back.

There was something he wasn’t telling her, some dark secret that accounted for the odd pauses, the faraway looks, the sudden withdrawals. She just hoped it wasn’t feelings for another woman. Connie came to mind on several occasions; although Amanda knew she had no way of putting dibs on him and worse, there would come a time when they would each have to go their separate ways. She also knew that she was in love with him—for better or for worse kind of love—the kind likely to last a lifetime.

She sighed. She would worry about that later. For now, she was going to make the most of him catering to her—hopefully all night long again.

When they got back to the ship, they had been boarded by the RBDF—the Royal Bahamas Defense Force—who were busily arguing with Raoul about something. Raoul’s hands were expressive and waving boldly.

"Does that look like trouble?" Amanda asked.

"Shouldn't be." Augustino picked up the pace and hopped onto the plank. Lending Amanda a hand, he walked over to the two officers and politely introduced Amanda and himself.

He took the customs officers aside for a private talk. Amanda saw him point amicably toward her and Raoul. Then Augustino went down to the safe in his office, came back and showed the papers Gary had brought with him. He then opened another folder and displayed forms Amanda had not glimpsed before. It was clear by Augustino's covert gestures that he didn't want her or anyone else to know what those forms represented.

Their little reunion lasted five more minutes, the time to verify everyone's passport before the authorities were on their way, seemingly satisfied and appeased.

"What was all that about, *amigo*?" Raoul asked Augustino. "They told me that we weren't supposed to be here one more day; that our papers weren't in order. Then you come along and they're all smiles and chuckles." Raoul was looking for answers.

"I told them I was here with my fiancée...that we had a long night." Augustino turned and winked at Amanda, smiling as he did. "Didn't get up early enough to leave on time."

"Oh yeah? What were those forms you showed them?"

"Leave it alone. We're fine, aren't we?" Augustino was adamant as he rounded up the papers to put them back in the locked file cabinet.

Amanda didn't dare say anything. She thought she might discuss the subject with him later, when the two of them were alone.

"Where is Gary, anyway?" Augustino wanted to know.

"I don't know. He and Albert went to town. Manuel is somewhere on the beach. He should be back in an hour. Should I have a key to that safe?" Raoul could not leave it alone.

"Hey, man. I said don't worry about it. All is well. No harm done."

Raoul recognized the tone and nodded with half a smile, giving Amanda a little hand salute as he went down to the galley.

Augustino glanced at Amanda. "Not you too," he warned pleasantly when he noticed her eyes the shape of question marks.

She shook her head, her face scrunched up with disdain. "Nah. Not interested one bit."

He knew she was lying—to please him. "Truth, Amanda. Remember our pact."

"Okay. So I'm interested—a little bit," she answered expectantly.

He smiled. He walked up to her and kissed her on the mouth. "Maybe later, okay?"

She nodded, placated—much more interested in his kiss than his explanations.

They ate on board by candlelight, leftovers from the day before, partly because Amanda wasn't very hungry and because Albert had returned too late to cook them anything new.

Gary was nowhere to be found. Amanda couldn't help noticing how worried Augustino was becoming. Not by what he said. More from a subtle fret in his eyes—him spotting his watch more often than usual. He jumped when Albert brought him the phone.

"Milo." Looking at Amanda across the table, he refrained from saying anything. He grunted and listened. Finally he added, "Good luck, friend. See you there."

"Was that Gary?" Amanda asked.

"Yes. He's going to meet us at Harbour Island."

"How is he getting there?" Amanda was curious.

Augustino looked at her strangely and took several seconds before answering. "Not with this ship, that's for sure." He knew that was lame. He couldn't chance any other reply for now.

It was enough for Amanda to get the picture. This top-secret stuff was annoying, she lamented silently. At least he wasn't lying to her. Of course, there were probably tons of omissions and maybe even little white lies—but she figured they were all part of the game.

Later Augustino told her he had an hour's work to do in his office. He excused himself but she called out to him just as he reached the top of the stairs.

"I'm turning in early, Augie. I'm tired and tomorrow will be another big day." She smiled at him, hoping he would give her some sign he wanted her to wait for him.

He walked back and kissed her on the top of her head. "I'll see you later, Amanda."

What was that, she wondered. Did he mean he would

wake her up when he got there? Would he be there before she fell asleep? Or would he simply slide into bed without waking her?

She still didn't know after soaking in the bath for forty-five minutes, or when she went to bed. She hesitated between wearing a nightgown and sleeping in the nude. It would be nice to stretch and feel his skin rub up against hers underneath the sheets. But being naked might make her appear desperate, especially if he wore clothing to bed. Although sleeping on deck with last night's cooler winds is what might have forced him to wear nightwear; somehow, under normal circumstances, she could swear he was a *buffer*.

She slid into bed and tried to stay awake, refreshing her memory with one of the scuba books he had loaned her. But as hard as she tried, it wasn't ten minutes before the book fell out of her lap and her head sunk deeper into two down pillows she had used to prop herself up.

By the time Augustino came to bed, he realized a little disappointedly that Amanda was sound asleep. As he watched her face, her soft, full lips and heard her steady breathing, his heart welled up with a tumult of passionate sensations—the memory of their previous night together still vivid. He also noticed that her head was twisted backwards and her neck bent in an awkward position. She would feel that in the morning if he didn't straightened her out somehow.

He hated waking her. She had had a rough couple of days. Gently he opted to remove the pillow closest to the bedpost. This way he wouldn't have to move her head. As he did, little Dino who had been sleeping, jumped up and began growling at him, barking fast and furious.

Amanda opened her eyes and smiled the instant she saw him bent over her, just happy he had come to bed and was kind enough to wake her. "Hi, I've been waiting for you," she told him, reaching up to press her lips against his.

He rose, a dubious look on his face. "You were sleeping soundly," he told her as he removed his bathrobe. She shivered when she noticed he was naked. She was glad she had opted to do the same. When he got into bed, she immediately cuddled up to him, her contented sighs deepening when he wrapped his arms around her.

"There, there," he told her, his husky breath warm on her forehead. He carefully kept his caresses to a minimum. "You should be sleeping, Amanda. With Gary gone, I thought of taking the guest quarters..."

She eyed him with such sad disappointment that his heart melted and he found the courage to explain. "It's been a long day. I caught you limping once or twice. You can't deny you still have discomfort."

"Hum!" she sighed, mollified at once. She began caressing his chest, working her way down to his stomach. Looking up at him with hungry eyes, she admitted, "I do have discomfort. My biggest one is this sensation of emptiness—not...being full," she added, tugging at his bottom lip with her finger.

"Goddamn it, Amanda. You're not making it easy for me to be considerate." He bent and sealed her mouth in a long hungry kiss. When he surfaced, he added, "Just the once, that's all. Okay? Do you agree to that?"

"Yes, sir," she teased him. "Once will do—for now..."

* * * * *

Amanda stood on deck leaning over the side. Her elbows resting on the railing, she stared at the choppy waters whirling and churning like in that deep boiling caldron Augustino had mentioned. A light windbreaker staved off the chill from an unusual northern breeze. Not minding the cool wind, wisps of her hair toyed with it playfully.

She wondered where everyone was. Augustino was nowhere. He hadn't even been there this morning when she and Dino had padded out of bed. It was the drone from the motors revving on and off at 6:00 that had waken her. She had not encountered Raoul either. She concluded he was probably in the engine room. But where were Albert and Augustino? Manuel, she knew, was sleeping. He had come back from partying very late the night before. As for Augustino, he must have gotten up before dawn not to wake her and be off the ship by the time she was out of bed. He was usually an early riser and certainly had no reason to be exhausted. Their night of passion had been tame compared to the previous one—though the *once* had escalated to *twice* easily enough, which was great. This meant Augustino had made strides in dropping that self-control of his. Actually, she smiled, he had proven much easier to handle than she had originally thought he would be.

She saw a taxi pull up, an old beat-up Cadillac. Augustino and Albert stepped out and headed for the trunk. Albert had done some shopping. Augustino was on his cell phone.

At the same time, Raoul came up on deck. "Just in time," he yelled at them, perching beside Amanda. "We're leaving in five."

"Were you waiting for them, Raoul?"

"Yeah. *¡Oye, tortugas!*" he yelled out to them. "He wants me to reach Harbour Island by lunch. With this wind and the Backbone to navigate..." Raoul may have felt like lashing out, but he kept smiling. He knew better than to argue with Augustino.

"I'm sorry, Miss Amanda. I'll have breakfast ready in a jiffy," Albert assured her, huffing and puffing as he came aboard.

"Don't bother, Albert. I've already had a couple of toasts and a muffin. I'm fine till lunch. But thanks anyway."

"Well, I'm starving, Alberto *mi amigo*," Raoul jumped in. "I'd love some of your eggs and ham."

Amanda tried to coin Augustino's attention, but he was on the phone and barely nodded in her direction. It's times like these when he made her feel like an intruder that she wondered if he didn't value his privacy above all else.

Raoul finally ate in the pilothouse, so anxious was he to be at sea. And just as Amanda was ready to give up on him, Augustino came out of hiding in his office to be with her on deck, slipping both arms around her waist as he surprised her from behind.

"It's a bit chilly out here this morning. But it'll warm up soon enough. Missed me?"

"Nope." She gave him an odd look, a slight shrug.

"Dino and I wondered where you were..."

"No sour grapes, Amanda." He pecked her cheek. "I kissed you this morning before leaving. You grunted and turned away. I suspected you'd had enough of me—so I left."

"You suspected right," she sassed him.

"It's okay to be turned off, you know," he added, nibbling her neck. "I understand. You know nothing about me, the man that I am—or very little. And I've spent the last few days groping and poking you as if you were the original Eve—the world's first clay creation. Frankly, I don't know how you can still put up with me."

That's the most he had confided in her since they had met. She would have loved to turn and see his eyes.

"Excuse me, Miss Amanda. You have a call." Albert handed her the phone.

"Who could be calling me at 8:00 in the morning?" Amanda gave Augustino a questioning look. He in turn urged her to pick up with a nod of his head.

She was surprised to hear Ginette at the other end. "Is everything okay, Gin?"

"Imagine my surprise...Hi. Hope you're having a wonderful time...when I come home last night and for the first time in two days decide to cook myself a little something to eat instead of hauling take-out. It took me one hour to find dishes...no, not true; it took minutes to find the pots and pans; more precious minutes to hunt for *my* dishes and an hour to replace everything. Please tell me that's not your idea of a joke?"

Amanda bit down on her bottom lip not to laugh.

"Sorry, Ginette. It's a bit of a long story. I'll explain when I get back." She eyed Augustino and mouthed the word *dishes*. He smiled and rolled his eyes.

"Speaking of owed explanations...ask me why I'm calling you so early?"

Ginette's shift was from 10:00 in the morning to 10:00 in the evening. This was early for her. "I give up, Gin. Why?"

"Because every social misfit in the county seems to have our number. Okay. I'm exaggerating. But there have been at least four calls in the last hour from work-buddies of yours. Here's a flash, girlfriend. You're not supposed to give out your private home number to hobos..."

Amanda gritted her teeth. "For god's sake, Ginette. You're a nurse; you're supposed to show some compassion. You clean bedpans for some of these hobos."

"My compassion stops at sleep. When I sleep, all bets are off. This REM time was my time to rest. Seriously, Amanda, are we going to have to change our number? What the hell's going on?"

"I wish I knew, Gin. Fiona Christian assured me that she would look into it. I have no idea how these people got my number."

"Newsflash. A Mr. Sanchez says you gave him our number."

"He's lying, Ginette. I can't imagine what he would have to gain by lying, but he is. It's the only explanation."

"You want me to blast Fiona? You just say the word and I'll do it. I never liked her, Amy. She's a two-faced bitch."

"Don't...don't...do anything like that." Amanda sighed

and checked Augustino's face. "Can you live with it for a few more days, Gin? I promise to take care of it the minute I get home. Meanwhile, take the phone off the hook. If I need to talk to you, I'll call your cell. The hospital always uses your beeper anyway."

"Okay. Look, I'm sorry for blowing up. Just...rewind this whole episode. Put it down to morning breath meets morning manners. You know. First toothpaste then coffee, I haven't had *any*."

"I hear you. Play nice with the other children and I'll bring you back a souvenir," Amanda laughed at her a little as she hung up to eye Augustino with a worried frown on her face.

He was staring at her in the oddest way. "What was all that about—I don't mean the dishes. I got that. But about Fiona?"

Amanda hesitated. She didn't like discussing work. Problems or not, the intricate workings inside the center were of a confidential nature. Complaining about Fiona would not help matters. But the eyes peering at her were the eyes of the man she loved, brimming with empathy, she thought—and some other element...curiosity perhaps?

"The morning you came to get me—Wednesday morning—Mr. San...a client called me at home. I was surprised. People we help at the center aren't supposed to have our private home numbers. But what was more disturbing is that he said I gave it to him..."

"Why would he say that?"

"That's just it. I have no idea. I would never give out

that kind of information."

"Who's the client, Amanda?"

She shook her head, meaning that she could not divulge that information.

"Sanchez? Juan Sanchez?"

"How...?" Amanda was more worried than surprised—preoccupied that this information had traveled much faster than she had anticipated. Augustino's eyes were probing and his expression unyielding—not foreboding, though. There was a definite solicitous tinge to his facade as he leaned toward her.

She remembered their night together, his gentleness and his thoughtfulness and trembled from the weight of a problem she had not foreseen to be this huge—not until now.

Mirroring herself in his eyes, she sidestepped the audacity that was intrinsic to her makeup. His willingness to help and his take-charge attitude clipped her sails, and for the first time in her life, her voice matched her thoughts—timid and tremulous. "When I reported this to Fiona, she seemed to think that maybe I had...given it to him...I mean, by accident. She even had me double-guessing myself; but then a couple of other clients called me at home."

Amanda bit her bottom lip. She wasn't going to shed tears over this—not in front of him. Crying was so not her thing. She dipped into her strength and continued. "That's when I knew there had to be a leak somewhere. I asked her to have Sinclair investigate." Amanda drew in a long shaky breath and after the slightest of hesitations, confided.

"Sanchez even had the name of our agent who lines up the job interviews for the people we place. That's information treated very confidentially."

Augustino searched her face with sharp, unwavering eyes. He then took her by the hand and nodded for her to follow him. Once in his office, he closed the door and offered her the chair directly in front of his. "Take your jacket off, make yourself comfortable. What would you like to drink? Orange or apple juice?" he asked her as he stood in front of the small refrigerator.

Amanda just shook her head. She was too interested in what he had to say. She knew it concerned work—but how?

"Tell me about Fiona," he asked, not looking directly at her while pouring himself a glass of orange juice.

"Fiona Christian? I thought you and she were friends." Amanda eyed him suspiciously. "Why don't you tell me exactly what you want to know? That would be easier, Augie. And how do you know about Sanchez?"

"Let's just say we are keeping an eye on *Señor* Sanchez. As for Fiona, she and I met four years ago through a mutual friend." He replaced the juice container in the sideboard refrigerator. "The FBI had her under surveillance for months when I was sent in to...befriend her." He sat down, legs sprawled, seemingly relaxed yet observing her every move.

"Why was she under surveillance?" Amanda had paled and was searching his face as much as he was hers.

"They suspected her and some of her superiors of falsifying papers to process undesirables into the country. We assumed she might even have ties to that mole I mentioned to you. The one responsible for creating positions with phony corporations—fronting for terrorist farms."

This was unbelievable, right out of a horror film—only Augustino made it sound real. Horror because she knew these people, had befriended them. She had worked side by side with Fi and Sinclair to help a slew of newcomers; all of them in terrible situations. They had laughed and cried together—lived through hectic deadlines. She could only hope Augustino was wrong. She knew he wasn't jesting; he was too stern and determined to be anything else than dead serious.

"You're speaking in the past. I imagine this means you have since cleared these people?"

Augustino shook his head. How could he tell her that she was the one the FBI had really wanted to investigate? That since she had shown up on his boat, they had gone back to the drawing board to re-examine her friends—that Sinclair and Fiona were guilty of murder and terrorism—that her friends were responsible for Emilio's murder. "The investigation is back on. That's all I can say for now."

"But how does this involve the center? Are you saying the Miami Center is part of your investigation?" Even as she formulated the question, Amanda shook her head, rejecting that very possibility. There had to be a better explanation.

He toyed with a pen that was lying on the armrest. "The center could be the vehicle she or they might use to legitimize their transactions. The Bureau had discarded Fiona as a potential problem these last years. I...didn't necessarily share their views. How did you get the job on my ship?"

She shrugged, recounting how Fiona had offered her the position and asked her not to tell anyone. “Twice a week, she had me bring fresh flowers and a few other little knick-knacks on board. She told me never to show myself to the owner. He doesn’t wish to have anyone see his face, she told me; not unless he had cleared them first—security, she said.”

Augustino shook his head with a dubious smile. “What kind of gizmos did she have you bring on my ship? Anything to do with a telephone prong?”

Amanda nodded and smiled. “Sure. You know. You’re the one who requested it...Fi said,” she shrugged. “You needed a double prong connector instead of the single one you...” She sobered and stopped in her tracks. Augustino’s eyes were ice-blue and piercing through her very soul. “What is going on?”

“What about Sinclair?” he asked. “Have you ever met him? Did you run errands of the sort for him?”

“Yes, of course I’ve met him. Augie, we worked together—on several projects. And no, never—no errands.”

“He ever do anything out of the ordinary?”

This felt like an interrogation and Amanda threw him a sidelong glance. “Not that I know of...although...” She stopped to think, remembering something that had puzzled her senseless. “...Now that we’re on the subject, a few times I questioned Fi as to why she reported to Neil on projects he had no authority to handle. They were totally out of his jurisdiction. Like the time she had asked for his approval to clear Trans State Transport as one of our job suppliers. It was none of his business—not in his department...”

"Trans State Transport? What is that exactly?"

"I was told they're an outfit not averse to hiring...non-Americans..."

"Like Cubans that cross our borders. Know who is in charge?"

He kept interrupting her with quick questions. Amanda felt pressed and leery of supplying too much information. She shrugged. "I'm not sure. He came to the center a couple of times. They call him Gary. It was always hush-hush when he did...come."

"Gary? That's it?"

"I think that's what it was."

Augustino rose abruptly and turned to the sideboard refrigerator. "Sure you don't want any juice?"

Amanda wasn't deterred by his tactic of changing the subject or by his sudden urge to hide his expression from her. "Augie, I've tried to answer your questions. Can you please tell me what's going on? I really need to know. Please?"

She sounded anxious, he thought dejectedly. *Gary! His name is Gary!* As he turned to face her, he had to steel himself to look through her—avoid those warm brown eyes that displayed worry and hesitation. Her whole demeanor craved reassurance and enlightenment he couldn't give her. Fists clenched for dear life by his side, he needed to remain impartial and keep his distance if he was going to resist taking her in his arms, confessing what he knew and cuddling all her fears away.

When no answer was forthcoming, Amanda took another tack with him. "You know Fiona always did the same thing to me—what you're doing now. She took pleasure in reminding me that her dealings were none of my business...out of my league, I believe were her exact words..."

"There's no need to compare me to Fiona Christian, Amanda," Augustino told her with barely hidden impatience. "I think I've demonstrated to you on more than one occasion that I do trust you." He nodded, his eyes branding their mark in hers. "The leap of faith is in your court right now. You're the one who is going to have to trust me."

His warm sustained glance created tingles all the way up her spine. But she didn't look away. She just had to know. "Are you investigating the Miami Center?"

He shrugged, trying to reflect nonchalance. "Obviously, we've known for a while that it's the ideal setup for someone to foster illegal aliens into the country. What better way for these entrants to show their appreciation than to swear allegiance to the better-paying mercenary groups." He could see that Amanda's eyes, her features and her body language were fast becoming hostile. He needed to tone down his approach.

"We're not investigating the center per se. This would mean suspecting everyone who works there." He conveniently omitted to say that they had already investigated the legitimacy of the center and found it to be authentic.

Amanda's shoulders relaxed somewhat. She still didn't understand what the fuss was about. "Why Fiona? What is she doing that is any different from what...Midge Parker is doing or...Neil Sinclair for that matter. They all exercise supervisory functions that are identical. They follow strictly monitored, preset rules. Any deviation would bring attention to themselves—in fact, would launch an *internal* investigation."

"Why is Juan Sanchez calling you at home?" He smiled, trying to put her at ease.

"I have no idea..." Amanda stared at him with wide eyes brimming with suspicion. "How do you know his full name?" she breathed. "That's confidential information, Augustino." Now she was more than wary, she worried that she had already said too much to him. Why couldn't he come clean with her?

Augustino also worried that he had said too much. He wasn't one for dancing around the totem pole when he needed information. Being forced to wear white gloves with Amanda curtailed his efforts.

He decided truth would best help her understand—part-truth at least. "Juan Sanchez is Conchita's husband. He's under close watch. Has been for the last two weeks." He waited for her to make the connection.

"Conchita—your...? I mean Connie? The woman I met?"

He laughed wryly. "She is not *my* Connie, and yes, one and the same."

"That's why she looked familiar. I had a photo for the files—obviously not a recent one," she said more as an afterthought when remembering the picture's youthful face and large mane of hair. "So that's why Sanchez never brought his wife with him."

"Connie always found an excuse not to go," he added.

"But why? Wouldn't it be easier for her to collect information if she followed him wherever he went?"

"She found other ways of gathering knowledge from his activities. If she had tagged along, first sign of trouble or proof of leaked information, he would have suspected her immediately. Besides, she didn't want to risk being recognized..." He trailed off. "We knew he was smuggling for years. Just never knew he was doing it through the center....How long has he been your client?" His tone was incidental as he tried to obtain information without ruffling her feelings.

"But why is he trying to enter our country through legal channels...if he is a smuggler? Is Conchita allowed into the US?"

"The Sanchez family is huge. Some family members, like Conchita and her two brothers, have dual citizenship. Others came through with investors' visas. Juan is using relatives and non-relatives as an excuse to bring undesirables into our country."

"I see."

"How long has he been your client?" Augustino would not be deterred.

"A couple of months. Fiona has been giving me more and more responsibilities. She says that it's time I expand my knowledge with new duties. Unfortunately, Sanchez is one client I don't need. I find him extremely difficult to deal with. For one, he's a liar. He came in the other day with a twenty-eight year old woman he claimed was his daughter, Maria..."

As he listened to Amanda rattle on about her problems with Sanchez, relief slowly settled on Augustino's features. A contented smile dawned on his face, lighting up his expression. Amanda had never been a suspect on his list and now, he had proof. Gary would have to swallow his phony accusations now that he could point the finger in the right direction.

Fiona Christian, the true suspected *white tiger*. She always had been. She and Sinclair were the only two capable of bypassing the system without being flagged. "I'm sorry," he apologized for his wide grin. "I'm not making fun of your predicament," he added, noticing the hard glint in her eyes. "It's just that I know what a hassle Sanchez can be. And for him to materialize a twenty-eight year old daughter, it's just funny—a grotesque sort of funny." *Obviously Fiona is unloading some of the burden on Amanda to try to finger her in the future. Why else would she leak her personal information to Sanchez? The idiot's only too happy to oblige, claiming Amanda gave him the number.* Were they scuttling this route in favor of adopting another one? "Does Fiona know you and I have met?"

"Don't know. I've never mentioned it to her..."

"Of course she knows," Augustino said more to himself. *That little listening device was her handiwork,* remembering what Bob had told him on the phone a couple of days earlier.

"She mentioned you'd told her you wanted to hire me—because you enjoyed my attention to detail. Did you ever tell her we'd bumped into each other?"

Augustino shook his head, deep in thought. So, Fiona was operating with the certainty that Amanda and he knew each other—probably counting on it and plotting around it.

Only with the connector removed, Fiona and Sinclair were driving blindfolded. "I'd like you to contact Ginette and warn her that if she ever speaks to Fiona or anyone else at the center, she not say where you are or who you are with."

Amanda nodded. "I'll call Gin right away..."

"Can you change your answering machine in Miami to say that you've gone home for the holidays—to New Jersey? Can you do that?"

"I can change my machine message from here....Augie?"

He looked at her, interrupting his musing. "Uh-huh?"

"Am I in any kind of trouble?" She searched his face and added. "Please tell me the truth."

"None whatsoever. Of course, except for the fact that you're working with barracudas and they can be unpredictable when threatened; but I won't let anything happen to you, Amanda. You have my word on that."

She nodded, a pale smile proving she trusted his chivalry to be sincere. "That's what I meant—by trouble. If Fiona is guilty of...whatever, and she knows I'm onto her, things could get rough."

"Hey." Augustino dragged his chair closer to hers. "I don't want you to worry. No one's going to harm you. Are we clear on that?"

Amanda nodded, a little color coming back to her face. His steel blue gaze was reassuring as she stared back at him with huge trusting brown eyes.

"Come on. Let's go on deck. It'll get your mind off of this; and we'll be able to help Raoul navigate around Devil's

Backbone."

She placed her small hand in his and admired his long tapered fingers. Clearly she recalled how skillful those fingers were at causing her body to quiver and tingle and she clasped his warm hand firmly. When she smiled up at him, he nuzzled the tip of her nose.

Coming upstairs, Augustino noticed that they had passed Ridley Head, avoided the three coral reefs off Ben Bay Beach, leaving them well to starboard, and were continuing past the Wide Opening and the three beaches, well on their way to Harbour Island.

"You're doing great, Raoul. We're dead on course." Augustino glanced at the charts, and Amanda helped by watching the landscape immediately surrounding the *Milan*.

"I don't like that expression—dead on course. I don't know why you didn't spring for a pilot." Raoul was sweating despite the on-deck pilothouse being sealed and strongly air conditioned.

"A pilot?" Amanda asked.

"You can charter a small plane with an experienced pilot to help you navigate the Backbone; or bring a captain for hire aboard," Augustino supplied with a smile. "Stop being such a wimp, Raoul. This way is more sporting."

"If I crash us on that rocky outcropping, you won't think so," Raoul added, ill at ease and not amused.

"The fact that you've spotted it is perfect. Leave it to starboard. And just make sure you leave the reefs on portside at a proper distance. We've engaged the Backbone now, and we've got no more passes until we reach the south of

Harbour Island."

"Look!" Amanda pointed a finger ahead. "You'll have to get closer to the beach." She was peering at the expanse of ocean with binoculars. "The water gets dark green closer to the beach and lighter green as you head out." She handed the binoculars to Augustino, proud she had retained her first lesson.

"She's right, Raoul. It looks like you have to tuck within 70 to 80 feet of the beach. We're passing Preachers Cave."

"Thanks, man. I thought you were never coming up." Raoul breathed noisily, relieved and happy to have company to share his misery. "I followed the familiar landmarks Captain Charles mentioned. Those that I can find. *¡Oye!* It's not easy to do. "

"That's what three pairs of eyes are for, Raoul. Relax, you're doing fine." Augustino slapped him on the back, trying to encourage him. "You want me to get you something to eat?"

"No, *amigo*. Albert just came up with refreshments."

Augustino kept his eyes on the charts. "In about fifteen minutes you'll have to increase your offing to avoid the shoal off Hawks Point. Two hundred yards north should do the trick." He handed the binoculars to Amanda. "The worst is over," he exaggerated to boost Raoul's moral and to tease him a little. "Amanda will direct us in the narrow passage headed to Monument Stake." He turned toward her. "Just identify the dark green blotches from the lighter ones," he smiled.

"How about I follow these bearings Captain Charles gave us," Raoul answered sarcastically.

"It's one way to go." Augustino mocked, obviously in a jocular mood.

Twenty minutes later, peering through the glasses, Amanda reflected. "What must that be like?"

"What's that you're staring at?" Augustino asked.

"Three lone houses on an island; talk about living in a remote area."

"Is one of them pink?" Augustino asked.

She looked at him, surprised; then returned to the glasses. "How did you know? One of them is pink—the biggest one."

"That'll be Pierre Island," Raoul was glad to know. "Thanks, Amanda. All I have to do is head for Prominent Beach and then follow Charles' instructions *exactly*."

The rest of the journey was accomplished in quasi-silence as they gazed at shivers of sharks swimming in the turquoise shallow waters, and further out in the open sea, Augustino pointed out to Amanda pods of dolphins dancing the bob in perfect synchronicity.

Nevertheless Raoul was glad when the time came to veer 90 degrees into Government Dock, by Dunmore Town. The traffic around the docks was considerable. But Raoul waited his turn, happy to arrive in one piece.

"Dunmore is three hundred years old." Augustino told Amanda who was searching the place with avid eyes. "It was once the capital of the Bahamas."

"It looks absolutely charming." She picked up the binoculars. "The sand is so white here the glare hurts your eyes."

The crossing of Devil's Backbone had taken them nearly two hours, Raoul not wishing to drive any faster.

Manuel stepped off the ship to begin mooring it carefully. "Your timing is perfect, Raoul," Augustino patted him on the back. "We're here in time for lunch and early enough to explore the local shops." Then turning toward Amanda, he smiled contentedly. "*Cara*, I am yours for the entire afternoon."

"What happens this evening?" she asked, noticing he had conveniently left it blank.

"I have a meeting with Gary and a few other people," he answered briefly.

She guessed the curt answer meant no invitation to either discuss it or attend it. She toyed with the idea of putting up an argument, but opted against it. She was here for a couple of days and intended to enjoy herself immensely. Especially since the earlier conversation in his office had left a sour taste in her mouth—one she intended dissipating quickly.

With Dino in tow they strolled down Bay Street, then up the hill to the Harbour Lounge. Lunch was their first port of call. Augustino had skipped breakfast and he was famished.

The girl invited them to a table beside a panoramic window overlooking the harbor, and got them a little bowl of water to accommodate Dino. Amanda was happy to be ashore and bask in the glow of Augustino's presence.

"It's breathtaking—the view from here," she added to answer his look of curiosity.

"I'm just glad you like it." He was glad the incident in

his office had not dented her appetite for adventure. She was a trooper and he was proud of how exceedingly brave she was. She had rallied quickly, agreeing to relegate the event to the back of her mind, it seemed. He was going to make certain she enjoyed her trip. Still, he was looking forward to their meeting with the fink—especially after what Gary and Bob had told him during their meeting aboard.

"Did you hear what I said, Augustino?"

"I'm sorry, *cara*." He bent over the table and kissed her lips. "I was thinking how beautiful you are in this sunny climate."

"Flatterer," she accused him. "You were not. You were somewhere else entirely." She caressed his hand on the table. "I asked you what you were going to have."

"That's easy. The lobster roll. You should try it. Manuel tells me it's good here." He smiled at the sun toying with the gold mesh in her hair. "That gold mesh—is it natural?"

She nodded. "It's an oddity, I know. But then again, I'm the only dark one in my family. The others all look like my mother, light colored hair and blue eyes. I guess I needed something to show I belonged—although my dad and I are identical—in coloring," she added wryly to wipe the raised eyebrow smirk off his face.

"I'm sure in other aspects you resemble more your mother," he couldn't resist adding.

"So what's this meeting this evening? And who are the people attending?" She asked buoyed by his good mood.

He placed their orders with the girl and took his time before returning her gaze. "Gary, Bob and I will be exchanging strategies; but first, a couple of locals are meeting with us to tell us what they know. They were the bigger reason for this trip."

"What kind of information?" she formulated, regretting it immediately.

He smiled. "More of that top-secret gibberish I have to keep secret for a while."

She nodded with a sheepish motion of her eyebrows.

"Jose Arroyo—you met him. He'll be there with some suggestions and valid input...and Connie."

Had he punched her in the gut, it wouldn't have had a more caustic result. Especially that he had added Connie's name as an afterthought, clearly knowing she would find it distasteful. But Amanda smiled. She wasn't about to allow anything to perturb this day. She was as tough as nails, she reminded herself as she bit into her lobster roll, ignoring his statement. "I hope you can clear up this mess—for all our sakes," she told him nonchalantly between two bites.

If Augustino was surprised, he hid it well. She spotted it though; paying specific attention to eyes that darted back to her—quizzical, probably wondering if she had heard him. But he added nothing. And she was happy with her decision to ignore the hurt; because the rest of the afternoon was lovely.

He lavished affection on her as they toured the sights, like the Governor's Mansion and the shops in the straw market where he bought her a few souvenir trinkets. They even stopped by Picaroon Landing to plan the next day's dive.

By the time they returned to the ship the sun was a timid orange ball and their midday snack long gone. Albert had fussed and prepared them a Bahamian fare of conch salad and mahi mahi filets soaked in rum, limejuice, onions and spices, with a side dish of pigeon peas and rice. The dining room table had been thoughtfully set for two and the smell of bread warmed in the oven wafted up from the galley.

"This is beautiful, Albert," Amanda smiled appreciatively. "I'm just going to freshen up quickly. I feel like the day's dust is blocking all my pores.

She scooted down to the stateroom and piled her soiled clothes in the basket under the sink. It felt good to take a shower and feel the water rinsing off her tired aching muscles. They had walked for hours under the hot sun, never stopping to rest other than to shop, curiosity blindly urging them on.

Humming to herself, the water spray jaunty and effervescent over her face and limbs, she never heard Augustino enter the head. Not until he opened the glass door prepped and ready to share the shower. She jumped, shocked to see him there. She somehow never believed he could be this familiar with her—at least so soon in their relationship. He smiled at her and set her heart aflutter.

"I hope you don't mind?" he asked tentatively, "since we are pressed for time. Albert will have a fit if we let the fish get cold....I thought it would be okay," he added.

"Of course," she answered timidly.

"Turn around," he told her with eyes on fire. "Actually, you are lucky that we *are* pressed for time," he teased. He took the sponge from her and washed her back gently and firmly. He moved in closer and encircling her with his arms, he poured more lotion over the sponge to wash the front of her as well.

Amanda closed her eyes as he slithered against her soapsuds back and exhaled little gulps of hot, sensuous breath on her neck. He spread the loofa sponge over her breasts, round her stomach and between her legs. Suddenly, the fish didn't seem so appetizing. She much preferred having Augustino on the menu.

"Now I'm only hungry for you, Amanda. I guess this wasn't such a time-saving idea after all," he added in her ear, echoing her own thoughts.

"I don't think we should disappoint Albert," she added in a soft moan.

He grunted a mumbled acceptance before moving away, quickly using the sponge on himself and leaving, allowing her to rinse in peace—or rather, in shattered pieces.

"I'll shave while I wait for you, Amanda." He dried while she rinsed. And when she reached for her towel from the bar, he interrupted his strokes with the blade to teasingly grab it and hold it at bay.

She gave him a wry look. "You would have me beg?" She asked him.

He laughed and unfolding the towel, wrapped it snugly around her, molding her every curve.

It was clear he was in a playful mood and she rued the fact he had to be out for most of the evening.

Enjoying dinner with him, sharing discussions about the lovely sights they had seen, comparing notes about the magic of this day spent together, was friendly and pleasant;

it left her worries of intrigue and espionage in the lurch, but it in no way dispelled the sexual tension he had revived in the shower, just one hour earlier. It was as thick and potent as dusk's humidity rising off the water.

"Don't wait up for me, Amanda." He told her as he kissed her goodbye. "I don't expect to be back before the early hours of the morning. I may even stay at the inn. Gary has a room there."

She nodded, her throat too constricted to talk. Connie's name was never mentioned, but she loomed between them as true to life as if she had been there in the flesh.

Barely thirty minutes after Augustino's departure, Amanda was already moping around—like an empty vessel without a purpose. She hadn't realized she was until Raoul pointed it out to her, derogatorily.

"What's a charmer like you doing alone on a gorgeous Bahamian night, smack dab in the middle of a pleasure island with no one around to show her a good time?" He wanted to know. He wasn't openly criticizing Augustino, but Amanda sensed he was happily trying to score himself good-guy points.

She shrugged with an ironic smile. "I've been left to entertain myself; and I'm lousy at it." All she could visualize was sensuous hungry Conchita hanging her arms around Augustino's neck—an ignoble waste of time, she realized.

"What do you say you and I go dancing?" Raoul was still wound up from his morning feat and desperately needed to let off steam. He was younger than Augustino, a couple of years, she guessed, and he was the same height as she, stocky, with pleasant Spanish features.

She laughed, thinking he was joking. But he insisted and she found herself staring into his smiling eyes, apprais-ing what Augustino might say faced with the same decision. Well, he was with Connie, wasn't he? He had no difficulty ex-plaining that he might be away all night—sleeping at the inn. And they weren't really engaged. This meant she was free to do as she pleased.

She looked down at the short skirt and off-the-shoul-der blouse she had put on for dinner and decided they were perfectly designed for schlepping around a dance floor. "Lead the way, Raoul." She raised her chin and looped her arm in his. "On to dancing."

"*¡Ole!*" He cheered beaming an excited smile.

CHAPTER FOURTEEN

Gary poured the third round of coffee. Augustino, Bob and he sat in his suite, their table fronting a panoramic view of a streak of pink sky quickly turning a dark shade of mauve over the harbor. Diligently they compared notes on new twists and turns, sorting through compiled information and searching for the quickest and easiest way to bring the two groups to their knees.

Jose sat alone in a small alcove, silent, his eyes glued to the palm trees below studded with the blinks of hundreds of minuscule white lights; he had been unusually sullen and generally moody since he had first arrived.

"So, you're saying that the Gary Amanda mentioned could be short for Garrison? Judd Garrison?" Augustino needed this cleared up.

"Not *could be*, Augie, *is*." Gary was bent from his chair, rummaging through papers on a small coffee table. "Hey! I hope you guys never thought that was me...?" Gary asked as an afterthought.

Augustino smiled with raised eyebrows and a dubious look on his face. "Mother T, jumping the fence? I don't think so." He laughed.

"He was spotted coming to and from the center—a couple of employees ID'd him. His appointment was with Neil Sinclair," Bob supplied.

"Kind of sloppy of him to let himself be seen like that." Augustino added.

"Hey! They never figured we'd find them out," Gary snorted. "That's like looking for a stupid word in a dictionary. First you have to *know* how it's spelled before you can find it and *see* how it's spelled."

Augustino nodded. "And Fiona?"

"It's confirmed," Bob added. "Jim phoned while you were having dinner. She's in cahoots with Hank Williamson—same as your Brad."

And when Augustino gave them both a knowing look, Gary added. "Please don't rub our noses in it. We're just as glad as you are about Amanda's innocence."

A knock on the door signaled that Captain Pike, lawyer Joe Frake and his client Henry Monet had arrived. Monet, a resident of the island, was the boatman Pike had fingered. Monet swore he was unaware that the clients who had hired him were human traffickers.

Augustino let them in, and after the usual greetings, the six men sat on opposite divans, ready to talk.

"You are well within your rights to have your lawyer

present, Mr. Monet," Gary began. "But if you maintain that you didn't know the group you were working with was smuggling people...to mercenary camps, then why would you need representation?"

Bob was quiet, leaving Gary to pose the questions. Discreetly he scribbled notes on a small pad while a tape recorder sat on the coffee table, its red light indicating it was hard at work.

Henry Monet was in his late forties, a huge black wall of a man whose nerves had him fidgeting with his keys and bathing in sweat despite the ice-cold temperature of the air conditioned room. "I'm not an educated man. Taught myself to read and write. I'm not familiar with the law."

Gary's back jerked from the comment. "You are familiar with what's right and what's wrong, I presume. Carrying human cargo from Cuba to the United States via Eleuthera is wrong, Mr. Monet..."

"My client has already told you that he didn't know the shipment left Eleuthera for the southern coast of the United States. It's not an obvious trajectory and I don't think you have to ask him again, Mr. Flint."

Gary nodded, surreptitiously looking toward Augustino. If there was a time he needed him to jump in with a line...

"Mr. Monet, can you describe the person who hired you for this particular job?" Augustino asked, scratching the question about why Monet hadn't noticed the transgression when Captain Pike, the one-time captain for hire, had spotted irregularities on his first trip with them.

He shrugged shyly. "I don't want any trouble." He looked toward his lawyer who nodded for him to continue. "I have a wife and three children. They need to eat. They need to be safe."

"No one will know you said anything to us, Mr. Monet. We will keep you out of the loop." Augustino smiled to reassure him. "We plan to put an end to their operation within the next few weeks—if not earlier. You will be a hero, not a villain. Your family will be proud of you, Henry."

"It's okay, Henry," Frake told him. "You're getting immunity for your testimony."

The big man nodded. Then he pulled a picture wallet from his jacket pocket. "These are my children," he smiled—a big bright grin. "My oldest boy is twelve. I'm proud of him. He's in school—doing good."

Augustino took the flap the man handed him and smiled when looking at a mirror image of Henry Monet, only younger and shorter. "Do it for him, Henry. He's a good-looking boy. He's worth it."

The big man nodded. "This Schneider fellow hired me. He said he was transporting tourists from Punta Cruz to the northern tip of the island. At first I believed him. Then, I had my doubts..."

"Don't say that," Frake interrupted. Turning toward Gary and Bob, he reiterated. "You can't use anything he says against him. We have a deal."

"Relax, Freak..."

"It's Frake," the lawyer corrected with a murderous look.

"Yeah, Frake. That's what I said." Gary shrugged. "Anyway, we told you. We don't intend prosecuting your client. Please continue, Henry," Gary added.

But Henry hesitated.

"What made you suspect they weren't tourists?" Augustino asked calmly.

Another shrug from Henry. "I found a weapons locker on one of the trips. Lots of guns and weapons. Then I heard a Spaniard fellow..."

"Sanchez–Juan Sanchez?" Augustino wanted to know.

Henry Monet shook his head from side to side. "Fernandez. He talked about the military camps..."

Gary, Bob and Augustino stared at each other. "Would you know where these military camps are located?" Gary wanted to know.

Monet stared at his shoes for a few seconds. "I remember they talked about two locations..."

Bingo! Gary mentally enthused. "We've got them."

"I'm not sure I can recall the names–exactly," Henry added.

"Wait a minute," Augustino suddenly wondered out loud. "Do you happen to know this Fernandez's first name?"

"No. They used a nickname. Hawk. He looked strange with his red hair. Didn't look Cuban."

"Sweet Mary Joseph!" Gary sprang up and began pacing, hitting his fist against a glass hutch.

"There's your mole." Augustino told both FBI agents. He got up and walked the ten feet to the small kitchen.

The three of them stared at each other then looked toward Jose Arroyo and Captain Pike. Nothing more was said. Now was not the time to air out the department's dirty laundry. "I'll notify Internal Affairs," Bob said simply.

"Wait before you do," Augustino suggested as he got up to walk the ten feet that separated them from the kitchenette. "The effort will have to be a coordinated one."

Wheeling a cart carrying a tray of refreshments towards the two groups, Augustino asked the three men sitting on the opposite divan to be discreet with whatever they heard in the room. "Help yourselves. There is soda in the refrigerator if you don't like beer," he added, seeing Henry Monet hesitate with a choice of beverage.

"Thank you." Henry Monet was quiet as he threw a side-glance to the men in the room. He opted for a soda instead.

"Sure, Henry," Augustino told him, sensing the man had a lump he needed to get off his chest. "Come, I'll show you where the glasses are." He waited for Henry to rise and follow. Once near the kitchenette's counter, away from prying ears, Augustino told him matter-of-factly. "I got the feeling you wanted to keep those locations to yourself, Henry...those military locations." He added when Henry's eyes questioned him. "You were smart to do so. It's good not to let everyone know. I'm right aren't I?"

Henry hesitated. "No one can know I told you, Mr. Milan," he whispered. Reassured by Augustino's assent, he admitted. "One of the locations is the air strip on Walker's Cay."

"Walker's Cay?" Augustino asked.

"Forty miles north of the Grand Bahamas Island, there is an air strip that takes up most of the island. Behind one of the main hangars, there is a huge shell where they have training facilities, weapons; also in one of the three smaller hangars, I heard them mention it. And they use the airport as testing ground for new flyers."

Augustino acknowledged with a slight nod of his head. *That's why they ship these people via Eleuthera. The training is done on these islands.* "Anything else on that island?" Augustino whispered as he poured him the soda.

"Usual tourist places. And great fishing." Henry's bright, wide smile was back. "My cousin caught an eighty-pound dolphin there in '89. It was a record."

"I see," Augustino smiled back. "The other place?" He asked, trying not to appear too eager.

"Charles Island—on the south side. I heard them say they had their headquarters supplied by one of the locals. Someone who has property there."

"Hey, what are you two whispering about over there?" Gary asked, his question drawing the attention of Henry's lawyer, Joe Frake.

"You're not being harassed are you, Henry?" Joe asked.

"Mr. Milan was showing me a selection of drinks," he answered gruffly.

Trailing Henry back to the living room nook, Augustino endeavored to catch Gary's eye. He had vital information to share with him and Bob—information that could not be discussed in front of Jose Arroyo. Time was of the essence. They had to find a way to dismiss their party of three and to conclude their discussion with Jose, before they could safely take a stab at Henry's intelligence.

Sitting on the edge of his seat, he patiently waited for his guests to down their glasses. He looked at his watch several times—a sign they had predetermined—meaning they needed privacy and had gathered enough information.

Thirty minutes later, Gary finished with the list of questions he had lined up sensing Augustino had the goods he needed. He got up, politely thanked the three men for their cooperation and, with a thin smile on his blond face, extended his hand in readiness—his haste to close the meeting evident to all. He waited as the trio rose and reciprocated the polite gesture. "We appreciate you taking the time and trouble, Mr. Monet." Gary concluded.

Augustino did the same. "Thanks, Pike. It's men like you that make it possible for others like Henry here," he patted Monet on the back, "to get out from under." He shook Pike's hand vigorously.

"My pleasure, Milan. If you ever need a good captain, you know where to find me."

"Frake," Augustino continued, "Thanks for your cooperation. Can we call again on Henry's help in the next few days—should he remember those military sites?" He didn't want anything mentioned in front of Jose Arroyo, nor did he want Frake to know that Henry had already handed him the locations.

Frake checked with his client; Henry Monet gave a

hesitant nod and a sad smile. He would help. He wanted to help, he repeated when he shook Augustino's hand.

After their departure, Gary and Bob began listening intently to the taped conversation. As for Augustino, he nodded surreptitiously to Gary's silent question. Without fanfare, his narrowed eyes elicited him to be discreet. They would talk later.

Jose sat in a corner brooding, utterly surpassed by the previous events. "All I know is that you people need to better protect us." He suddenly spoke aloud, not encouraged by the recent meeting. "Had it not been for Anton, I would be dead by now." Jose was angry. His bodyguard had taken a bullet for him at the airport. "Lucky he was wearing or he'd be dead too."

But Augustino ignored Jose's rantings. Gary, Bob and he had played babysitter since the beginning of their meeting—long before their three visitors' arrival. "I'm telling you," Augustino got up and began pacing, "in my mind, especially after what our informants just told us..."

"Why are *they* so important? We—my people were once all you needed." Jose spewed.

Augustino threw Jose a sobering look that had him shrug and taper off. Shaking his head, Augustino repeated as if dazed. "You guys found your mole." He still couldn't believe that fact, in awe of how readily they had been handed the information. "After four years of searching. It hardly seems possible." He sighed, silently consulting with Bob and Gary—not wanting to say too much in front of Jose.

"Why, you think it's too easy—that it's a plant?" Gary

added.

"No. Not at all. I think it fits perfectly. I'm just sorry we didn't discover this four years ago." Augustino was relieved.

Bob had not said a word. When Gary and Augustino looked his way, he shrugged. "What? I don't know what to think." He added. "After what we've just heard, with what Jose's people have corroborated and after our epiphany with Jim and Fred, I worry they're getting ready to scuttle the route. They're all of a sudden loose with this stuff. I mean, it's coming out of the woodwork—they can't be too panicked—one week, two tops, someone pulls the rug...again..."

"I disagree. We know who the players are. They can't run and hide...or blame anyone else. We've got them." Augustino nodded emphatically.

"I'm with you, Augie," Gary added enthusiastically. "They'd have to shovel shit awfully fast to dig a disappearing hole this time—not to mention make time to stake a couple of patsies or willing sacrificial lambs."

"Like the Cole girl," big burly Bob sneered. "They've hung so many nooses around her pretty neck, she'd be the first to go down—if we didn't know better," he added, putting up his hands to calm the storm brewing in Augustino's eyes.

"Brad's another patsy. You can bet Hank's going to leave him out to dry. And I hope to hell they screw Sanchez to the wall," Gary added.

"Sanchez is a likely candidate," Augustino said. "Although, he'd have to hand over damn good evidence if he wanted to cut a worthwhile deal...he's in this up to his eyeballs—one of their key players."

"I pray Hank's their little lambkin. There's nothing I'd like more than to see that son of a bitch go down," Gary stated ruefully.

"He's the one likely to collect heads on a stick, not be their scapegoat," Augustino added. "Anyway, forget about the scuttle. The likelihood of them making a run for the hills is out. Since we now know that the two groups are working together, we join forces with Jim and Fred on this one." Augustino rose and began pacing the small room. "Newsflash! I'm not letting them skedaddle. I'll go to hell and back if I have to. I mean, we had Fiona Christian and Neil Sinclair in our grasp...." Augustino showed the palm of his hand clenched tightly. "Then Hank gets Emilio killed—I still can't believe that idiot got away with this for so long." Augustino hung his head. "Then with the bullshit they serve us, we become suspicious of other people."

"When Amanda Cole showed up at that party with a ticket belonging to Fiona Christian—yes. That little bit of travesty threw a wrench in our wheels," Bob admitted. "I mean, she leaves the party with Emilio and Emilio is shot and killed not ten days later..."

"Yeah, well, if your intel hadn't told us Amanda was Fiona, we could have avoided a lot of this crap," Augustino countered.

"How the hell were we supposed to know that?" Bob countered back, feeling the sting of Augustino's words. "She had Fiona's ticket and played it like she was her. And Fiona and Sinclair checked out. They had alibis for the time of the murder and were in no way related to the thugs who killed

Emilio—at least that's what it looked like."

"Come on! We spent weeks thinking that she was," Augustino added. "Then I meet the real Fiona and discover that the girl at the party is a phantom—lost, never to be found again."

"We didn't even know we had to hunt her down," Bob added, "until all the evidence was completely destroyed. Can we help it if the girl was a ghost? We couldn't collect fingerprints or anything else after the party was a wash...no one could identify her picture...." As an afterthought he added. "What didn't help was Emilio sousing her with alcohol. She was so far gone he couldn't get an address or even a name from her. I was afraid to stand too close to her with a lit cigarette, is how drunk she was."

"Rookie mistake," Gary conceded. "Emilio mistook innocence for hard core resistance."

"Can we leave my brother out of this? His soul rests in peace and I don't want his name shoved around by you people." Jose's mood was deteriorating.

"Sorry, Jose. Emilio was my friend too," Augustino muttered. Shaking his head, he smiled ruefully. "That first day I met Christian, I almost had a heart attack."

"We all know why...," Bob added with a dig in his voice.

"Let's keep this friendly, guys." Gary warned, leaning against the wall. He smiled, looking at Augustino. "Well, at least you've found her," he said kindly.

Augustino threw them both a brooding stare before sitting back down.

"Listen," Bob told him, "after what you found out from Amanda, and from what these people have just told us, it would seem they've been setting her up for quite a while... satisfied?" Bob was trying to make amends. "They've probably done the same to others. Now all we need is proof."

"Yeah, well it seems Jose was right after all," Augustino added. "The Havana Club is to be blamed for the deaths. They may not have been the ones who pulled the trigger, but they're just as guilty as if they had."

Jose was quiet.

"What are you *not* telling us, Jose?" Bob asked. "Whatever it is, you've been choking on it all evening."

"He knows what Conchita told me last Tuesday evening," Augustino announced. "What Gary risked limb and life to retrieve yesterday morning."

Gary nodded in Bob's direction. "I didn't have time to say anything, man. Sorry. But we're even 'cause I don't know the whole story."

Augustino continued. "Conchita overheard Sanchez talking to one of his lieutenants. He was talking about never having retrieved a key from Emilio. One was arguing that it was lost, the other was cautioning that it could still be out there."

Jose was unhappy and determined to show it. "I don't know why you didn't let my sister in here. Why she has to wait downstairs, in her room—like an intruder." He felt he needed to come to Connie's defense. "She's been a big help. That's why she's here today. She risked her own life to do this. Now, she's scared."

"My god, man," Bob insisted. "Does this mean that Sanchez ordered the hit on Emilio? How hard must that have been for her to hold it together...when she heard...?" He glanced at Jose with a little more compassion in his eyes.

Augustino shook his head. "He was nowhere near Emilio when he was shot. Not him or anyone who works for him."

"What's this key?" Bob asked.

"Conchita remembered that one was included with Emilio's belongings when they sent her brother's things to her. I guess the guy who killed him didn't have time to do a thorough search. Alejandro must have scared him off that night."

"It was me," Gary added. "I scared him off. Go on."

"It opened a safety deposit box at Bank of A downtown Miami. In it was nothing out of the ordinary. A couple of papers and a roll of film marked, 'family picnic, summer 1990'. The caption had been written by Armando."

"I escorted Conchita to the bank," Gary explained.

"Okay...." Bob hesitated. "So what does that have to do with our problem?"

"For some reason, Armando never had it developed. Then Armando is killed. And Emilio never gave two hoots about it. He had told Conchita about the film and had decided not to bother with it, leave it where it was. She forgot about it until Sanchez brought it up."

"And...? Geez! Would you look at me," Gary smirked. "I'm holding my breath here."

"The last I heard, Conchita was having the film

developed by a trusted friend."

The three of them consulted silently, and of a common accord glanced at Jose for enlightenment.

"Is this what you've been dying to tell us all evening, Jose?" Augustino asked him point blank.

"Never mind the pictures," Jose Arroyo continued in the same whining tone of voice. "My sister has them. And yes, they have been developed...but we cannot find any proof of anything on them."

"You should let us be the judge of that, Jose," Augustino admonished. "We might be able to recognize some of the players on these pictures."

"Well, you're not getting them from me. Conchita will need to give her consent. She will give them to you...if you do not treat her like *una inadecuada*." He got up, reached for his briefcase and threw a folder on the table in front of them.

Augustino reached for it. "More withheld evidence? What's in the folder, Jose?"

"You have my permission to look at it, Milo. It is not withheld since I have just received it from my sister—more of Conchita's hard labor of the past few days." He spoke with his hands. "She has sacrificed much for this cause. Now, she can no longer return home." His words were solemn and his voice strained. Having finally spit up the chunk that had soured in his belly all evening, he sat deep in the lounger next to the sofa and dropped his face in his hands.

Augustino sat next to Gary and Bob, gazing at the first few pages of a stack of memos and letters. The missives were handwritten, in poor Spanish and faded in certain areas; but he could still make out their content. He straightened with eyes wide and darkly sullen.

"It's a contract to kill," continued Jose when Augustino didn't utter a word. "That's why Connie had to leave in the middle of the night—abandon her children. She's heartbroken. She tried to tell you on the phone the other day, Milo. You wouldn't listen."

Augustino shook his head. "I swear to you. She never mentioned this. She was angry when she discovered Amanda was accompanying me to the Bahamas. That's all she ranted about; besides, there's a contract to kill Amanda here as well." Augustino appeared ashen under his tan. He stared at each of the men with a hard glare. "Did any of you know about this?" He asked them, swallowing hard.

Both Gary and Bob swore they knew nothing.

"I only found out tonight," added Jose.

"The double murders again. Their diabolical payola system." Gary slammed his fist down on the table beside him.

"It says here," read Augustino, "that she's scheduled to go north by car for the holidays...they must have called her machine," he muttered to himself. "It describes an accident...a plant of incriminating evidence in her car and in her apartment—that's probably why the home phone number was given out—in readiness."

"And when it is written in ink by one of my countrymen, it's as good as written in blood!" Jose shouted.

"I guess you foiled their attempt by having her with you," Gary added. "You best keep an eye on her, friend." When

Augustino eyed him strangely, Gary continued, "Look, Augie, we all know how you feel about her—how you really feel; I mean she's a wonderful person; we all know that now. But like it or not, she's in this up to her eyeballs—if unintentionally, mind you. But until this is clinched, you should make sure she's permanently glued to your hip, buddy..."

"By the look of these letters, we have enough to indict." Augustino changed the subject with more pressing matters, not wanting to have his personal life discussed openly in front of Jose.

"You can't." Jose was pacing frantically. "Connie's children are on the island. If she moves left or right..."

"The man wouldn't kill his own children," Bob protested.

"The rat would kill his own mother to get away," Jose clamored, turning several shades of red.

"I thought you said he didn't know that Connie had this file," Augustino asked.

"It is true. He does not know she copied the file. Until he does, he's not going to run or try to harm anyone," Jose added as he stared at the three men. "But if you make a move to indict your pathetic friends at the other end, then he will hide out there and hold the children for ransom."

"He's right." Gary told them. "He hasn't crossed stateside since Amanda last saw him in her office."

"How do you know this?" Augustino was surprised.

"Hey, we've been busy." Bob added. "We've had a tail on key players and border guards have been on the lookout for a list of people. Sanchez is one of them."

Augustino smiled. "That means we're right. We've got their asses on a burner and they know it."

Gary and Bob both nodded, the information dawning on them as well.

"Where are the children now?" Augustino asked.

"They're on Charles Island—a little atoll off the coast of Spanish Wells. He has a hacienda there that they've used as a holiday home for years."

Juan Sanchez's house—the property Henry mentioned. No wonder he wants to get rid of Connie. Maybe she knows more than she is letting on.

"It's one of those gingerbread houses," explained Gary. "Not especially big or likely to be booby-trapped."

"*Si, Si*. This is correct." Jose harped, downing the dregs of his scotch. "Unfortunately, it is like a fortress because he owns acres of land around it; land that is so flat he would see anyone coming for miles. And the local authorities will not touch him unless we can *prove* beyond the shadow of a doubt that he has done something wrong."

Augustino shook his head. "Even if we showed the locals this incriminating evidence, it would take weeks before they'd even agree to set the ball in motion."

Bob was curious. "How is he planning to...well, to get rid of his wife?"

"It talks about a Cessna incident," Augustino explained. "I imagine they own a small plane?"

Jose nodded, hands in his pockets, deep in thought.

"It describes problems with the fuel line." Augustino was curious all of a sudden. "Who flies this plane?"

"My nephew Eduardo. Connie of course. Mostly Eduardo. He learned to fly he was barely ten years old. I can't believe Juan would do this to my sister and to his own children—to leave them motherless...to threaten them... "

"Relax, Jose." Augustino tried to calm him. "He's more likely to keep them away from Connie—isolate her with this plane accident. Does Eduardo know his way around a plane?" Augustino was hoping he did. Usually small plane operators needed to know their craft inside and out should anything happen to leave them stranded.

"Yes, he does. Why, you have a plan?"

Augustino looked at each of them, the etching of a smile lighting-up his face. "Gentlemen, I think we can begin to envisage the light at the end of a long and dreary tunnel. It's going to take some quick planning and urgent action—the sweeping kind—if we're going to throw a net over all the intended parties before the rats can run and hide."

He glanced at Gary and Bob who consulted with each other before turning back to Augustino to nod their tacit agreement of full cooperation.

Turning toward Jose, Augustino asked. "What day is Eduardo's birthday exactly?"

"How did you know? It's on Wednesday." Jose eyed him suspiciously.

He shrugged. "Connie told me. She plans to surprise him with a nice gift—she just doesn't know how nice." Augustino turned the paper around so Gary could read. "According to this scribbled note in the margin, Juan plans to send Connie to Abacos with the two-seater—maybe to run an errand."

"So?"

Augustino smiled. "This is where it'll get interesting." Turning toward Gary and Bob, he added. "If we orchestrate our roles with extreme precision, we can lay down the law and serve these bastards with indictments sooner than we think. The trick will be to use the smallest net possible to reel them in; I don't want *anyone* escaping through a loophole." He turned toward Jose. "Come on, let's go get Connie."

Augustino knew that to thwart these people was to prevent any accident from harming Amanda. Amanda's death would be the one thing he knew he would never survive. As Gary already suspected, he loved her deeply. She was all he had thought about for so long—almost four years. Now that he had slept beside her, known the sweet ecstasy of loving her, she was more vital to him than food and water. So why had he not told her, he had berated himself on many occasions. It meant admitting he had fallen in love with her previously, admitting who he was and talking openly about his covert operation. He had put it off until the time was right. And now that the time was right there, broaching the subject flustered him more than taking on all of Sanchez' men. What if she took one look at his tortured soul and saw him for the pathetic lovesick idiot that he was? Would she lose interest in him?

Connie leapt on Augustino the minute she saw him. He bent to disentangle her arms from around his neck. "Conchita, please. All of us are here to talk to you, to help. Behave yourself," he admonished as she pouted openly as soon as she was free.

The men decided it would be better to discuss their plan out in the open than in Jose and Connie's room. They opted to take a table in the lounge of the bar, left of the lobby. The rhythmic raucous sound of tight-skinned bongos and the strident winces of guitars from three locals decreased their risk of being noticed or overheard.

Connie agreed wholeheartedly with the men's decision and sat beside Augustino. Her hand resting on his lap, she looked up at him with sad, bewildered dark eyes and begged for his help.

"Of course we're going to help you, *cara*. I have a plan. All of us need to refine it, is all."

"Should we tape this, Augie?" Gary asked.

"By all means. These steps lay the groundwork for all the *rest of it...our own efforts* we need to coordinate," Augustino specified, raising his eyebrows toward Gary and Bob. They understood that more information would need to be factored in after Jose and Connie's departure.

"Let's tape *and* take notes." Bob surmised when he glanced at Gary, eyes wide with meaning.

Not an hour into their meeting, Connie noticed a couple gliding on the dance floor nearby, attracting the attention of onlookers with some fancy steps. She recognized Raoul. She had danced with him many times and knew his style well. She wasn't sure who his partner was but she called out to him excitedly, partly to attract Raoul's attention, partly to let the others know the handsome Spaniard was on the premises.

Augustino glanced in that direction and held his breath when he recognized Raoul's partner. It was Amanda. She had just thrown her head back and was laughing as she endeavored to follow Raoul in executing a perfect mambo. Both immersed in the music, neither of them had heard Connie's call. Augustino disciplined the pain he felt at the sight of Amanda at ease and amused in the arms of another man. So, this was jealousy, he thought. He cringed, realizing he had no right to refuse her the pleasure of dancing with whomever she wanted. And he wouldn't have minded had Amanda's heart belonged to him. As it was, their engagement was bogus to her. She had no concept of how he felt which at the moment was tortured and deeply lonely.

"Isn't that Amanda?" Gary asked. "If it is, you should warn her, Augie. She shouldn't be out in public without protection—not until we've cleared this mess."

"How dare she come here!" Connie was on the warpath. "She follows you to spy on us. She is a traitor."

"Calm down, Conchita." Augustino told her, his eyes not straying from the twosome in front of them. "She's just enjoying herself. There's no law against it." As he finished saying those exact words, Amanda looked up and saw him, her smile quickly waning. The pain dug deeper inside his chest as if she had wedged a knife in his heart, driving it in further, without mercy. Why did the sight of him not thrill and excite her—at least as much as Raoul's presence seemed to make her laugh? Why was she suddenly sullen and quiet—worried even?

He excused himself, got up and strode toward them.

He smiled when he approached her. He told Raoul to go look at the bar for a drink with his name on it.

"What are you doing here, Amanda?" His voice was surprisingly soft and she physically stepped back from the odd sadness in his eyes.

"I could ask you the same question? I thought you had a meeting; and here you are in a dance bar cozily sitting beside modern-day Lolita." She couldn't believe she had just said that. Only the worse nag would have snapped those petty words. "I'm sorry, Augustino. I can see you're busy...and rightly solving complex matters..."

He smiled teasingly, a little ray of hope back in his eyes. "You wouldn't be jealous now—would you?"

It wasn't a question. It was more like a statement he desperately wanted her to acknowledge. The man was strange, she decided. But he could still make her head spin. She shook her head. "Your spare time is your own affair, Augie—just as mine is," she asserted. She literally wished those last words not be true, even as self-preservation demanded she show him nonchalance. But had he played truth or dare with her this exact minute, he would've caught her nose extending a few inches.

"Well then," he mocked her with the tilt of his head. "How about a dance with a modern-day Casanova?"

She bit her bottom lip, but then gave in and laughed. "That you are, my friend. That you are."

When the dance was over, Augustino bent and kissed her lips, tenderly at first, then hungrily driving his tongue deep inside her mouth. She moaned and quaked against him, returning his kiss with equal ardor, so glad he had taken the initiative.

"Can you do me a favor, Amanda?" He asked, catching his breath and leaning his forehead against hers.

Eyes closed, she nodded without speaking, dazed and trying to steady her wildly beating heart.

"Please have Raoul take you back to the boat. I can't tell you why right now." He saw she wasn't about to comply without an explanation. He caressed her arms, shaking her a little, staring deeply into her eyes. "I'll explain tomorrow," he told her. "I did say *please*," he smiled, prepared to beg for her cooperation.

She nodded. "Shall I wait for you...tonight?" She asked, trying not to seem too eager.

He shook his head, his eyes darkening. "I still don't know how long I'll be." He kissed her forehead and motioned to Raoul who was standing by the bar, impatiently looking on for his cue to return. "Take care of her for me, *amigo*."

Amanda watched as he rejoined the little group at the table. It was strange how little Raoul's presence meant to her after all.

She had come there on a lark, the excitement more in thwarting Augustino's sensibilities than dancing with Raoul. Secretly she had wished him a little jealous. But he had passed with flying colors, she thought ruefully. He had been remarkably calm and pleasant—indifferent was the word that unavoidably sprang to mind. What else could she expect? Their union was a sham.

She thought of the words Albert had told her once

concerning Augustino's feelings for her and shook her head, disavowing them completely. He had made a mistake. There was no other explanation.

At the table, Connie's face was mutinous. The feral femme fatale was in the throes of a painful discovery. She had witnessed the all-consuming kiss between Augustino and Amanda. The kiss Augustino had refused every female since she had met him, since he had first started hanging with her brother. He had even refused to so much as peck her on the lips. Her eyes were dark as she watched Amanda and Raoul leave. She would think of some way to discredit the intruder, to tear the two of them apart. With her husband out of the way, Augustino was going to be hers, she vowed.

CHAPTER FIFTEEN

Amanda had her wet suit in the bag next to all the other equipment Augustino had just rented for her from one of the larger diving schools on the island.

She had refused to let him to purchase the gear outright, even though he had extolled the virtues of possessing the equipment. She first wanted to sample a couple of dives.

Seated in the small boat about to bring them to a bigger rig, they were waiting for other would-be divers to file in and fill up the rows of stripped wooden laths posing as benches.

"We're just going down twenty to twenty five feet for now," he told her, scrunched down beside her. "But first," he smiled at her wide-eyed expectancy, "we're going to go over what we discussed earlier."

She nodded, staring at the handsome picture he made in his bright yellow sleeveless top and black bathing suit. As he continued giving her vital instructions, she couldn't help wonder where he had spent the night. He had already eaten when she had gotten up at 8:00 and was busy in his office. Had he come back in the early hours of the morning? Or had he slept elsewhere and arrived in time for an early breakfast? She didn't want to think about Connie. That would've spoiled her day right and proper. Now he was waiting for her to acknowledge and she hadn't heard a word he had said. "I'm sorry." She told him sheepishly. "Can you repeat what you've just said? My mind was wandering..."

He shook his head, breathing out a little frustration, put his equipment down and sat next to her. He stared at her and she smiled at him. But sensing he still didn't have her attention, he cupped her chin in his hand. "What's on your mind, Amanda?"

"Nothing—I mean, not anything important. I'm looking forward to this dive—honest."

He watched her closely, the eager smile, the need to please. "Truth," he said, melting a little from liquid soulful brown eyes. "What's really bothering you?"

She tugged at his arm to free herself and looked away. She supposed being as tough as nails meant not fearing the truth. "I went to bed late. I'm just a little lightheaded."

"You waited up for me; after I'd specifically asked you not to." He couldn't help a crooked smile.

"I'm not a child, Augustino. You don't need to remonstrate to me as if I am. So I unconsciously waited for you, I guess," she admitted. "I just couldn't sleep."

The impulse to berate her was strong. But the contrite gleam in her eyes and the warm, tingling thought that she had yearned for him inspired him more to nurture. "Had I known you were waiting for me, *cara*, I would have joined you." His voice was a whisper and he felt the tugs of an equally strong yearning—the burning, aching need to confess to her how he really felt. He adored her and hated concealing it from her. Omission *was* an untruth, he recognized, able to cloud and shroud the purest of intentions.

"I came in around 2:00. I looked but saw no light under your door. So I crashed in the guest stateroom." The love oozed out of his every pore when finally he saw the relief in her eyes. He smiled at her, grateful she was eager to believe him.

"Thank you," she nodded and smiled, stroking his cheek with shy fingers. "Thank you for telling me. You didn't have to, you know."

"I know." He caught her hand and kissed it. "Now can we get back to this dive?"

"Absolutely. I'll be the best student ever...I guess you had a lot to discuss with your friends..."

Augustino couldn't tell her that Jose and Connie had left around 12:00, and that Gary, Bob and he had continued planning and strategizing for two more hours—not without explaining why. "We worked out a lot of details," was all he added with a smile and a shrug. There was also no point in cranking up her interest at this juncture. Not until he had secured his operation. "So how about you recap for me the pointers I gave you." He sat, arms crossed and laughing at her a little.

"Okay." She flexed her fingers. "I know. The reason

for the wet suit is to protect from the coral, other floating debris and from the varying water temperatures—not to annoy me or make a foul fashion statement." She laughed when she saw him shake his head and roll his eyes with a dubious smirk. "I can adjust my BCD," she added as she pointed to it, "for buoyancy; and my weight belt will help me stay down." When he nodded, she continued. "Never, never hold my breath under water—especially when surfacing. Never climb too quickly—slower than my bubbles. Or I'll get the...bends?"

"Amanda," he intervened. "Pretend that your body is a soda bottle. Under water, it becomes pressurized and extremely sensitive—like when you shake a pop bottle. If you depressurize too quickly—remove the cap—the nitrogen in your blood bubbles—overflows and is released through your system. These bubbles lunge for your joints and arteries. It can be extremely painful; can even cause death..."

"Like the mess caused by spilled soda," she exclaimed, a light tease in her voice. "What?" She added to his pointed stare. "It's extremely sticky—very difficult to wash off the floor..."

"This is serious, Amanda."

"I know, I know."

"You remember how to clear your mask?"

She nodded. "And I remember how to unblock my ears. I pinch my nose and blow out through it. Why do we have to go out with a group?" she asked, noticing the clunky boat filling up fast with all types of people. "They all look so much more experienced than I am."

"They'll go their way. You and I will stay together.

They're going down to see the wrecks. There are many. Some as shallow as twenty feet. But all we're doing is letting you get comfortable with the equipment, okay?"

She nodded. She was worried about the mild claustrophobia she had suffered as a child resurfacing. But the instant she bit down on her regulator and plunged to follow Augustino. At once she fell in love with the liquid freedom the peaceful swab-colored ocean dispensed. The silence enveloped her and calmed all her apprehensions. The only problem she discovered—which Augustino silently pointed out—was her tendency to hold her breath. It was strongly ingrained. She would have to remind herself constantly to inhale and exhale.

He pointed out two small plastic baubles floating in front of them and she thought they might be part of a wreck from some ship. But she enjoyed more gazing at the multitude of fish in all sizes and colors swimming alongside. At one point she followed a school of yellow tiger fish while the slew of them gathered around her. She would have loved to know all the names to their particular species. Where was that underwater camera she had purchased at the souvenir shop? She fidgeted to find it on her outfit but realized she had left it on board the small boat. The next thing she realized was that Augustino was nowhere around. She was lost.

He had taught her how to read her compass. A lot of good that did her when she didn't know from which way they had started. Right now she wished she had paid more attention to his lecture. She had turned around to stare at the fish, and now she didn't know which way was back or which way was forward. They had discussed this contingency. She would swim another ten minutes or so, then, if she couldn't get her bearings, she would very slowly surface.

As she swam, she found it strange that she couldn't spot any of the other divers. She looked above her and couldn't see the sun anymore. Maybe it was getting cloudy. Too bad, because she could've used that sun to help her navigate. Before setting out any further, she checked her compass—in case she ever needed to double back. The important thing was not to panic, which is what her lowly brain very much wanted to do right now.

As she swam on, she noticed it was getting darker and wondered if she wasn't going deeper by mistake. She could not tell up from down anymore, as it was just as dim above her as it was below. She was laboring to breathe and that was annoyingly impossible—with the regulator refusing to dispense more air than it should. Frantically taking in more air would not help find Augustino, she reasoned. She would have loved to call out to him right now or see him appear in front of her. She would head out for another five minutes in the same direction, then double back.

Having executed what read like the planned five minutes on Augustino's diving watch he had insisted she wear, she noticed a bright ray of light ahead that looked to be close. She swam toward it and noticed on her compass it was coming from the east, always further and further away. She headed in that direction, and after ten minutes—an eternity it seemed—she came to an opening the size of a large person. She hesitated a moment, looked at her surroundings and concluded she was in some sort of cave. Out there was where she had to be. She swam through the opening the other side and in the distance spotted other divers—no Augustino—but life other than the gilled kind.

Looking back, she wondered how she had entered a cave without realizing it. No wonder the sun had disappeared. And had she tried to surface, she would have been in for some surprise. Tricky, this vast ocean, she surmised, very tricky.

She decided she would swim toward the group of divers rather than surface, not sure of where she was. As she rounded a corner, she heard a strange noise—high pitched like a reverberating muffled clank of metal.

Unable to determine what that was, she lunged forward to meet up with the swimmers she had spotted in the distance. At least they were *human* salt-water dwellers.

But her swift kicks mounted to nothing more than a slow crawl. The ocean's dense placidity dampened her impatience, which was just as well since upping the pace with all her apparatus was difficult. She tempered her reckless breathing. It wouldn't do to run out of air before she got there. It felt like plodding against a gutsy wind, held in check by Mother Nature. And the high-handed efforts to reach her destination quickly plucked her spirit, leaving her tired, worn—and not a little bit giddy.

She felt something grab hold of her fin. Was she stuck in a crevice, caught in some vines, or had some bigger fish dubbed her as lunch? She panicked. She squirmed and twisted, trying to turn to face her enemy.

Once the bubbles had cleared her mask, she saw that

the fish face behind her struggles was Augustino, closing in on her fast. He wasn't smiling and was—green around the gills, she thought, dizzy and feeling the urge to laugh while hilarious strips of comedy danced through her head. He took hold of her belt and tugged her along. He motioned for her to breathe slower as they began their ascent.

As soon as they surfaced, he took his mask off and told her to follow him and swim ashore. They beached on an abandoned stretch of sand, maybe half a mile from the marina where they had started, and as they took off their suits in silence, she wondered why he seemed so furious.

"What's wrong, Augustino?" She felt spent from raw nerves and relief—an odd mixture of sensations tingling all the way down to her toes. She laughed as she stared at him sitting in the sand with his face in his hands.

"Do you know what you put me through?" he finally uttered, looking at her with a contorted grimace. "I thought I had lost you. I looked everywhere—behind me, beside me... didn't you remember...my signal? Didn't you hear me tapping on my tank with my knife? Where were you?"

"Will I get a cigar if I answer that?" She laughed at the look of shock on his face. "I'm sorry." She continued laughing, flopping down on the sand beside him, holding her sides from splitting. "It's nerves I guess. I can't stop laughing. And it's not even funny." After bouts of giggles, her smile changed to a frown and tears began pouring down her cheeks.

"You're shaking," he muttered. He scooped her up in his arms and held her tightly until her sobs subsided, rubbing some warmth back into her senses.

"I'm sorry," she hiccupped. "I got into this cave by accident and then it was like the whole ocean was closing in around me." She mumbled incoherently. "I missed you so much. I thought I was never going to see you again."

"Oh, Amanda!" He kissed her cheeks, her neck and her ears and molded her snugly to niche against him. "Never in all my years did I witness such a lamebrain performance."

She gently jabbed her fist in his back. "Hey, watch the name-calling," she complained in a teary voice.

"Sweetie, you had to follow me closely. That was the whole idea of this exercise."

"I tried. You were swimming too fast."

He moved his head back to kiss her teary eyes and salty lips. "From now on, I don't want you further than one step behind me, at all times; understood?"

"How about one step *beside* you," she added pointedly, sniffling into a tissue he had handed her from his pouch.

He smiled and readily agreed. "Nice to see the ocean hasn't dampened your spirits," he remarked with a dry chuckle.

Gazing at her dewy eyes and pouting lips, his touch suddenly took on the sensuous feel of a hungry burn. His fear of losing her, the worry of Sanchez' threats and overseeing her safety had compounded and grown, transforming a need to reassure into a physical need to assuage.

Before she had time to protest, Augustino sealed her lips in a long and ardent kiss. And when he surfaced, he stared into her eyes as he plopped her down against the hot, silky sand. Deliberately he tucked down the top of her bathing suit. He cupped her breasts, avidly taking a hungry mouthful of any piece of her he knew to be soft and pliant—to prove the taste and smell of her was urgent and foremost on his mind. No one and nothing could take her from him when he bore her this close.

She tried to complain that they were on the beach; that anyone could see them. But insistent fingers probing inside the bottom half of her suit, deftly, sensuously exhorting her legs to spread melted all her inhibitions.

It was then that she spotted it. Half dazed, wallowing in the pleasure of Augustino's caresses, she caught the vague outline of a large dark figure cropped against the glare of the sun. Her muffled scream—still a sharp dissent above the ocean's roar—curbed his ardor.

Was he hurting her? Breathlessly he apologized and searched her tortured eyes for clues.

But she shook her head, her eyes indicating someone staggering toward them on the beach not fifty feet away.

Augustino rose quickly, leaving Amanda to fasten the top of her bathing suit. Sensing trouble, he ran to the broad figure emerging from the froth of waves barely able to walk a straight line toward them.

Bending over the slouching man, Augustino recognized Henry Monet. He was bruised and battered, laboring to breathe. "What happened, Henry?"

"They picked me up off the pier...took me out to sea...tried to kill me. I jumped overboard." He was gasping, speaking in short spurts. "Frake's dirty." He breathed the words out seconds before he slumped to the ground, bleeding profusely and clutching his left arm with a grimace of pain

Augustino searched the ocean for a ship or a bobbing craft. “Did they see you get away?”

Henry shook his head, his wild eyes large and haggard. “My family needs protection, man. You need to help my family. They shot at me. I think they think I’m dead.” Those were the last words he uttered before he collapsed and lost consciousness.

“We’ll get you out of this, Henry. Don’t worry.” He walked over to Amanda and calmed her down with the wave of his hand. He picked up the cell from his satchel and called Gary.

“Who is that man, Augie?”

“Part of the cavalry...Gary, Henry Monet’s lying on the beach near Picaroon Landing. He’s been beaten and shot in the arm. He needs a medic—and protection. How fast can you get here? Oh, and don’t let anyone know he’s here, especially not the lawyer.”

Amanda wondered if she shouldn’t head over to where the man was lying, his face buried in the sand, barely out of the surf. She might be able to help.

But Augustino ran back toward Henry, ripped off a piece of his shirt using his pocketknife, and applied a tourniquet to Henry’s arm. Then he yelled at her to leave—to leave her gear on the beach, and head toward the marina. Manuel would pick her up to take her back to the ship. He would see to the scuba gear.

It was during the long walk back to the ship with

Manuel that Amanda concluded that overall her first diving experience alarmingly resembled her first love-making experience—a stumble in the dark, over in a jiffy and not a little bit scary.

Even scarier was Augustino's call after lunch, informing her that they were dining on board with Gary Flint, Bob Farrell, Jose Arroyo and Connie as guests. Eating aboard ship she didn't mind. She had not been spending a lot of time with little Dino lately and she missed him. But seated at the same table as Connie she did mind.

"We're probably going to talk shop this evening, Amanda. Don't be alarmed by what you hear or what you don't understand, okay?" Augustino was putting on a white smoking jacket over a light blue shirt she had picked out for him. He knew she was only partly paying attention. "Amanda, are you listening to me?"

"Uh-huh," she answered automatically, too engrossed with the charming way he looked to care about any trivial, boring piece of news they were likely to discuss around the table.

She turned her back to him so he could tie the diamond clasp at the back of her dress. He had suggested she wear the same little number she had worn on Paradise Island and she had agreed, just happy to please him. "Is that man going to be all right?" She had heard the ambulance as she had obediently walked toward the marina. Her thoughts at the time had been mostly about Augustino. How she would play the church mouse if it helped smooth his troubles, ease his burden. She worried about him. That he was in some deep dark sort of trouble. The kind he couldn't discuss with her—which did not augur well, a nagging little voice kept repeating.

He sat on the bed, asking her to sit beside him. "Amanda, there are a lot of...details I haven't...explained to you yet. Like the reason I was so concerned about the man we encountered on the beach. His name is Henry Monet, and...he... was shot. Someone tried to kill him."

"I heard you tell Gary that he needed protection..."

He nodded with a frown. "And someday, I'll tell you all about him....In the meantime, if you hear something that doesn't make sense this evening, I would rather you shove it under the rug for now. You know, not ask for any explanations at the table. Can you do this for me?" He smiled at the earnest way she was staring at him and knew her mind was still on the couple of hours they had just spent in each other's arms. He knew. Because he found it just as difficult to return to normalcy after reveling in the oneness they had just shared. He kissed her lips. "I don't know how you do it," he told her roughly. "Somehow, making love to you gets better each time we're together."

"I agree," she whispered in his ear.

"Amanda," he shuddered, "I promise I'll give you chapter and verse tomorrow. It's just that it's a long story. I can't go into it before everyone arrives."

"I understand, Augustino," she told him softly.

"I had planned to do it earlier. But then...well, we spent the afternoon otherwise engaged...don't take it as a complaint." He pleaded when he noticed the rise of winged eyebrows. "I wouldn't change one minute of the time we shared this afternoon. I think you know that," he cooed, eyeing the creamy white curve between her neck and shoulder.

"I just wish we didn't have to entertain all these people tonight," she answered, rising and walking to the commode to pick up her watch. She stared at their image reflected by the mirror above the dresser, and held her breath at the sensuous glint his brooding eyes deployed as they polished the back of her. She closed her eyes, basking in the warm feelings he churned up inside her and valiantly told him. "Let's get this show on the road."

Albert had outdone himself. They had lengthened the dining room table and the porcelain and cutlery were a pristine white and gold, shining from the soft glow of large candles. Manuel was tending bar and Amanda spotted two magnums of champagne in large ice buckets on each side of the counter.

On the menu was roast pork, roast duck, and conch chowder, accompanied by peas, spiced kidney beans and rice. There were also a variety of salads and fresh rolls.

"This looks like a celebration dinner," Amanda smiled. "What's the occasion?"

"Hopefully reaching the end of a very long tunnel," Augustino replied. "We've found solutions to our four year old dilemma. At least, we hope we have."

"Of course we have," thundered Gary as he entered the dining room. He was slightly shorter than Augustino but slim enough to appear tall. He kissed Amanda's hand and gave

Augustino a warm pat on the back. "Thanks to this man of yours, Amanda. He is a tactical genius."

"Beady-eyed lawyers usually are," Augustino supplied.

"That can't be true," Amanda argued with a smile. "You don't have beady eyes."

"You have wonderful eyes, *querido*," Conchita Sanchez affirmed as she confidently made her regal entrance into the dining room, her arm looped in her brother Jose's. She threw Amanda her darkest and most scathing glance. She had imagined her red sheath would be most revealing and very sexy; even so, she realized it was not as enticing as Amanda's chiffon.

"Good evening, Conchita," Augustino greeted her with a peck on the cheek. "Jose, glad you could make it." He quickly resumed his place beside Amanda. "I hope we can reach a consensus during this wonderful dinner Albert has prepared," Augustino patted him on the back as he was carrying in more goodies, "with Manuel's help, the talented man who can do just about anything." He smiled at the younger man who was always available to lend everyone a hand. "Didn't Bob come with you, Gary?"

"No. He's taking a cab later. He's arranging round-the-clock surveillance for Henry Monet while he's at the hospital—and for his family. They've been moved," was all he said on the subject. "Plus the last I heard, he was still trying to get clearance for your...plan. That's a big ticket item."

"I've already told you which route we'd take if they don't release the budget," Augustino said. "I'll end up using it instead, if need be."

"That's big of you, man. We'll just have to play it by the book for now," Gary added.

Augustino was right, Amanda thought. She didn't understand a thing they said during dinner. He had specifically asked her not to comment or ask for explanations. She didn't. She just hoped no one would ask for her opinion.

Connie, on the other hand, seemed perfectly knowledgeable with every little detail. And as dinner unfolded, Amanda realized the topic of conversation revolved around her. She gathered her children were in trouble; that Sanchez was trying to harm her and that they were discussing ways of communicating with Eduardo—her eldest son. A slew of names were mentioned, all of them strange to her except for Henry Monet. She gave up trying to make sense of their conversation.

For the rest of the meal, she tried not to listen; and she found it was much less frustrating. Nevertheless, she was glad when the ordeal was finally over. She had been as quiet as a mouse, trying not to show her ignorance of the matter.

Trying not to choke on her last gulp of coffee, she juggled with mixed feelings of awe and anger, glancing at Augustino seated at the head of the table. He had had all this time to brief her. Why hadn't he told her something—anything? She felt as helpless and dumb as a fish out of water—or more precisely, like an Amanda *in* the water—swimming with fins and scuba gear.

When time came for everyone to retire, it was very late. Augustino smiled at her and gathered her up in his arms.

"You were wonderful," he whispered. "I promise to clear all this up for you tomorrow, okay?"

She nodded, her cheek rubbing against his chin, still more than miffed.

"What's wrong, Amy?" He drew back when he felt her stiff and rigid instead of yielding and tender.

"Nothing's wrong, Augie," she edged without looking at him. "I've had a very long day."

He watched her in silence for a few seconds. He knew she was lying to spare his feelings, to avert an argument—that she was angry, confused, and not about to admit it.

"How about I use the guest quarters tonight? It'll give us both time to...rest. Get a good night's sleep."

She looked up at him and nodded, her bottom lip quivering at the thought of not spending the night in his arms. He was right. They both needed time off from each other to think. She also realized how disappointed he was with her answer. His eyes grew somber and the little muscle in his jaw began twitching—a sign she had come to read as deep frustration. She knew how much he wanted her. She could feel his desire pulsing against her hip.

But he smiled, kissed the back of her hand and walked away. She stood there for a good five minutes, unable to rid herself of a wrenching sense of loss. A morbid, inner hunch screamed at her that she was never going to see him again; which was ridiculous. He would explain everything in the morning. Then they would be back to...what? What were they exactly? Best of friends—no, that wasn't it. They hardly knew each other. They weren't star-crossed lovers—nothing as glamorous. Perhaps two partners who happened to be sexually compatible—very compatible as it turned out. Well, she couldn't speak for Augustino, but she was in love with him. She sighed, aching for his presence, thinking that she should have followed her earlier goal to ignore the hurt and grab the pleasure. If only he had given her a little time after the others had left, time to regain her senses, swallow her damn pride. She even wondered if it was too late to change her mind.

She ran down the stairs but saw that the hallway was dark. She walked down the corridor that linked her room to the guest quarters and noticed the light underneath his door. She heard a soft rendition of *Harbor Lights* playing somewhere on the docks outside and applied her hand to knock on his door. She feathered the texture of the wood instead, caressing it with the tips of her fingers. She hesitated, turned and left quietly. The pride she couldn't quite swallow had grown to choke all her good intentions.

She did find sleep. Exhaustion had her out like a light in minutes; and when she awoke, she rubbed her eyes and looked at the clock. It was nearly 9:00. She got up, quickly showered, put on a bright-colored summer dress and donned flat sandals. She rushed upstairs with her hair still wet, in a hurry to catch Augustino before he left. She knew he was meeting with Gary and Bob this morning.

"Hi, Albert," she smiled, trying to hide the pain of her disappointment. Albert was having breakfast in the dining room, which could only mean that Augustino had already left.

"I'm sorry, Miss Amanda." He rose apologetically. "I thought you had eaten."

"No, Albert. I haven't. Can we eat together?" she asked, not wishing to interrupt his meal and needing the company.

"Certainly," he answered politely.

"Hey, Amanda," Raoul called out to her from the top of the stairs, bending over the railing in the pilothouse. "You're a sleepyhead this morning. Augie told me to tell you that he's coming back around lunchtime. To stay put until he returns." He executed a little army salute indicating he weighed Augustino's orders very carefully. She acknowledged with a little laugh. The day was brightening up. He wanted to see her the minute he returned.

"I guess he had to leave early this morning...," she said more to end the long silence between them.

Albert smiled politely and nodded. "Would you like something more generous?" He indicated the toasts and croissants. "Eggs and ham, perhaps?"

"No, this is fine. I'll have a little of that orange juice." She pointed to a half-full pitcher on the counter next to Albert.

Albert reached up to fetch it for her.

"Coffee?" he offered while he was up.

She nodded. "Thank you, Albert." Hesitantly, she continued, "I guess you don't know much about what he and Gary are up to—or do you?" She hated asking Albert about details Augustino had not yet supplied. But she needed to validate that he cared for her, even in a remote sort of way.

"Very little I'm afraid, Miss Amanda. But I do know

that Master Milan is a fair and decent fellow. He will explain when he feels the time is right."

"I'm sorry for asking, Albert. I certainly don't want you to betray Augustino's trust."

He said nothing.

"I guess you heard about our encounter on the beach yesterday—Henry Monet?"

Albert shook his head. If he had, he wasn't saying.

"It's just that last night...everyone seemed to be aware of...well, of whatever is going on—everyone except me."

"Life is strange, Miss Amanda." He paused with an enigmatic smile on his face. "Just when you believe you are nothing but an innocent bystander, deliberately kept on the sidelines—at bay from a brewing storm, you look up and discover you're in the calm of the eye of that same storm."

Amanda stared at him, a puzzled frown across her brow. Did he mean to say that she was at the center of this whole confusion? That didn't make sense. He couldn't mean she was at the center of Augustino's universe. Was this his way of saying that she was kept unaware as a form of protection? That if she was to move left or right from that eye, she would be in danger? What was he saying? Why was he speaking in riddles?

Just as she was about to test Albert's comment, putting down her second piece of toast for later, a black Mercedes pulled up. The driver stepped out to open the passenger door and Connie emerged, looking fresh and proper in white cotton pants and a pale pink crewneck shirt. She waved the driver off and came aboard.

"*Hola*, Alberto," she greeted him, surprised to see him at the table with Amanda. "Would you be so kind as to make me your special breakfast? You know the one I like," she cooed.

"My pleasure," Albert answered, putting his plate and coffee mug on the tray to carry them downstairs.

Amanda had the impression his term of *my pleasure* was broad and vaguely exaggerated; but she bit down on a wide smile at the look of commiseration on Albert's face as he brushed past her.

Determinedly, curiosity thrown in there somewhere, she turned her attention to the woman seated in front of her. She examined her yet again. And yet again she marveled at the fact that Connie had four children, one of them a teenage son. She barely looked out of her teens herself. "If you're here to see Augustino, he's at a meeting with Gary and Bob," Amanda told her, not knowing why else the girl would be there.

"I know. I've just left him," she replied cattily.

So, Amanda thought. She had come to gloat.

"I realized last night at supper that you knew very little of what is going on," she added, pouring herself a cup of coffee from the urn. "So, I've come to make amends." Her smile was bitter honey, and Amanda was immediately on her guard.

"If it's for your awful manners around me," Amanda told her matter-of-factly, "you needn't bother. I didn't and don't really care." She looked her straight in the eye.

"You can't really blame me—for my bad manners, I mean." Conchita had straightened in her chair and her tone was contrite, yet haughty. "I hated you for so long, thinking you were responsible for Emilio's death."

Amanda smiled with raised eyebrows. "Excuse me?" The girl was nuts.

"You know, the suspicious way Emilio died not ten days after that party..."

"What party?" What was she trying to tell her?

"The Simon—the statue party in July 2000. When you left with him. My brother died not ten days after taking you to a hotel; we all thought you were responsible."

Emilio! That was his name. Amanda sighed. He was the young man she had left the party with that night. "What does that have to do with you?"

"Don't you recognize me? I was there...with Augustino."

Amanda searched her eyes and knew she was telling the truth. She cast her thoughts back to that evening. It took her a few minutes, but staring at Conchita's face, suddenly she did remember. She was that wild Spanish girl hanging on the arm of the most attractive, handsome man...at the time she had dubbed him the man of her dreams...that's where she had seen Augustino before. That's why he looked so familiar to her, why she wanted so much to be with him. The stranger with the deep blue eyes that had haunted her for months. Had she not been so inebriated that night, she would have remembered him immediately—when she first saw him on his boat. "Emilio was your brother?"

Connie nodded. "That's when Augustino dropped everything he was doing to hunt down his killer. That's why he first approached you," she added softly with candid eyes.

"Are you saying that Augustino first approached me because he thought I was...?" She just couldn't finish her sentence. "You're lying."

"What would I have to gain by lying?"

Amanda could think of at least half a dozen reasons. "What you're saying doesn't make sense. All they had to do was arrest me if they thought I had anything to do with... Emilio's death." She had vowed she would not let this girl get to her, but what Connie was saying was seeping through.

"He wanted to make certain that he got to the leaders of the organization. To arrest you would have meant revealing their cards too early in the game. Besides, they all thought you were Fiona Christian. You went to the party under her name."

"Well, yes. Because she gave me the invitation..."

"First, they discovered you weren't the real Fiona Christian when Augustino arranged to meet her. That's when she told Milo that she had lost the invitation when her purse was stolen. He checked with the police and there was a report for a stolen purse made out by Fiona."

"Why are you telling me all this?" Amanda asked in a small voice, on the edge of her chair and ready to bolt. "You just want me out of the picture so you can sink your teeth into Augustino," she rasped.

"Having a contract on your head makes you see life in a different perspective," Connie told her tearfully.

"What are you talking about?"

"Here, you have one too. We're both in the same boat." Connie showed Amanda the two memos she had copied from the file at Gary's expense. "We've both been...pried by Augustino...for information and eventually, he'll dump you just as he did me."

Amanda read the notes and her rudimentary Spanish was enough to understand what was written. She sat back down, deflated, her legs feeling like two boulders of lead underneath her. She already knew Augustino had used sex to pump Conchita for information. He had told her himself.

"There is a contract out to kill me—and one for you," Connie continued. "I could tell last night that Augustino had not told you. He doesn't care, that man." She wiped her nose with a tissue. "All he wants is to play his little games..."

Amanda remembered the first time she had met him on his boat. He had talked about playing games. He must have been shocked—and furious—thinking he was meeting up with the girl who'd....No wonder he sounded crazy.

"...they are conquerors," Connie continued. "They want to win at all cost." She paused, waiting to see if she had Amanda's attention. She placed a hand on hers and told her softly. "He told me about your engagement being bogus—you know, to extort a confession out of you—anyway he could, he added." She shook her head in disgust.

That would certainly explain the odd pauses, the blank stares and the feeling he was...not quite with her sometimes. Slowly but surely, the discovery of his treason spilled into her heart and invaded Amanda so strongly that she had no tears, no complaints, simply a deeply sad and depressing numbness—and a very dry and overwhelming desire to be elsewhere. He had told Connie about their bogus arrangement. What else had he bragged about? And she had given Augustino everything; her heart, her body, her soul even.

CHAPTER SIXTEEN

"Amanda, it's been three days. Don't you think we should talk about what happened?" Ginette was pressing her a little each day to get her to come out of her shell. It wasn't easy. Amanda was mutinous, having decided to spend the rest of her vacation in robe and slippers. She wasn't taking any phone calls and refused even to talk to her sister Meg.

"All right," she exclaimed, "if it'll get you off my back."

Truth was she needed to air out some of her frustrations. Desperately wanted to confide in someone. She was tired of feeling the pain of regret gnawing at her ribs. She had lost three pounds and didn't even care. She was just thankful Ginette had been patient enough to keep harassing her about it.

She recounted briefly part of the trip, the navigating through the Devil's Backbone, the scuba lesson. She talked about Paradise Island and all the places indelibly stamped on her brain. Then she told her about Connie's last visit.

"So you left, just like that. How'd you get here?"

"Connie knew a pilot with a small plane. She paid him—my credit cards were maxed," she added, teary-eyed. "He left me in Miami at a small private airport, near Biscayne Bay. I took the bus home."

"Just like that, without speaking to Augustino? Did you tell Albert or Raoul?"

"I told them I had to leave—a family emergency." She inched a look at Ginette who was shaking her head. "I had no choice. What was I going to say? That Augustino is a liar, that he took advantage of me and used me in the worst possible way?"

"Consider the source of your information, Amy. You could have at least given him the benefit of an explanation. Slipping out like that was so rude."

"You call me rude! What do you call his behavior?"

"I reserve judgment until I know for sure. All I know is when I saw that man, he was puppy-dog sick over you. He loves you Amanda, how can you not see that?"

"Remember that monstrous self-control I told you about? Well, strangely enough, he had none with me."

"Doesn't that prove he loves you?"

"It only shows me that he turns it on and off at will, meaning that he is still very much in control. Just plays it differently with different people."

"You're not making any sense, Amy." Ginette held out her hand to her. She didn't grasp everything that had happened over there. But she knew that she had never seen Amanda so miserable. She looked genuinely frail.

"Where's the ring he gave you?"

"I left it on the dresser in the master stateroom. He's bound to see it there. I wouldn't want him to think I was a thief as well as a murderer." She cuddled Dino in her arms, a tear falling on her cheek.

Ginette turned away. She fought back tears herself. She just couldn't believe that the man would do this to her. There had to be some sort of explanation. "You actually saw a paper saying that these Sanchez people are trying to kill you?"

Amanda nodded. "Has he called? No. Is he worried that I might be killed? Obviously not. That should sum it up for you easily enough."

"What are you going to do about work?" Ginette asked her softly.

Amanda shrugged. "I don't know. Face the music, I guess."

"I have a little money saved up. You could look for another job—or go up to your folks for a couple of months. I can manage the rent."

Amanda reached for Ginette's hand and held it tightly. "You're a real friend; thanks. But I have to get back on the merry-go-round, Gin. I'll go nuts if I don't."

Ginette got up to freshen up their pot of coffee. She heard a car door in front of the apartment and glanced to see who it was. She was expecting friends to pick her up to take in a movie. "It's the neighbor across the street. I'm going to call Jen to tell her I'm not going with them," she said.

"Don't not go on my account," Amanda told her.

"Nah. I just don't feel like going—there's that guy again. The one I told you about. He's forever parked on our side of the street in his annoying, stupid Porsche. Every time I come home from work he's sitting there, lurking at our building. That's my parking spot. God knows they're few and far between around here." All of a sudden Ginette and Amanda's eyes met. They had flashed on the same idea at the same time.

"You don't think...," Amanda started.

"It's not a Jag, Amy. Don't get your hopes up."

Amanda got up and joined Ginette at the window. "Ginette, do me a favor. Go downstairs and get this guy to step out of his car."

"How am I supposed to do that, exactly?" Ginette was nonplussed. For all they knew, this guy was an escaped psycho-sicko. "He's not Augustino, Amy. That's for sure. I saw him walking up and down in front of our house a couple of times. He's cute, but barely." But staring at Amanda's sad, disappointed expression, she ignored her saner side. "You think you would know who he is?"

Amanda looked at her with a pale smile. "There's one way to find out."

The phone rang and Ginette picked up. "You're circling—you can't park?" Ginette nodded toward Amanda. "Jen and Carol," she whispered. "I'm not surprised. There's never any parking around here. Hey, I'm about to dislodge a crank from my parking space. Want to watch?"

Amanda shook her head. She didn't feel like being the

focal point of any form of entertainment right now.

"Tell you what, Jen, why don't you and Carol go without me. I'll catch up with you guys later. Don't worry. I won't be long."

Ginette hung up the phone. Then she took a deep breath, smiled at Amanda and told her on her way out. "On me in three."

Once in the street, Ginette opted for the direct approach. She tapped on the man's window and signaled for him to exit the car. Amanda noticed a slight altercation as Ginette argued with her hands and the car's driver did not budge. Suddenly, a policeman walked by and Ginette made a motion to grab his attention. Immediately the man exited his car.

Amanda caught her breath. It was Jeff Nichols, from the marina. Why was he down there watching her apartment? Then she realized Augustino must have sicked him on her—the nerve of him. That was the only explanation.

Quickly she shoved robe and slippers in the bathroom and put on shorts, a top and her slinky sandals. In lightening speed, she gave her hair two strokes of the brush and without even looking, dabbed color on her lips. She flew down the stairs and Ginette nearly had a heart attack when she turned and bumped into her.

"God! You scared me...I was just telling this...person, Amanda, that he is trespassing. This is my parking space."

"Hey, Amy." Jeff ignored Ginette and riveted his focus on Amanda. "Looking good." He smiled at her in his usual corny way.

"You know this creep?" Ginette was happy, the façade

be damned.

"Yeah, I do. I can take it from here, Gin. Thanks a million." She pecked her on the cheek. "You should hurry to catch up with your friends."

Ginette nodded, and backing up, she raised her eyebrows in Jeff's back for one more affirmation from Amanda. Amanda nodded emphatically and shifted her attention to Jeff.

"So, why are you down here stalking my apartment? And don't even say you're not; and just so you know, there are laws against this." Amanda blurted out, animated by nerves.

"Slow down," he smiled. "I know the sight of me can sometimes cause excitement, but this is overdoing it a bit." He chuckled at the dubious look on her face and her hands-on-hips stance. "The big guy sent me—as if you didn't know."

"I suppose by big guy you mean Augustino Milan?" She couldn't believe how pronouncing his full name aloud got her hot and flustered.

"He's worried about you. Manuel has the night shift..."

"Manuel? But he was on the ship..."

"Left an hour after Augie discovered you were gone. Been with you ever since."

She leaned back against the side of his car, just now realizing the commotion her departure must have caused. "How is he bringing the ship back? Manuel was indispensable."

"A...Captain Pike sailed it back. He arrived in Miami yesterday. Augie had unfinished business over there. He kept Raoul with him."

"And Albert?"

"Came back with Pike's crew."

Jeff was certainly well informed, she thought. She wondered how much more he knew. "Anything else you should be telling me?"

He shrugged. "Hey, I'm not here to explain. Just to protect," he smiled. "But if you don't mind me being the buttinsky, I'm not surprised one more woman stormed out of his life."

Suddenly he had all her attention. She needed this type of reinforcement, when one more good deed from Augustino was threatening to have her hurl with panic, thinking she had made the wrong decision. *Bring it on*, her eyes conveyed.

"I've seen a slew of gorgeous women leave him already. Don't get me wrong. The guy's a saint—truly," he added when he saw her eyes conspicuous slits. "But he just can't commit. It's like he loves women for one reason only; then, when he's finished with them, he irritates the hell out of them until they leave. Is that what he did to you—what Connie is famous for complaining about?"

"I don't know what you mean, Jeff—it's none of my business."

"You know, she's always whining that he doesn't pay attention to her," he lowered his voice to a whisper, "even nags that he won't kiss her." He nodded to reinforce his words.

Amanda picked herself up off the car. She was disgusted with Jeff, even more with herself for having humored him this long. This ended their conversation. "You may want to park elsewhere while you're here on...assignment. This is my roommate's parking spot." She rubbed the car dust off the back of her shorts.

"I don't see her name tattooed anywhere or any sign marked *reserved*," he argued. "And you won't find any dust on this car," he added, as he saw her checking her back for dirt.

"What's a...young guy like you doing with a Porsche, anyway?"

"Big guy gave it to me," he smiled.

"Excuse me?" she asked him, more than skeptical. "Augustino gave you a Porsche!"

"Yep. It's all mine. Beauty, ain't she?" But Amanda was still shaking her head in disbelief. He just had to wipe the scowl off her face.

He scuffed the ground with his shoe, staring at the few sand pebbles his motion dislodged onto the pink sidewalk and admitted. "I was a teenage runaway, turning tricks. He picked me up off the streets in Baltimore. He gave me a job as a gofer in his office, found me a family to stay with—then one day, I am arguing this big case with him and he says I have talent. So he sent me back to high school. Now, I'm one year away from passing the bar."

Amanda was speechless. She couldn't believe her ears.

"Hey, I'm not the only one. He enlisted Manuel while he was filling tin cups at the corner of Flagler and First. He's studying computers now, working for Augie in the summer." And as if one more good deed might mask the fact that he was one of these troubled souls Augustino was helping, he added. "Raoul was an ex-con. Augie's office prosecuted him and he was going down—third time convicted. He pulled some strings and got him off. Gave him a job...at the salary he gets, Raoul's going to be a millionaire before he's forty."

"Stop," she insisted. This was not what she needed to hear. Here she was working as a social worker while this guy was *living* as a social worker. She had made the right decision, she consoled herself. The man was a freak. He had to be. What kind of person would go around giving Porsches...?

"He gave me that boat too," he was proud to add.

...And...and boats and scholarships..., she sighed. She would, if she had the money. "That has to be one lucrative law practice," she mumbled to herself.

"Nah. It makes money, for sure. But he inherited from his grandfather. A gazillion or something. I don't know."

"One thing I do know," she added staring at him squarely. "I don't think you should be telling me all this."

"You're the first person I've told. Honest." He crossed his heart, faced with her skeptical frown. "I thought he really liked you, that you two were going to make it. I was rooting for you, Amy. Now, well, I'm just sorry that you're not."

"You seem to know that for a fact..."

"Hey, I've never seen Augustino this angry with anyone before, not since I've known him—seven years."

She trembled at the sound of his words. She closed her eyes and saw Augustino's sculptured features and dark blue eyes. She could well imagine him angry. She was suddenly sorry it was because of her—very sorry. "Wait a minute. How did you *see* him?"

"He came with Manuel. A couple of hours behind you. He had called me before leaving, so we met at the house. Twenty minutes and he was gone again."

Amanda regretted having engaged in conversation with Jeff. The effect she had hoped to achieve had boomeranged in the worst way. Doubts concerning Connie's statements were seeping through her tightfisted logic and threatening to crumble her wall of self-esteem. She told herself that the man could very well be a philanthropist and a fink at the same time—for the right cause. He had dropped everything to avenge his friend Emilio—perhaps even his scruples. He had admittedly befriended Fiona for that purpose, slept with Connie for the same reason. A man with a mission could be as dangerous as a runaway missile. At least he had hit the target precisely where she was concerned.

Nevertheless, this information didn't make for breathing easier. "Thanks for the talk, Jeff. I've got to go. Thanks for looking out for me too."

"Don't worry. It's only until tomorrow."

"Why, what happens then?"

"They've apprehended Sanchez today. Hopefully, he'll talk and point the finger. They've got another guy who's also ready to spill." He smiled and waved her off.

She turned and ran toward the building. Inside, she paused and took a few shaky gulps of air before taking the stairs to her apartment. They had never been this steep to climb. What was it that Augustino had called her—the original Eve, the first clay creation? She was dumber than the first Eve. At least *she* had been chased out of paradise—Amanda

Cole had run out, of her own free will.

For the next couple of days, she tried not to let these feelings pervade. It was hard enough dealing with the loneliness and the reticence of heading back to work after the two worst weeks of holidays of her life. That was unfair. Parts of those two weeks had been memorable. She had always wanted to go sailing the ocean to exotic ports of call. She had gotten her wish.

Besides, the two worst weeks of her life were probably ahead of her. She now had to face the junta at work. The *who-dun-it* qualms would be widely dispersed and difficult to ignore while she didn't know what would happen with the files of her most recent clients.

When she got to work on the following Monday morning, Amanda received warm greetings from everyone. Big cheery smiles and peace signs made up the offering and she wondered why people were so expressive. It had only been two weeks after all, and here they were shaking her hand and opening doors as if she was the prodigal employee finally returned to work.

The girl who had replaced her, Maria, sprinted the minute she saw her to give her a big bold bear hug. Amanda had to ask. "What's going on? Why is everyone so ecstatic to see me? The feeling is not mutual—not that I don't love you guys," she told Maria and two other co-workers, "but I'd much rather still be on vacation."

"We heard about your cooperation in apprehending Fiona Christian and Neil Sinclair. They were indicted last

Thursday morning, arrested right here at the office." Maria was out of breath, jubilant to be the one handing her the news.

"Apparently, they'd been smuggling in terrorists from all different countries. I guess I don't have to tell you that," Tomas Perez added. "The list grows longer each day. Two FBI men were here on Friday and seized a huge number of files. They're due back today."

"Fiona never even argued or put up a fuss. I think she knew," Maria added.

Amanda was shocked. She had never imagined things would be resolved so quickly, nor her name mentioned as one of the contributing factors to the arrest. She had done absolutely nothing to warrant this praise.

"Congratulations, Amanda," Midge Parker was saying on her way to her office. "Peter Franklin wanted to see you the minute you arrived," she told her with a smile.

Amanda pointed to herself with disbelief. Peter Franklin, the operation's vice president, wanted to see her. She was amazed he even knew a lowly employee like her existed.

Straightening her jacket and skirt, she knocked on Franklin's door and entered when invited to do so.

"Miss Cole. It's a pleasure to welcome you back. Please, come in and have a chair."

"Mr. Franklin," she sat, propped on the edge of a lounger after shaking the man's hand. "I don't know what you've heard, but I assure you I had very little to do with the..."

"He warned me you were a true heroic spirit. That you'd make fie of all this glory. Well, Miss Cole—may I call you Amanda?"

"Please," she smiled, still frowning in disbelief.

"Amanda, over the years, as you well know, we've garnished our supervisory and principal positions with fresh candidates gleaned from outside the fold—from the corporate mainstream." Peter Franklin was rocking back and forth in his office chair, and every now and then he would toy with his moustache, curling and twisting its long scraggly ends. "People with psychology degrees," he continued in one long litany, "law diplomas, even the occasional commerce students to act as consultants; we have not promoted one single person from our little labor group—not a one—not in the last decade. Clearly we should have. With Sinclair and Christian gone—we still hope good lawyers can clear them of these dastardly charges, mind you—terrible indeed." He paused to lend drama to his words. "But with these two postings being vacant, we would like you to accept Fiona Christian's supervisory mandate. We may even expand your responsibilities to include some of Sinclair's curriculum. We understand the two of you worked together on several projects. Needless to say, salary and benefits will be adjusted to befit your new position."

"I...I don't know what to say, exactly."

"Simply say yes." He smiled politely. "Midge will help you settle in. She's familiar with both positions. And the rest is up to you. Although you're by far the youngest supervisor this agency has ever employed, you come highly recommended..."

"Mr. Franklin, just what were you told was...my

contribution in this investigation...?"

"There's no need for such modesty, Miss Cole," he told her.

"Mr. Franklin, I'm at a loss. I truly have done nothing that could warrant such praise...or such a promotion."

"Let me refresh your memory," he said condescendingly. "We were assured that you bravely compiled information—at the peril of your own safety—and were able to keep it under wraps, only to come forward when you felt the time was proper. Sound familiar?" He smiled.

Amanda refused to acknowledge, preferring to wait for him to continue. He obviously relished the sound of his own voice, she thought.

"We were also told that during the course of apprehending the alleged culprits, you were greatly inconvenienced during the last few weeks and suffered the loss of your vacation. We were very sorry to hear about that mishap."

"My vacation was fine...," she finished lamely, deciding it was a bad idea to mete out personal details of her trip to her boss.

"Tut-tut. We heard otherwise and we intend to compensate you by giving you extra leave of absence—paid of course."

"Of course...," she added ruefully. "Who told you...? I mean, who highly recommended me for this position?"

"The head of the operation—of course. Mr. Augustino Milan."

Amanda's heart sank down to her toes. "He was the head of this operation?"

"You are a modest girl," he added. "He is a very prominent, politically connected lawyer. He ran this investigation and swears that without your cooperation, none of this would have been possible."

"I assure you, Mr. Franklin. He is much too kind. He has exaggerated my collaboration...tenfold." Amanda was seething. If this was his way of laughing at her or making her feel petty, he was succeeding. "If my new promotion is based solely on his word, I don't think it would be proper for me to accept it." That felt so much better, she sighed.

"On the contrary. FBI agents Gary Flint and Bob Farrell support Mr. Milan. They agree wholeheartedly."

Amanda let out an enormous, frustrated breath. It was a conspiracy. They had obviously found a way of apologizing for having thought her guilty for so long. Still, to accept the position would only serve their maniacal egos—men! She inwardly cursed. They always had to have the last word.

"The center won't take no for an answer, Miss Cole. They told me you might react this way..."

"They did, did they?" Typical, she thought.

"And we believe you are by far the best person for the job with or without the kudos of this investigation," he finished, extremely insistent on having his way. Why did this not surprise her?

He poured himself water and invited her to do the same. "As you know, they will be rummaging in your department's files and cases for the next few weeks. And although your promotion is effective as of this date, we suggest you take your two weeks paid leave immediately, seeing the authorities will be traipsing in and out of your office—making a thorough mess of things."

Amanda found his missive sounded more like an order than a suggestion. There was no doubt about it; he was dismissing her for the duration.

"What you're saying, Mr. Franklin, is that they won't be needing my testimony? Doesn't that seem a bit odd to you? That having been this...pivotal player, I'm suddenly sent home?"

He smiled. "Not at all. You've done more than enough. Mr. Milan specifically suggested that you not be bothered with the nitty-gritty of proof. They have all they need." He tossed the file in front of him. Obviously he considered the matter closed.

What was she going to do with herself? She had looked forward to occupying her mind and getting back to a normal routine, one that didn't include a constant barrage of thoughts about Augustino Milan.

Ginette was surprised to see her home at lunchtime. But she found the idea of her paid vacation extraordinary. "You're lucky, Amanda. Not only did you get a promotion—how many rungs of the ladder did you skip to get there?" Ginette suddenly thought to ask.

"A few. I'm telling you, Gin, I came dangerously close to shoving the position back in their faces. Anyway, I thought I'd fly up to see my folks for the next two weeks. What do you think?"

"I think it's a great idea. I'll even drive you to the airport." Ginette was pleased that Amanda was seeking a reprieve from her ordeal—of her own volition. She knew home would stabilize her mood and put her adventure in perspective.

The next morning, as promised, Ginette got up early to drive Amanda to the airport. While she waited for her to get dressed, she sat in front of the TV., watching the latest breaking news on the story of the Miami Shelters. The commentator was relating how two of the shelter's directors had allegedly paved the way for undesirables to enter the US illegally. Three analysts were seated around a table, debating the situation. "Actually, Paul, we're told a dozen people have been indicted in the last few days. Hank Williamson, one of Quartain Tech's directors..."

"I think he was Vince Morello's right arm, wasn't he?"

"Yes he was, Tom. He was also the whistle blower who jump-started the investigation of Quartain Tech's alleged illegal arms market."

"I've always maintained that whistle blowing can be a tricky affair," Tom Brooks added.

"He's going to have to perform some tricky footwork now, Tom." Julie Harris added. "He has just been brought in for questioning. He was identified by several people as the potential leader of a group of terrorists—the very same group he accused Vince Morello of supporting."

"And I'm told, Julie, that Judd Garrison was nowhere to be found when they tried to serve him early this morning. He is also alleged to have been a key figure in the demise of Quartain Tech's CEO, Vince Morello."

"That's right. By the way, I've just received word that

we're about to hear from our correspondent in Washington, John Marks. He is attempting to interview one of the key players in this investigation. Go ahead, John."

"Good morning, Julie. I'm standing here on the steps of the J. Edgar Hoover Building, waiting for the star investigator in this case to come out of his meeting. Theories among my fellow reporters as we line Pennsylvania Avenue," the camera showed a quick glimpse of the entrance to the building crammed with people, "are running rampant. As you know, Mr. Augustino Milan, the man of the hour, has refused to give any observations to the press. As for the director of the FBI, Jack Doyle, his only comment so far has been...no comment."

"Do you think they might be going from their meeting directly to the press room?"

"We can only hope so. Speculation is that it does not appear it will be today. As you can see," he designated other reporters milling on the sidewalk, others leaning against their cars—the camera showing a few of them sitting with their heads in their lap, "all we can do is be patient."

"John, we have heard rumors about an investigation within the Bureau walls. Anything concrete on that?"

"Nothing yet. I suppose that's why we're out here and they're...in there. Back to you, Julie."

"Thanks, John. That was..."

"Gin! What are you doing? I told you I didn't want to see any of this!" Amanda yelled. Ginette, as engrossed as she was, jumped out of her chair.

"Geez Louise! I'm sorry." She quickly flicked the

remote and changed the channel. "You almost gave me a heart attack. I thought you were still in the bathroom." Throwing the remote on the sofa, she griped, "I can't believe you're not interested in this. It's the news of the hour and you're missing it."

"You can watch it when I'm gone. I told you, I don't want to risk seeing...him. I thought you understood that."

"Okay. Okay. You ready?"

Amanda nodded.

Ginette picked up one of her bags and secretly wished for home-sweet-home to sprinkle a little sweetness on Amanda while she was there. That she might come back rested and a tad more sensible.

But when Amanda returned two weeks later, Ginette couldn't believe how thin she looked. "Did you lose more weight?"

"I don't know. But I've never been to so many beach parties. We had a blast," she smiled. "Mom says hi, by the way; and so does Susan. And," she added, unpacking her case, "I brought you back a souvenir."

Ginette gazed at the mug with the Pleasantville logo and smiled. One more to add to an extensive collection. "Thanks, Amy. You're a doll. So, did you meet anyone interesting at those...beach parties?" Ginette asked without much hope. Amanda's face was paler than when she had left and the lighthearted mood she flashed appeared forced and superficial.

She shrugged. "Would you believe Johnny the Jock

just got married? To Loralee, the assistant librarian. I'm telling you. Pleasantville seems to have shrunk."

"By the way, *you've* got mail," Ginette announced with the singsong internet tone. She handed the letters to Amanda, drawing her attention to the top one.

"It's from...a law firm...in Baltimore...," Amanda breathed.

Ginette nodded excitedly. "Open it, quick. I've been dying to see what's inside."

Amanda's fingers fumbled miserably. Why was it that interesting mail was always so perfectly glued? When she finally tore open the envelope, she found a polite letter, brief and to the point that stated. 'Due to the contract between Mr. Augustino Milan and Miss Amanda Cole, please find enclosed a check for the amount owed of $6,000.00, the equivalence of three weekends' compensation'.

The check was included and Augustino had signed it. Amanda stared at it, her heart hammering in her chest while war drums beat inside her head. She checked the postmark. It had arrived three days after her departure. "Well, I'm not cashing it. I've done nothing to deserve this. More ways to ridicule me. I'm telling you, Gin. That man is mean and vindictive. I think he spends his time dreaming-up ways to humiliate me."

There was no point in arguing with her. Not when her usual sharp logic was this painfully skewed. "A Midge Parker called for you yesterday. She said to make certain you were at work first thing tomorrow morning."

The request surprised her. The next day was Friday.

She had not expected to go back until Monday.

Another sunny day woke Amanda from a sound sleep—Miami's one drawback, she pouted as she turned a dull eye to the play of rays on her wall. Unconcern for a fool's broken heart. Any fool. It should have been raining, pouring and cloudy—thundering even—all better matches to reflect her foul mood.

The first person she spotted at work, in the corridor leading to her office, was Midge. She signaled Amanda over. "Amanda, I hate to spoil your last weekend away," she whispered, her glasses askew on the bridge of her nose, "but there is someone in the boardroom who absolutely wants to talk to you." She smiled, a conspirator's look in her eyes, and Amanda choked on the pumped up adrenalin her beat-skipping heart welled up inside her.

She stopped by the ladies' room and feverishly checked her hair and make-up in the long foggy mirror. She had worn her dark blue dress today, the plain one, and it only served to accentuate her paleness and haggard lost expression. She sighed dejectedly, wishing she had paid more attention to her attire, but there was little she could do now. There was no remedying the situation other than hurrying to meet her visitor.

Inside the boardroom, casually sitting at the head of the solid cherry-wood table was Gary Flint, shuffling through a stack of papers.

"Thanks for coming in, Amanda. I'm lost in these files. I need your help desperately. Can you afford me a few hours?"

Nothing came out of her mouth, so expectant had she

been at seeing Augustino's handsome face, having his eyes brand into hers.

"I have to catch a plane this afternoon for a meeting with my superiors. Can you help me?" He smiled, only now taking in her sullen expression. "You look tired. Is everything all right?"

She dug deep into her bag of quick responses. "You know how it is when you're on vacation. You overdo it and get more tired than you were before you left. You need to go back to work just to recover."

He chuckled. "That's a problem I would love to have. I told Augie; after this stint, it's a long overdue break for me."

She was dying to ask about Augustino. Instead she said, "How have you been, Gary?"

"Great, now that all this is finally out of the way. Did Augie run you through the mechanics?"

She shook her head. "I've been away."

"I know. To that family emergency. I hope everything is okay." He seemed genuinely concerned. And only when he noticed her half-hearted nod did he continue. "Well, we finally got word out to Eduardo, Conchita's son. He was secretly able to mend the fuel line. Then Connie arrived on the island with a four seater Cessna—compliments of Augustino Milan...that man has done more for this investigation...the plane being her gift to Eduardo. Anyway, Sanchez asked her to pick up the gift he had for Eduardo in Abacos. She agreed and suggested Eduardo try out his new toy at the same time. He gave the other children a ride and innocently followed his mother to the southern coast of Florida. Once there, Eduardo called his father in a panic saying that his mother's plane had crashed and that he wanted to be picked up. The rest you can probably deduce." He smiled. "Of course, I'm giving you the Cliffs Notes version."

"Once Sanchez on American soil, I imagine he was arrested?"

He nodded. "He's been talking ever since."

"What about Connie and her children?"

"They're safe. They're staying at Augie's house, in Coral Gables—until the lawyers can set her papers straight—which shouldn't be too long considering the large sums of money she stands to receive."

"Who thought up this brilliant plan?" She asked, but already knew. She just needed the conversation to veer back to the one person her mind was brimming with.

"Augie." He smiled, as proud as if he had been talking about himself. "If it hadn't been for him...." He stopped his filing and stared at her. "You know, had it not been for Augie's unflinching belief in you, we would've put out an all-points-bulletin on that gorgeous mug of yours two years ago."

Amanda sat down beside him. She didn't want him to see how weak her legs suddenly were. "An APB on me? Why?"

"We thought you were the mysterious woman who had stolen Fiona Christian's purse to get to that ticket. Emilio took you on as an assignment that night and found that you were an extremely hard nut to crack—so he said."

Amanda blew out a nervous laugh. "I had nothing to say—didn't know anything. Even worse, I was drunk. I never drink. I guess he spiked my drinks...to get me to talk...ended up achieving the complete opposite. I'm surprised he never noticed."

"We know that now. Still, when Emilio turned up dead and Augie found out that you weren't the real Fiona Christian, he had a tough time convincing us not to sketch your pretty picture to put it on the wire. We knew he had fallen for you. It showed in that gooey way he eyed you all night...at that party...So Bob and I questioned his better judgment, thinking it might be screwed...excuse the expression," he laughed.

"You were there?" Amanda was breathless. She couldn't believe what he was saying about Augustino.

"Yep. And we all saw it. He gets shy when he meets up with a woman he really likes, which isn't often, so it's noticeable when he does. But that night, he was tongue tied, literally." Gary laughed. "I'd known him too long not to catch that *Cupie* arrow reaching its mark." He shook his head and rolled his eyes. "Bob gave him hell, more than once—those two always inches away from an all out war—you know..."

"Over me..."

"Over the fact that he trusted a perfect stranger. Anyway, that's when it all started. Augie volunteered his services. He called it a trade—him for you. We agreed. It was a bargain. He left his Baltimore firm in the hands of a junior partner, bought a house down here, a boat and started sniffing for clues." He sat back in his chair, deep in thought. "At first I thought he was doing the Miami thing...to try to find you. But you know, even when I told him how it'd be a cinch to find you once your picture ran out to all corners, he wouldn't budge. Go figure."

"Exactly, go figure," she repeated in a small voice. "I don't think a man can fall in love so quickly. Sometimes women do...," she said more to herself, wringing her hands to stop them from shaking.

"Bah! Augie's built different. He knows what he wants the minute he sees it. If I had one tenth of his insight, I'd be a decorated man. Look how well it turned out." He smiled as he designated her.

She nodded. There were no words. None that she could say to make this ache less painful or have the numbness of remorse disappear. "Let's go through these files," she mouthed instead.

CHAPTER SEVENTEEN

It was August. But the days weren't getting shorter for Augustino Milan. They were fast becoming long and longer links in a chain of formality that stretched from 7:00 each morning to unspecified times most nights.

Between piecing his practice back together, the meetings and briefings he held to ease the media frenzy, the unending questions and forms he filled out to serve an onslaught of authorities, he had little time left for a personal agenda—or at least he rejected one as much as he could. While his evenings were punctuated with soirees and necessary functions, his nights had him fighting for his sanity—alone in his room, between the sheets—when thoughts of Amanda would have him hurl the rich food he had ingested a few hours prior. Sleep was fitful and restless. The pain of her betrayal colored everything around him until all his leisure time needed to be filled with work—the personal agenda be damned.

"Augustino?" Samantha walked into his office after knocking for form. The door was ajar. "Brad is being arraigned today. Should I send someone from the firm to the courthouse to take notes?"

"It's already being taken care of."

She watched his bent head, looking over the files Lisa had just brought him. He had changed. He hardly smiled anymore and his eyes had lost their luster. But to Samantha Craig, this enigma that surrounded him only made him more charismatic. She had never wanted him more. She smiled to herself, thinking that with this added vulnerability he would be a cinch to nab. "Oh! And Gary Flint is on his way up. He called from the lobby."

He looked up from his work. "Thanks, Sam. Please see him in and close the door behind him."

She nodded, even though he was no longer looking at her. She doubted he would have heard a word she said. When he was this engrossed with work, there was no reaching him.

Gary entered Augustino's office with his usual flourish. He was happier than he'd been in years and he didn't mind sprinkling some of that gaiety around. "Hey! Pal. You were right."

Augustino looked up at his friend's huge smile and knew things had gone from good to better. "What's up?"

"Frake and Garrison met in Eleuthera. How the hell you knew...." Gary shook his head in amazement.

Augustino shrugged. "Frake's a crooked lawyer. The only sort Garrison can use right now. Plus, extradition from the Bahamas can be tedious."

"Who needs extradition when we've got Jose Arroyo!" Gary laughed at Augustino's puzzled expression.

"The man's totally climbed the chart of my hit-parade list. He can be a take-charge little man when he wants to be. He rounded up a gang of his merry men and literally kidnapped the two creeps."

Augustino smiled and sat back in his lounger. "I can believe it of the son-of-a-bitch. He can be rough around the edges—irritating most times—but useful once every blue moon. Where are they now?"

"In custody. Being questioned as we speak. Frake's an asshole. Claims he was paid to keep an eye on Monet and nothing else. Not saying much. But Garrison has a lot to lose. He's already cutting a deal with the prosecuting attorney for his cooperation and all the information he's handing over."

Augustino opened one of his desk drawers. "Here." He handed a folder over to Gary. "Make sure the prosecutor asks him these pertinent questions. A lot of them have to do with the brief I'm putting together to have Morello and a few others retried."

"I read that Quartain Tech was sold?"

"It was."

"All that money for their underwater technology...." Gary shook his head. "Whatever happened to Morello's project?"

"Shelved—pleasing some UBS branch no end. At least it's collecting interest."

"I heard that the endeavor is worth a hell of a lot more these days. The Australian government has just allocated some $264 million to provide their own version of our robot friend Kevin." Gary added.

"There are several countries aiming for this new breed of robots that will work autonomously under inhuman conditions." Augustino looked up from his files. "They're not so far in our future. They'll be able to warn us against hurricanes, tsunamis—even better, they'll give us a glimpse into why they happen—how they work."

"What about Kevin? Jim says he can't be sold?"

"The conglomerate that purchased Quartain has also purchased the going interest for the underwater project. Hence our friend Kevin has a new owner."

"I thought the money was tied to Vince Morello. Jim told me that without Morello's strict supervision of the project, the funds can't be released—sort of a catch 22 wouldn't you say?"

"Indeed. That is why the conglomerate has agreed to sit Vince on its board, provided he's cleared—at any cost, was their mandate. No doubt about it. It's still Morello's baby."

"Then, hurry up and get him off. If anyone can, Augie, it's you." Gary smiled. "You look tired, Augie. When are you going to make time for that girl of yours?"

Augustino looked up and gave him a half smile. He hadn't told anyone about Amanda's true reason for running. Keeping up the pretence was another task slowly driving him to the brink. "There'll be time enough for playing later," was all he said, continuing to scan through his files.

"Speaking of playing, Sheila Purdue admitted that Pete Schneider was the one who paid her to finger Attorney

General Sam Bigelow. You'll be happy to learn that they're letting her go in exchange for her testimony." Gary raised his eyebrows up and down a few times.

Augustino shook his head and snorted a little laugh his way. Gary had no conception of devotion, commitment or loyalty to any one woman. He was a gentle and affable man who believed in spreading the love around. "Then you should ask her out, Gary. You know you're dying to. I hope you're not waiting for my blessing."

"Nah. I don't want to ask her out." He shrugged. "Just want to have her in...," he laughed. "I'm glad you don't mind." Gary waited for a response. When none came, he added. "Why aren't you happy? You're so gloomy—for a guy who's the toast of Washington....You know how much publicity your firm will derive from this?"

Augustino nodded. Putting his pen down, he looked straight at Gary. "Jim Dunbar tells me De Marco and his lieutenants are liable to get away with the murders they committed. Short of reaching an arm into Cuba to grab the bastards."

Gary raised his shoulders. "I know how you feel. Fidel assured us he would get the lot of them tried in Cuba; but we know what that means. They'll probably get a pat on the back and be handed a medal."

"First they've got to find them." Augustino shook his head, disgusted with this turn of events. "Bringing terrorists into our country might have been their own government's initiative. Who knows?" He interrupted his thoughts to answer his phone. "Okay, Lisa. Please see him in. Bob's here."

Augustino sat back in his chair. "Internal Affairs finish cleaning house in your department? Where's Hawk?"

Gary rubbed his hands together. "Done and done. He's going away for a long time. No deal for him, that's for sure."

Bob entered, imposing as usual, smiling from one to the other. "I'm glad you're here too, Gary. I'll be able to brief you both."

"Hey, Bob." Augustino acknowledged his presence. "Have a seat." He buzzed Lisa on the intercom. "Lisa, can you bring us a pitcher of coffee with cream and sugar, please?"

Bob sat down and opened his briefcase. He had a grin on his face, which was rare for him. He nodded, looking particularly pleased with himself.

"What did you go and do, Bob?" Gary asked with a tease in his voice.

Augustino rose and invited them to the round table at the other end of his office—the one near the tall windows overlooking Clifton Park.

As the three of them sat at the table, Lisa came in with coffee and a pitcher of water. There was also a platter loaded with sandwiches and cookies.

"Thank you, Lisa. This is wonderful." Augustino smiled at her.

"This *is* nice, Augie." Gary added once Lisa had left. "I haven't had lunch." Gary grabbed a couple of sandwiches and poured himself a cup of coffee. "So, are you going to let us in on your little caper?" He asked Bob with his mouth full.

Bob took a sip of his coffee. "Hum, this hits the spot. Well, I spent the last two weeks reviewing Sanchez's testimony—his written affidavit. I took a peek at Lewis' transcript..."

"Who's Lewis?" Augustino asked.

"A two-bit shadow who follows Sanchez everywhere," Bob added.

"I know the runt," Gary said. Turning toward Augustino, he explained. "He's the guy Conchita saw that day arguing with Sanchez about the key to the safety deposit box."

When he saw Augustino nod, Bob continued. "I noticed that nowhere in either of their testimonies was there any mention of the key, the content of that safety deposit box or the roll of film. I found that strange. And I also remembered that during our meeting in the Bahamas, Jose had been adamant about insisting there was nothing interesting on that film. And I'm thinking...it doesn't add up. Something's up with that. Maybe something he doesn't want us to see." He stopped and took another satisfying gulp of his hot coffee.

"Not to mention that I nearly got my head blown off, trying to help Connie retrieve that bloody negative," Gary added.

"Go on." Augustino was more than curious.

"Well, I went to the source. I figured if Jose wouldn't give me the time of day, maybe Conchita would." He smiled. "I was right. By now, she was in dire need of a friend." He stared at Augustino with a pointed look. "She said you're angry with her."

"She did, did she?"

"Didn't say why...you know Connie. All drama and waterworks. Anyway, she said to 'give the pictures to Milo. He would understand'." Bob tried to imitate Conchita's sultry voice; and he and Gary laughed. "Anyway, I'm thinking she is hoping you'll be grateful enough to...thank her...properly."

Augustino ignored the comment as he took the stack of pictures he was handed. Flipping through the photos of a summer picnic, he noticed on several of them the faces of Armando Arroyo and a younger version of Jose Arroyo. There were a lot of people in the background. But what took his breath away was the sight of the man in four of those pictures, standing between Armando and Jose—his arms wrapped around their shoulders. There was no mistaking his stature, his undeniable presence. *El Presidente*, Fidel Castro himself. Augustino raised his eyes and stared at Bob in shock. He handed those few pictures to Gary.

"There is more," Bob told them. "There's one with Conchita stretched up against him, her arms around his neck, clinging to him in one powerful lip-lock."

"No wonder Armando was hiding this in a safety deposit box. He had to. He wouldn't have been granted citizenship with known ties like these," Augustino breathed.

"Apparently, both families go back a long way. They are true friends," Bob announced.

"Hey! This means there's a chance the government might go after the Havana Club," Gary added as an afterthought. "At least bring down De Marco and his four goons. That would dismantle their operation."

Bob smiled. "Our friend Conchita is determined to make amends." He glanced at Augustino. "She has already set Fidel straight as to who murdered her father and brother."

"Maybe..." Augustino was pensive. "We might be gloating too soon, though. De Marco and his captains can hide out for years. They'll be difficult to find."

"That's what I thought," Bob added with a broad smile. "Then I began thinking. Why would Sanchez be worried about these pictures? The propaganda of having ties with the Cuban government can no longer hurt Armando. So it wasn't to hold them over his head. Can't harm Jose—hell, he's a hero now. But then I figured that maybe these pictures could be held over Sanchez' head." He stared at Augustino, waiting for him to figure the rest.

Augustino looked at Gary, then Bob, and a smile slowly lifted his tired features. "Print these photos in the Havana Journal with a nice little caption about the deaths...." Augustino's smile stretched as a contented look dawned in his eyes.

"Geez! Every desperado in Cuba will be turning in evidence. There won't be a hole where these guys can hide." Gary was excited.

Bob laughed. "The process has already begun. Two of De Marco's men were turned in this morning," Bob paused for effect, "by their own families."

Augustino shook his head in disbelief. "Fidel still commands more loyalty than the almighty dollar." He rose, exhorting Bob to do the same. He shook his hand vigorously. "Excellent work, Bob. I hope they nail the bastards to the wall."

"Oh! They'll be nailed to the wall alright. Nailed with a hail of bullets. Firing squad." He nodded vigorously. "Country's not big on lengthy trials."

CHAPTER EIGHTEEN

For Amanda, August went by in a flash. With all her new responsibilities, spending time in meetings, trainings and briefings, Amanda was at work sixty hours a week. She wasn't used to two secretaries and an administrative assistant. She needed to learn to delegate—or not so carefully comb through all the work that they did. Still, by Labor Day she felt more comfortable, more at ease with her workload and grateful for not always having to think about work when she wasn't at work.

She had marked off each day on her calendar as one more day Augustino had not called her. At least Ginette had stopped talking about it—even though she was still thinking about it—they both were. It wasn't every day that a woman ran out of paradise; or valued the opinion of someone she despised over someone she loved.

She had picked up the phone so many times to call

him. She had worried that Connie would answer. She had worried that no one would answer. She had worried that Augustino would answer and refuse to talk to her. After all, her logic in believing Conchita may have proven to be flawed. She had certainly been wrong not to trust him or not to give him the benefit of an explanation. But he hadn't called her either. And judging by what Jeff had told her about his anger, remembering the three-line letter she had received from him with the check, he was holding a grudge. He wasn't giving *her* the benefit of an explanation. A little voice told her maybe he simply considered the chapter closed. He had returned to his law practice, most likely had sixty-hour weeks himself and indifference had replaced infatuation. Obviously he had merely been infatuated. How else could he have forgotten about her so quickly?

These were the thoughts that spun round and round in her mind, poisoning her leisure time and sucking her joy out of life.

"If you continue to lose weight, you're going to have to buy a whole new wardrobe," Ginette told her a couple of days before Halloween. "You have to slow down. I never see you anymore. At least when I do double shifts I have a slew of days off afterwards."

Amanda shrugged, clearly refusing to discuss it. "I feel fine. Stop nagging."

"You just keep going like that energizer bunny and you'll end up in one of my wards."

Ginette gave up. It was useless. Amanda was just going to read that damn paper and ignore everything she said.

"Your sister called yesterday. She wants to know if you can take little Jerry out for trick or treating. Her morning sickness is worse in the evenings."

Amanda sighed. Meg was pregnant again. She should have been happy for her. She and Jerry had been trying to have a second child for so long. "I guess. I don't know why Jerry doesn't take him out. Him and his stupid sports. There's probably a game on TV or something."

Ginette looked away, quickly dabbing at a tear. She couldn't bear to see Amanda hurting this much. She whose lust for life and heart for helping others was unparalleled. She didn't know how to help her. One thing she did know. If Augustino was too stubborn to talk to her or at least call in the next little while, her best friend would wither away.

By the time November rolled around, Ginette was in a sound relationship and happier than she had ever been. Amanda was extremely pleased for her. And although she had asked Ginette to bring Jen around more often, Ginette spent most of her time at Jen's house. It was more convenient was all she would say. It made sense, Amanda thought, since Jen lived alone. This meant that Amanda had to slash her working hours or bring little Dino with her whenever she could to prevent him from being alone, days on end. The rest of her leisure time she spent at Meg's. Her sister's pregnancy was proving to be a difficult one. She needed all the help Amanda could spare. This made for long days and extended evenings.

A week before Thanksgiving, on one of her extended Fridays, Amanda jumped to see how late it was when she parked the car in front of her apartment. Where did the time fly! Eight o'clock and she hadn't eaten since lunch. Juggling Dino, her purse, her briefcase and a couple of bags, she flicked the alarm on her Bug and walked toward her building.

Rounding the stairs to the second floor, she cursed the building's lack of elevators. Meg was so lucky with her first floor apartment, she sighed.

At eye-level with the second floor landing, she stopped, spotting a conspicuous pair of leather loafers on the stoop. As she allowed her eyes to roam upward, she nearly fell backwards in the stairway with all her packages. Augustino stood there, handsome and charismatic in a dark colored sports jacket, an open shirt and dark colored dress pants, seemingly waiting for her.

She noticed he wasn't smiling as he ran down a few steps to help her with her bags. In front of her door, she put down Dino and her briefcase to fumble for her keys, her eyes mesmerized by his. She wanted to ask what he was doing there but couldn't utter a single word. She just stood staring at him, the intensity of his eyes making it difficult for her to look away.

"May I come in?" he asked.

She nodded, still stunned as she turned the key in the lock. She had forgotten how deep and sensuous his voice could be.

Inside, she deposited her bags on the sofa, unable to ignore that he was posted at her back, waiting for her to acknowledge him somehow. She turned, ready in spirit yet physically unprepared, though she had rehearsed for this meeting a hundred times. "You're lucky to find me at home.

I'm not often here."

"I know. It's my third try in as many days." He still wasn't smiling. "I can't stay long, Amanda. I have a dinner engagement." He checked his watch. "I...just thought we might talk?"

She nodded and sat down at the table, inviting him to do the same.

But he shook his head. "I really can't stay. Truth is I've been waiting here for a while. I was just about to leave when you came in."

"I still have a telephone," she answered, a little miffed by his cool approach. "It would have been better to call ahead..."

A small crooked smile relieved the stern look on his face. "I didn't know how I would be received. Plus, what I have to say...is best said in person." He hesitated, then sat down on the edge of her sofa, his forearms resting on his knees. "First, I want to apologize for not...for having been so angry with you...for not calling..."

She put up her hand. "That's okay. I'm the one who should apologize. I've wanted to for some time." She smiled at him, a little of the old mischief returning to her eyes. "You had your reasons for not using the telephone...well in my case the damn thing was too heavy to pick up."

He smiled outright. "I understand." Then his eyes darkened and a telltale muscle moved in his jaw. "I still feel like wringing your neck...." He didn't continue, taking in the sheepish look on her face. "Don't you even want to know why?"

"That's easy." This part she had rehearsed. "For failing to see that you could never deliberately hurt me. That you're incapable of deceit—at least where I am concerned....How am I doing?" She asked in a small voice. "Getting warm?"

He shook his head. "It surprised me...that you never knew how much I loved you, Amanda. I flat out told you the first night we made love..."

"I thought you were...too tired to mean what you were saying." All she focused on was the past tense of his love declaration.

"Albert told you. I confirmed it several times—each time I kissed you after putting emphasis on the fact that I hadn't kissed a woman in years. The intimate, personal way I made love to you, touched you—I...did things a man would never do with a casual fling. Still, Connie's jealousy should've been the clincher, Amy. She was so crazy jealous of you..."

"So that's why you were angry. It could have been so easily solved had you simply been more explicit."

"That's not why I was...still am angry." He watched as she tensed up and immediately regretted his choice of words. "I realized very early that you were in love with me, Amanda. It's there in those beautiful eyes when you look at me," he said softly. "I sensed it when you touched me and made love to me. I knew it in the way you disliked Connie—sweet Amy who doesn't have an enemy in the world. But to love me so much," he smiled at her sad eyes, "and not be able to trust me...that deflated me, angered me out of my mind. I thought if she can't trust me loving me as much as she does..."

"So, why are you here?" She had stiffened and her

voice was a thin whisper.

He lowered his head and let out an enormous sigh. "Ginette called me—two weeks ago."

Amanda was shocked. She got up and began pacing. "Why do people think they have the right to meddle?" She strapped her arms around herself. "I told her to stay out of it." Then she turned to face him. "What did she tell you?"

"You mean, after she took a breather from calling me every curse word under the sun?" He smiled at the laughter in her expression. "She basically gave me the same failing grade I had given you. She said forgiveness is big between lovers. She also reminded me that you didn't know who the real me was—that you'd fallen in love with an illusion. *That* scared me."

He got up and slowly walked toward her. "I was coming back to Miami in January, Amanda. I had planned to get in touch with you then. I hurried back...I just don't want to lose...sight of you. I don't know. I thought we might become friends? Get to know each other?" It was a clear question. He waited for her response.

She wanted them to be closer than mere friends. She supposed it was a start and she certainly didn't want him to think her ungrateful. As she stood up, she acquiesced. "Friends would be good. I'm sure I can handle friends." She smiled at him expectantly when all she wanted to do was kiss his lips and feel his arms around her.

He came closer and noticed her disappointment. "Some projects are worth developing slowly," he told her softly, flicking her chin with his finger. "Believe me, I know.

I've just spent the last few months in Baltimore, nursing my firm back to health. It was in—well, disarray is a kind word. One of the juniors, Samantha Craig, a wonderful young woman...did the best she could. She thought I would be there until the New Year. She was sorry to see me leave, I can tell you. I told her I had...a family emergency." He smiled knowingly, a bright twinkle in his eyes.

"You said you were still angry with me," she reminded him, a little breathless.

He shook his head. "Just a little vexed. That you weren't the one berating me over the phone instead of Ginette."

He looked at his watch and strode to the door. "May I take you to dinner next weekend?" He asked, turning back before leaving.

"Next weekend...!" What was wrong with this weekend, she thought, berating that thought just as quickly. He had a life—plans. Not everyone was as pathetic as she was. "It's Thanksgiving weekend, Augustino. I'm going to Pleasantville to be with my folks." Then she remembered that he had no family. "Would you like to come...?"

She regretted her invitation immediately when she saw the raised eyebrows and stunned look on his face. "That's silly. Forget it. Come to think of it, I can stay in Miami for the holidays. Meg and her husband aren't coming up this year. She's pregnant and too nauseous to fly, too sick to drive and Jerry's not a strong driver. He wouldn't make it all the way there on his own." Why was she babbling? And how desperate did that sound...when he had told her he was already late, she sighed.

Patiently, his hand still on the door handle, he smiled at her. “Don’t change your plans for me, *cara*. Flying there?”

She nodded. He had called her *cara*—the only word she knew in Italian—her favorite Italian word. She loved it when he used the endearing term. But now, she wasn’t going to be with him.

“I’ll talk to you when you get back. Take care, Amanda.”

She stood staring at the place he had vacated. She closed her eyes, still feeling his presence and the musky smell of his aftershave lingering mildly. She was doomed to spend the next week and the whole Thanksgiving weekend pining for him. He hadn’t kissed her, hadn’t made a move to show he still loved her. An olive branch of friendship was the only gift he had extended. And she had embarrassed him by inviting him to spend Thanksgiving weekend with her and her family. She cringed as she vividly recalled her prattling plea to change her plans just to accept his dinner invitation. Well, if he couldn’t interpret that pathetic behavior of hers, he was deaf, dumb and blind. At least they were on speaking terms again.

She hurried to the shadow of her window in time to watch him get into his car. She wondered who the lucky person was, having dinner with Augustino Milan. She closed her eyes, praying it wasn’t Conchita Sanchez.

CHAPTER NINETEEN

"Are you sure you won't come, Gin?" Amanda was feeling so much better knowing she would soon see Augustino again. She was looking to spread the joy. "Just consider it my way of thanking you for...meddling." She gave Ginette a crooked smile.

Ginette shook her head. "Say hi to your mom for me. I'd just be in the way. Besides, Jen and I have plans."

"You wouldn't be in the way, trust me. My parent's home may be old, but it's huge. There are seven bedrooms aside from the sleepers in the den."

"I love you for asking, Amy. You just have a super time."

Half an hour later, Amanda ran through Miami airport with her coat on her arm and a woolen sweater for Dino between the clutches of her handbag. She was traveling light.

She kept clothes in her old room at home.

The flight was uneventful. She tried to focus on the movie that was playing instead of replaying Augustino's last visit in her mind—over and over. The more she did, the more aloof he became and the more remote seemed the possibility of them ever being lovers again. By the time her plane landed, she felt as tired and drawn as if she had flapped her arms and flown there herself.

She took a cab from Atlantic City International Airport, twenty minutes away instead of ten because of the five o'clock traffic, and smiled in spite of herself when her folks' house appeared in the distance.

They lived in an older sector of the small city where the clapboard houses were bigger and trimmed with mature trees. The oaks and maples were bare this time of year, which left all homes exposed to the full strength of autumn winds.

She paid the taxi driver and noticed that most of the houses' chimneys on her street were spewing smoke. The fireplaces had their bellies stocked with logs and dry kindle, working overtime to provide heat and comfort. She smiled as she took in a whiff of burned cedar and the sounds of boys, two houses down, whistling and yelling as they played street hockey.

Just a few hours in the sky and presto, her surroundings had magically transformed from the warm sunny ocean and exotic palm trees to early nightfall, bitter cold and frozen ground laying bare pumpkin patches and decimated apple trees. Both scenes pleased her. This time of year was when as a child she had waited with feverish anticipation for the fall of the first snowflakes.

"Hey, everyone," Amanda signaled her arrival. And a host of people stampeded the hallway, shoving to be first to bombard her with hugs and kisses. Dino was excited and jumping up and down, showing off his new sweater. Amanda's mom wore an apron covered with flour and splatters of crushed cranberries. Susan was beaming her bright, blond smile; and gangly Shawn, eleven months her senior, was standing around waiting for his turn to hug his baby sister. When the little group finally dispersed, she spotted Michael in the background talking to...her brain froze. "Augustino?" For a moment, he looked so out of place in her house, wearing dark cords and a burgundy turtleneck, she almost couldn't place him. "What are you doing here?" she breathed, conscious of everyone's eyes on her.

"You invited me, remember?" He was smiling, a jubilant gleam in his blue eyes.

"You love to do this, don't you?" She was glaring at him, torn between jumping in his arms and slapping his face. "Catch me off guard..."

He chuckled. "This way's more fun. While your back is turned I get to hear the skinny on you by people who know you well. They know the type of people you like."

She laughed, unable to repress it. He was quoting back the line she had served him when Albert had confided in her. She turned toward Michael and the others. "Okay, what did you tell this man?"

They laughed and went about their business, tacitly affording them privacy. Her family members were thrilled she had brought a friend home for the holidays. "Sorry, sis. It's confidential." Michael came up to her and gave her a big hug.

"Good to see you, Mike. I missed you in July. How's Brenda?" Brenda was Michael's wife who had just given birth to a big baby boy the night before.

"She's great. You're going to have to come see her and Mike Junior. He's so cute."

"I bet he is, sweetie," she said. She turned from Mike and her gaze reverted to Augustino, whose eyes were glued to her every move. "Can you and I talk now, or do you have some other pressing engagement you need to attend?"

"I did promise your mother I'd help her carve the turkey." Clearly he was having fun at her expense.

"Upstairs. In my room." She urged him to follow. As an afterthought, she turned and asked him, "Or did my mother already assign you a room?"

Slowly he shook his head. "I think she assumes you and I are together; that we'll be sharing...." He smiled. But she knew that smile, underlining the dark sensuous quality of eyes on fire. That revealing little twitch was prominent in his left jaw. His breath was shallow and labored.

Scouring the area, she was relieved to see they were alone. "Come, I'll show you where you can put your bag," she said softly.

Inside her room, Amanda closed the door behind her and momentarily leaned against it as she watched the tall proud man survey the private sanctuary of her childhood memories. Delicately, so as not to disturb him, she walked over to the bed and perched herself on the edge, following his every move as he picked up her old teddy off the shelf, thumbed through the jackets of well-read books and admired a collection of plates from the many cities she had visited. He smoothed his hand against the pink Thumbelina wallpaper and checked the stack of games and old music tapes she had on her dresser. She waited silently with baited breath as if this search through her personal possessions needed to meet with his approval. When he got to the window, he peered through whirls of frost at what little he could see from the lights of streetlamps and turned to smile at her. He sat down on the window seat and patted the space beside him. “You wanted to talk,” he told her quietly, succinctly.

She knew that tone of voice. He was controlling a bustling tide of strong emotions and she hesitated, not knowing if they’d be able to talk impassively in such proximity. But desire had been welling up inside her as well. She no longer had the strength or the foresight to think logically. She walked over to the seat and perched herself on the edge.

Seeing her nervousness, he leaned back against the opposite wall and propped his foot up on the wooden seat, encircling his leg with his arms. He was glad to see her relax. And for the longest time, he simply stared into her eyes, the silence engulfing them in a world of their own.

“So,” she finally said softly, hating to break the spell between them. “How did you get here? I didn’t see your car out there. I imagine you caught an earlier flight?”

He shook his head, his smile widening to reach his eyes. “I drove up. My car is parked in your father’s garage.

He insisted."

She opened wide eyes. "Daddy took his car out so that you could park yours? In his precious garage? He's never done that before. Where is he, by the way? I didn't see him downstairs."

He shrugged. "I think he went shopping with Jerry—something about getting Meg a warmer bathrobe and a couple of warm sweaters."

Amanda slanted her head, the stunned frown on her face making him laugh. "What is it with you? Do you always have to do that—shock the hell out of me?" The more she said, the more he laughed. So she waited for him to explain, wearing a mutinous look on her face, trying hard not to laugh herself.

"I remembered what you said, about Jerry not being good to drive up on his own. So I offered to take them with me."

"How...?"

"I asked Ginette for Meg's number..."

"So Ginette knows about this?"

He nodded, an expression in his eyes that tickled her all the way down to her feet. "I called Meg and told her I was your...boyfriend..."

"Wait a minute," she told him, a little frustrated, "why did you have to lie to her...?"

"I figured it was the only way she would give credence to anything I said. After all, I was about to offer her, her husband and their son a two-day ride to their parent's house."

He had a point. "Did she sound strange over the

phone?"

"You mean, did she think *me* strange over the phone?" he laughed. "Well, she did invite me over to meet them. Tuesday night I had a deliciously home-cooked meal."

"That's why she didn't want me over all week."

"I told her it was a surprise. She agreed to go along. Said...," he leaned toward her, brushing her cheek with the back of his hand, "she wouldn't miss my surprise for anything."

"And she did," Amanda smiled sadly. "She wasn't there when I arrived. Where is she by the way?"

"She's sleeping. And she hasn't missed anything. She'll see it later, when she wakes up." He dropped his leg and slid to sit next to her. Gently he cupped her face in his hands. "I hope you're not upset by all this. I know you're a private person, modest about displaying your...good times, inner heart—whatever you call it...." He let go of her face, still unsure of her reaction.

"I just don't like deceiving my family. Already it's causing problems. Augie, my mother thinks we're sharing a room."

He nodded, taking in her silk blouse and the soft way it clung to her breasts, the gentle curve of her neck, and slipped his fingers behind the curtain of her hair, his right thumb caressing her ear lobe. He smiled when he saw her close her eyes, enjoying his caresses. "Would it be so terrible if we did share?" he asked in a broken, breathless voice.

She shook her head, having difficulty finding her breath. She opened her eyes to look at him and the dark hungry look in his blue eyes drew a soft moan from her. "I thought you wanted us to be friends," she breathed against his cheek.

He snorted. "Friends first, yes! We've got to be friends, trust each other. 'Cause I can't ever go through that again, Amanda. I felt as though someone had reached inside and torn the heart out of my chest, *cara.*" He shuddered, his breath uneven and raspy.

She stroked his face, his hair. "Can you forgive me—really forgive me? I love you so much, Augustino." She heard him groan, felt him tremble and then she was in his arms, finally pressed against him, rubbing her face against his chest, moaning aloud as his arms squeezed her tightly against him.

He grasped her, possessively stroking her back and rocking her inside his arms for a long time, afraid to let her go. When he disentangled to look into her eyes, she protested slightly. "I love you, Amanda. I adore you. I never want to worry about losing you again."

She nodded, a tear rolling down her cheek.

"First time I lost you was at that damn party. When I found out that you weren't Fiona, I didn't know who you were or where you were." He kissed the tip of her nose and smiled. "Then when I came back to the *Milan* that day...Albert told me you had a family emergency. I couldn't understand what had happened. I was terrified. Then I found the ring in the stateroom..."

He stopped talking. There were no words. Only his eyes reflected the pain. "Raoul told me Conchita had come to visit....Then I started worrying about that damn contract Sanchez had on you..."

"I'm so sorry," she told him with a teary voice. "I had no idea you loved me or that you had fallen in love with me that night....Augustino, to me our engagement was bogus—a sham. I had to fight to remember that...all the time we made love."

"I know, *cara mia*. I think I was angrier with myself for failing to tell you the truth sooner. To me our engagement was real. That's what I wanted to explain that morning when I had Raoul tell you to expect me around lunch."

She was just now realizing how frustrated he must have been. "And here I was, thinking I was in love with a man who cared nothing about me—at least that way."

He kissed her lips. "Well, there'll never be such a misunderstanding between us again—not of that magnitude—ever—if I have to wait a year before I make love to you again."

She moved away from him. "What does one have to do with the other?"

"Come on, Amanda. For me, making love to you on the ship was a...gesture of love, a means to a conclusion—one I already knew. To you, I was this horny bastard who grabbed and clutched at you every chance he got. And this while we were at sea, miles from everywhere, you at my mercy and at the mercy of that damn heart of yours that cares more about everyone else than herself."

She took in a deep breath, her bottom lip quivering. "But you talked about sharing this room?"

"Yes. That's what I meant, sharing the room. You give me a pillow and I'll sleep on the floor. I'll be very comfortable. I sometimes prefer it."

There was a knock at the door. "Who is it?" Amanda asked.

"It's Shawn. Supper is ready. Mom wants us all downstairs."

They looked at each other and knew this conversation would have to keep. Amanda didn't mind. Now that she knew that Augustino loved her.

The aromas wafted all the way up to the second floor. "Go on, Augie; I'll meet you down there, okay?"

He smiled and fingered her hair.

She watched him go down the stairs she had taken so many times as a child. She could still hear the echo of Shawn's laughter as he would run down behind her. There he was, the man of her wishing well. Amanda shivered as she turned to stop by Meg's door. She knocked lightly and entered when she heard her sister's voice acknowledge.

"Hey, Meg. I'm glad you could make it." She rushed to help her get up and gave her a big hug. "I'm only sorry I didn't suggest being you guys' second driver. It never dawned on me—work's got my brain fried."

"Are you kidding? And miss riding up here with Adonis? Amanda, he's gorgeous. I mean, don't let Jerry hear me, but this man looks like he stepped out of Cosmopolitan. He's thoughtful, sexy as hell, charismatic and he drives a Jag."

"I'm glad you like him."

"What does he do? I was afraid to ask."

"He's a lawyer." Amanda didn't want to go into the details of him owning gazillions of dollars—as Jeff had put it.

"Come on. Mom asked us to hurry. You know how upset she gets when we let everything get cold."

Everyone was seated. Meg and Amanda were the last ones to arrive. Amanda bent and hugged her dad, planting a big kiss on his cheek before taking her place beside him.

"I warn you, Mom. I might not be able to eat much," Meg complained.

"That's okay, dear. It's the thought that counts." Her mother's blue eyes twinkled with mischief and kindness.

Amanda thought that even though she had inherited her father's coloring, she was glad she had been blessed with her mother's nurturing qualities.

"Now everyone," Mommy tapped on her glass to rivet their attention. "As you know, usually our Thanksgiving dinner is on Sunday at noon. Exceptionally, we are having it Friday evening because this particular Sunday, Brenda's coming home with her new baby." She paused as everyone cheered and Michael took a bow. "And tomorrow, we might even have leftovers to munch on." Again, she waited for all the laughs and comments to subside. "Also, we would like to welcome Amanda's new friend, Mr. Augustino Milan, to our humble table." There were rounds of welcome around the table. Then she pointed to her husband. "Daddy has something to say."

Amanda was surprised. Her father rarely talked at the table. He had always left that to Mommy. He cleared his throat and looked at Amanda, Augustino, then at the others. "You've all flown the coop," he mumbled gruffly. "Except for Shawn there who'll probably live with us forever." They all laughed at Shawn, who smiled from ear to ear and got a pat on the hand from Mommy. "But it's a crazy day—happy and sad—when a man loses his baby girl."

What was Daddy rambling about, thought Amanda. For once she had brought a man home—hadn't even brought him, in fact. It didn't mean she ought to get this fishbowl treatment. It was embarrassing.

He continued. "I just met Augustino—haven't gotten used to his name yet," another gusto of laughter shook the table, "but when he made his intentions clear concerning my baby girl, I thought him honorable to do so." He turned toward Amanda. "It's up to you, little dove." He patted her hand. "You're the only one who can set him straight."

She noticed all eyes on her and huge smiles on everyone, as if they were all in on some humongous gag. "Augie, what's going on?"

He stared at her and for the first time in his life, felt concern facing one of his decisions. He knew how private she was about her emotions.

He reached in his jacket pocket and extracted a small container she had seen before. From it he pulled the ring she had left behind, in the master stateroom of the *Milan Milend.*

Suddenly all she could see were his eyes, a bright teary blue. And she bit down hard on her bottom lip not to cry. "Amanda Lisa Cole, will you marry me?"

She shook her head as she glanced at the ring's beauty, remembering how she had regretted taking it off. She smiled and nodded while two big tears rolled down her cheeks.

He was so relieved he unconsciously let out an

enormous sigh—which in turn drew the others' *ahs.*

Bending toward her to put the ring on her finger, he spoke in her ear. "It's never coming off, *cara.*" Then looking into her eyes, he whispered. "I thought that if I asked you in front of all these witnesses, you would banish the word *bogus* or *sham* from your vocabulary." He cracked her half a smile, kissing her lips.

Amanda nodded and smiled at him amid the boisterous applause and congratulations that came from all sides. With gusto, everyone around the table happily attacked the bounty set to feast their thanks.

Later that evening, Augustino and Amanda took a drive and ended up at one of the piers along the beach. The wind had died down, but it was icy cold as they stood on the bluff overlooking the ocean. The occasional wave gleamed translucent in the glow of a full moon and the frozen smiles of millions of stars.

"Soon," she said, "this vast expanse of sand will be covered with ice and snow. There's something so sad and desolate about a cold, barren and unattended beach. When I was a little girl I would ask Daddy to take me to visit it, so it wouldn't feel lonely—especially in December." She pulled herself out of her reverie and gave him a sheepish smile.

"Don't be embarrassed, Amy. The ocean remembers and is grateful. That's why it brought the two of us together."

"That's right," she told him, happy he understood how she felt. He hadn't teased her. "It drew me to Miami because it wanted me to meet you," she laughed.

He smiled and gave her a little squeeze. "You'll soon be back on the *Milan*, my love. We'll try scuba again if you like, and I'll bring you back to the Atlantis."

"I'd love that, Augie." She thought about her job, wondering when she would be allowed more time off. "I never thanked you properly for the leg-up you gave me at work. At the time, I thought you did it to rub my nose in it."

He laughed and looked into her eyes. "At the time, you weren't absolutely wrong. Now I wish I'd gotten you fired." He paused, waiting for her reaction. "We're going to have to find a way to be together. My life's empty without you, *cara*. That's why I'm opening a law firm in Miami."

"That's going to be hard work," she told him.

"For the coming year. After that, I'll make sure it runs itself. By then, perhaps you'll be able to take an extended leave of absence. See how it plays out?"

She nodded. "I might like that, Augie." She noticed he hadn't yet told her he was financially independent. She also noticed there were many other things that needed sorting between them. "Has...Conchita left your house yet—in Coral Gables?" She had tried to bite the question back—ever since she'd first laid eyes on him. But it rolled off her tongue and nothing she could do now could take it back.

"I saw her off last Monday," he answered as casually as he dared, the question in his eyes wondering how she knew about this detail.

"Was she your dinner engagement? You know; the reason you couldn't stay and talk last Friday night—when you showed up at my door?" Amanda turned to look at him and witnessed the waning of his smile and the growing of a frown on his brow.

"Would it matter terribly if she were?"

His eyes bore into hers and she regretted her stupid curiosity. This was before they had reconciled. So what if Connie sat down and had a meal with Augustino? She shook her head and smiled. "It doesn't. I'm sorry. I had no right to ask."

"I'm glad you did, Amy. No more secrets. That's how we got in this mess in the first place. And we're engaged now. We should be able to tell each other everything."

"In principle," she added teasingly.

"In principle," he agreed. He gave her a warm little squeeze. "Besides," he added, an amused glint in his eyes, "Conchita wasn't the one I was meeting that night. My late dinner affair was in the Bahamas, in Abacos. I met with Henry Monet and his family. Gave them a leg-up—financially, gratefully. Without his cooperation, we wouldn't have been able to indict so quickly."

"I guess I owe him a ton of thanks too," she added.

He nodded. "You know, Amanda, after you left the ship, I had a very small window to react..."

"I know...some of it. Jeff told me how you and Manuel flew to Miami. The rest of it I heard on the news and read in the papers. You've become quite the famous attorney."

He nodded, staring into her eyes. "I was livid and scared. And so confused, I nearly lost it—you know? Almost gave up on the investigation to rush and patch things up with you. All I could think of was getting to you, tying you to me—if I had to, in part to protect, in part to never let go.... I would have shackled you had I caught up to you that day. It wouldn't have been pretty....Then as time elapsed I began feeling sorry for myself. And the more I felt sorry for me, the angrier I became with you. In any case, Conchita got the brunt of my temper. I was furious with her. I lashed out at her every chance I got, and once the indictments meted out, I ordered her out of my life for good.

Then a little voice reminded me of what you had said once. How maybe she was in love with me." He paused to caress her face with his eyes. "I knew how hurt I felt from the knife-twist you had given me...don't worry," he added, noticing the sadness in her eyes. "I know I had a lot to do with putting myself under the blade. Anyway, there we were on the *Milan* one night...she was crying...she didn't want to return to the island and it was actually unsafe for her to do so....I offered her to stay at my house, in Coral Gables. It seemed proper. I was living and working in Baltimore..."

She nuzzled his left ear with her lips. "I love you, Augustino Milan. I had the pleasure of discovering who you are while you were absent—out of my life."

There was a twinkle in her eyes as she faced his puzzled look. "It seemed as though the universe was concocting against me. Out to prove what an idiot I had been. Every day there would emerge this gallant, altruistic picture of you... made clearer and clearer by all your friends, your associates....All I *thought* I knew about you...gradually changed.... Then one morning, it was different. Anyway, that's when I learned about Connie living at your house."

"What else did you learn from my many *irreverent* friends?" he mocked.

She laughed. "That you were this generous if somewhat love-'em-and-leave-'em womanizer...the patron saint of good old boys." Again she laughed, faced with the perplexed expression on his face. "Jeff's own words—or close enough," she explained.

"Ah!" He nodded while staring into her eyes and Amanda shivered, reliving the passion they had shared on the ship when plunging into stormy, steamy blue eyes.

"Cold?" he whispered in her ear, hugging her warmly.

"A little," she added, giggling as she tucked her ice-cold nose into his warm neck.

Augustino trembled as he led her to the car, his arm wrapped firmly around her waist. That's when Amanda realized he hadn't kissed her since she had arrived—not a real kiss. There was all this talk of love and promises of a wonderful future, but no physical demonstration—except for his tender cuddles and intense yet chaste little kisses.

Even as they got ready for bed, he came in the room after taking his shower wearing a t-shirt and a pair of jogging pants.

She laughed at him a little and quipped. "The house is drafty but we do have central heating."

"Not allowed making fun of my sleep...system while you're wearing that cotton nightie. Throw me a couple of pillows, please."

"You're kidding, right?"

As an answer, he walked over to where she was sitting

in the bed and kissed her on the cheek. "Goodnight, Amanda." He grabbed the pillows, a comforter he had borrowed from the hall closet and lay down on the carpeted floor.

He wasn't kidding. They were officially engaged; this time it was real—she fingered her ring for the umpteenth time—and he was sleeping on the floor. "How long do you intend to keep this up?" She asked more than a little peeved.

"For as long as it takes. Goodnight, Amanda. Could you get the light? I've had a long day."

He was already lying down with his eyes closed. She laughed—a dry, frustrated little laugh. But she turned off the light and lay down hard with a loud drawn out breath. "Tell me again why you're doing this?"

It was his turn to emit a frustrated breath. "To prove to you that I am not just a pig—that I have self-control. This is to prove to you that I loved you on the ship. That I would not have made love to you had I not. Now goodnight."

"But I believe you, Augie. I told you that."

"This way you'll never be jealous of Connie or any other woman again."

This was rich. She had to be truthful with him. "Did it ever occur to you that I maneuvered to have you give up that rotten, damn control of yours? That it pleased me no end to have you throw caution to the winds—that I lusted after you? You said yourself that I was in love with you. Why wasn't it me that wanted you inside me as much as you did? Are women not supposed to have these kinds of needs?"

He snorted. "Nice try, *little dove*," he jeered.

"Listen, Milo." She had to get his attention. "Just

because I'm a softy and a pushover and...and consider other people, as you say, doesn't mean I don't have my own brand of fire. That I don't burn for the man I love." She waited, but he said nothing. Why did he have to pick tonight to be so mulish? Their engagement night?

If there was ever a time she needed to admit to him, knowing about....She thought she had buried the episode forever. It was too embarrassing to discuss with him. But now, in the dark, this was her chance. "Remember that first Friday you saw me on your ship?" She waited but he didn't answer. "Well, I was hiding in your closet when you and Connie...Augie?"

"I'm listening," he said expectantly.

She almost preferred he had been asleep. "I heard you guys on the bridge. I had gone back because I had forgotten Dino. Anyway, there was no time for me to leave and Fiona had said I would lose my job if the owner ever saw me there; so I hid in the cedar closet—the one with the louver doors?" Surely now he knew what she meant.

"Go on," he told her.

"I can't believe you don't remember this. You came into the room with her. She was drunk. She stripped and put her arms around you and...and did something with your finger and asked you..."

"You saw this?" His voice was low and gritty.

"I closed my eyes for the most part; but I heard...all her screaming....That's when I peeked a little. I saw your face. You had such a blank expression. I actually felt sorry for her. And I remember thinking that you were a monster. Then I noticed the...lump in your pants and knew that you were simply a monster of self-control." She was finally getting this out. And it was easy, like talking to herself out loud.

She heard him curse in Italian under his breath. But she continued even though she knew he was fuming, buoyed by the darkness, by the joy of this weight lifting off her chest. "Well, I told Ginette that my one worry about accepting this... your assignment was the fate-worse-than-death incident. We laughed about it. You know, where you would be lying beside me, I would crave for you to touch me and love me...then you would flatly refuse me like you had Connie. Oh! Nicely enough, probably. But just the same, you'd wield that damn self-control in front of my nose and then...the fate-worse-than-death would rear its head...where I would have to beg you to make love to me." She took a trembling breath. "I was so happy on the ship, Augustino. I didn't have to beg once."

She heard him get up and mumble a string of not so courteous epithets; and worried that he was livid and liable to trip in the dark she turned on the bedside lamp.

He stood over the bed, his eyes tortured, rasping as if he'd just run the four-minute mile. "Why in the hell didn't you tell me this before? It would have explained your disdain of Connie, your perspective of this whole mess...." He snorted. "And I was worried about...shocking you with my intimacy."

She shook her head and smiled. "That's not a particular concern of mine—you know," she told him wickedly, scrunching her nose as she said it, "deep, probing, intimate lovemaking."

He cursed as he dropped on top of her, kissing the

breath out of her. Deftly, he removed her nightgown while she pulled on his pants. Coming up for air, he slipped his shirt over his head. The feel of her soft, silky skin rubbing against his drew a loud groan from him. "There's something I haven't told you," he murmured hoarsely, his hands gently cupping her breasts. "You never have to work again if you don't want to."

"I know," she nodded, running both hands down his back, stretching to reach past his waist. Gently she kneaded his buttocks, pressing him down against her—so impatient was she to feel him inside her.

"None of your family members do," he moaned as she moved one hand to tug at the hair between his legs. "Stop!" he cautioned her. "I didn't bring protection," he breathed.

"Why not?" she protested.

"I wasn't going to do this," he smiled. "Are you okay with this—no condom? Are you on the pill?"

She shook her head. "I never do this. But it's okay, Augie. It's the wrong time of the month...or the right time...." She was becoming impatient. She knew he was good for hours but she couldn't wait anymore. Climaxing with him was overdue and foremost on her mind.

He knew she wasn't thinking rationally. So he took his sweet time penetrating her, affording her the chance to reconsider. "This feels good!" He moaned as he finally settled inside her. "I'll have you know I'm a virgin; I've never made love to a woman without a piece," he added as he slowly stoked her furnace until she was hot and fast getting hotter.

"And I'm so ready for you...for you to explode inside

me...don't make me wait too long," she breathed in his ear.

"You're an impatient little vixen," he whispered as he moved inside her, his hands caressing her thighs. "There's no hurry, Amanda. We've got all night."

"Shh," she whispered, running her tongue in his ear, enticing him to go faster. "Don't make me beg."

The distant moonbeams and faraway dance of gleaming stars peering through the frosted windowpanes were the only witnesses to the heat of their embrace. And the cosmic orchestra played discreetly, quietly weaving its spell, solemnly promising it would never tell.

Fervently, Augustino capitulated to exult all of Amanda's wishes—those shyly spoken and those silently coveted. No matter how long the night, darkness and loneliness they would fell together.

You can guess the rest.

PIEEYE PUBLISHING INC.

www.pieeyepublishing.com

To e-mail the author, jrteasdale@pieeyepublishing.com